Stalking Jack the Ripper

Kerri Maniscalco

JIMMY PATTERSON BOOKS
LITTLE, BROWN AND COMPANY
NEW YORK • BOSTON

JIMMY Patterson Books / Little, Brown and Company
Hachette Book Group
1290 Avenue of the Americas, New York, NY 10104
JimmyPatterson.org

First Paperback Edition: September 2017
First Edition: September 2016

JIMMY Patterson Books is an imprint of Little, Brown and Company, a division of Hachette Book Group, Inc. The Little, Brown name and logo are trademarks of Hachette Book Group, Inc. The JIMMY Patterson name and logo are trademarks of JBP Business, LLC.

Photographs courtesy of Wellcome Library, London (pp. 2, 16, 90, 290); John Walker (p. 32); John M. Clarke, The Brookwood Necropolis Railway (p. 176); and William Whiffin, Tower Hamlets Local History Library and Archives (p. 200).

Library of Congress Cataloging-in-Publication Data
Names: Maniscalco, Kerri, author. Title: Stalking Jack the Ripper / Kerri Maniscalco.
Description: First edition. | New York : JIMMY Patterson Books/Little, Brown and Company, 2016. | Summary: A gothic murder mystery set in gritty Victorian-era London, where an intrepid society girl finds herself embroiled in the investigation of a serial killer known as Jack the Ripper.
Identifiers: LCCN 2016006139 | ISBN 9780316273497 (hc) | 9780316464284 (large print) | 9780316273510 (pb)
Subjects: | CYAC: Mystery and detective stories. | Serial murderers—Fiction. | Jack the Ripper—Fiction. | London (England)—History—19th century—Fiction. | Great Britain—History—Victoria, 1837–1901—Fiction. | BISAC: JUVENILE FICTION / Horror & Ghost Stories. | JUVENILE FICTION / Historical / Europe. | JUVENILE FICTION / Mysteries & Detective Stories.
Classification: LCC PZ7.1.M3648 St 2016 | DDC [Fic]— dc23 LC record available

at https://lccn.loc.gov/2016006139

Printing 25, 2025

LSC-C

Printed in Indiana, USA

For Grandma,
Who always loved a good whodunit

FOREWORD

The book you're holding in your hands represents a lot of firsts.

It's the first acquisition that I am publishing under my new imprint for young readers, JIMMY Patterson Books.

It's the first young adult novel I chose, thanks to its fresh and compelling take on the ever-fascinating Ripper mystery.

It is author Kerri Maniscalco's first novel.

And it was when I read her very first line that I knew I was going to love this book.

Kerri's clever, vibrant voice and unerring grasp of suspense and emotion came through right from those opening words. *Stalking Jack the Ripper* is an atmospheric tale full of chilling twists and unsettling turns, and I assure you it more than lives up to the promise of that mesmerizing first sentence. It may be set in Victorian-era London, but you'll find the brilliant and impassioned Audrey Rose to be inspiringly modern, even by our standards.

Part of our mission at JIMMY Patterson is to create books that young readers will finish and then immediately say, "Please give me another book." I have no doubt that *Stalking Jack the Ripper* will be the first of our offerings to fulfill that mission, but it certainly won't be the last.

—James Patterson

"It will have blood; they say, blood will have blood."

—*MACBETH*, ACT 3, SCENE 4

WILLIAM SHAKESPEARE

Stalking JACK THE RIPPER

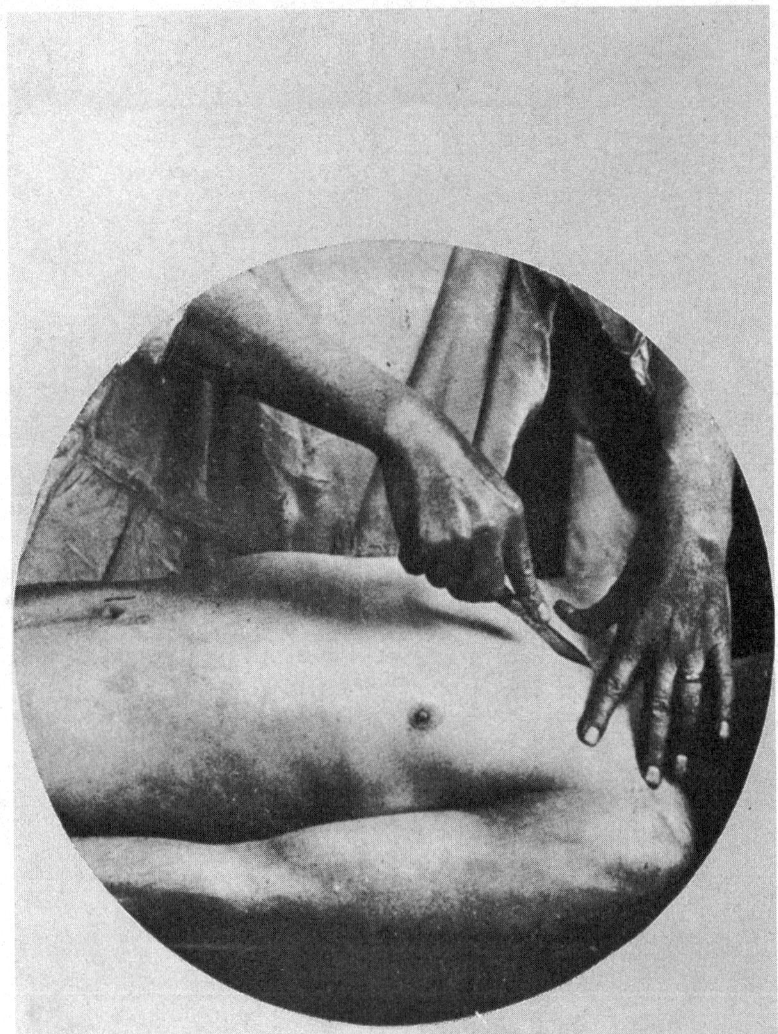

Fig. 3. Shewing the stretching of the skin, and the method of holding the knife in the preliminary incision.

J. M. Beattie, *Post-Mortem Methods,* 1915

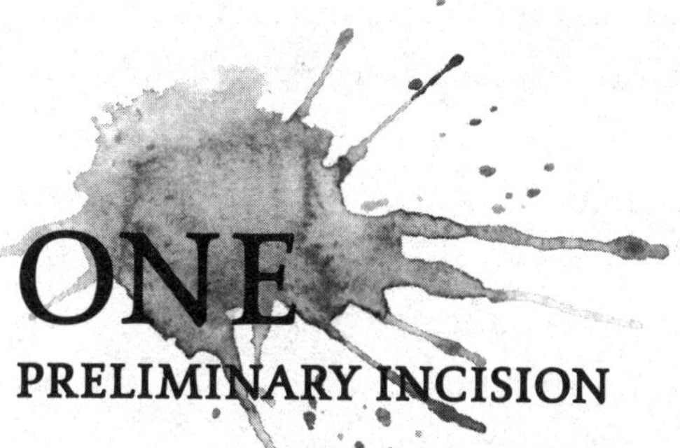

ONE
PRELIMINARY INCISION

DR. JONATHAN WADSWORTH'S LABORATORY, HIGHGATE
30 AUGUST 1888

I placed my thumb and forefinger on the icy flesh, spreading it taut above the breastbone as Uncle had showed me.

Getting the preliminary incision correct was imperative.

I took my time eyeing the placement of metal upon skin, ensuring proper angling for the cleanest cut. I felt Uncle hovering behind me, studying my every move, but had my view set entirely on the blade in my hand.

Without hesitation, I dragged the scalpel from one shoulder to the sternum, taking pains to push as deeply as I could. My brows raised a fraction before I schooled my face into an unreadable mask. Human flesh flayed much easier than I'd anticipated. It wasn't much different from cutting into a pork loin prior to its roasting, a thought that should have been more disturbing than it was.

A sickeningly sweet smell wafted from the incision I'd made. This cadaver wasn't as fresh as others. I had a sneaking suspicion not all our subjects were obtained through proper legal or voluntary measures and was regretting waving away Uncle's earlier offer of a breathing apparatus.

Foggy wisps of breath escaped my lips, but I refused to give in to building shivers. I stepped back, my slippers lightly crunching sawdust, and examined my work.

Blood barely seeped up from the wound. It was too thick and dead to flow crimson, and too foreign to be truly frightening. Had the man been dead less than thirty-six hours, it might've spilled onto the table then onto the floor, saturating the sawdust. I wiped the blade on my apron, leaving an inky streak in its wake.

It was a fine incision indeed.

I readied myself for the next cut, but Uncle held a hand in the air, stalling my movement. I bit my lip, despising myself for forgetting a step from his lesson so soon.

Uncle's ongoing feud with Father—neither one claimed to remember its origin, but I recall it well enough—had him wavering on continuing my apprenticeship. Proving myself incapable would not help my case, especially if I hoped to attend school the next morning.

"One moment, Audrey Rose," he said, plucking the soiled blade from my fingers.

A sharp scent sprung into the air, mixing with the stench of decaying organs as Uncle uncorked a bottle of clear liquid and splashed it onto a cloth. Antiseptic was pervasive in his basement laboratory and amongst his blades. I should've remembered to wipe the other one down.

I would not make the same mistake again.

I glanced about the basement, where several other bodies were lined up along the wall, their pale limbs stiff as snow-covered branches. We were going to be here all night if I didn't hurry, and Father, the all-important Lord Edmund Wadsworth, would send for Scotland Yard if I wasn't home soon.

Given his station, he'd probably have a small army out patrolling for me.

Uncle recorked the bottle of carbolic acid, then handed me another scalpel resembling a long, thin dinner knife. Its edge was much sharper than the last blade's was. Using the sterilized tool, I mimicked the same incision on the opposite shoulder, then made my way down to the deceased's navel, stopping just above his belly button.

Uncle hadn't warned me how hard it would be, cutting down to the rib cage. I stole a glance at him, but his gaze was fixed hungrily on the corpse.

At times the darkness in his eyes terrified me more than the dead we butchered.

"You'll need to crack the ribs open before reaching the heart."

I could tell Uncle was having a difficult time restraining himself from doing the deed. Corpses kept him company most nights, like intriguing textbooks; he cherished dissecting them and discovering the secrets held between the pages of their skin and bones. Before obsession could override his lesson, I quickly broke the rib cage apart, exposing the heart and the rest of the viscera.

A foul odor hit me full in the face, and without meaning to, I staggered back, nearly placing a hand over my mouth. It was the opening Uncle had been waiting for. He moved forward, but before he could push me aside, I shoved my hands deep into the abdomen, feeling around in squishy membranes until I found what we were looking for.

I steeled myself for the task of removing the liver, then accepted the blade from my uncle once more. After a few slices and tugs, the organ came loose.

I plopped it onto a waiting specimen tray with a slick thud, resisting the urge to wipe my hands on my apron. Having Uncle's servants wash a little blood was one thing, the gooey blood and mucus now coating my fingers was quite another.

We couldn't afford losing another lot of maids, and Uncle could ill afford having any more rumors flitting about. Some people already thought him mad enough.

"What is your medical deduction on how this man expired, Niece?"

The liver was in ghastly shape. Several scars ran along its length and width, giving the appearance of dried-out rivers and tributaries. My first guess was this man had been no stranger to his drink.

"It appears he died of cirrhosis." I pointed at the scarring. "His liver has been shutting down for quite some time, I believe." I walked around to his head and pulled one of his eyelids back. "Slight yellowing around the whites of his eyes is also present, furthering my suspicion he's been dying quite slowly for several years."

I walked back to the liver and carefully removed a cross section to study under the microscope later, then rinsed it and set it in a jar for preservation. I'd need to label it and add it to the wall of other pickled organs. It was important to keep meticulous records of every postmortem.

Uncle nodded. "Very good. Very good indeed. And what of—"

The door to the laboratory crashed against the wall, revealing a silhouetted male. It was impossible to see exactly what he looked like or how old he was, with a hat tugged so low over his brow and his overcoat practically touching the ground, but he was very tall. I dared not move, hoping Uncle would brandish a weapon, but he seemed unimpressed with the dark character before us.

Ignoring my presence completely, the male focused only on my uncle. "It's ready, Professor."

His voice was smooth, and hinted at youth. I arched a brow, intrigued by what a student and my uncle were up to.

"So soon?" Uncle checked the clock on the wall, looking at the body on the table and then at me. I had no idea who the rude boy was or what was ready, but had a feeling it couldn't be anything good at this late hour. Uncle rubbed his chin. After what felt like an eternity, he addressed me with a calculating stare. "Are you capable of closing the cadaver up on your own?"

I stood taller and thrust my chin up. "Of course."

It was truly absurd that Uncle would think me incapable of such an easy thing, especially after I'd been fishing around inside the dead man's viscera well enough on my own. Out of all my tasks this would be the easiest.

"Aunt Amelia says my needlework is quite impressive," I added. Except she didn't have skin stitching in mind while praising my embroidery, I'm sure. "Anyway, I practiced suturing on a boar's carcass over the summer and had no trouble forcing the needles in and out of its derma. This won't be any different."

The dark figure chuckled, a damnably pleasant sound. I kept my expression calm, though I was quietly seething underneath. There wasn't anything funny about that statement. Whether stitching skin or linen, the craft was what counted, not the medium.

"Very well." Uncle slipped a black overcoat on and removed something I couldn't quite see from a box near his desk. "You may close the body up. Be sure to lock the basement on your way out."

The young man disappeared up the stairs without a backward glance, and I was happy to see him go. Uncle paused at the door, his scarred fingers tapping a nervous beat against the frame.

"My carriage will take you home when you're through," he said. "Leave the other specimens for tomorrow afternoon."

"Uncle, wait!" I ran around the examination table. "What of school tomorrow? You said you'd let me know tonight."

His attention flicked to the gutted cadaver on the table, then back to my expectant face. I could see his mind strategizing and coming up with a thousand reasons why I should not attend his forensic medicines class.

Propriety being the least of his worries.

Father would tear him limb from limb if he discovered my apprenticeship.

Uncle Jonathan sighed. "You're to come dressed as a boy. And if you so much as utter *one* word, it will be your first and last time in my classroom. Understand?"

I nodded vigorously. "I promise. I'll be as silent as the dead."

"Ah," Uncle said, putting a hat on and tugging it low, "the dead speak to those who listen. Be quieter than even them."

TWO
BLOOD VENGEANCE

HARROW SCHOOL FOR BOYS,
LONDON
31 AUGUST 1888

There wasn't as much blood as one would expect from such a violent throat slashing, according to my uncle. I barely kept up with his account of the gruesome scene he'd attended early this morning, and my notes were looking rather scattered, much like my thoughts.

"Tell me, boys," Uncle Jonathan said, moving about the low stage in the center of the gallery, his pale green eyes pausing on mine before continuing, "what does the evidence suggest if the blood found under the body was already coagulated? Better yet, if there was barely enough blood found to fill but half a pint, what might that say about our victim's end?"

The urge to call out the answer was a miserable beast longing to break free from the cage I'd agreed to lock it in. Instead of exorcising that demon, I sat quietly with my lips pressed shut and my hat pulled low. I hid my annoyance by scanning my classmates' expressions. I inwardly sighed. Most of them were the same shade of artichoke and looked a breath away from vomiting. How they'd stomach dissecting a cadaver was beyond me. I subtly scraped dried blood from my nail beds, recalling the way it felt to hold a liver in my hands, and wondered what new sensation today's postmortem would bring.

A boy with dark brown hair—as carefully sculpted as his immaculately pressed uniform—raised his hand, straight as an arrow in the air. Inkblots covered much of his fingertips, as if he were too entranced with writing notes to be bothered with delicacy. My gaze had lingered on him earlier, fascinated by the methodical way he took notes. He was nearly manic with learning—a trait I couldn't help admiring.

Uncle nodded toward him. The boy cleared his throat and stood, confidence pulling his lean shoulders back, as he faced the class instead of my uncle. I narrowed my eyes. He was also quite tall. Could he be the mysterious visitor from last night?

"It's rather obvious, if you ask me," he said, his tone bordering on disinterest, "that our murderer either propositioned the deceased for illicit acts to lure her somewhere private, or sneaked up on her—as she was clearly inebriated—and dispatched her from behind."

It was hard to tell, since he'd barely spoken yesterday, but his voice sounded as if it *could* be that of Uncle's late-night visitor. I found myself leaning closer, as if proximity might spark recognition in my brain.

Uncle Jonathan cleared his throat to stall the arrogant boy and sat at his wooden desk. I smiled. Posing as a boy certainly had its merits. Talk of prostitutes always put Uncle on edge, only now he couldn't scold anyone for speaking freely in front of me. He pulled a drawer open, taking a pair of spectacles out and rubbing smudges from them on his tweed jacket before settling them on his face. Leaning forward, Uncle asked, "Why might you believe our victim was assaulted from behind, Thomas, when most of my colleagues believe the victim was lying down when attacked?"

I glanced between them, surprised Uncle had used his Christian name. Now I was almost positive he was the late-night stranger. The boy, Thomas, drew his brows together.

Golden-brown eyes were perfectly set into an angular face, as if Leonardo da Vinci had painted him himself. If only my lashes were as luxuriant. His chin was squared, giving him a look of steadfast determination. Even his nose was thin and regal, giving an air of alertness to his every expression. If he weren't so infuriatingly aware of his own intelligence, he'd be quite attractive, I supposed.

"Because as you stated, sir, the throat was slashed from left to right. Considering most people are, in fact, right-handed, one would imagine from the downward trajectory you described, and the statistical probability our perpetrator was indeed, right-handed, the easiest way to commit this act would be from *behind* the victim."

Thomas grabbed the student sitting beside him, and wrestled him to a standing position, demonstrating his point. Chair limbs screeched against the tiled flooring as the boy struggled to break free, but Thomas held tight as if he were a boa constrictor with its prey.

"He probably placed his left arm across her chest or torso, dragged her close, like so"—he whipped our classmate around—"and swiftly dragged the blade across her throat. Once, while standing, then twice as she fell to the ground, all before she knew what was happening."

After simulating the near beheading, Thomas dropped the boy and stepped over him, returning to both his seat and his former disinterest. "If you were to investigate blood splatter at a slaughterhouse, I'm sure you'd find something like an inverse pattern, as livestock are typically killed while dangling upside down."

"Ha!" Uncle clapped his hands with echoing force.

I jumped at his outburst, relieved most of the class jolted in their wooden seats along with me. There was no denying Uncle was passionate about murder.

"Then why, naysayers cry, didn't blood splatter all over the upper portion of the fence?" Uncle challenged, pounding a fist in his palm. "When her jugular was severed, it should've rhythmically sprayed everything."

Thomas nodded as if he'd been anticipating this very question. "That's quite simple to explain, isn't it? She was wearing a neckerchief when first attacked, then it fell away. Or, perhaps the murderer ripped it from her to clean his blade. He might possess some neurosis or other."

Silence hung thick as the East End fog as the vivid image Thomas created took life inside each of our minds. Uncle taught me the importance of removing my emotions from these types of cases, but it was hard to speak of a woman as if she were an animal being brought to the slaughterhouse. No matter how far she'd fallen from polite society.

I swallowed hard. Thomas had a disturbing way of both predicting why the murderer acted as he did and turning emotions off when it suited him, it seemed. It took a few seconds for my uncle to respond, but when he did, he was grinning like a madman, his eyes two sparks of fire set ablaze in his skull. I couldn't stop a twinge of jealousy from twisting in my gut. I couldn't tell if I was upset Uncle looked so pleased and I wasn't responsible or if I wished to be interacting with the annoying boy myself. Out of everyone in this classroom, he at least wasn't cowed by the violence of this crime. Being afraid wouldn't find justice for the family—this boy seemed to understand that.

I shook my thoughts free and listened to the lesson.

"Brilliant deduction skills, Thomas. I, too, believe our victim was attacked from behind while standing. The knife used was most likely between six and eight inches long." Uncle paused, showing the class about how big the blade was with his hands. Uneasiness crept into my blood. It would've been around the same size as the scalpel I'd used last night.

Uncle cleared his throat. "Judging from the jagged cut in the abdomen, I'd say the wound was inflicted postmortem, where the body was discovered. I'd also venture our murderer was interrupted, and didn't get what he was originally after. But I've an inkling he might be either left-handed or ambidextrous based on other evidence."

A boy sitting in the first row raised a shaking hand. "What do you mean? What he was originally after?"

"Pray we don't find out." Uncle twisted the corner of his pale mustache, a habit he often indulged while lost in thought. I knew whatever he'd say next wouldn't be pleasant.

Without realizing it, I'd grabbed the edges of my own seat so hard my knuckles were turning white. I loosened my grip slightly.

"For the sake of this lesson, I'll divulge my theories." Uncle glanced around the room once more. "I believe he was after her organs. Detective inspectors, however, do not share my sentiments on that aspect. I can only hope they're right."

While discussions broke out on Uncle's organ-removal theory, I sketched the anatomical figures he'd hastily drawn on the chalkboard at the start of our lesson in order to clear my mind. Dissected pigs, frogs, rats, and even more disturbing things such as human intestines and hearts adorned the inside of my pages.

My notebook was filled with images of things a lady had no business being fascinated by, yet I couldn't control my curiosity.

A shadow fell across my notebook, and somehow I knew it was Thomas before he opened his mouth. "You ought to put the shadow on the left side of the body, else it looks like a pool of blood."

I tensed, but kept my lips shut as if they'd been sewn together by a reckless mortician. Flames quietly burned under my skin, and I cursed my body's reaction to such an aggravating boy. Thomas continued critiquing my work.

"Truly, you should erase those ridiculous smudges," he said. "The streetlamp was coming from this angle. You've got it all terribly wrong."

"Truly, you should mind your own business." I closed my eyes, internally scolding myself. I'd been doing so well keeping quiet and not interacting with any of the boys. One slip could cost me my seat in class.

Deciding one should never show a mad dog fear, I met Thomas's sharp gaze full-on. A small smile played upon his lips, and my heart trotted in my chest like a carriage horse running through Trafalgar Square. I reminded myself he was a self-important arse and decided the stutter in my heart was strictly due to nerves. I'd rather bathe in formaldehyde than be ousted from class by such a maddening boy.

Handsome though he might be.

"While I appreciate your observation," I said between clenched teeth, taking careful pains to deepen my voice, "I'd like it very much if you'd be so kind as to leave me to my studies."

His eyes danced as if he'd discovered a vastly entertaining secret, and I knew I was a mouse that had been caught by an all too clever cat.

"Right, then. Mr....?" The way he emphasized *mister* left no room for misunderstanding; he was quite aware I was no young man but was willing to play along for God only knew what reason. I softened a bit at this show of mercy, dropping my disguised voice so only he could hear, my heart picking up speed once more at our shared secret.

"Wadsworth. My name is Audrey Rose Wadsworth."

A flash of understanding crossed his face, his attention flicking to my uncle, who was still inciting a heated discussion. He held his hand out, and I reluctantly shook it, hoping my palms wouldn't give away my nervousness.

Perhaps having a friend to talk over cases might be nice.

"I believe we met last night," I ventured, feeling a bit bolder. Thomas's brows knit together and my newfound confidence plummeted. "In my uncle's laboratory?"

Darkness shifted over his features. "Apologies, but I haven't a clue what you're referring to. This is the first time we've spoken."

"We didn't exactly speak—"

"It's nice to meet you, Wadsworth. I'm sure we'll have much to discuss in the near future. Immensely near, actually, as I'm apprenticing this evening with your uncle. Perhaps you'll allow me the pleasure of testing out a few of my theories?"

Another crimson wave washed over my cheeks. "Your theories on what, exactly?"

"Your scandalous choice to attend this class, of course." He grinned. "It isn't every day you meet such an odd girl."

The friendly warmth I'd been feeling toward him froze over like a pond during a particularly frigid winter. Especially since he appeared completely unaware of how irritating he was, smiling to himself without a care in the universe. "I do love the satisfaction of solving a puzzle and proving myself right."

Somehow I found the strength to bite my retort back and offered a tight smile in its place. Aunt Amelia would be proud her lessons on etiquette stuck with me. "I am very much looking forward to hearing your scintillating theory on my life choices, Mr. . . . ?"

"Gentlemen!" Uncle barked. "If you please, I'd like each of you to write down your theories on Miss Mary Ann Nichols's murder and bring them to class tomorrow."

Thomas gave me one last devilish grin and turned back to his notes. As I closed my journal and gathered up my things, I couldn't help thinking he might prove an equally vexing mystery to solve.

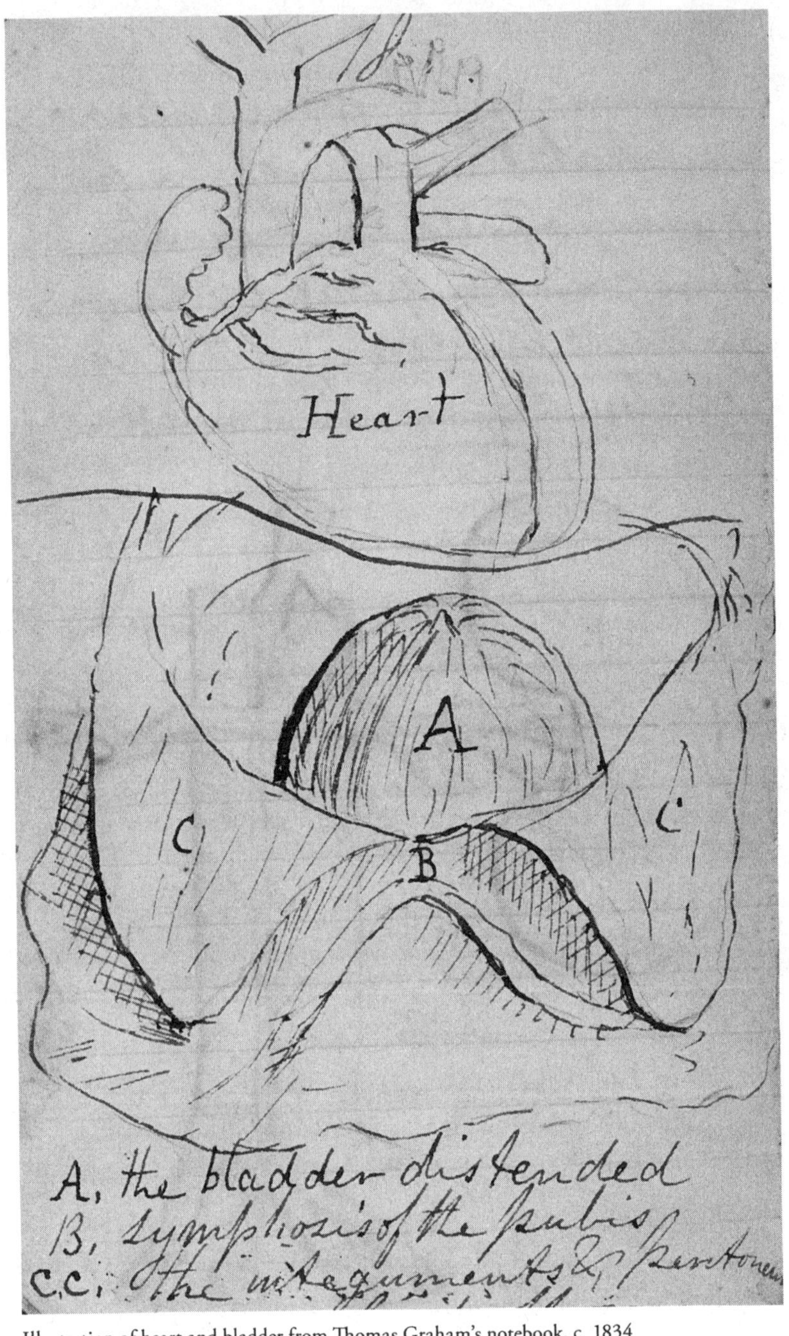

Illustration of heart and bladder from Thomas Graham's notebook, c. 1834

THREE

TEA AND AUTOPSIES

WADSWORTH RESIDENCE,
BELGRAVE SQUARE
31 AUGUST 1888

"Where are you running off to at this hour?"

Father stood near the grandfather clock in the foyer—his tone striking the same nervous chord as the beastly antique—while he checked his pocket watch. Only a handful of years separated Uncle and Father, and up until recently they could have passed for twins. A muscle in his square jaw twitched. Worse questions were coming. The urge to flee back up the grand staircase was suddenly overwhelming.

"I-I promised Uncle Jonathan I'd join him for tea." I watched him inhale a sharp breath and added quietly, "Turning down his invitation would've been rude."

Before he offered any more thoughts on the matter, the parlor door swung open and my brother waltzed in like a beam of sunshine set against the backdrop of a gray day. Taking quick note of the situation, he pounced.

"I must say, everyone appears so downright cheerful this afternoon, it's rather disturbing. Give me a proper scowl, good man.

Ah—" he smiled at the glare Father leveled at him— "that's the spirit! Excellent job, Father."

"Nathaniel," Father warned, his glassy focus darting between us. "This matter does not concern you."

"Are we terrified to let the girl out of the protective bubble again? Heaven forbid she catch pox and perish. Oh, wait," Nathaniel cocked his head. "That's happened before, hasn't it?" He dramatically grabbed my wrist, checking for a pulse, then staggered back. "By God, Father. She's quite alive!"

Father's pale hand shook, and he blotted at his brow with a handkerchief, which was never a promising sign. Nathaniel usually managed to diffuse Father's anxiety with a well-placed quip. Today wasn't one of those days. I couldn't help noticing extra lines around Father's mouth, dragging his lips into a near-permanent frown. If he'd only let some of his endless worry go, it would erase a decade from his once-handsome features. Strands of gray hair were also slipping in between his ashy-blond locks more and more lately.

"I was just telling Father I'm on my way to the carriage," I said as pleasantly as I could manage, feigning ignorance of the volatile atmosphere. "I'm meeting Uncle Jonathan."

Nathaniel clapped his gloved hands together, a sly smile spreading across his face. He couldn't resist assisting me with my chosen medical studies. Mostly because my modern stance—on why girls were equally capable of having a profession or apprenticeship—offered endless amusement.

My brother's love of arguing made him an excellent barrister-in-training, but his fickle attention would lead him elsewhere soon enough. His prior whims included a few months studying medicine, then art, then a horrendous effort with a violin—which went badly for all who had the misfortune of hearing him practice his scales.

Though, as heir to our family legacy, he needn't learn a trade at all. It was merely something to pass idle hours and afternoons besides drinking with his pompous friends.

"Ah, that's right. I recall Uncle saying something about tea earlier in the week. Unfortunately, I had to decline his invitation, what with my studies and all." Adjusting his gloves and smoothing his suit, Nathaniel stepped back and grinned. "Your dress is exceptional for today's weather and special occasion. Seventeen now, right? You're stunning, birthday girl. Don't you agree, Father?"

Father scrutinized my ensemble. He was probably searching for a lie to prevent me from traveling to Uncle's home, but he wouldn't find one. I'd already packed the carriage with a change of simpler clothing. If he couldn't prove I was going to practice unholy acts upon the dead and risk infection, he couldn't very well stop me.

For now, I was dressed in proper afternoon tea attire; my watered-silk gown was the same shade of eggshell as my silk slippers, and my corset was tight enough to remind me it was there with each painful breath I took.

I was suddenly grateful for the rose-colored gloves that buttoned up to my elbows; they were a fashionable way to hide how much my palms were sweating.

Father ran a hand over his tired face. "Since it's your birthday you may go there for tea and come straight back. I do not want you going anywhere else. Nor do I want you engaged in any of that"—his hand fluttered about like an injured bird—"that *activity* your uncle is involved with. Understood?"

I nodded, relieved, but Father wasn't through.

"Should anything happen to your sister," he said, staring at my brother, "I will hold you responsible."

Father held Nathaniel's gaze for a moment longer, then stalked from the room, leaving us in the wake of his storm. I watched as his broad form disappeared down the hallway and until he slammed the door of his study shut with one backward swipe of his hand. I knew he'd light a cigar soon and lock himself away until morning, thoughts and memories of Mother plaguing him until he fell into a troubled sleep.

I turned my attention to Nathaniel as he pulled out his favorite silver comb and ran it through his hair. Not one golden strand could ever be out of place, else the universe might possibly explode. "A bit warm for leather gloves, don't you think?"

Nathaniel shrugged. "I'm on my way out."

As much as I wanted to speak with my brother, I had serious engagements that needed attending. Uncle was a creature of many habits, and tardiness wasn't tolerated. No matter that it was my birthday.

Personally, I didn't think the dead would mind waiting five minutes to be cut open and explored, but I didn't dare say so out loud. I was there to learn, not ignite the demon sometimes lurking within him.

Last time I questioned this rule, Uncle had me sopping bloody sawdust up for a month. I wasn't keen on receiving that punishment again; blood had crusted my nail beds and was terrible to clean away before supper. Thank goodness Aunt Amelia hadn't been visiting, she would've fainted at the sight.

"Do you want to have lunch tomorrow?" I asked. "I can tell Martha to prepare something for us to bring to Hyde Park, if you'd like. We can even walk round the Serpentine."

Nathaniel smiled a bit sadly. "Perhaps we can take a belated birthday stroll around the lake next week? I'd certainly like to know what you and Uncle Cadaver are up to in that house of horrors." His eyes sparkled with a hint of trouble. "I worry about you seeing all that blood. Can't be good for your fragile womanly temperament."

"Oh? Where in a medical dictionary does it say a woman cannot handle such things? What is a man's soul made of that a woman's is not?" I teased. "I had no idea my innards were composed of cotton and kittens, while yours were filled with steel and steam-driven parts."

His voice softened, getting to the heart of what was truly bothering him. "Father will go berserk if he discovers what you're really doing. I fear his grasp on reality is most delicate these days. His delusions are becoming... worrisome."

"How so?"

"I—I caught him sharpening knives and talking to himself the other morning when he thought everyone was still asleep." He rubbed his temples, his smile fading. "Perhaps he thinks he can stab germs before they enter our home now."

This was troubling news indeed. Last time Father got this way, he'd made me wear a facial mask each time I left the house to avoid breathing contagions. While I'd like to fancy myself above things such as vanity, I'd hated the stares I'd received when venturing out. Going through that again would be torturous.

I plastered on a big smile.

"You worry too much." I kissed him on the cheek before heading for the door, my own tone lightening again. "If you're not careful, you'll end up losing all of your luxuriant hair."

Nathaniel chuckled at that. "Duly noted. Happy birthday, Audrey Rose. I do hope you have a wonderful time with whatever it is you're up to. Be careful, though. You know Uncle can be a bit... mad."

Twenty minutes later I was standing in the basement of Uncle's laboratory, getting acclimated to the smell of someone else's nightmare.

Dead flesh had a sickeningly sweet undertone that always took a bit of time getting used to. Fresh, unharmed bodies gave off a scent similar to a raw chicken. Bodies deceased for a few days were a bit harder to ignore, no matter how much experience one had with them.

Miss Nichols was murdered less than a day ago, but the strong dead rat scent confirmed her injuries were brutal. I said a silent prayer for her troubled soul and ravaged body before fully stepping into the room.

A gas ceiling lamp threw sinister shadows against the brocade wallpaper, while two familiar figures peered over a corpse laid out on the mortuary table. It didn't take a genius to deduce the body belonged to our subject from class and the extra person in the room was my infuriating classmate.

I knew from experience not to interrupt Uncle while he was examining evidence and was especially grateful for that rule when he described the mutilated neck again—in even greater detail—for Thomas. There was something familiar about the woman and I couldn't stop myself from imagining her life prior to ending up before us.

Perhaps there were people who loved her—a husband or children—and were mourning her loss this very moment, no longer caring that she'd fallen on hard times.

Death was not prejudiced by mortal things such as station or gender. It came for kings and queens and prostitutes alike, often leaving the living with regrets. What might we have done differently if we'd known the end was so near? I shut those thoughts off. I was wandering dangerously close to an emotional door I'd already locked.

Distraction was something I needed, and thankfully, this was the perfect place for that very thing. Mahogany shelves lined the walls around the room with hundreds of glass specimen jars. They'd been carefully catalogued and displayed in alphabetical order—a task I was given last autumn and had only recently finished.

Overall I'd counted nearly seven hundred different samples, a brilliant collection for a museum, let alone a single household.

I trailed a finger over the preserved body nearest me; the label written in my tiny cursive identified it as a cross section of a frog. The dulled ammonia scent of formalin permeated everything in the subterranean lair, even the sweetness of decay, but was strangely comforting nonetheless. I quietly picked up the liver I'd removed yesterday and added it to the shelves. It was my very first addition to them.

My attention snagged on what I assumed were Miss Nichols's clothes. Bloodstains were hard to see on the dark material; however, given the nature of her attack, I knew they were there. Small, lace-up boots were covered in mud, smudging the table on which they rested. They were well-worn, telling of her poverty.

A chill—having nothing to do with the macabre scene unfolding across the room—crawled down my spine. Keeping the temperature quite low in this part of the house was essential, else the specimens rotted too fast.

The less constricting muslin dress I was wearing now offered little in the way of protection against the chilly air, but I preferred working in it over my finer corseted one, even as I rubbed the goose-flesh from my arms.

I scanned the wall opposite me containing medical journals and tools that, to an outside observer, might seem a bit frightening. The curved, scythe-like blade of the amputation knife, the bone saws, and the imposing glass and metal syringes wouldn't be out of place in a gothic novel such as both Nathaniel's and my childhood favorite: *Frankenstein*. They could easily be thought of as the devil's design, if one was inclined to think such superstitious notions... like Father.

The room's eerie silence was broken as Uncle called out basic facts such as height, gender, and hair and eye color while scouring the body for other traumas sustained during the murder. Facts I had already memorized from my journal entry.

I watched Thomas write notes onto a medical sheet with mechanical precision, his fingers more ink stained than they were in class. Note taking was generally my area of assistance during these procedures. I stood patiently, breathing in the chemical air and listening to the gentle sounds of flesh splaying, trying to ignore the sick churn of my gut. Settling my nerves always took several moments.

A few breaths later, Uncle noticed me standing in the corner and signaled for me to grab an apron and join them.

As I moved closer to the cadaver, it was as if a door had closed between my heart and head, sealing all emotions on the opposite side. Once I was standing over the body, I no longer saw the person she was in life. I only saw the shell left behind, and curiosity took hold in the worst of ways.

She'd morphed from a kindly enough looking woman into another faceless corpse; I'd had plenty of experience with them this summer. Strips of cloth covered parts of her to keep her decent, though there wasn't anything decent about her state.

Her skin was paler than the finest hand-painted pottery Mother had inherited from her grandmother in India, except along her jawline where dark bruising was evident. Hard living stole the softness I imagined she once had, and death was not gentle when it took her in its unforgiving embrace.

At least her eyes were closed. That was where the semi-peacefulness ended. According to Uncle she was missing five teeth, and her tongue had also sustained a laceration, indicating she was likely struck to either stun or knock her unconscious before the throat slitting. Those were the kinder injuries.

My gaze drifted to her lower abdomen, where a major injury was located on her left side. Uncle Jonathan hadn't exaggerated in class;

this cut was jagged and extremely deep. A few smaller slices ran along the right side of her torso but weren't nearly as bad, from what I could tell.

I saw why Uncle thought someone who had use of both hands might be responsible. The bruising on her jaw indicated someone had grabbed her face with the left hand, and the incision on the left side of her body was most likely made by someone using the right. Unless there was more than one butcher on the loose...

I shook my head and focused on her upper body again. The knife wounds to her neck told of an attack bred by violence. They were surprisingly easy to look at in my new emotionally detached state, however, and I wondered briefly if Aunt Amelia would say that was another strike against my moral character.

"Girls should be concerned with lace, not moral disgrace," she'd say.

I dreamed of a day when girls could wear lace and makeup—or no makeup at all and don burlap sacks if they desired—to their chosen profession without it being deemed *inappropriate.*

Uncle suddenly jumped back and sneezed. Thoughts of contracting airborne diseases crowded into my brain. I collected myself for a minute. Father's fears would not become my own and hold me back from what needed to be done.

Uncle snapped his fingers, pointing to one of four surgical knives lying on a metal tray. I snatched it up and handed it to him, grabbing each used tool and setting it in an alcohol bath after he was through with it. When it came time for the organ removal, I had individual trays and specimen glass ready before Uncle asked for them.

I knew my job well.

He grunted his approval then weighed the kidneys one at a time.

"The left kidney is approximately one hundred and thirty-seven grams." Thomas scratched the information down, quickly returning his focus to my uncle's next words. He was silent while absorbed in his work, my presence like a piece of furniture, wholly unnoticed until needed. "The right is a bit on the small side, coming in around one hundred nineteen."

Uncle removed a small piece of each organ, placing them on Petri dishes for further testing. This same routine went on for the heart, liver, intestines, and brain. My uncle's clean white apron gradually became bloodier, but he methodically washed his hands after each dissection to avoid contaminating the evidence.

There was no proof such contaminations could occur, but Uncle had his own theories on the matter. "Conventional society be damned," he'd bellow. "I know what I know."

Not much separated him from a butcher in appearance. I supposed even deceased humans were nothing more than animals being flayed open in the name of science instead of nourishment.

Everything looked the same when you removed its top layers.

I nearly laughed out loud at my absurd thoughts. Twice a year Aunt Amelia and cousin Liza stayed with us. Part of their visit included socializing me with girls my age by hosting lavish tea parties. Aunt Amelia hoped I'd continue attending them on my own, but I'd put an end to that. The girls at tea didn't understand my mind, which was precisely why I'd declined their invitations over the last several months. I hated the pity in their eyes and couldn't imagine explaining my afternoons to them.

Some of them found it obscene to dip their butter knives into lemon curd. What horror they'd feel at seeing my scalpel disappearing into bloody tissue!

Something cool and wet seeped into the bottom of my shoes. I hadn't noticed the pool of blood I'd been standing in. I quickly fetched a bag of sawdust and sprinkled it across the floor like a fine layer of tan-colored snow. I'd have to get rid of my slippers before I went home later, no need to frighten my newest lady's maid any more than I normally did when I came home splattered in the day's work.

Uncle snapped his fingers, returning me to the task at hand.

Once I'd disinfected the bone saw Uncle used to open the cranium and laid it back on the shelf, the autopsy was complete. Uncle Jonathan stitched the body together like a skilled tailor whose medium was flesh instead of fine fabric. I watched as the Y incision he'd made earlier turned from darkened crimson to black thread.

Out of the corner of my eye, I saw Thomas furiously sketching the body in its last state. His pencil slowing, then speeding across the paper. I grudgingly had to admit his drawing was really quite good. The details he captured would aid us with the investigation once the body was taken back to the morgue.

"Do you recognize the deceased, Audrey Rose?"

My attention snapped to Uncle. He was removing his apron, his gaze locked onto mine. I bit my lip, studying the woman's mangled face. There was that gnawing sense of familiarity, but I still couldn't place her. I slowly shook my head, feeling defeated.

"She worked in your household. Briefly." Guilt sunk its claws into me—I still didn't recognize the poor woman. What a wretched thing; taking no notice of someone in my very own home. Miss Nichols deserved better from me. And the world. I felt utterly terrible. Uncle turned to the sink. "You would've been ill at the time."

Thomas jerked his attention up, reading my body for any signs of lingering disease. As if he even cared. He was probably worried this news might pose some sort of potential hazard for himself. My face burned, and I busied myself with the specimens.

"What have either of you learned from our little exercise today?" Uncle Jonathan interrupted my thoughts, scrubbing his hands and forearms with a block of carbolic soap. "Any interesting theories?"

I jumped at the opportunity to speak my mind now that we

weren't surrounded by students. A small part of me was also excited for a chance to show off my theories in front of Thomas. I wanted him to see he wasn't the only one with an interesting mind.

"Whoever is responsible for the murder must have some sort of training in the medical field," I said. "He might even be a mortuary student. Or someone who's taken surgical classes at the very least."

Uncle nodded. "Good. Tell me more."

Feeling bolstered by Uncle's approval, I circled the body. "She might've been grabbed by her face, then received a blow rendering her unconscious." I thought of the incisions and areas of the body that were injured. "Also, she might have been brought elsewhere. Our murderer needed time to perform his surgery without interruption."

An image of our former servant being beaten, then dragged to some forgotten cellar or other damp, shadowy place set my skin crawling around my body like worms in a graveyard. Though I didn't remember her, the mere thought of her living and breathing and working in my house made me feel responsible for her in a way. I wanted to help her now in death, though I'd failed her miserably in life. Maybe she'd still be alive and reputably employed if I'd been brave enough to speak out against Father's chronic need to change staff every few weeks.

My hands fisted at my sides. I refused, absolutely *refused* to let this cruel treatment of a woman stand. I'd do everything in my power to solve this case for Miss Nichols. And for any other voiceless girl or woman society ignored.

Mother would've done the same.

All other thoughts left my mind in place of the horrific reality we were dealing with. "He must have slit her throat in a location where a large amount of blood wouldn't draw attention. Possibly he took her to the slaughterhouse and did it there."

Thomas snorted from his station near the body. I whipped

around to properly glare at him, removing the ties from my apron with as much venom as I could inject into the action, and tossing it into a laundry bin. I knew my face must be flushed again, but hoped he'd misinterpret the cause.

"Why is that funny, Mr. . . . ?"

He composed himself and stood.

"Mr. Thomas Cresswell at your service, Miss Wadsworth." Bending slightly at the waist in a mock bow, he came to his full, impressive height and smiled. "I find it amusing because it's an extraordinary amount of work for our murderer. Hauling her off to the slaughterhouse *after* he went through the trouble of knocking her unconscious." He tsked. "Seems rather unnecessary."

"Pardon me, but you don't—"

Thomas closed the journal he'd been sketching in and walked around the corpse, rudely speaking over me. "Especially when he could easily slice her open at the river, allowing evidence to wash away without dirtying his hands further. Not to mention"—he pointed to her soiled boots—"the mud caked onto her heels."

I scrunched my nose as if something worse than rotten flesh was in the air. I hated the fact I'd missed making the connection between the dirt on her boots and the muddy banks of the river. I hated even more that Thomas hadn't missed it.

"Hasn't rained here in almost a week," he went on, "and there are a number of dark corners near the Thames ripe for Leather Apron's picking."

"*You* just stated it was ridiculous to presume he killed her at the slaughterhouse," I said, narrowing my eyes. "Now you've gone and called him a leather apron?"

"I was referencing *the* Leather Apron. Haven't you seen a paper this afternoon?" Thomas studied me as if I were a specimen he'd possibly like to dissect. "Surely choosing the perfect silken shoes isn't more important than finding a blood-crazed murderer. Yet... look at those things on your feet, getting all stained and gory. Is your interest in science simply an attempt at finding a husband? Shall I grab my coat, then?"

He flashed a roguish grin at my scowl. "I'm sure your uncle won't mind stopping his investigation to chaperone us"—he turned to Uncle—"would you, Dr. Wadsworth? I do admit your niece is quite beautiful."

I averted my gaze. I'd forgotten less frilly shoes in my mad rush to exit the house. Not that there was anything wrong with my slippers. If I chose to wear them to postmortems it was my choice and my choice alone.

Perhaps I'd do it from now on simply to irk him.

"You know an awful lot about how this murderer thinks," I said sweetly. "Perhaps we should investigate *your* whereabouts that evening, Mr. Cresswell."

He gazed at me, a dark brow arched in contemplation. I swallowed hard, but held his stare. A minute later he nodded as if coming to some sort of conclusion about me.

"If you're going to follow me around at night, Miss Wadsworth"—his attention flicked to my feet—"I'd advise you to wear more sensible shoes." I opened my mouth to retort; however, Mr. Thomas Cresswell spoke over me again. Brash fool. "The Leather Apron is what they're calling our murderer."

He moved around the examination table, stalking closer to where I stood. I wanted to back away, but he held me in his magnetic orbit. He stopped before me, a softness briefly flashing across his features, and my heart picked up speed.

Lord help the girl he set those eyes on for good. His boyish vulnerability was a weapon, powerful and disarming. I was thankful I wasn't the kind of girl to lose my mind over a handsome face. He'd need to work a bit harder to gain my affection.

"To answer your earlier question, Dr. Wadsworth," he said, tearing his gaze from mine, his tone more serious than before, "I fully believe this is only the beginning. What we have on our hands is the start of a career murderer. No one with that kind of surgical prowess would commit one murder then stop."

His lips quirked slightly when he noticed my incredulous expression. "I know I wouldn't. One taste of warm blood is never enough, Miss Wadsworth."

The Princess Alice, c. 1880s

FOUR
A DANCE WITH THE DEVIL

WADSWORTH RESIDENCE,
BELGRAVE SQUARE
7 SEPTEMBER 1888

Leather Apron and the Whitechapel Murderer were the headlines of the last week.

Everywhere I looked, a new theory was introduced by another supposed expert in the field. Detective inspectors had several doctors examine the body of Miss Nichols and, for the most part, they'd all come to the same conclusions as Uncle Jonathan.

Most everyone disagreed with Uncle's theory of her being assaulted while standing, however. They did agree her throat was slashed prior to the incisions made along her abdomen, and that whoever was responsible was unlikely to simply stop now.

East End residents were terrified to go out after sunset, fearing every shadowy figure was the depraved murderer. Prostitutes were warned to be on high alert, but their need to pay for lodging kept them from completely abandoning the streets.

My father was worse than ever, coming unhinged, it seemed, every time I left the house. It was becoming harder to sneak about or come up with excuses for leaving that he didn't question. He'd let go of all our maids and hired a whole new lot, his paranoia of them infecting our family with Lord only knew what overshadowing his reason. There was no point telling him that new servants were more likely to bring infection in, as they'd been outside our home and in the scary, disease-spreading world.

Pretty soon I feared he'd be escorting me everywhere himself. Unfortunately, that meant attending Uncle's forensic medicines class had become nearly impossible, though I was fortunate I could still make it to the laboratory.

"I fully believe this is only the beginning." Mr. Thomas Cresswell's ominous warning replayed through my mind each passing day. It felt like the uneasy stillness before the storm, and I found myself even more restless than usual at night. I had a hard time fully believing his theory, though. The thought of any more murders taking place was simply out of the question. I'd never heard of a career murderer before.

It seemed Thomas was looking for another outlet to show off his brilliance, and I wanted nothing more than to prove him wrong, potentially earning more of Uncle's respect in the process.

Between my desire for Uncle's approval and my connection to Miss Nichols, I was determined to help solve this case.

I tried approaching my brother to discuss his thoughts on it, but he'd been preoccupied with studying and couldn't spare any time. Which left me with too much time to think about death and the finality of it all.

Nathaniel always assured me what happened wasn't my fault, but his comfort didn't take the sting out of my chest each time Father stared at me with such overwhelming fear. As far as he was concerned, it was his duty to protect me against everything in the world. Mother didn't die nursing Nathaniel back from scarlet fever, after all. He didn't have to watch her face flush with that horrible rash and see her tongue swell because my brother had been weak. Her already damaged heart didn't break fully because Nathaniel had brought infection to our home.

I couldn't help feeling as if I were Father's useless, murdering daughter who looked too much like her mother—a constant reminder of all he'd lost. Of all I'd stolen away from him the night I took my first fever-free breath, and Mother took her last.

I was the reason for his growing madness, and I never let myself forget it. When I closed my eyes, I still saw the hospital staff in their long dresses and starched aprons. Their solemn faces turning away from my earsplitting screams as Mother's chest stuttered and fell still forever. I banged on her sternum with both fists, my tears falling on her beautifully stitched dressing gown, but she didn't stir again.

No twelve-year-old should watch her mother's soul drift into the abyss. It was the first time I'd ever felt helpless. God had failed me. I'd prayed and prayed the way Mother always said I should, and for what? Death still claimed her in the end. It was then I knew I'd rely on something more tangible than holy spirits.

Science never abandoned me the way religion had that night.

Forsaking the Holy Father was considered a sin, and I did it repeatedly. Each time my blade met with flesh, I sinned more and welcomed it.

God no longer held dominion over my soul.

This evening my thoughts were treacherously loud and impossible to quiet down. I tossed back and forth in my thin nightdress, kicked my sheets off, and finally poured myself a glass of water from a pitcher on my bedside table. "Blast it all."

Sleep wasn't going to find me. That much I was certain of. My limbs itched with the need to get out and *do* something. Or perhaps I simply needed to escape from the confines of my room and all the woeful thoughts that came with the darkness.

Each day that passed was a failure to help Miss Nichols's family find peace. I'd already failed her once; I wouldn't fail again so miserably.

I clenched my fists. I could do the safe and reasonable thing, waiting in Uncle's laboratory until another victim showed up. Or I could act now. Tonight. I could gather clues that might help, impressing both Thomas and Uncle in the process.

The more I thought on it, the surer I became of my decision. Mother used to say, "Roses have both petals and thorns, my dark flower. You needn't believe something weak because it appears delicate. Show the world your bravery."

Mother had had a weak heart and was kept from much physical activity as a child, but she'd found other ways to prove her strength. One needn't be strong in only physical matters—a strong mind and will were fierce to behold as well.

"You're right, Mother." I paced along the deep gold Persian rug in my room, relishing the coldness of the hardwood when my soles found the edges of the carpet. Before I knew what I was doing, I found myself standing in front of my looking glass, dressed all in black. "It's time for bravery."

Pulling my dark hair into a simple braid and pinning it about my crown, I tucked a few wayward strands behind my ears. My dress was a simple design with long fitted sleeves, a small bustle, and light cotton fabric. I ran my hands down the front of it, enjoying the softness and fine craftsmanship of the garment.

I stared at the dark circles under my eyes that told of many sleepless nights. The paleness of my already sallow-looking skin was heavily contrasted by the black clothing, so I pinched my cheeks, giving them some much-needed color.

Mother never had to worry about doing such things. Her skin was a beautiful golden beige, showing off her ancestry from India, and mine was simply a paler imitation of hers. I reminded myself I need not be fashionable; I was going for stealth. Though my aunt would be pleased I'd taken an interest in my appearance.

Unbidden, a wretched thought flashed through my mind. Thomas and Uncle were out the evening of the first murder... they were interested in studying the human body. And Thomas had flat-out lied about it. If I discovered them doing treacherous things, would they harm me? I laughed, covering my mouth to stifle the sound.

What a ridiculous notion.

My uncle was not capable of such acts. Thomas, however... I couldn't say for sure, but refused to follow that trail of thought.

I imagined the murderer was a physician traveling abroad or someone who was working for a physician to locate organs for study. Or perhaps some wealthy man or woman was willing to pay dearly for a transplant of some sort.

Though, that science hadn't been effective yet. No one had ever accomplished a successful organ transplant. Either way, I doubted highly that Leather Apron was hanging around, stalking women of the night. I'd be fine, cloaked under darkness.

Without allowing myself a moment's hesitation, I swiftly sneaked down the stairs, crept into the drawing room, and latched myself in. Glancing about the empty room, I released a sigh. All was quiet. I tiptoed across the floor, then opened the window farthest from the door.

Placing both hands on the windowsill, I glanced over my shoulder, checking the lock once more. Father was sleeping, and he wasn't quite mad enough to check on me during the night, but the thought of being caught had my heart running double its speed.

A thrill twirled through my veins as I pushed off, dropping a few feet to the patch of grass set between stones. The few seconds of weightlessness made me feel as free as a bird soaring in the heavens.

I smiled as I wiped my soft leather gloves off and slunk into the shadows surrounding the building. Father would lock me in the old coal cellar if he knew I'd sneaked away so late, which made my night adventure all the more appealing.

Let him discover I was out at this indecent hour and was more than capable of taking care of myself. I welcomed the chance not only to ferret out helpful clues for our investigation but to prove Father's fears irrational as well.

Even if there was *potentially* a madman on the loose.

My quest began losing its appeal the longer I slipped in and out of the dimness of London's abandoned streets.

I couldn't take the carriage without Father learning of my shameful activities, and trekking through the cobblestone streets for nearly an hour wasn't as bold and daring as I'd imagined it to be. I was cold, and the streets stank of waste. Needles pricked between my shoulder blades. I had the horrible feeling I was being watched. I nearly fainted when a silly old cat ran into my path.

Down the block, I heard a commotion and slipped into the closest alleyway to avoid being seen. Voices carried over the rolling fog, adding a haunted feeling to the already eerie streets. I counted my breaths, waiting for the people to pass by, praying no one would slink into my hiding place. Wind tickled the back of my neck, raising gooseflesh. I didn't like being trapped between buildings.

I hadn't really thought of what I'd say should I encounter someone at this hour. All I'd been thinking was I'd spy on the pubs Miss Nichols had visited prior to her death, possibly learn some new fact or clue from the people deep in their drink, and outsmart Thomas Cresswell. Perhaps I should've prepared myself a bit more instead of being motivated by the desire to show off my own intelligence to such an obnoxious yet damnably brilliant boy.

I glanced up through the light fog at the cross street. Hanbury.

How had I gotten this far over? I was nearly to the Princess Alice but had traveled a touch out of the way. The next few streets should take me to Wentworth and Commercial.

Without waiting for the drunken couple to pass, I willed myself to take on the stealth of an apparition, floating soundlessly down the alley and across the road. My feet took sturdy steps, though a feather could have knocked me over my heart was pounding so hard. Halfway through the alley, a pebble knocked out of place behind me. I whirled to see . . . nothing.

No scythe-wielding murderer or drunken bar patron. Only an empty black space between buildings. Must have been a rat crawling through rubbish.

I stood for a few more beats, waiting, my heart thrashing against my ribs like a fish taken from water. I feared a monster would be standing behind me, breathing its rotten breath down my neck should I turn around, so I closed my eyes. Somehow, everything seemed easier to manage when I couldn't see. Though it was a foolish, foolish thing to do. Pretending a monster wasn't there didn't make it go away. It only made one vulnerable to its attack.

I listened hard. When no other sounds occurred, I moved swiftly away, tossing glances over my shoulder to be certain I was alone.

Once I saw the lively pub in front of me, I took a deep breath. I'd much rather take my chances with drunken ruffians than the shadows stalking the night. The brick building stood three stories tall and was prominently placed between two streets, giving it a triangular shape in the front.

Noise and the clinking clatter of plates and glasses filtered out through the front doors along with bawdy laughter and words no lady should hear. Sinking my teeth into my lower lip, I eyed some of the more surly patrons in view.

I rethought my earlier fear of shadows.

Some men were covered in soot, while others had blood splatter along the cuffs of their rolled sleeves. Butchers and factory workers. Their arms were corded with the look of hard labor, and their rough accents spoke of poverty. My fragile aristocratic bones stuck out even in my plainest dress. I cursed the bustle and finely stitched seams—apparent even in the dark—and contemplated turning back.

I refused to be defeated so easily by fear or a well-made garment.

Squaring my shoulders, I took one giant step toward the crowd before being dragged backward by an unseen force. I opened my mouth to scream, but was quickly silenced by a large hand covering the lower half of my face.

The grasp wasn't hard, but I couldn't gain enough leeway to bite down on my assailant. I kicked and jerked about to no avail. The only thing I managed to do was to wrap my blasted skirts about my legs, tumbling into my assailant, allowing him a bit more ease in his unholy mission. I was at the mercy of this invisible demon, powerless to break free of its supernatural grasp.

"Please. Don't scream. You'll ruin everything." His voice was far too amused given the situation. At least he wasn't an apparition, then. I wrestled with everything I had, twisting and knocking my head against his chest. If he wasn't so tall, I might have connected with his head. "We're going somewhere quiet. Then we can talk. All right?"

I nodded slowly, collecting my racing thoughts. Somehow, that voice was familiar. He gently pulled me into the shadows, our bodies pressed together most inappropriately, and even though I thought I recognized his voice, I didn't make his job easy. I'd show him how right my mother was about roses having both petals *and* thorns.

Digging my heels in, I kicked and tried scratching his arms, with little success. We stumbled into the alley, our limbs knocking together, and he *ooomphed* as my elbow connected with his stomach. Good. If I died now, at least I'd have some satisfaction of having injured the beast. My momentary victory was short-lived—my bulky skirts weighed down any more attempts at fleeing, and the monstrous fog finally swallowed us whole.

Once we were far enough away from the pub and the gas lamps lining the cobbled streets, my attacker released me as promised. My chest heaved with fear and rage. Bracing myself for a fight, I spun on my heel, blinking disbelief away.

Thomas Cresswell stood with his arms crossed at his chest, a slight frown turning down his handsome features. He, too, was dressed solidly in black, with the addition of a cap pulled low over his brow. His profile cast sharp shadows in the waning light.

There was an almost dangerous aura about him cautioning me away, but anger seethed through my veins. I was going to kill him.

"Are you completely mad? Was that necessary?" I demanded, both fists planted on my hips to avoid strangling him. "You could've simply asked me to follow you! And what do you think you're doing skulking along the streets at this ungodly hour?"

He eyed me warily, then ran a hand down his tired-looking face. If I didn't know any better, I'd think he'd possibly been worried. "I could ask the same of you, Miss Wadsworth. But I'd rather save that spectacle for your brother."

"My—" I didn't have time to finish my sentence before Nathaniel appeared like the Ghost of Christmas Past, looking less than amused. For once, I was without words.

Nathaniel nodded toward Thomas, then grabbed me roughly by my elbow, pulling me deeper into the shadows and out of earshot. I wrenched around, glaring, but Thomas's attention was fixed on the arm Nathaniel was latched onto, the muscle in his jaw clenching. His reaction confounded me enough to go along with my brother peacefully.

"Please spare me any of your ridiculous stories, Sister," Nathaniel whispered harshly when we were far enough away. "I don't even want to know *why* you thought it a fine idea to traipse around darkened streets while a murderer is stalking women. Do you have some sort of death wish?"

I got the impression this was a rhetorical question. I kept quiet by squeezing the material of my skirts between my fingers. What I wanted to do was shake his rough hand off my elbow where he was still gripping me a bit too hard. I also wanted to scold him for being as overprotective as Father and reacting hysterically.

But couldn't bring myself to do either of those things.

Nathaniel released me, then tugged at his fine leather gloves until his face slowly returned to a more natural color instead of the blazing red of the Queen's Guard.

He sighed, running a hand through his fair hair.

"Losing Mother was bad enough." His voice caught and he coughed the emotion away, yanking his comb out from beneath his overcoat. "Don't expect me to sit back and watch you recklessly endanger yourself, little sister." His eyes dared me to say one stupid thing. "It would destroy me. Understand?"

As quickly as my temper flared, my ire was quelled. For the last five years it was the two of us against the world. Father was too lost in sorrow to really be present. Putting myself in Nathaniel's place, I could see the minute cracks of my emotions shattering should I ever lose him.

"I'm sorry for worrying you, Nathaniel. Truly." I meant every word of the apology. Then a thought struck. I narrowed my eyes. "Why, might I ask, are you trolling around back alleyways with that devil Mr. Cresswell?"

"If you must know," Nathaniel said a bit haughtily, adjusting his collar, "we're not the only ones out here."

Now this had my full attention. I raised a brow, waiting while my brother scanned the abandoned area around us. "A group of us are doing a bit of our own inquiry. We've taken up posts throughout Whitechapel and are looking for suspicious persons. We're calling ourselves the 'Knights of Whitechapel.' "

I blinked. The only people who looked sorely out of place were my well-dressed brother and his ridiculous hat-wearing lackey. I could only imagine what the rest of the highborn boys looked like in this neighborhood.

"The Knights of Whitechapel," I repeated. My brother wasn't capable of hurting a common housefly; I hated imagining what some diabolical killer might do to him out here in the dark. "You cannot be serious, Nathaniel. What would you possibly do if you came face to face with this murderer, offer him a silver comb or perhaps some French wine?"

A dark look crossed my brother's face.

"You'd be surprised what I'd manage should the need arise." Nathaniel gritted his teeth. "He'd soon discover he's not the only one who can induce fear. Now, then"—he angled me back down the alleyway toward the lone figure standing near the end—"Mr. Cresswell will see that you make it home safely."

The last thing I wanted was to be escorted home by Mr. Thomas Cresswell. He was quite smug enough. "If you're staying out here, then so am I."

I planted my feet, refusing to budge, but Nathaniel simply dragged me behind him as if I were made of feathers.

"No, you're not." He handed me off to my classmate. "Take the carriage to my house, Thomas. I'll come back on foot later."

If Thomas was annoyed with Nathaniel bossing him around like a common servant, he didn't show it. He simply wrapped his long fingers around my arm, tethering me to his side. I hated the surge of my pulse at his touch, but no longer struggled to break free. I stole a glance, noticing the smirk on his face.

He didn't grip me as if I were an unruly child in need of scolding, choosing instead to hold me back from Nathaniel, as if *he* were the one in need of rescuing. It was high time *someone* noticed I was capable of looking after myself. Even if that someone was an infuriating boy. An intelligent, arrogant, handsome boy. I stood a little straighter, and Thomas chuckled—a delicious, rumbling sound I wouldn't mind hearing again. My brother spared me one last look.

"Be sure to place a stick atop that windowsill in the drawing room." He smiled broadly at the death glare I leveled at him. "Sorry, little sister. But I do believe you've had enough excitement for one evening. Count your blessings you encountered only the two of us out here and not someone more sinister."

"Come," Thomas said, directing me toward the carriage. "Your brother's right. Something wicked lurks in these shadows."

I twisted around to stare at him. "Something more wicked than you?"

Thomas opened his mouth before catching on to my teasing, then laughed in a way that set my heart racing again. Perhaps he *was* the most dangerous thing I could encounter out here, and my brother hadn't a clue. One fact was slowly taking shape: I was in jeopardy of admiring Mr. Cresswell against my better judgment. A gust of wind tangled my hair, bringing with it a chill that caressed my skin.

I glanced around for my brother, but he'd already been taken by the fog.

FIVE

DARK AND HIDEOUS THINGS

WADSWORTH RESIDENCE,
BELGRAVE SQUARE
8 SEPTEMBER 1888

"You're looking rather unwell this morning." Father glanced at me over his paper. "Perhaps you ought to return to bed. I'll send up some broth. Last thing we need is to have you coming down with an influenza or worse. Especially as winter draws near."

He set the paper down and wiped his brow with a handkerchief. Out of our family members, Father was the only one who appeared unwell. He'd been perspiring a lot lately.

"Are... are you feeling all right, Father? You look a bit—"

"How I look is not your concern," he snapped, then quickly amended. "You needn't worry about my health, Audrey Rose. Attend to yourself. I should like it very much if you didn't leave the house again for some time. I've heard more disease is spreading in the slums."

After adding a few drops of tonic to his tea, he continued reading the news. I wanted to point out that gaining an immunity to certain things would keep me healthier, and the only way to gain such immunity was by leaving the house, but he'd never tolerated my knowledge of science or medicine. Keeping me in a bubble equaled safety to him, no matter how wrong that notion was.

He sipped from his tea, his presence filling the room but not warming it. My attention drifted to the clock. I needed to meet with Uncle soon. Nathaniel was still sleeping, so I was on my own for leaving the house.

I politely cleared my throat. "I'm in need of some new dresses and shoes"—I dropped my gaze, peering up through my lashes, feigning embarrassment—"and other more delicate items..."

Father waved me off, thoughts of corsets and undergarments too much for him to hear about despite his fears of my poor health. He blotted at his nose with the same handkerchief, then returned it to his pocket.

"Do what you must," he said. "But be home in time for supper and your lesson on running a proper household. Your aunt says you showed little improvement last time she visited."

I fought the urge to roll my eyes at his predictability. "Yes, Father."

"Oh," he said, wiping his brow once more, "wear a mask when you leave today. There's talk of more East End sickness."

I nodded. The "mask" was nothing more than a cotton neckerchief I tied about my nose and mouth. I doubted it would protect me from anything. Satisfied with my obedience, he went back to reading, the sound of his teacup hitting the saucer, his sniffling, and the flipping of pages our only talkative companions.

GHASTLY MURDER IN WHITECHAPEL

I read the headline aloud to my uncle while he paced in front of the specimen jars in his basement laboratory. The deep burgundy wallpaper was normally a warm backdrop against the frigid temperature and even colder bodies adorning the examination table most days.

Today, however, the red tones reminded me of spilled blood, and I'd had my fill of that substance lately. I rubbed my hands over the thin sleeves of my muslin day dress and scanned the article. There was no mention of the new body they'd found this morning; it was still detailing poor Miss Nichols's death. The killer had taken mercy on her, compared to the nefarious acts he'd committed on victim number two.

I watched Uncle absently twist his mustache while doing his best to carve a path in the carpet. If he kept walking back and forth, I feared he'd wear through the wooden floorboards soon enough.

"Why position the body in such a manner?"

It was the same question he'd been asking himself since arriving from the latest murder over two hours ago. I had no theories to offer him. I was still trying to divorce myself from the abhorrent diagram he'd sketched on the chalkboard earlier.

My attention drifted to the disfigured image he'd created, drawn against my will like a magnet to the unimaginable gore.

I studied the words scrawled above the detailed drawing. *Miss Annie Chapman, aged forty-seven. Approximately five feet tall. Blue eyes. Shoulder-length dark brown, wavy hair.* An entire life distilled into five basic physical descriptions.

She'd been murdered on Hanbury Street. The very street I'd found myself on late last night. A chill worked its way deep into my bones, settling between my vertebrae like pigeons roosting on a clothesline.

Mere hours separated her untimely end and my dance with danger. Was it possible I'd been so close to the murderer? Nathaniel was right to be worried; I'd practically run into Leather Apron's all-too-eager arms by sneaking around like a child during the witching hour.

Should anything happen to me, Father would lose what was left of his mind, locking himself away in that study until he finally died of a broken heart.

"What of tossing her intestines about her shoulder?" Uncle paused before the diagram, staring past it at a memory not captured on the board. "Was it a message for the inspectors, or the easiest way to get what organ he sought?"

"Perhaps," I offered.

Uncle turned to me, astonished, as if he'd forgotten I was there. He shook his head. "Lord knows why I allow you to learn such unseemly things for a girl."

On occasion, Uncle would mutter such annoyances. I'd learned to ignore them for the most part, knowing he'd forget his hesitations quickly enough. "Because you love me?"

Uncle sighed. "Yes. And a brain such as yours shouldn't be wasted on frippery and gossip, I suppose."

My focus found the drawing again. The woman who'd taken my measurements earlier resembled the deceased woman's description nearly perfectly.

Keeping up the pretense of my whereabouts for Father, I'd stopped by the dressmaker's shop on the way in, picking out rich fabrics and new styles to be sent to the house. I'd decided on a walking dress made of deep navy with gold and cream stripes.

The bustle was smaller than my others and the hefty material would be perfect for the cooler weather. My absolute favorite was a tea gown I'd chosen, to wear when receiving visitors. It was the color of spun sugar with tiny roses embroidered along its front. A soft pink robe completed the loose-fitting gown, cascading to the floor.

Honestly, I couldn't wait for them to be ready. Just because I studied cadavers didn't mean I couldn't appreciate beautiful garments. My thoughts returned to the matter at hand. Had the seamstress not been reputably employed, she very well could have ended up on the streets and eventually in Uncle's laboratory, too.

Another cold corpse to slice into.

I crossed the room to where a tiny table stood nestled in the corner; a maid had brought in a tray of tea and a platter of scones with raspberry jam. I poured myself a cup of Earl Grey, adding a sugar cube with ornate silver tongs—the very opulence juxtaposed to our new case was nauseating.

I prepared a second cup for Uncle, leaving the scones untouched. The sanguine color of the preserves was revolting—I feared I'd never be hungry again.

Uncle jerked himself out of his next reverie when I handed him the steaming cup. The sweet herbal scent mixed with bergamot transfixed his attention for a few precious beats before he continued mumbling and pacing.

"Where is that blasted boy?"

He checked the brass—anatomically correct—heart clock mounted on the wall, frustration knotting his brow. It was hard to tell if he was more annoyed by the timepiece itself, or by Mr. Thomas Cresswell.

The clock was a gift from my father, a long-ago kindness he'd shown Uncle upon completing his medical degree. Father used to craft toys and clocks before Mother died, another joy her death had stolen from him.

Whereas I shunned religion for its abandonment, Father shunned his brother and science for their failure to save Mother. When she died, Father claimed Uncle hadn't tried hard enough.

Conversely, Uncle thought Father relied too heavily on a miracle he couldn't offer and was a fool to blame him for Mother's death. I couldn't imagine ever hating my brother that much and pitied them both for their animosity.

I shifted my focus to the time. Thomas had left over an hour earlier, inquiring after the members of his vigilante group. Uncle hoped one of them might have seen something suspicious because they were posted—like boys playing medieval knights—throughout Whitechapel until four in the morning.

Personally, I wondered why Thomas wouldn't already know if they'd come across something. That was the whole point of their little group.

When another half hour ticked by and Mr. Cresswell still hadn't returned, Uncle was practically mad with unrest. It seemed even the corpses and dead things surrounding us held their collective breaths, not wanting to wake the sleeping darkness from within him. I loved and respected Uncle, but his passion often toed the line of madness when he was under pressure.

Ten minutes later the door creaked open, revealing Thomas's tall, silhouetted form. Uncle practically vaulted across the laboratory, a rabid hunger for knowledge in his eyes. I swear if I had looked closely enough, I'd have seen white foam collecting at the corners of his mouth. When he got like this, it was easy to see why some people thought him odd, my brother included.

"Well, then? What news have you? Who knows what?"

A servant removed Thomas's long overcoat and hat before disappearing up the narrow staircase. Those uninterested in forensic studies never liked lingering down here for long. Too many dark and hideous things lurked in glass jars and on stone slabs.

Thomas eyed the drawing on the board before answering, purposefully not looking in Uncle's direction. "No one saw or heard a thing out of the ordinary, I'm afraid."

I narrowed my eyes. Thomas didn't sound very upset by this news.

"However," he added, "I tagged along with the inspectors while they made some inquiries. Paltry as they might be. This one jester pelted me with questions regarding your work, but I didn't offer much. Said he might call on you later this evening." He shook his head. "Screws and gears were discarded near the body. And . . . a few witnesses have stepped forth."

Uncle inhaled sharply. "And?"

"Unfortunately, the best description we received came from a woman who saw only a man from behind. She stated that the two of them were speaking, but she couldn't make out more than the deceased agreeing to something. As she was a prostitute, I'm sure you can fill in the lurid details."

"Thomas!" Uncle shot a glance in my direction; only then did my classmate acknowledge me standing in the room. "There's a young lady present."

I rolled my eyes. Leave it to Uncle Jonathan to worry about prostitution being too much for my feminine persuasion, yet think nothing of me seeing a body spliced open before I'd even had my luncheon.

"Sincere apologies, Miss Wadsworth. I hadn't seen you there." Thomas was nothing but a filthy liar. He cocked his head, a sly smile tugging at the corners of his lips as if he were privy to my thoughts. "I did not mean to offend you."

"I am hardly offended, Mr. Cresswell." I gave him a pointed look. "On the contrary, I am highly perturbed we're even discussing such fatuous things when another woman has been slain so brutally." I ticked off each injury on my fingers, accentuating my point. "Gutted with her innards tossed over a shoulder. Posed with her legs up, knees facing outward. Not to mention . . . her missing reproductive organs."

"Yes," Thomas agreed, nodding, "that was rather unpleasant, now that you mention it."

"You speak as if you've witnessed it firsthand, Mr. Cresswell."

"Perhaps I have."

"Thomas, please," Uncle scolded. "Do not goad her."

I turned my annoyance on Uncle. "By all means, let's continue wasting time speaking of my potential *discomfort* at her occasional profession. What is your issue with prostitutes anyhow? It's not her fault society is so unjust to women."

"I—" Uncle Jonathan stepped back, placing a palm to his forehead as if he might be able to rub my tirade out with a few soothing strokes. Thomas had the gall to wink at me over the cup of tea he'd poured himself.

"Very well." He raised an exaggerated eyebrow at Uncle. "The young lady has made her case, Doctor. From this point forward I shall pretend she's as capable as a man."

I glared harder. "Pretend I am as capable as a man? Please, sir, do not value me so little!"

"Also," he continued before I exploded, setting his teacup down on its matching blue and white Staffordshire saucer, "as we're now treating each other like equals and peers, I insist on you calling me Thomas, or Cresswell. Silly formalities needn't apply to equals such as we." He grinned at me in a way that could be considered a flirtation.

Not to be outdone, I lifted my chin. "If that's what you want, then, you're permitted to call me Audrey Rose. Or Wadsworth."

Uncle stared up at the ceiling rose, sighing heavily. "Back to our murder, then," he said, removing spectacles from a leather satchel and securing them on his face. "What else have either of you got for me besides the promise of a splitting headache?"

"I have a new theory on why this act was more violent than the last," I said slowly, a new puzzle piece slipping into place in my mind. "It occurred to me the scenes appear to be tainted with . . . revenge."

For once, I held their attention—as if I were a corpse with secrets to divulge.

"During our lesson you said first-time killers most likely start by murdering those they know." Uncle nodded. "Well, what if the murderer knew Miss Nichols and couldn't really let himself go as wild as he'd hoped? It's as if he wanted to exact revenge, but couldn't bring himself to do it once it came down to it. Miss Nichols was not as viciously mutilated as Miss Annie Chapman had been, leading me to believe Miss Chapman was unknown to our murderer."

"Interesting theory, Niece." Uncle absently stroked his mustache. "Perhaps Miss Nichols was murdered by her husband or the man she was living with."

Thomas took up my uncle's favorite habit of pacing in a wide circle around the room. With each movement he made, the scent of formalin and bergamot wafted through the air, creating a strange aroma that was both unsettling and comforting.

"Why is he taking their organs, though?" he muttered to himself. I watched silently as the gears twisted and ground their way through the maze of his brain. He was fascinating to study, no matter how much I pretended to detest that fact.

As if a light had illuminated the dark, he snapped his fingers. "He has a deep hatred for women, for what they represent to him, or something from his past. Somewhere along the line, a woman disappointed him greatly."

"Why attack prostitutes?" I asked, ignoring Uncle as he cringed at my improper word choice.

"First, they're easy, opportunity-wise. They also follow men into dark places eagerly." Thomas walked closer, his attention landing on me for the briefest moment before moving on to the cadaver. "Maybe he fears the threat they pose. Or perhaps he's some sort of religious zealot, ridding the world of whores and harlots."

Uncle slammed his hands down on the table, causing a specimen jar to slosh onto the wooden surface. "That's enough! It's improper enough to be teaching Audrey Rose such things, we needn't use vulgarity in the process."

I sighed. I'd never understand the way a man's mind worked. My gender didn't handicap me. Yet I was blessed that Uncle was modern enough to allow my apprenticeship with him, and so I would tolerate these minimal annoyances.

"I apologize, sir." Thomas cleared his throat. "But I believe if your niece can handle dissecting a human, she can handle intelligent conversation without fainting. Her intellect, though nowhere near as vast as mine, may prove useful."

Thomas cleared his throat again, preparing himself for Uncle's backlash, but my uncle quietly relented. I couldn't help staring, open-mouthed, at him. He'd actually defended me. In that annoying, roundabout way of his. But still. Seemed I wasn't the only one experiencing growing respect.

"Very well. Do go on."

Thomas glanced at me, then took a deep breath.

"He loathes these creatures of the night. Loathes they're alive, selling themselves. I wager the one he loves or loved has likely left him. Perhaps he feels betrayed in a way." Thomas picked his tea back up, taking a careful sip before setting it down again. "I wouldn't be surprised if his wife or betrothed committed suicide—the ultimate act of leaving him."

Uncle, returning quickly to his scientific mind-set, nodded. "He also feels he's entitled to take what he wants. Literally. He paid for it, after all. In his eyes, he's telling these woman exactly what he's after, therefore they're willing participants in his..."

"Murders." A sick feeling tied bows in my stomach. Someone was running about the streets tricking women into agreeing to be butchered. "Is it possible he's living out a fantasy?" I asked, thinking aloud. "Perhaps he's trying to play God."

Thomas almost fell over from stopping so short. He twisted on his heel and crossed the room in a few short strides. Clutching my elbows, he kissed my cheek, rendering me both speechless and scarlet.

My focus shot to my uncle as I touched my cheek, but he said nothing of this inappropriate behavior; his mind was latched on to murder.

"You're brilliant, Audrey Rose," Thomas said, eyes glittering with admiration. He held my gaze a moment too long to be polite. "That's got to be it! We're dealing with someone who thinks himself a god of sorts."

"Well done, both of you." Uncle's eyes shone with renewed hope and near certainty. "We've secured a possible motive."

"Which is what?" I asked, not fully following the motive they were talking about. I was having difficulty thinking of anything other than Thomas's lips on my cheek, and the grotesqueness of our conversation.

Uncle inhaled deeply. "Our murderer is using his religious views to determine these women's fate. I would be unsurprised if he were some closet crusader or perhaps he's a failed clergyman, killing in the name of God."

A new realization sat heavy upon my breast. "Which means there could be more victims." And a lot more blood before this was through.

Uncle shared a haunted look with Thomas, then me. Words needn't be said.

Scotland Yard would laugh us into the asylum if we went to them with this theory. And who would blame them? What would we say—"A mad priest or clergyman is on the loose, killing because God ordained it, and all of London won't be safe until we find a way to stop him"?

My uncle was famous, but people still gossiped behind his back.

It wouldn't take much for him to be seen as a man driven to murder from picking apart the dead like a carrion scavenger. People would cross themselves and say a prayer he lived out his days peacefully in a faraway place, preferably in solitary confinement.

Thomas and I wouldn't fare much better in the vote of public opinion. Our work was considered a desecration of the dead.

"It's essential we tell no one of this," Uncle said at last, removing his spectacles and pinching the bridge of his nose. "Not Nathaniel. Nor friends or classmates. At least not until we can prove ourselves to the police. For now, I want you both to scour the evidence we've collected. There has to be some clue we're missing, anything at all we can use to identify the perpetrator before he strikes again."

The murderer truly must be a madman if he thought what he was doing was helpful or righteous. And that thought was more terrifying than any other.

A knock came at the thick wooden door, followed by a servant bobbing a quick curtsy at my uncle. "Mr. Nathaniel Wadsworth is in the parlor, sir. Says it's urgent he see his sister straightaway."

SIX
DEN OF SIN

DR. JONATHAN WADSWORTH'S PARLOR, HIGHGATE
8 SEPTEMBER 1888

Nathaniel was pale as a corpse when I rushed into Uncle's stuffy parlor.

The dark greens and blue swirls of the wallpaper were meant to inspire a sense of tranquility, but did little to calm my brother. Sweat trickled down his brow, staining a ring around the starched collar of his shirt. His hair was as wild as his eyes; severe dark circles marred his normally flawless complexion. My brother hadn't slept all night, it seemed, but the sorry state of his hair worried me the most.

I gathered my skirts and collided with him halfway across the room, ignoring the way the boning on my corset dug painfully into my ribs. He wrapped me into an uncomfortably tight embrace, tucking his chin to my neck and breathing deeply.

"You're all right," he whispered, half mad. "Thank the heavens, you're all right."

I pulled back slightly, peering into his eyes. "Of course, I am, Nathaniel. Why would you assume I wasn't?"

"Forgive me, Sister. I just learned of the second murder and where it occurred. I knew the victim wasn't you, but couldn't shake the sense of foreboding gripping my heart." He swallowed hard. "Imagine my worry. You haven't the best history when it comes to sound judgment. I feared you'd been lured away someplace dreadful. The day has already been unkind to our family. I couldn't help fearing the worst."

"Why wouldn't you think of finding me here sooner?" I asked, clutching the last unraveling thread of my patience. How infuriating having to deal with such doubt all the time. If I were a man, Nathaniel certainly wouldn't be treating me as if I were incapable of looking after myself. "You know I spend most of my time with Uncle. Surely you can't have been running aimlessly around the streets all afternoon. And what has the day done to our family that's so horrid?"

Nathaniel's features twisted with anger. "Why indeed would I be flustered? Perhaps because my sister cannot bother to remain indoors like a normal, decent girl!"

At first his words stole the breath from me. Why must I either be docile and decent, or curious and wretched? I *was* a decent girl, even if I spent my spare time reading about science theories and dissecting the dead.

I drew myself up, sticking my finger in his chest. "Why in heaven's name would I leave a note Father could find? You know how he'd react to discovering my lies. Have you gone completely mad, or is this just a temporary spell of insanity?" I didn't allow him a moment to respond. "Thank goodness it seems to affect Wadsworths born of only the *superior* gender. My lowly womanhood shall save me from you brutes yet. Now what is this nonsense about the day? Has it anything to do with Father?"

The fight drained from my brother as swiftly as it had come. He stepped back, rubbing the tension from his temples.

"I don't know where to begin." Suddenly the floor was vastly intriguing to him; he stared at it, refusing to meet my eyes. "Father will be... away for a few weeks."

"Is he all right?" I touched his elbow. "Nathaniel, please, look at me."

"I—" Nathaniel stood straighter, meeting my worried gaze. "A superintendent called on our house this morning. Now, Audrey Rose, what I'm about to tell you is quite disturbing, steady yourself."

I rolled my eyes. "I assure you I'm more than capable of hearing whatever you've come to say, Brother. The only thing that might kill me is the unwarranted suspense."

Someone snorted from the doorway, and Nathaniel and I both snapped our attention to the unwelcome intruder. Thomas. He covered his mouth, but didn't bother hiding the fact he was shaking with laughter.

"Do go on," he managed between bouts of chuckling. "Pretend I'm not here if you must. This ought to be good."

"Must you intrude on other people's conversations?" I said, sounding snappish even to my own ears. "Have you nothing better to do? Or do you simply excel at being arrogant and unlikable in every manner?"

Thomas's smile didn't falter, but there was a noticeable shift as amusement left his eyes. I wished to crawl into the nearest grave and hide.

"Thomas, I do apologize. That was—"

"Your uncle asked that I check on the racket coming from this room. He wanted to make sure you weren't murdering each other on his favorite oceanic carpet." Thomas paused, adjusting his cuffs, his tone now cold and remote as the arctic tundra. "I assure you, young miss, I'd rather have my nails ripped from their beds, one by one, this very moment, than remain here, unwanted, a breath longer."

His attention flicked to Nathaniel. "Tell her about your father's dance with Scotland Yard this morning. I promise you, she's most equipped to handle it."

Without another word, Thomas inclined his head, then stalked from the room. It was clear I'd hurt him, but I hadn't the time to dwell on it. I swung around, facing Nathaniel. "What does this have to do with Father?"

My brother walked to the settee and sat. "Apparently, sometime after breakfast Father went into Whitechapel. Detective inspectors were scouring the neighborhood, what with the murders and all, and found him in a certain....establishment unbefitting to his title." Nathaniel swallowed. "He's lucky the man who discovered him knew who he was. The superintendent escorted Father home, suggesting he leave the city for a few weeks. Or at least until he gets his... affairs in order."

I closed my eyes, my imagination running away with astounding leaps. There were only a few different "establishments" in the East End. Pubs, brothels, and... opium dens.

Somehow I found myself collapsing onto the little couch next to Nathaniel. Father took laudanum—an opium tincture—every day since Mother's death. The doctor assured us it would cure him of his insomnia and other ailments, but it appeared to be having the opposite effect.

Images of him mopping his brow, walking the halls at night, and his growing paranoia flashed through my mind. I couldn't believe I hadn't associated Father's souring moods and behavior with the abuse of his precious tonic.

I picked at stray threads on my skirts. "How is Father?"

"To be quite honest, he wasn't in any condition to discuss anything when I left," Nathaniel said, shifting uncomfortably. "The superintendent is taking Father to the cottage in my stead."

I nodded. Our "cottage" was a sprawling country estate in Bath named Thornbriar. It was beautiful and extravagant, like most things Lord Wadsworth had inherited. It was the perfect place to recover one's... sensibility.

"He's been very discreet and helpful, the superintendent," Nathaniel added.

I clamped my mouth shut. Father probably paid this policeman for his silence in the past, and his kindness was a result of hoping for more monetary gain. "Is there anything you need me to do?"

Nathaniel shook his head. "Superintendent Blackburn, I believe his name is, was getting Father's things together with the new valet and said I should focus on finding you. They set off about an hour ago."

I stared at my brother for a beat. Father had already left. No matter how hard he made life at home, I couldn't stop myself from worrying after him. I took a deep breath. Dwelling on things out of my control when there were murders to solve and bodies to be studied was a luxury I could ill afford.

"Will you be all right without me for a little while?" I asked, standing and brushing down the front of my bodice. "I really must get back to assisting Uncle if there's nothing to be done at home."

Nathaniel's focus drifted toward the door leading to the laboratory. God only knew what was running through his mind. According to my brother, Uncle was "one case away from crossing into the darkness" he so loved studying.

Instead of instigating another argument, I clutched his hands in mine and smiled. He softened a bit and my smile grew. Aunt Amelia's lessons on how to persuade the opposite gender came in handy after all. I'd need to attempt even better tactics with Thomas if I hoped to repair his bruised feelings.

"I'll be home in time for a late dinner. We can discuss a treatment plan for Father then." I stood back, letting a bit of humor creep into my voice. "Besides, you really should address the matter of your hair, Brother. You're a wreck."

Nathaniel looked torn between laughing, demanding I return home with him, and allowing me the freedom he knew I so strongly desired.

Finally, his shoulders slumped. "I shall send the carriage back at precisely seven o'clock, no arguments. While Father's gone, I'm in charge. Until Aunt Amelia arrives, that is."

Despite everything going on, this was rather pleasant news.

I could handle Aunt Amelia and all her etiquette lessons. Her mornings were filled with visits to the shops, afternoons with teas and gossip, and she retired early enough, claiming her need of beauty rest, but I knew she truly enjoyed a few spirits before bed. She'd be coming and going more than I was. Freedom would be a blissful thing.

Somehow in the midst of Father's addiction, a career murderer, mutilated women, and buckets of blood, I managed a small smile.

"You're pleased your father will be gone."

Thomas wasn't asking, merely telling me how I felt with more confidence than anyone had the right to possess. Ignoring him, I scanned the notes my uncle had scratched down at each crime scene. Something had to stand out.

If I could find that one connection before Uncle returned from Scotland Yard...

"You've had quite a poor relationship with him, probably for a few years." He paused, dropping his attention to where I twisted my mother's ring.

It was a pear-shaped diamond—her birthstone—and one of the few possessions of hers Father actually allowed me to keep. Or, I should say, one of the few items he could part with. Father had a sentimental heart.

Growing up, I'd always wished my birthday was in April, too. Diamonds were everything I hoped to be; beautiful, yet containing unimaginable strength. Somehow I was more of a Herkimer diamond, similar in appearance to the real thing, but not quite authentic.

A sad smile tugged at Thomas's mouth. "Ah. I see. You haven't been on good terms since the death of your mother." His smile faded, his voice growing quiet. "Tell me, was it…difficult for you? Did he beg your uncle to fix her with science?"

I stood so abruptly my chair fell to the ground with a clatter that would awaken the dead, had there been any in the laboratory.

"Do not speak about things you know nothing of!"

I balled my fists to keep from thrashing out at him. His mask of indifference fell away, revealing honest regret. After a few breaths, I calmly asked, "How did you come to know these intimate details of my life? Have you been asking my uncle about it, purposely to hurt me?"

"It seems…you must realize how much—" Thomas shook his head. "Hurting you wasn't my intent. I apologize, Miss Wadsworth. I thought perhaps I could…" He shrugged and fell silent, leaving me to wonder what he thought he could do by bringing up such a terrible subject.

I inhaled deeply, curiosity getting the better of my anger. "All right. I'll forgive you this once." I raised a finger at the look of hope blossoming in his features. "Only if you tell me, *truthfully*, how you knew that."

"I believe I can manage that. It was quite easy." He pulled his chair around the table, toeing the line of what polite society deemed decent. "You simply need to hone your powers of deduction, Wadsworth. Look at the obvious and go from there. Most people ignore what's right before their eyes. They believe they see, but oftentimes only view what they want. Which is precisely how you missed your father's opium addiction for so long."

He patted the front of his jacket and pants pockets, knitting his brow when his search returned no results. "It boils down to mathematical equations and formulas. If the evidence is *e* and the question is *q*, then what equals *a* to get to your answer? Simply look at what's before you and add it up."

I drew my brows together. "You're saying you figured all that out by simply watching me? Excuse me if I find that extremely hard to believe. You can't apply mathematical formulas to people, *Cresswell.* There's no equation for human emotion, there are too many variables."

"True. I've no formula I can work out for certain... emotions I feel around you."

That lively spark was back in his countenance. Leaning away, he folded his arms across his chest and grinned at my deep blush.

"However, upstairs when your brother said your father would be gone, you smiled, then immediately frowned, causing one to believe you were covering up your elation at being left alone for a few weeks. You didn't want to seem an insensitive monster, especially since your poor father is unwell."

"How did you see that?" I asked, eyes narrowed. "You'd already left the room."

Thomas didn't reveal the answer to that question, but a flicker of amusement was there and gone, so I knew he'd heard me. Spying scoundrel.

"Now, when I mentioned your poor relationship," he continued, "your eyes darted to that ring you were absently turning round your finger. Judging from the style and fit, I deduced it was not originally your ring."

He paused again, rechecking his suit pockets. I hadn't the

faintest idea what he was looking for, but his agitation was growing. He shook his hands out.

"Whose ring was it, one might ask? Considering the somewhat old-fashioned style, it's not hard to believe it belonged to someone old enough to be your mother," he said. "Since you sneak about in the late-night hours and spend time in this laboratory, coming to the conclusion your mother is no longer living and your father doesn't know your whereabouts wasn't hard."

Thomas bit his lip, seeming lost for how to continue. Now I understood the way his mind worked. Cool detachment was a switch he flipped while working out problems. I braced myself for something unpleasant and waved him on. "Go on. Out with it."

He studied my face, gauging my sincerity. "What kind of father doesn't know where his daughter is? One who doesn't have the best relationship with said daughter because he's likely too consumed by his own grief or addiction to really care."

Thomas sat forward, intrigue and possibly even esteem lighting his gaze. "How might a young woman such as yourself become obsessed with the macabre? By bearing witness to a scientific act of desperation meant to save a life. Where would you come into contact with that, I wonder?"

He purposely glanced around the room, driving his point home. "See? All the answers I sought were plainly visible. I didn't know until now your uncle was involved with your mother's..." He trailed off, realizing he was straying close to a sensitive subject. "Anyway. You simply need to know where to look for the questions. An easy mathematical formula applied to *Homo sapiens*. And behold! Science reigns over nature once more. No emotions needed."

"Except you're wrong," I whispered, shaken by the level of his accuracy. "Without humans and nature, there's no such thing as science."

"That's not exactly what I mean, Wadsworth. What I'm talking about is trying to solve a riddle or crime. Emotions play no role there. They're too messy and complicated." He leaned on his elbows, staring into my eyes. "But they're good in other situations, I suppose. For instance—I've not yet figured out the formula for love or romance. Perhaps I shall learn one day soon."

I gasped. "Would you talk this indecently if my uncle were present?"

"Ah, there you are," he said, picking up a journal and ignoring my last question. I lifted my chair from the ground before reading through my uncle's notes again.

Or pretended to, at least.

I stared at Thomas until my eyes crossed, trying to force some clue to rise to the surface about him or his family. The only thing I could deduce was that he was unabashedly bold, his comments bordering on impropriety.

Without lifting his head from his own journal, he said, "Not having any luck figuring me out, then? Don't worry, you'll get better with practice. And, yes"—he grinned wickedly, eyes fixed on his paper—"you'll still fancy me tomorrow no matter how much you wish otherwise. I'm unpredictable, and you adore it. Just as I cannot wrap my massive brain around the equation of you and yet adore it."

Every retort I was thinking fell from my thoughts. As if sensing the shift in the room, he glanced up. If I expected Thomas to feel ashamed by his forwardness, I'd be cursedly wrong again. Brow quirked, his look held a dare.

I wasn't the sort of girl who backed down, so I kept my gaze locked on his. Issuing my own challenge. Two could play his game of flirtation.

"Are you quite through being a detective, then?" he finally asked, pointing to a passage in Uncle's journal dated nearly four months prior to the first murder. "I think I've found something of great note."

My skin prickled with our proximity, but I refused to move away as I leaned over and read.

The victim, Emma Elizabeth Smith, was assaulted by two or possibly three attackers, according to her own testimony in the early morning hours of 3 April 1888. She either didn't see or, as authorities believed, purposely refused to identify the perpetrator(s) responsible for the horrific act committed on her person. An object (rammed inside her body) proved to be the cause of death one day later as it ruptured her peritoneum.

I swallowed bitter bile down as quickly as it rose in my throat. The third of April was my mother's birthday. How horrid something so despicable could happen on such a joyous day.

A peritoneum, if memory served me correctly, was the abdominal wall. I had no idea why Thomas thought this was related when, clearly, this was an act committed by some other savage wandering the London streets. This murder occurred in April and our Leather Apron had only just begun his rampage in August.

Before I gave him a proper tongue-lashing, he pointed to the most monstrous part of all. "Yes. I found that rather disturbing the first time around, Cresswell. No need to revisit the horror again, unless you're deriving sick pleasure from watching me nearly vomit." I couldn't stop the venom from injecting itself in my tone.

"Take your emotions out of the equation, Wadsworth. Having a heart that gets distracted by such frivolous things won't aid you in this investigation," Thomas said softly, reaching across the short distance separating us, as if he longed to touch my hands and remembered his place. "Look at it as if it were simply a puzzle piece with a very unique—albeit gruesome—shape."

I wanted to argue that emotions were not frivolous things, but my interest was piqued by his detachment during investigations. If his method worked, it might be a useful switch to flip on and off in myself when needed.

I read the journal again, this time my focus snagging on the repugnant details in a clear manner. Thomas might be mad, but he was a mad genius.

On the surface this crime didn't resemble either Miss Nichols or Miss Chapman. The timeline didn't fit. The woman was still alive when discovered. No organs had been removed, and she was not a brunette.

It did, however, fit with our theory of a man driven by his desire to rid the East End of sin. She was nothing but a lowly disease-spreading prostitute, and she did not deserve to live.

Had I not already turned myself into an immovable block of ice, I was certain chills would be raking their talons down my spine.

The detective inspectors were wrong.

Miss Nichols wasn't our murderer's first victim.

Miss Emma Elizabeth Smith was.

SEVEN
A STUDY IN SECRETS

WADSWORTH RESIDENCE,
BELGRAVE SQUARE
10 SEPTEMBER 1888

I pushed the herbed potatoes around my plate until they formed a question mark in my gravy.

Two days had passed since my father had been escorted to the country and Thomas and I had discovered our murderer's actual first victim. Not much progress was made in the interim. Now the space at night formerly haunted by the ghosts of things I couldn't control was filled with questions I couldn't answer. I swear I ate them for breakfast, lunch, and dinner. When I thought I'd had my fill, an entire new course brimming with more questions was served on a silver platter.

Nathaniel watched me over the rim of his wineglass, his expression a mixture of worry and annoyance. Our aunt and cousin were arriving within a week, so I needed to get myself together by then. I hadn't made for an amusing housemate, and my brother's patience was quickly evaporating. Uncle swore me to secrecy; even if I wanted to share my thoughts with Nathaniel, I couldn't.

Not to mention, the subject matter was hardly appropriate for the dinner table. Discussing missing ovaries, then asking him to pass the salt would be revolting for anyone, let alone a girl of my station.

I took a small bite, forcing the food down as best I could. Martha did an exceptional job making roast turkey, braised carrots, and rosemary herbed potatoes, but the aromatic scent and congealing dark brown gravy was turning my stomach. Giving up all pretense of eating the vegetables, I pushed my turkey around the crisp white plate instead.

Nathaniel slammed his glass down, rattling my own with the force. "That's quite enough! You haven't eaten but a few bites in the last two days. I'll not allow you to continue assisting that madman if this is the result."

I stared at him, fork poised over my uneaten dinner. We both knew it was an empty threat. Nathaniel broke away from our locked gazes first, rubbing circles in his temples. His suit was exceedingly fashionable this evening, made of imported fabrics and tailored to his frame perfectly. He called for a servant to bring in a bottle of his favorite wine, crafted in a year not even Father was alive in.

I could tell by the way his shoulders slumped slightly forward, as if they were growing weary from carrying a heavy load, that Father's ill health was weighing on him.

He'd always been the more sensitive and kind one, setting every bug that found its way into our house free. Feeding each stray that ended up on our doorstep more food than it needed, while I imagined what the insides of the animal would look like should it expire. He saw a butterfly as an object of beauty, deserving to flutter about the world, sharing its multitoned splendor. I saw the shiny metal needle I longed to slide into its body, pinning it to a board for further scientific inspection.

He took after our mother.

"I cannot have you starve, Sister." Nathaniel pushed his own plate forward, pouring himself another glass of wine from the freshly filled crystal decanter set before him. I watched, fascinated, as little spots of red splashed onto the white tablecloth like blood splattering on the walls near the victims' heads.

I closed my eyes. Everywhere I looked there was some reminder of the atrocious acts being committed in Whitechapel.

Perhaps I was too preoccupied with death. I sincerely doubted my cousin, Liza, would think of blood splatter. She'd probably bid an attendant to come and address the stain before it had time to set. Aunt Amelia had raised her well and was undoubtedly hoping I'd turn out the same with a little polishing.

Nathaniel took a long pull from his drink, then set it down gently. His fingers tapped a slow beat against the stem of the glass while he came up with another tactic to dissuade me from my studies. This deliberate show of parental guidance was growing tedious.

Like a white flag, I held my hand up and waved it, too tired to argue when he got this way. If keeping myself away from Uncle's laboratory for a few days would appease my brother, then so be it. I didn't need to conduct my research from there.

But he needn't know that.

"You're right, dear Brother. Some time away from all this unpleasantness is precisely what the doctor ordered." I offered him my most sincere smile, pleased to see him slowly return it with one of his own. "I promise I shall have a snack before bed later." I placed my napkin on the table and stood. "If you don't mind, I think I'll retire for a bit. I'm exhausted."

Nathaniel rose and tipped his head forward. In his mind as long as I was eating and sleeping regularly, I was bound to feel right as the sunshine on a summer's day. "I'm very pleased you're listening to your big brother for once. A little time and distance from all the misery in the world will do you good, Audrey Rose."

"I'm sure you're right." I gave him one more smile before leaving the room. The servants closed the wooden doors behind me, securing my brother and themselves on the other side. I took a few breaths, then glanced down the darkened hallway.

There was another reason for my early departure from dinner. Father kept records of all our servants, and I was hoping to discover something useful regarding Miss Mary Ann Nichols.

I crept toward Father's study, carefully avoiding every spot in the floor that creaked. I didn't want Nathaniel or any of the servants knowing about this. Pausing at the door, I stared at the ornate handle. Father would murder me should he ever find out I'd sneaked into his private workspace.

While it had never been expressly stated, it was a known fact Father's rooms were all off-limits after Mother's death. I was like an unwelcome shadow lurking around corners in my own home.

A clanking din rose from the back staircase, where most of the servants were below cleaning up from supper. Now was the ideal time to sneak into the study undetected. My palms itched with the need to turn the brass handle and slip inside, but I couldn't bring myself to do it.

What if he could tell I'd been in there? I doubted he'd come up with anything elaborate, but perhaps he'd set some sort of trip wire up to sound an alarm...

I leaned against the wall, nearly giggling. How absurd! To think Father would do such a thing, especially when maids would be in and out cleaning. I was being a foolish child, terrified of unknown things hiding beneath the bed frame.

Taking a deep breath, I steadied my heart. I hadn't realized how it had accelerated its beat in the last few moments. Surely if I could wander the streets at night while a murderer was on the prowl, I could sneak into my own father's study while he was away.

Voices sounded from the kitchen, growing louder. They must be bringing up a decadent dessert course for Nathaniel. My pulse galloped through my veins.

It was now or never. As the voices came closer, I shot across the hall, turned the knob, and slipped inside, closing the door with a slight click that sounded much too like a bullet sliding into its chamber for my comfort.

I stood with my back pressed firmly against the wooden door while the sound of footsteps echoed, then disappeared down the corridor. For added measure, I turned the key, locking myself in and anyone else out. The room was exceptionally dark.

I blinked until I was acclimated to the blackness covering everything like spilled ink. Father had had the deep green drapery pulled shut, keeping both the cool September chill and evening light out.

The result was a room as welcoming as a crypt.

Even Uncle's laboratory with its cadavers had more warmth between its walls. I rubbed the coldness from my arms while slowly making my way toward the fireplace, my silk skirts rustling treacherous whispers behind me.

The smell of sandalwood and cigars evoked the ghost of my father, and I couldn't stop myself from continually checking over my shoulder to be certain he wasn't standing behind me, waiting to pounce. I swear eyes watched me from the shadows.

A few tapers in hurricane lamps dripped waxy tears and a giant candelabra decorated the mantel next to a photograph of my mother. We had very few images of her, and each one was a treasure I held dear to my heart.

I studied the graceful curve of her lips, tilted into the sweetest smile. It was like peering into a looking glass showing me in the future; even our expressions were similar. A heart-shaped locket with tiny gears was clasped in her hands, and on her finger was the very ring I never took off. Tearing my gaze away, I returned to my purpose.

All I needed was to light one of the lamps so I could go through Father's records; I hoped no one would notice the slight flicker coming from under the door.

As I picked up the base of the hurricane lamp, an object clanked to the floor. Every muscle in my body froze. I waited a few beats, certain I'd be discovered by someone—anyone—but the solemn sound of silence echoed back at me. Forcing myself into action, I lit the lamp. The hiss of the flame sparking to life had me holding my breath a second time; every little sound seemed like a cannon going off, announcing my whereabouts. Finally, I bent and retrieved a small brass key.

How odd.

Not wanting to waste precious moments figuring out what it opened, I quickly replaced the key and grabbed the lamp again.

I held the light up, my eyes trailing over every object in the room as if it were the first and last time I'd ever see them. I longed to catalog each piece within the shelves of my mind and visit them whenever I'd like.

A large portrait—presumably of one of our ancestors—was mounted on the wall between floor-to-ceiling bookshelves. His chest was puffed up with self-importance and his foot rested atop the carcass of an enormous bear he'd slain. Strange it hadn't been there the last time I was here, though it had been quite a while.

"How charming," I whispered to myself. An ocean of blood surrounded the furry corpse island he was standing upon. The artist captured a deranged essence in our ancestor's eyes that chilled the very marrow in my bones.

I scanned the room again. Everything was dark: the wood, the rug, the large settee, a few spots of brocade wallpaper visible from behind artifacts collected over several lifetimes. Even the marble making up the fireplace was a deep green with darker veining. No wonder Father couldn't move past his grief; darkness was his constant companion.

I walked over to his desk, a mammoth thing taking up most of the room, threatening me with its hulking form. I rolled my eyes. Leave it to me to give an ordinary desk that much of a villainous personality. Hulking form indeed.

Sitting in Father's plush leather chair, I set the lamp down, taking great care not to disturb any of the papers scattered about. I couldn't help noticing Father had made quite a few mechanical sketches. The detail he managed to capture using only charcoal and paper was astounding. I swear I almost heard the cranking of gears and smelled the oil greasing their parts.

There was beautiful destruction all across the page.

Flying ships with guns bolstered to their sides and other miniature wartime toys took up each inch of paper. Shame he stopped creating clockwork pieces; judging from the images I saw, he hadn't lost his talent.

I stopped ruminating and slid open each drawer of the desk, searching with renewed purpose for files he kept on all our servants, both past and present. Even though our butler tended to the records, as was customary, Father was quite insistent he have his own. When I reached the bottom drawer, I discovered it was locked. I leaned closer. It looked as if Father had created the locking mechanism himself.

"Where would I hide something important?" I tapped my fingers on the arms of the chair. Then I remembered the key that had fallen from beneath the lamp. Running to the mantel, I obtained it, then quickly ran back to his desk.

Time was ticking away, and dessert was nearly over and servants would be busy in and out of the hall shortly.

It was a long shot the key would work, but I had to try.

I shifted the light closer. With shaking hands, I slowly pushed the key into place. I turned it to the left, certain it would have opened already if it were the correct one, when a small 'click' sounded and the drawer cracked open. Thank the heavens.

Opening the drawer fully, I ran my fingers over the tops of files, which were smashed together. There were so many I feared it'd take all evening to locate what I needed. I couldn't even recall how many maids we'd gone through over the last five years. Luckily, Father organized this drawer better than the top of his desk.

Little name tags peeked out above the folders like islands breaking through an ocean of ink on paper. I thumbed through them once, then twice before finding Miss Mary Ann Nichols's folder.

Checking over my shoulder to be sure the door was still locked, I pulled the file out and quickly read a lot of... nothing. There was only a ledger with her payments.

No background reference. No letter of recommendation.

Not a single glimpse into her life prior to working for us. I couldn't believe Uncle had recognized her so easily. According to Father's records, she'd been in our employ for only a fortnight. I slumped into the chair, shaking my head.

I removed a random file, drawing my brows together. This was for our cook, Martha, also our longest servant, as she didn't interact with us often and Father loved her black pudding.

It contained a letter of reference from her previous employer, a letter from Scotland Yard stating she'd never been under investigation, her monthly wages, allowances, and board wages, and a photograph of her in her typical cook's attire.

I scanned a few more files, finding they all resembled our cook's.

On a hunch, I dug around in the drawer until I found another servant who'd been dismissed for no better reason than having stayed with our family more than a month. Her file looked precisely like Miss Nichols's, confirming my suspicion that Father must clean out the majority of their information once they were no longer employed.

I closed the folders, taking pains to place everything back exactly where I'd found it.

Cursing my father for keeping pointless records, I wished I could set the whole mess of papers ablaze.

As I slid the last file into place, a familiar name caught my attention. I hesitated briefly before removing the folder and flipping it open. It contained a lone newspaper clipping. A brutal coldness enveloped me where I sat.

Why did Father have an article on Miss Emma Elizabeth Smith's murder?

EIGHT
BRING OUT YOUR NEARLY DEAD

GREAT WESTERN ROYAL HOTEL,
PADDINGTON STATION
11 SEPTEMBER 1888

The tearoom in the Great Western Royal Hotel was unbearably warm.

Or perhaps it was simply the fiery rage burning inside me. Sitting with my hands folded politely in my lap, I prayed for the strength I'd need to stop myself from reaching across the table and wrapping my fingers around a neck instead of cucumber sandwiches and petits fours. "You look as if you've not slept, Mr. Cresswell."

"Who said I did, Miss Wadsworth?"

I raised my brows. "Doing subversive things at indecent hours?"

"Would it offend you if I were?" Thomas smiled at the waiter and leaned in, whispering in his ear. The waiter nodded, then marched off.

Once we were alone, he turned his steady focus on me, calculating a thousand things simultaneously. I lifted the porcelain cup to my lips, forcing a sip of tea down.

I'd agreed to meet him here only to go over case details. Now he was doing that infuriating thing where he'd inevitably guess my secret plans, and I'd have to murder him. In front of all these witnesses, no less. What a pity.

"Sir." The waiter came back to the table, presenting Thomas with three things: a silver ashtray laid out with cigarettes, matches he produced from his black trousers, and an orchid. Thomas handed the flower to me then plucked a smoke from the tray, allowing the waiter to light the end. A gray cloud puffed into the air between us. I purposely coughed, batting the smoke back toward his side of the table.

"I cannot believe you'd buy me a beautiful flower only to ruin it with smoking," I said, scowling. "How incredibly rude."

Smoking in front of a girl without her permission was against social mores, but Thomas didn't seem to care for that rule one bit. I set the orchid down, staring at him through a fringe of slitted lashes, but he only took another drag, slowly letting the toxic air out before dismissing the waiter.

He reminded me of the caterpillar from *Alice's Adventures in Wonderland,* sitting upon his giant mushroom, lazing about without a care in the world. If only he were small enough to squish beneath my boots.

"That's a disgusting habit."

"So is dissecting the dead prior to breakfast. But I don't scorn you for that unseemly habit. In fact"—he leaned closer, dropping his voice into a conspiratorial whisper—"it's rather endearing seeing you up to your elbows in viscera each morning. Also, you're quite welcome for the flower. Do place it on your nightstand and think of me while dressing for bed."

I dropped my finger sandwich onto my plate, shoving it away with as much vehemence as I could muster. Thomas pulled in another lungful of smoke, meeting my gaze with a flash of defiance and something else I couldn't quite read.

"Well, then. I see there's nothing more to say. Good day, Mr. Cresswell." Before I stood, Thomas's hand shot out, gently circling my wrist. I gasped, drawing my hand back, and glanced around. Thankfully, no one had seen his indiscretion. I swatted away his second attempt to hold me, though I didn't exactly mind his touch. "I see your addiction has addled that brain of yours."

"On the contrary, dear Wadsworth," he said between puffs, "I find nicotine gives me an added boost of clarity. You ought to try it."

He flipped the awful thing around, offering it to me, but there were limits I'd set for myself as far as amateur sleuthing was concerned. Smoking was one of them. He shrugged, returning to his nicotine intake.

"Suit yourself," he said. "Now, then, I'm coming with you."

I looked him squarely in the eye. Thomas was no longer showering me with cool indifference; he was warm as an August afternoon, his lips turned up at the corners.

A flame flared across my body when I realized I was studying the shape of his mouth, the way his bottom lip was slightly fuller and all too inviting for a girl without a chaperone to take notice of.

I collected my thoughts like specimens to be dissected further. Clearly, I was experiencing some sort of degenerative medical condition if I was thinking such indecent thoughts about the scoundrel. He was likely goading me into a kiss.

"I'm going... home. *You* most certainly are not invited." I dared to meet his gaze in spite of my momentary lapse in judgment. "Nathaniel won't approve of finding a boy in our home, no matter how innocent our work situation may be."

"Going home, are you?" Shaking his head, he *tsked*. "Let's promise each other one thing." He leaned across the table, reaching for my hands, which I quickly stuck under the table. "We always tell each other the truth. No matter how harsh it may be. That's what partners do, Wadsworth. They don't bother with preposterous lies."

"I beg your pardon," I whispered harshly, not particularly

enjoying the casual use of my surname he kept tossing about, though I'd permitted it. "I didn't *lie*—" Thomas held a hand up, shaking his head. Fine. "What makes you sure I even need a partner? I'm quite capable of doing things on my own."

"Perhaps it's not you who would benefit from our partnership," he said quietly.

His response was so unexpected, I covered my mouth with the back of my gloved hand. The very idea he might need someone, and chose me out of everyone in London, sent foolish notions dancing through my head before I banished them.

I would not fancy Thomas Cresswell. I would *not*.

Watching him stub his cigarette out, a deep sigh worked its way out of me. "You ought to buy a ticket, then. We'll be leaving for—"

Pulling a folded ticket from his jacket, he flashed a mischievous grin. My jaw practically hit the table. "How in the name of the queen did you know where we'd be going?"

Thomas folded the ticket up, securing it back in its safe place, his look smugger than a mutt stealing a Christmas goose. "That's quite a simple question, Wadsworth. You're wearing lace-up leather boots."

"Indeed. So simple." I rolled my eyes. "If I don't murder you this afternoon, it'll be a gift sent directly from God Himself, and I vow to attend services again," I said, holding a hand against my heart.

"I knew I'd get you to church eventually." He brushed the front of his suit down. "I'm impressed with how swiftly you've relented. Though, I *am* hard to resist."

He sat straighter like a peacock showing off its colorful plumage. I imagined him preening himself as if he had a fan of bright feathers growing from his backside.

I motioned for him to get on with it. "You were saying."

"On a normal day, you wear silk shoes. Leather is better suited for rain," he said, matter-of-factly. "Since it's not raining in London yet, and according to the paper, Reading has been pouring buckets all morning, it didn't take much to deduce you'd be heading there."

I so badly wanted to say something cutting, but Thomas wasn't finished impressing me yet.

"When you first rushed through the lobby your attention shifted to the clock mounted on the wall; you hadn't seen me standing near, waiting for you. Leading me to believe you were in a hurry." He took a sip of tea. "A quick check of the departures board and I noted the next train leaving for Reading was at twelve noon. Quite easy, as it was also the *only* train leaving at that time."

He sat back with a self-indulgent grin plastered across his face. "I paid the waiter to fetch me a ticket, ran to our table, then ordered our tea all before you had your duster checked."

I closed my eyes. He really was an enormous test of my patience, but he might prove useful with my next task. If anyone would be able to read a situation, it'd be Thomas Cresswell. I wanted answers regarding Miss Emma Elizabeth Smith and her association with my family, and could think of only one person who might know about her. I stood, and Thomas joined me, eager to move onto our next mission.

"Hurry along, then," I said, grabbing my orchid and securing it safely in my journal. "I want to sit by the window."

"Hmm."

"What now?" I asked, losing patience.

"I usually sit by the window. You may have to sit in my lap."

Within ten minutes, we were standing below gigantic wrought iron arches that spanned Paddington Station like iron bones holding the glass flesh of the ceiling up in a show of man-made perfection. There was something thrilling about the cylindrical shape of the station as it teemed with people and huge steam-breathing machines.

Our train was already waiting on the tracks, so we climbed aboard and situated ourselves for the ride. Soon we were off. I watched the gray, fog-filled world blur by as we chugged our way out of London and across the English countryside, my thoughts consumed with a million questions.

The first being, Was I wasting my time? What if Thornley knew nothing? Perhaps we should have stayed in London and pored over more of Uncle's notes. Though it was too late for turning back now.

Thomas, once he'd woken from a disturbed nap, fidgeted in his seat enough to draw my attention to him. He was like a child who'd eaten too many sweets and couldn't sit still.

"What in heaven's name are you doing?" I whispered, glancing at the passengers around us, who were tossing dirty looks Thomas's way. "Why can't you act properly for an hour?"

He crossed then uncrossed his long legs, then did the same with his arms. I was starting to think he hadn't heard me when he finally responded. "Are you going to enlighten me on where exactly we're going? Or is the suspense part of the surprise?"

"Can you not deduce it, Cresswell?"

"I'm not a magician, Wadsworth," he said. "I can deduce when facts are presented to me—not when they're purposely obscured."

I narrowed my eyes. Even though there were a thousand other things I should be concerned with, I couldn't stop myself from asking. "Are you feeling ill?" His attention shifted to me before moving back to the window. "Do you suffer from claustrophobia, or agoraphobia?"

"I find the act of traveling very dull." He sighed. "Another moment of the inane conversation of the people behind us or the blasted chugging of the engine, and I might lose my mind altogether."

Thomas grew silent again, accentuating his point about the annoying conversation and overwhelming sound of the train.

"Perhaps this is our murderer's motivation for killing," he mumbled.

I laid my head against the seat and eavesdropped. According to society, this was precisely what young women were supposed to be concerned with. Shoes, silks, dinner parties, and who might be the handsomest duke or lord in the kingdom. How one might secure an invitation to an important ball or tea. Who was in the queen's favor, who wasn't. Who was old and smelly but worth marrying anyway.

My daily worries were so far removed, I feared I'd always be shunned amongst my peers. While I enjoyed finery, I tried imagining myself chattering on about a napkin design, but my thoughts kept turning to deceased bodies, and I laughed at my failure to even *picture* being a so-called normal young lady.

I was determined to be both pretty and fierce, as Mother had said I could be. Just because I was interested in a man's job didn't mean I had to give up being girly. Who defined those roles anyhow?

"Truly, Thomas," I said, trying to contain a laugh. "People needn't debate rhetoric in order to be interesting. Is there nothing you fancy outside of the laboratory?"

Thomas was unamused. "You aren't exactly the queen of intellectually stimulating conversation this afternoon."

"Feeling neglected, are you?"

"Perhaps I am."

"We're going to see my father's former valet, you insufferable thing," I said. "I've reason to believe he might have information regarding one of our victims. Satisfied?"

Thomas's leg stopped bouncing and he swiveled to face me. I sincerely disliked when he studied me so openly, as if I were a complex mathematical equation he had to solve. He absentmindedly tapped his leg, leaving me to conclude his brain was working furiously.

The train whistle blew a steam-filled warning that Reading

station was approaching at the same time a flourish of rain pelted our windows, as if on cue.

He smiled to himself. "Looks like this afternoon just became a bit more intriguing."

Horse hooves clacked on the wet stones of Broad Street as our rented carriage moved up the hill to Aldous Thornley's residence. My stomach flipped with each jolting sway, and I feared I'd lose my lunch on the rain-soaked cobblestones. I pulled the navy curtain back, focusing on our surroundings instead of my growing nausea.

The town was filled with people selling wares despite the unpleasant weather. Awnings covered vendors from the elements; I watched as a woman haggled with a man over a basket of seeds she was selling.

Thomas pointed to a large building on our right, purposely leaning over my shoulder, his breath tickling the high lace collar covering my neck. "Reading. Famous for its three B's of business. Breweries, Bulbs, and Biscuits. That's the Huntley and Palmers factory."

"Their biscuits are my favorite for tea," I said. Though I didn't absorb much of what Thomas was saying regarding the history of their company. I twisted my hands until I popped a button off my gloves, then stopped.

If he noticed—which he most likely did—Thomas didn't comment on my display of nervousness. I was grateful he didn't ask me to explain anything further about our trip and even more grateful for his attempt to distract me by pointing out every factory we passed.

Another giant building puffed smoke into the rainy sky, like a man exhaling a cigar into the atmosphere.

This morning I'd been sure coming here was the best course of action; now, little buds of doubt were blossoming in my mind. Each drop of water hitting the top of our carriage echoed loudly in my ears, setting my nerves on edge.

"Maybe Miss Emma Elizabeth *did* work for my household prior to her fall into destitution," I said. "Maybe that's where her connection to my father ends."

"Perhaps," Thomas said, studying me. "It's best knowing for sure, though."

I chewed my bottom lip, hating myself for worrying so much. Was I mostly worried about being wrong or being horrendously wrong in front of Thomas? The latter half of that question bothered me. Since when had his opinion of my intelligence become so important? I could barely stand him. What he thought of me should mean absolutely nothing.

But it did matter. More than I cared to admit.

Then there was the even darker question I didn't want to acknowledge at all. What connected my father to these two murdered women? I couldn't help fearing the odds were stacked against this being some bizarre coincidence. But how everything fit together remained a mystery.

"Well, if anyone in our household knows intimate details of my father's life before Mother's death, it's Mr. Thornley," I said.

He'd dressed my father for every occasion and knew when and where he was at all times. He probably knew my father as well as—if not better than—my mother had. If he hadn't gotten too old to perform his duties, I'm sure he'd still be right by Father's side.

"Everything will be fine, Wadsworth. We'll either have answers or we won't. But at least we've gone out and tried."

A flash of lightning lit the dark sky, as if the Titans were clashing in the heavens. Thunder followed, reminding me of my parents. When I was younger and terrified of the storms that blew through London, I'd curl into Mother's lap while Father told me thunder was the sound angels made when they played skittles. Mother'd call down to the cook, fetch us some curry and flatbread reminiscent of

Grandmama's homeland, then fill my head with stories of heroines from faraway places. From then on I almost enjoyed thunderstorms.

Soon the carriage ride was blessedly over. We huddled beneath an umbrella in the doorway of a small stone house sandwiched next to twenty other identical homes that looked like cowsheds. Thomas knocked, then stood back, allowing me to greet Father's former servant first.

The door creaked open—its hinges in desperate need of a good oiling—and the unpleasant scent of boiled vegetables lazily wafted out. I expected to see familiar wrinkles around kind eyes and snow-white hair.

I did not expect a young woman with a child hoisted on her hip, looking less than pleased by the unannounced afternoon interruption. Her ginger hair was pulled into a braid coiling around the nape of her neck; her clothing was well worn, with patches on her elbows. Stray hairs fell around her face and she blew them back with little luck of keeping them out of her eyes.

Thomas quietly cleared his throat, spurring me to action.

"I... pardon me. I—I was looking for someone," I stammered, glancing at the number twenty-three on the door. "It appears I've got the wrong address." There was something intimidating about the way she was standing there staring, but we'd come all this way and I wasn't about to let someone with a sour attitude get the better of me. Her gaze traveled slowly over Thomas. Twice.

She reminded me of someone who was being tempted by a succulent-looking steak, and I didn't care for it one bit. I cleared my throat as another flash of lightning rushed across the sky. "You wouldn't happen to know where I could find a Mr. Thornley, would you?"

The baby picked that moment to start wailing, and the young woman shot me a glare as if *I'd* spurred the devil out of him instead of the booming thunder. Cooing to the screeching demon on her hip, she patted its back gently. "He's dead."

Had Thomas not grabbed my arm to steady me I might have fallen backward. "He's... but... when?"

"Well, he isn't fully dead yet," she admitted. "But he isn't much longer for this world. If he makes it through the night it'll be a miracle." She shook her head. "Poor thing doesn't hardly look himself anymore. Best you keep the memory of him untainted, else you'll have nightmares for years to come."

The warm sympathetic part of me wanted to say sweet words for our former servant's imminent passing, but this was our only chance to gain insight about my father's whereabouts during the murders and his potential connection to Miss Emma Elizabeth Smith.

I stood taller, imagining the veins flowing through my body were nothing more than steel wires, cold and unfeeling. Now was the time to find that scientific switch Thomas relied on. "I really must see him. It's of the highest importance. You wouldn't deny me saying good-bye to a dear friend—especially not one who's in the throes of death, would you?"

The young woman stared open-mouthed before snapping her jaw shut. She bumped the door open with her unoccupied hip, gesturing us inside with an impatient wave of her hand. Pointing to a holder in the corner, she jerked her chin.

"Put your brolly there and suit yourself, then," she said. "He's upstairs, first door on the right."

"Thank you." I crossed the tiny foyer with Thomas on my heels, heading up the worn staircase as quickly as I could. The scent of boiled cabbage followed us as we ascended, adding to the ill feeling churning in my stomach.

When my foot reached the top step, the woman called out in a mocking tone, "Nightmares will be your bedmates tonight. All the fancy sheets in the world won't make a lick of difference. Don't say I didn't warn you, my lady."

This time when I heard a crash of thunder, I shuddered.

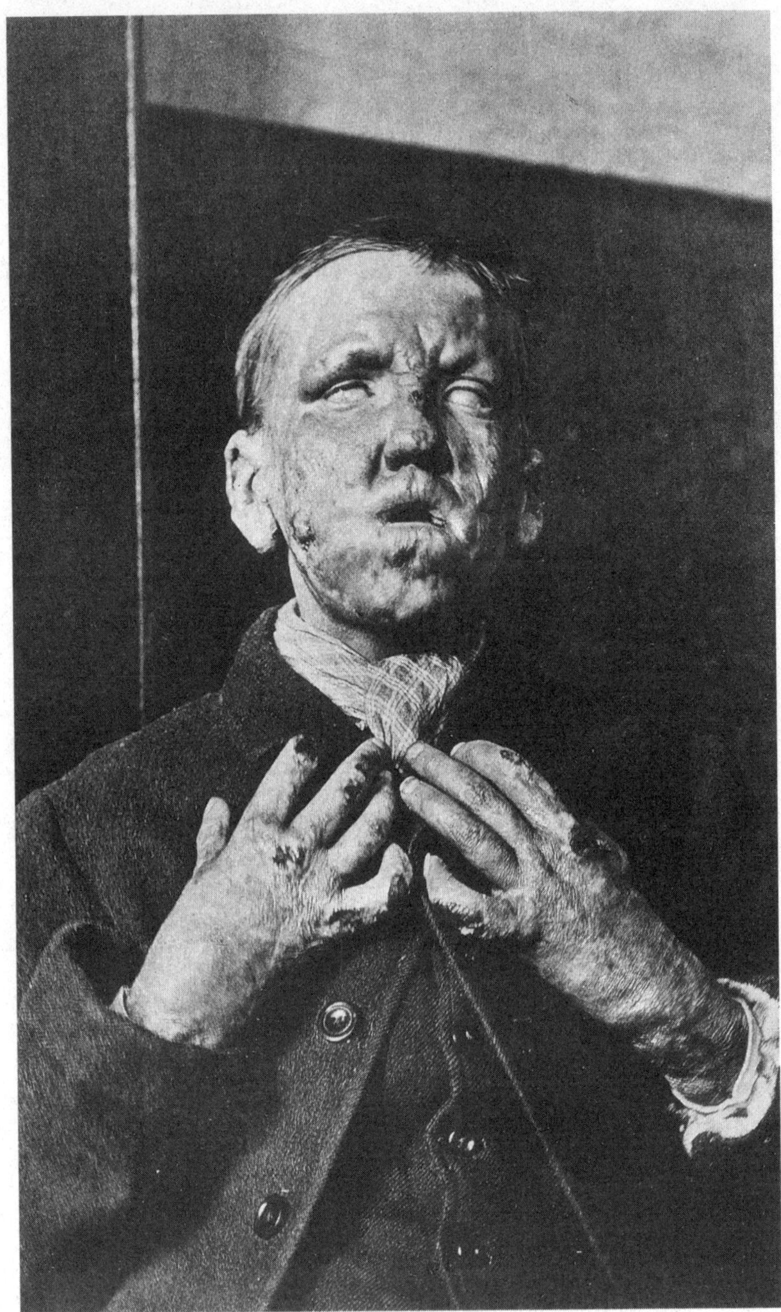

Tubercular leprosy, c. 19th century

NINE

MESSAGE FROM THE GRAVE

THORNLEY RESIDENCE,
READING
11 SEPTEMBER 1888

Gauzy curtains—that had possibly been white once—billowed toward us as if they were two decaying arms desperately reaching for release.

If I were forced to stay in this tomblike room for long, I'm sure I'd become as desperate. Drops of rain splattered onto the sill, but I didn't dare close the window.

A small wrought iron bed with a striped mattress displayed a skeletal body that barely looked alive. Poor Thornley had withered away to nothing more than graying skin pulled taut over fragile bones. Open sores on his torso and arms oozed a mixture of blood and pus reeking of fetid meat even from the doorway. It was hard to say for sure, but he looked to be suffering from a form of leprosy.

I covered my nose with the back of my hand, catching Thomas doing the same from the corner of my eye. The smell was overwhelming at best, and the sight before us was by far the worst thing I'd ever seen.

Which was saying a lot, as I'd witnessed the putrid insides of the departed on countless occasions during Uncle's postmortems.

I closed my eyes, but the rotten image was burned onto the backs of my lids.

I would've thought him long deceased, but the slight rise and fall of his chest defied what my eyes told me to be true. If I were a superstitious person, I'd believe he was one of the undead haunting the English moors, searching for souls to steal.

Or possibly eat.

All my life I'd been interested in biological anomalies, like the Elephant Man, gigantism, conjoined twins, and ectrodactyly, but this seemed a cruel act of God.

The young woman was right. This was the place nightmares came to be inspired.

The curtains inhaled wet breaths, then slowly exhaled—their dampness sticking to the wood before rustling free with the next gust of storm-drenched wind.

I took a breath through my mouth. We needed to either run back downstairs—and preferably all the way to the train station while screaming bloody murder—or speak with the poor man immediately.

The former had my vote even if it meant running in the rain, in heeled boots and possibly breaking my neck, but the latter was inevitably what we were going to do.

Thomas nodded encouragement, then walked fully into the room, leaving me propped against the door frame with nothing but my wits supporting me. If he was capable of facing this, then so was I.

If only my body would catch up with my brain's courage.

He pulled two chairs close to the bed—their limbs scraping in protest—before motioning for me to have a seat. My legs carried me across the room, seemingly of their own volition, spurring my heart into a steady gallop. I buried my hands in the folds of my skirts once

I sat down. I didn't want poor Thornley seeing how badly they were shaking; he was going through enough as it was.

A vicious cough raked his body, forcing veins on his neck to stand out like tree roots being yanked from the earth. I poured a glass of water from a pitcher next to the bed, carefully bringing it to his lips.

"Drink this, Mr. Thornley," I said gently. "It'll soothe your throat."

The old man slowly sipped from the glass. Water sloshed all over his chin, and I dabbed it with a handkerchief to avoid giving him chills on top of his other ailments. When he'd had enough, his milky eyes turned to mine. I had no idea if he was blind, but smiled at him nonetheless. Recognition filtered into his features after a moment or two.

"Miss Wadsworth." He coughed again, this time less violently than before. "You're as lovely as your mother. She would've been pleased with how fine you turned out, Lord rest her soul."

Even though I'd heard it all my life, it still brought the sting of tears to my eyes. Reaching out, I smoothed his thinning hair off his forehead, mindful of avoiding the open sores. I didn't think he was contagious, but took no chances and kept my gloves on. He closed his eyes, his chest stilling.

At first I was terrified he'd crossed into the afterlife, then his eyes fluttered open. I exhaled. We needed answers straightaway. I hated myself for jumping right into things, but feared he'd quickly lose energy and be unable to speak much longer.

I said a silent prayer that my ticket home was still heading directly for London and not detouring into Hell.

Thomas watched the valet with complete detachment, ignoring everything else altogether. It chilled me, seeing how unaffected he was by our current situation; how capable he was of flicking his emotions off on command. No matter how useful it was, it was still unnatural and reminded me of how little I knew him beyond Uncle's laboratory.

As if sensing my distress, Thomas drew out of his deductions long enough to meet my worried gaze and nod. It jolted me from my thoughts. I leaned closer to the bed, tying my nerves into knots.

"I know you're unwell, Mr. Thornley, but I was hoping to ask you a bit about my father." I took a deep breath. "I'd also like to know who Miss Emma Elizabeth Smith was."

He stared, his eyes—and whatever memories played behind them—shuttering before me. His attention shifted to Thomas. "Are you betrothed to my dear girl?"

Thomas actually turned scarlet, his well-armored demeanor shaken. He stuttered through a response, looking in every direction but mine. "I, um, well—we're—she's..."

"Colleagues," I supplied, unable to stop myself from enjoying how flustered he'd gotten. In spite of the purpose of our visit, and how odd his behavior could be, I was quite pleased something rattled him. All the more because it was over me. He rolled his eyes when I grinned at him. "We're both apprenticing under Uncle, that is."

Thornley closed his eyes, but not before I caught a flash of disapproval. Even straddling death's doorway, he was appalled by my association with Uncle and his unholy research. Apparently the fact that I wasn't spending more time securing a husband was another strike against me. I'd have felt shame if I hadn't had a greater purpose for being here. *Let people think what they like*, I thought crossly, then immediately cringed.

The man was dying. I needn't worry about his opinion or scorn him for it.

I sat straighter, my tone kind but strong. "I need you to tell me how Father knew Miss Emma Elizabeth Smith."

My father's former valet stared over my shoulder and through the window, the rain streaking down like tears. It was hard to tell if he was ignoring my inquiry or losing consciousness. I glanced at Thomas, whose torn expression mirrored my own. Pushing a dying man was a horrible thing to do, and if Thomas Cresswell was second-guessing our being here, then I'd really strayed from doing the proper thing.

Perhaps I was the deplorable creature society thought me to be. I could only imagine what Aunt Amelia would have to say or how many times she'd cross herself, telling me to pray for my sins. Religious fiend that she was.

Deciding I'd put him through enough, I stood.

"I must apologize, Mr. Thornley. I see I've upset you and that wasn't my intention." Releasing my skirts, I clasped his cold hands in mine. "You've been a great friend to our family. I cannot thank you enough for serving us all so well."

"Might as well tell them, Grandfather."

The young woman who'd answered the door now stood with her arms crossed at the foot of the bed, her voice gentler than I'd have thought possible.

"Clear your conscience before taking that last journey," she said. "What harm can come of telling her what she wants to know?"

Now I saw the strong family resemblance. They both had the same thick brows that held two enchantingly large eyes, and perfectly high cheekbones. The red tint to her hair hinted at their Irish roots and the handful of freckles tossed across her nose made her more girlish than I'd originally thought.

Without the child marring her demeanor, I'd say she wasn't much older than I was. Part of what she'd said replayed in my mind.

"Do you know anything about it?" I asked. She stared blankly, as if I'd spoken another language. "About why he'd need to clear his conscience?"

She shook her head, shifting her focus to her grandfather's restless form. "He hasn't said anything specific as such. Just frets about at night is all. Sometimes when he's sleeping he'll mumble a bit. I've never been able to make sense of it."

Thornley scratched his arms so roughly I was afraid he'd tear himself open. That explained some of the sores—he was giving himself scabs, then picking them until they were infected. It wasn't leprosy, then. It simply looked like it. I swallowed nausea down in one unpleasant gulp. His pain must be unimaginable.

Grabbing a tin of lotion from the bedside table, his granddaughter hurried to his side and lathered it on his arms. "His organs are shutting down, causing him to itch something terrible. Least that's what the doctor said." She applied another generous amount of the cream and he quieted down. "Lotion helps, but doesn't last long. Try not scratching it so hard, Grandfather. You're ripping your skin to shreds."

Thomas shifted in his chair, the telltale sign he was growing antsy to share his opinion. I gave him a withering look that I hoped conveyed the amount of pain *he'd* be in should he act like his usual charming self around the Thornleys.

He ignored me and my glare.

"What I recall of my studies, it's all part of the death process," he said, ticking each symptom off on his fingers. "You stop eating, sleep more, breathing becomes labored. Then body itches begin, and—"

"That's quite enough," I interrupted, shooting Thornley and his granddaughter sympathetic looks. They knew the end was imminent. They needn't hear explicit details of what came next.

"I only thought to help," he whispered. "Clearly, my services are unwelcome." Thomas lifted a shoulder, then returned to quietly assessing the room.

We would need to work on his "helping" skills in the future. I turned back to my father's valet. "Really, anything you can tell me about that time period would be immensely helpful. There's no one else whom I can turn to for answers. Some recent... events have occurred and it'd ease my mind."

Thornley's eyes welled up. He motioned for his granddaughter to come closer. "Jane, my love. Would you mind getting us some tea?"

Jane narrowed her eyes. "Wouldn't be trying to get rid of me now, would you? You haven't asked for tea in days." Her tone was more playful than accusatory, garnering a small smile from her grandfather. "Very well. I'll go fetch some tea, then. Behave yourself until I get back. Mum will hang me if she thinks I've mistreated you."

Once Jane was out of the room, Thornley took a few labored breaths, then looked at me, his focus clearer than it was a few seconds earlier.

"Miss Emma Elizabeth Smith was a dear friend of your mother's, Miss Audrey Rose. You probably don't recall her, though. Stopped coming around when you were still a little thing." He coughed, but shook off my offer of more water. "She also knew your uncle and father. The four of them were thick as thieves in their younger years. In fact, your uncle was betrothed to her at one time."

Confusion wrapped its fingers around my brain. The way Uncle's notes were written made it seem as if he didn't know the first thing about her. I'd never have guessed she was an acquaintance, let alone someone he'd been close to marrying. Thomas raised his brows; apparently that was something not even he saw coming.

I faced Thornley again. "Do you have any idea why Father would've kept track of her?"

Thunder crashed above us, booming a warning of its own. Thornley swallowed, his attention darting around the room as if he were afraid of something horrid reaching for him from beyond the grave. His chest swelled before he lost himself in another bout of coughing.

If he kept this up, I was certain he'd lose the ability to communicate altogether.

His voice was like gravel crunching beneath horse hooves when he managed to speak again. "Your father's a very powerful and wealthy man, Miss Audrey Rose. I don't presume to know anything about his personal inquiries. I only know two things regarding Miss Smith. She was betrothed to your uncle, and—" His eyes grew so wide they were mostly white. Struggling to sit back in bed, he kicked and coughed himself into a frenzy.

Jumping up, Thomas tried holding the old man down to prevent him from injuring himself with his convulsions. Thornley shook his head violently, blood collecting at the corners of his mouth. "I... just... remembered. He knows! He knows the dark secrets hidden within the wall."

"Who knows?" I begged, desperately trying to figure out if this was part of an elaborate delusion, or if his rant held any merit for our investigation. "What wall?"

Thornley closed his eyes, a guttural whine seeping out of his mouth. "He knows what happened! He was there that night!"

"It's all right," Thomas said, in a warm tone I'd never heard him use with anyone else before. "It's all right, sir. Take a breath for me. That's it. Good." I watched as Thomas held the old man steady, his touch forceful yet gentle. "Better? Now try and tell us again. This time slower."

"Yes, y-yes," he wheezed, "can't blame him, t-though." Thornley gasped, struggling to get more words out while I rubbed his back, trying miserably to sooth him. "N-no, no. Can't, c-can't blame him," he said, coughing again. "Not sure I'd be m-much better, given the c-circumstances."

"Blame whom?" I asked, not knowing how to calm him down enough to gather coherent information. "Whom are you speaking of, Mr. Thornley? My father? Uncle Jonathan?"

He wheezed so hard his eyes rolled into the back of his head. I was terrified it was all over, that I'd just witnessed a man die, but he thrashed about, sitting up fully, grasping the sheets on either side of his emaciated body. "A-Alistair knows."

I was more confused than ever. Alistair was a name I was unfamiliar with, and I wasn't even sure Thornley knew what he was saying any longer. I gently patted his hand while Thomas looked on in horror. "*Shhh. Shhh,* now. It's okay, Mr. Thornley. You've been immensely—"

"It's . . . because . . . of that . . . cursed—"

A shudder went through his body so turbulently it was as if he'd been flying a metal kite during the lightning storm going on outside. He convulsed until a steady stream of blood trickled down the side of his mouth and escaped from his nostrils.

I jumped back, shouting for his granddaughter to come back and help us, but it was too late.

Mr. Thornley was dead.

TEN

THE *MARY SEE*

THE SERPENTINE,
HYDE PARK
13 SEPTEMBER 1888

"Of course I recall an Alistair that Father knew. I can't believe you don't remember him," Nathaniel said, looking to me for an explanation I wasn't quite ready to offer. "Why the sudden curiosity?"

"No reason, really." Avoiding his gaze, I watched a flock of geese fly over the glasslike surface of the lake toward the Royal Humane Society receiving house, their V formation as perfect as the crisp fall weather. They were undoubtedly on their way south, seeking a more moderate climate.

I longed to understand the innate mechanism warning them of the coming winter months. If only women roaming the cold streets of Whitechapel could sense the same danger and fly to safety.

I picked a few blades of yellowing grass, twirling them between my pointer finger and thumb. "Hard to believe in a few weeks winter will destroy the grass."

Nathaniel looked exasperated. "Yes, well, until next spring when it stubbornly pushes its way out of its frozen grave, hope for life ever eternal."

"If only there were a way to cure life's most fatal disease," I mumbled to myself.

"Which would be what, exactly?"

I glanced at my brother then looked away, shrugging. "Death."

Then I could revive Thornley and ask him all the questions he'd left me with. I'd even have a mother if it were possible to bring the dead back like perennial plants.

Nathaniel's eyes were fixed worriedly on mine. He probably thought Uncle's eccentricities were poorly affecting me. "If you could, would you... attempt such a thing with science? Would death become a thing of the past, then?"

The boundaries of right and wrong were so less certain when a loved one was involved. Life would be unimaginably different with Mother still alive, yet would the creature ever come close to the real thing? I shuddered to think what could happen.

"No," I said slowly. "I don't suppose I would."

A tiny songbird chirped from a branch stretching lazily above our heads. Tearing a piece of my honey biscuit, I tossed it over. Two larger birds swooped in, fighting for a nibble. Darwin's survival of the fittest on full display until Nathaniel crumbled his entire biscuit up, throwing a hundred pieces over to the squabbling birds. Each of them with more food than they knew what to do with now.

"You're hopeless." I shook my head. He'd make for a horrible naturalist, constantly altering scientific data with his kindness. He brushed his gloved fingers off on a hand-stitched napkin, then sat back, watching as the little birds bobbed and plucked each morsel up, a satisfied smile plastered across his face.

I kept staring at the napkin. "I admit, I'm dreading the arrival of Aunt Amelia."

Nathaniel followed my gaze and waved the napkin in the air.

"It'll be a grand time, I'm sure. Least she'll be pleased with your embroidery. She needn't know you practice on the dead."

Aunt Amelia, aside from her daily lessons on tending a proper household and attracting a decent husband, had an inexplicable thing for stitching monograms in every bit of cloth she could find. I hadn't a clue how I'd manage sewing a lot of useless napkins along with apprenticing for Uncle.

Between that and her constant religious outbursts, I was certain the next few weeks were going to be more tedious than I'd originally thought.

"Where was it you ran off to the other day?" Nathaniel asked, dragging my thoughts away from sewing and other roaring good times. He wasn't about to let up his own inquest so easily. "Honestly, I don't know why you don't trust me. I'm quite offended, Sister."

"Fine." I sighed, knowing I'd have to reveal one secret in order to hang on to more important ones. "I sneaked into Father's study the other night and came across Alistair's name. That's all. Really."

Nathaniel frowned, pulling at his soft leather gloves but not taking them off. "What in the name of the queen were you doing in Father's study? I can't protect you from your own stupidity, Sister. There's no medical cure for that as of yet, much to my dismay."

I ignored his jab, plucking a grape from our picnic hamper, which Nathaniel had ordered from Fortnum & Mason. It was packed full of mouth-watering delicacies, from imported cheeses to hothouse fruit.

To appear less eager for information, I slowly pulled the cheese and bread from the cloth bundle and set the plate on the blanket in front of us. "He was a servant, then?"

"Alistair Dunlop was Father's old carriage driver," Nathaniel said. "Surely you remember him now? He was kind, but very eccentric."

A crease formed between my brows. "Sounds vaguely familiar, but Father changes staff so often it's hard to keep everyone straight."

I spread brie and fig preserves across toast points and handed it to

Nathaniel, before repeating the process for myself. Each time I was certain I'd resolved an important item to my satisfaction, it became clear it wasn't as it seemed.

I wished to find one blasted clue that could point me in a fruitful direction. It'd be even better if murderers, psychopaths, and villains simply held a sign up for inquiring minds to spot easily. It bothered me such a savage could be walking amongst us.

Nathaniel waved a hand in front of my face. "Have you heard anything I've said?"

"Sorry?" I blinked as if emerging from a daydream—one that didn't involve murders, and dying old men. My brother sighed again.

"I *said* Father fired him shortly after Mother's..." Death was what he didn't want to say. Neither one of us liked saying it out loud, the wounds still too raw to cope with, even after five years. I squeezed his hand, letting him know I understood.

"Anyway, he was dismissed abruptly. I never knew why," Nathaniel said, shrugging. "You know how Father can be at times, though. Mr. Dunlop used to teach me chess when no one needed him."

My brother smiled, the pleasant memory lighting his whole mood. "Truthfully, I've stayed in touch with him. He couldn't continue as a coachman after being turned out by Father without a proper reference. I've met him a few times to play chess, wagering money and purposely losing, just to help him out some. His circumstances are sadly reduced, and I cannot help feeling responsible somehow. These days he works the deck on the *Mary See*."

"Another life condemned to hard times, thanks to Lord Edmund Wadsworth and his own eccentricities," I said. I wondered what the coachman could've possibly done to end up a lowly deckhand. His only crime was probably being too kind to my brother.

It seemed when Father dismissed servants, their lives were never the same in the very worst of ways. At least Alistair was still breathing. Miss Nichols would never inhale the unwholesome air of the Thames again.

Misinterpreting my silence, Nathaniel wrapped an arm around my shoulder, pulling me into a comforting embrace. "I'm sure he's happy enough, little Sister. Some men live for the kind of freedom that comes with swabbing the decks of a great ship and hauling cargo chests. No responsibilities. No need to worry about teas and cigar rooms—white tie versus black tie and all that upper-class nonsense. The rush of wind through their hair." He smiled wistfully. "It's a noble life."

"You speak as if you'd like to throw away your good name and swab the decks yourself."

Nathaniel would make a terrible sailor, and we both knew it. He might entertain the notion of leaving behind the finer things in life for freedom, but he cherished his imported brandy and French wine too much. Giving all that up for cheap ale in dank public houses wouldn't suit him in the slightest. I smiled just picturing him sliding up to a bar, ordering something as common as a pint, his hair in complete disarray.

Before he teased me back, our coachman approached, bending to whisper something in my brother's ear. Nathaniel nodded, then stood, brushing down the front of his tailored suit. "Afraid we must end our lunch early. Word has come that Aunt Amelia and cousin Liza have arrived. I assume you're in no hurry to get on with your 'proper lady' duties. Will you be all right if I leave you here to finish your luncheon?"

"I hardly need a babysitter," I said. "But you're right. I'd like a little time to enjoy my remaining freedom."

I grinned, knowing full well that if Nathaniel had it his way, aside from my maid and the footman who were present, I'd have a bodyguard, governess, nurse, and any other attendant he could think of watching out for me.

"Go," I said, shooing him away. He stood there tapping his sides, uncertain. "I'll be fine. I'm going to enjoy the fresh air for a bit, then I'll head home." I crossed my heart. "I assure you I won't be sitting down to tea with any brutal killers between now and supper. Stop looking so worried."

A smile warred with a frown but eventually beat it out. His lips twitched. "Your assurances somehow leave me feeling anything but comforted." He tipped his hat. "Until this evening. Oh," he paused, eyeing my clothing. "Might want to change into something a bit more . . . suitable for Aunt Amelia's tastes."

I waved good-bye, uncrossing my fingers from behind my back once he'd disappeared from view. I'd most certainly head home and change out of my riding habit and into a new dress. That was, after I made a detour to the docks to speak with the mysterious Alistair Dunlop and sort out secrets he might be harboring on the *Mary See.*

"Honestly, I don't know why you insisted on bringing that wretched beast with us," I complained to Thomas as the leash nearly tripped me for the third time. "It's hard enough maneuvering around in these cursed heels without the added obstacle of having my limbs tied together every five seconds by a nearsighted dog."

Thomas eyed the silver buttons lining the front of my black riding habit, coaxing a scowl from me. His look implied my choice of attire—including a pair of matching breeches—should make for an easier time walking about.

"I'd like to see *you* carry on with a corset digging its bones into your rib cage," I said, returning the favor and eyeing his clothing. "And manage a skirt still covering most of your breeches and whipping around your thighs in this wind."

"If you'd like to see me out of my breeches, simply ask, Wadsworth. I'm more than happy to accommodate you on that front."

"Scoundrel."

He'd supposedly been taking the lop-eared, brown-and-white mongrel for a walk around the lake when he happened upon my picnic—an excuse I'd found highly suspect. Especially when he'd *happened* to run into me while John, the footman, was repacking the hamper. Thomas had snatched a few pieces of braised pork for his canine companion to snack on. I sent the empty hamper home along with John and my maid, both of whom looked only too pleased to be escaping one of my schemes.

When I pointed out the unlikelihood of the coincidence, Thomas stated it was serendipity and to be thankful for his "gentlemanly company while parading around in front of pirates and ruffians."

He should be thankful I didn't accidentally stab him with my hat pin. Though I was secretly pleased he'd sought me out.

The cobbled street was wide yet awkward to navigate with so much commotion going on. Men hoisted chests off the side of large ships, the wooden boxes dangling precariously from ropes above their heads. Barrels of wine were rolled into warehouses, along with large metal bins of tobacco; women shouted out specials on what they were selling a few streets over—everything from baked goods to mending torn sails.

We crossed from one basin into another separating the next set of ships. Shop after shop was dedicated to maritime adventures, boasting in the windows golden compasses, sextants, chronometers, and all other ship-themed paraphernalia one could desire. I watched a custom house officer check cargo coming off the nearest vessel, the brass buttons on his jacket winking in the afternoon sun.

He smiled, tipping his cap as I neared, causing my cheeks to pink.

"Come now." Thomas snorted. "He's not nearly as handsome as I."

"Thomas," I hissed, jabbing him with my elbow. He feigned injury, but I could tell he was pleased my attention had been restored to him.

Stores gave way to shabby houses piled together like nesting rats.

Refuse stunk up the gutters in this neighborhood, mixing with the scent of dead fish washing ashore. Thank goodness for the strong breeze coming in off the water, whipping my onyx locks and testing the fit of my velvet hat.

"Toby," he said, responding to a question I didn't ask, while observing the cacophony going on around us. "He's more intelligent than half the police force at Scotland Yard, Wadsworth. You should be kissing the very ground I walk upon for bringing such a fine animal. Or perhaps you could just kiss my cheek. Give the officers and ruffians a bit of a thrill."

Ignoring his attempt at improper flirting, I watched the dog waddle down the road and onto the dock, amazed it hadn't walked itself right off the piers. It was the clumsiest animal I'd ever encountered. I much preferred cats and their insatiable curiosity. "Is *Toby* your family's dog, then?"

Thomas counted off boats, reading names under his breath as we made our way down to the *Mary See.*

"I borrowed him." He stopped in front of a new basin of ships, the forest of masts looming high above our heads, swaying and creaking with the rolling tide.

This section was noisier; I could hardly keep a thought in my head without it turning into some sailor's boisterous tune. Nathaniel would be horrified if he knew I was hearing such vile language, making it all the more appealing, somehow.

Goats bleated and exotic birds cawed from the deck of one ship, encouraging me to crane my neck until I caught a glimpse of brightly colored macaw feathers flapping against a cage. On the very same boat, an enormous elephant trumpeted, stomping its feet as a slew of deckhands tried unloading it.

Names on the crates suggested they were part of the traveling circus arriving in town. Up until the last few weeks, I'd been looking forward to attending the event with my brother. The human curiosities attractions were world famous and boasted of several "must-see-to-believe" acts.

"I've heard rumors of a man who swallows fire," I said to Thomas as we passed the ship. "And another who's got four legs, if such things are to be believed."

"You don't say," he said. "Personally, I'd rather stay in, reading."

Queen Victoria was a great fan of the circus, and would make an appearance on opening night. Everyone who thought themselves important—and some who actually were—would be in attendance.

"Look," I pointed to the ship we'd been seeking, "there it is. The *Mary See.*"

"Stay close, Wadsworth," he said. "I don't care for the look of these fellows."

I peered up at Thomas, a subtle warmth spreading through my limbs. "Be careful, Mr. Cresswell. Someone might think you're beginning to care for me."

He glanced in my direction, drawing his brows together as if I'd said something particularly strange. "Then I should like to meet that person. They'd be quite astute."

Without uttering another word he walked forward, leaving me gaping after him a moment, stunned. What a horrid liar he was! I gathered myself and hurried after him.

The ship was the size of a small man-made island of steel, gray and desolate as a normal London day. It was easily twice the length of every other ship at dock, and the crew looked twice as mean.

As we approached the captain, a burly man with black eyes and broken teeth, docile-seeming Toby took on the ferocity of a dire wolf, baring his canines and growling loud enough to be intimidating.

The captain took a look at the dog, then passed a quick glance over us. "This ain't no place for a young lady. Move along."

I had half a mind to bare my teeth as Toby had—it was working wonders for him—but smiled sweetly, showing just the right amount of my pearly whites. Aunt Amelia always said men could be charmed easily. "I'm looking for an Alistair Dunlop. We were told he's under your employ."

The captain—vile creature he was—spit into the water, eyeing me suspiciously. "What's it to you?"

Thomas tensed beside me, his hand flexing at his side.

I smiled again, this time staring purposely at a point over the captain's shoulder. I tried my aunt's cunning and polite way; now it was time to do things in my own manner.

"I'd hate to make a scene and call that charming custom house officer over here," I said. "Really, one shouldn't operate such an important ship without the proper documentation for *all* their cargo. Wouldn't you agree, Mr. Cresswell?"

"Certainly," Thomas said, letting Toby's leash go slack. The captain took an unsteady step away from the growling mutt. "Not to mention it'd be catastrophic if men hiring such a ship discovered part of their cargo was being sold on the side. Doesn't your family know most of the aristocracy in Europe, Miss Wadsworth?"

"Indeed," I confirmed while the captain visibly squirmed in his boots, "we do. You come from equally good stock, don't you, Mr. Cresswell?"

"Indeed," he answered, smiling, "I do."

A look of pure hatred crossed the captain's face. Apparently, he wasn't someone who enjoyed being bested by a clever-mouthed boy and girl. The captain grunted. "He's making a delivery at the Jolly Jack. Should be unloading round in the alley."

ELEVEN
SOMETHING WICKED

JOLLY JACK PUBLIC HOUSE,
LONDON
13 SEPTEMBER 1888

Thanks to poor directions given by the unpleasant captain, we wandered down a few dead-end streets before finding ourselves at the disreputable but lively public house.

A painted wooden sign depicting a grinning white skull on a black flag hung over the door. Inside, men sat hunched over tankards, swigging pints and wiping their mouths with torn sleeves, while women slunk around like wild cats on the prowl. Giving up any pretense of fitting in, I strode through the room with my head held high, stares and whispers rolling in my wake.

Most highborn women didn't roam around in all-black riding ensembles with leather boots and gloves. While wearing riding habits when one wasn't riding was slowly coming into fashion, the color of my attire and material was what set me apart.

I hoped I inspired a sense of unease, even if it was fleeting.

Once we reached the back alley, we were met with nothing but the sounds of our own beating hearts and Toby's panting. I removed my gloves and rubbed behind his furry ears.

"Do you see him?" I asked, taking quick stock of our surroundings.

An open crate sat on top of several others that must have been unloaded recently, but there was no one here. I walked over to the wooden box and glanced inside. It was filled with rows of glasses; I imagined rowdy patrons broke a lot of them once they were well into their cups. Not exactly what I expected the captain to be selling on the black market, but profitable for him nonetheless.

Thomas knit his brows, staring at the crate. "Seems a bit odd that Mr. Dunlop would leave these goods unattended."

"Perhaps he's inside?"

Without waiting for his response, I turned on my heel and marched back into the noisy pub. I leaned over the scored wooden bar, practically shouting to get the barkeep's attention. The rotund woman wiped her hands on a dirty dishtowel, running her gaze over me as if I were a complete waste of time.

So much for fear-inspiring ensembles. Might as well have dressed in my Sunday best and left the leather for butchers.

"Shot of bourbon, miss?" she sneered, wiping out a pilsner glass with the rag, filling it with dark amber liquid and sliding it to a burly man at the end of the bar.

I watched him take a deep pull of the drink. I couldn't control my lip from curling at his ability to ignore the cesspool of filth that had been wiped all around the glass. God only knew what kind of disease he was potentially being exposed to. I longed to take the rag back to Uncle's laboratory and run a series of tests on it.

The group of men closest laughed, pulling me into the present. I gripped my fist, digging my nails into my palms for crescent-shaped serenity.

"Where's the man who's delivering the glasses? He wasn't out back, and his employer has a message for him." I leaned closer, dropping my voice to a stage whisper. "I suspect it has something to do with the custom house officer who boarded his ship with a contingent of men, looking for stolen goods. They may be heading here as we speak." I let my suggestion hang in the air.

Her eyes went wide in her ruddy cheeks. I kept my expression neutral, though I was quite pleased the way the lie came so naturally, and at the reaction it fostered in a woman who looked scarier than some of the sea-wrecked men.

Swallowing audibly, she pointed toward the door to the alley. "He's just outside."

Producing a large knife from under the counter, she hacked a fish apart on a wooden carving board. "I'll gut 'im next time I see 'im. You tell 'im next time he see Mary, he better run." That explained the name of the ship. She waved the knife in the air, hollering at an impatient patron holding his empty mug in her line of sight. "Keep swinging that in me face and it won't be the only thing I chop off, Billy."

I slipped out the door again, shaking my head at Thomas before quickly filling him in.

Thomas knelt beside a crate, sticking his finger in something wet and rubbing it between his thumb and forefinger. I gulped down a rising sense of panic when I noticed what he'd found. "Perhaps he broke a glass and went to get a bandage."

Thomas didn't dignify that with an answer. He stood, leading Toby close to the blood. "Toby, find," he gently commanded the animal.

I watched in amazement as the dog obediently sniffed around until he picked up the scent. His tail wagged so hard I thought he'd take off like a bird, flying through the cross streets and alleyways. Thomas let the leash go and we trotted behind the dog while he ran down one alley, then the next.

We'd gone only about five streets over when I saw a heap of tattered clothing propped against an abandoned building.

A man was sitting with his legs outstretched, his chin resting on his chest, eyes closed peacefully. His hand dripped spots of blood onto his shirt. I breathed a sigh of relief. A miserable drunk with a small cut was something I could deal with. Toby stopped a few feet from the man, growling low in his throat.

"Audrey Rose, wait." Thomas grabbed for my coat sleeve, but I maneuvered out of reach.

I thought it odd Thomas finally used my Christian name, but didn't stop to ponder it or his worried tone. It was getting late in the day. Nathaniel would be expecting me for supper shortly, and I didn't want to explain why I was only just arriving home after our lunch at the park.

Walking right up to the indisposed man, I cleared my throat. He didn't move. I tried again, a bit louder this time with the same results.

Blasted sailors and their love of all things liquid. I heard Thomas saying something behind me, but ignored him, bending to tap the man's shoulder. Honestly, I didn't appreciate all the males in my life thinking me incapable. I'd show every one of them I could handle anything they could, possibly even better.

I tapped him a bit more. "Excuse me, sir. Are you—"

I'd barely touched him when his head swung back, revealing a sinister crimson smile slashed across his neck.

It wasn't his hand that was cut after all. Someone screamed; perhaps it was me. Though it would have made me happier if it were Thomas Blasted Cresswell.

Thomas pulled me back, rocking me gently in his arms, and I didn't even care that it was vastly inappropriate. "Divorce yourself from emotions, Audrey Rose. See it like an equation that needs solving. That's all it is now. It's going to be all right."

When I looked at my hands I knew that was a horrible lie.

Everything was most certainly not okay, and this was no mathematical equation; my hands were covered in sticky blood. I frantically wiped them off on my bodice, but it was no use. Blood stained my fingers in a crimson accusation.

Somehow, some way, I was responsible for this man's death.

Nathaniel sat with his arms crossed tightly over his chest, looking more serious than a man facing a firing squad.

When the detective inspector showed up on our doorstep with me covered in blood and shivering beneath a horse blanket, he'd gone deathly pale. My aunt had nearly fainted herself when she'd seen me and ushered her daughter into their rooms, promising a thorough discussion on proper behavior once I was decent.

Something else to look forward to.

Each time I closed my eyes the scene replayed in my mind. The horrid, gaping smile taunting me. I'd heard police mention his neck was almost severed completely.

A few tendons and ligaments were barely saving him from decapitation, a fact I was well aware of. I shivered. There was something infinitely worse about touching a still-warm dead person as opposed to cutting open the cold ones in Uncle's laboratory.

"Here. Drink this." Nathaniel pressed a hot cup of tea into my hands. I hadn't seen him cross the room. I stared at the steam rising off the pale, almost golden liquid.

It was impossible, but I swear I could've almost heard the last few strained beats of the man's heart as he bled out in front of me.

Thomas assured me even if we'd arrived moments after the attack, he'd likely have died almost instantly. There was an agonizing feeling deep inside of me, wondering if I'd held a cloth to his wound instead of knocking his head askance if it could've saved his life. What kind of girl was so accustomed to blood she paid it no mind? A terrible one.

"If there's anything else we can do, Detective," Nathaniel said, ushering the man from the drawing room. I'd forgotten he was even there.

I heard snippets of conversation as they made their way to the front door. An identification card was found in the man's pocket, confirming my worst fears: someone got to Mr. Dunlop before I could question him. Guilt wrapped itself so tightly around me, I could scarcely breathe. How many men needed to die before I discovered the truth?

I sipped the fragrant tea, letting the warmth slide down my throat all the way into my gullet, heating me from the inside out.

I knew nothing regarding Mr. Dunlop and his personal life, so I hadn't the slightest clue who would wish him dead. Was it someone he worked with?

The whole crew of the *Mary See* certainly appeared capable of murder, but looks had a troubling way of being deceiving. Mother used to read stories from books she'd brought from Grandmama's. At first I'd turned my nose up at them, thinking nothing good could come from such battered covers. I'd been snobbish and wrong.

The words written between those crinkled pages were magical; like a fairy princess hiding amongst paupers. Mother taught me judging something from its outward appearance was silly, a lesson I tried remembering often.

Recalling the way I'd curl up in her lap brought on a new wave of sadness. How much death and destruction must one girl go through in a lifetime? As the door opened and closed, I blinked tears back, angry with myself for not being tougher.

Nathaniel sank into the high-backed chair across from me,

leaning over to look me in the eyes. I half expected him to scold me for venturing out, being reckless as I was prone to be; instead, he smiled.

"You're the bravest person I know, little Sister."

I couldn't stop myself from snorting. I was a sniffling, teary mess—hardly the mark of bravery. Thomas had held me the entire carriage ride home just so I wouldn't break apart. I'd siphoned his strength and missed it terribly now. Nathaniel shook his head, easily reading my thoughts. Well, I hope not the one regarding Thomas with his arms around me.

"Half the men in Father's circle wouldn't have dared to question men who work the docks," he said. "It takes an extraordinary amount of courage to do what you did." He dropped his gaze. "My only regret with your outing today is the horror of seeing that man with his—I'm truly sorry you were the one to find him."

I held a hand up to stall him. I didn't want to think about finding poor Mr. Dunlop anymore. I lifted my chin, chasing the would-be tears away.

"Thank you." I stood, setting my teacup down on the table, and hugged my arms to my chest. I needed to get out of this room and clear my head.

Reaching down to gather my skirts, I realized I was still dressed in my blood-smeared riding habit and breeches. Perhaps the news of my grisly discovery wasn't the only thing that had made my aunt nearly faint.

First thing I needed to do was change into clean clothing. Even the strongest soldier in the queen's army wouldn't run around in battered trousers, I assured myself.

Nathaniel got up from his own seat. "Where are you going?"

I smiled. "To change. Then I'm calling on Thomas. There are

things I need to discuss with him, and I'm afraid they cannot wait until morning."

Nathaniel opened his mouth, ready to argue, but stopped himself. I'd just discovered a mutilated man in an alley on the docks. Calling on Mr. Thomas Cresswell late in the afternoon was the least of his worries.

He glanced at the clock, then back at me. "I'm leaving shortly myself. I probably won't be home until after you're already asleep. Please, for my sake, try to get home before it gets dark out. We've both had enough excitement for one evening. Were I to have another fright like it, I might end up dying on the spot."

As we stepped into the hallway, I really looked at my brother.

Stress was still getting the better of him. Little lines were deepening around his eyes; exhaustion taking an even greater toll on him than it had a few nights ago.

I felt horrible adding to his already full plate. He was always busy studying, and now with Father gone he was tending to the house and me all while some murderer was running around, slaughtering women. I wasn't making his job any easier by sneaking out at night and finding dead men in the afternoon.

I twisted Mother's ring around my finger one way and then the next.

"How would you feel if I asked Thomas to come by here for a bit instead?" I knew it was an outrageous question since he wouldn't be home to chaperone us, but figured it might ease his mind knowing I wouldn't be leaving the premises after all. Plus, Aunt Amelia and Liza were in the house; it wasn't as if I'd be all alone with him.

"Audrey Rose... I'm not certain about that."

He stared at me for a painfully long few seconds, struggling with what was socially proper and what would make him inevitably feel better. He pulled his favorite comb out, running it through his hair, then placed it back in his jacket pocket before finally answering.

"Very well. I'll telephone him on my way out. You're not to close any doors." He took a deep breath and glanced down the hall. "Please keep to the dining room and parlor. Be sure to stay a decent length apart. Last thing we need are rumors circulating. Father will be home in less than two weeks. He'll slay us both if your reputation is tarnished. Especially since he's..."

Nathaniel snapped his mouth shut and turned. He wasn't getting away with keeping secrets that easily. I charged after him and grabbed his sleeve, tugging him back around.

"Especially since he's what?" I demanded. "What aren't you telling me, Nathaniel? Has he been back in London? Is he still unwell?"

My brother looked as if he'd rather be speaking with the detective inspector again, and an awful feeling bubbled up my throat. I shook his arm, my expression pleading. He sighed. It never took long for him to give in to his only sibling, and I felt only slightly terrible for exploiting that weakness.

"Your father has been receiving callers in both town and country," Aunt Amelia said, emerging, it seemed, from out of thin air. She looked like a feminine version of my father and uncle; tall, fair, and beautiful.

One would never imagine she was in her early forties. Aunt Amelia embodied the very essence of what a woman should strive to be at all times. Everything from her neatly styled hair to her silk-adorned feet was immaculate and delicate.

Even the disapproving, pinched expression on her face was royal-looking. "Though after tonight's debauchery, and the rumors surely following, I'm not sure he'll have much success. If I didn't know any better, I'd assume you were trying to ruin *all* of your prospects."

I stared from my aunt to my brother. "You said he hadn't left Bath at all."

"A young man's been writing to Father for weeks now. From what I've gathered his family is very well connected politically." Nathaniel straightened his suit. "The merging of our families would make sense. Father returned to London to meet with him, but it was only for a day."

It was as if the ground had split open in a giant yawn that swallowed me whole. I couldn't stop thinking about Father secretly meeting potential husbands while he was supposed to be recuperating.

"But I haven't even come out in society yet!" I said. "I've got an entire year before worrying about balls, and parties. How am I supposed to deal with this on top of working for Uncle and the murders going on in Whitechapel? I cannot possibly entertain the notion of anyone courting me."

Except for possibly one boy with mischief in his soul. Then a thought struck... Thomas's family was connected politically, as far as I knew. And we had been interacting for weeks. Could his flirtations be real, then?

Aunt Amelia crossed herself. "It will be a miracle if they remain interested in that merger now. You've got some serious mending to attend to. I'm organizing a tea for tomorrow afternoon. It'll do you a world of good, interacting with girls your age who are interested in decent things. There'll be no more childish games or discussions of murder. Certainly no 'working' for your uncle and his unnatural science. If your father learns of this he'll relapse. Have I made myself perfectly clear?"

I stared at my brother for assistance, but he was preoccupied. "But—"

Nathaniel checked the clock in the hallway, then gave me a sympathetic look. "Try not to dwell on it now. I'm sure it'll all work out fine. I really must be off. I was supposed to meet the head barrister half an hour ago."

Without waiting for my response, my brother tipped his hat to Aunt Amelia and me, then walked briskly down the hallway and out the front door, leaving me alone to deal with the aftermath of the bomb he'd just dropped on me.

Why was Father taking a sudden interest in marrying me off, and who was the mystery man writing about me? If it wasn't Thomas, then who was it? An uncomfortable feeling slithered like snakes through my gut. I didn't like this turn of events one bit and would do everything in my power to stall any courting. I clenched my fists.

"Arranged marriages have gone out of fashion," I stated, hoping to appeal to my aunt's vanity. "People would surely gossip about it."

"First things first," Aunt Amelia said, clapping her hands and ignoring me altogether. "Time to get rid of those disgusting blood-soaked garments. Then we'll address the matter of your hair."

She scrunched her nose as if she were observing a rodent rummaging through rubbish. I cringed. My hair had been the last thing on my mind after finding a man dead.

"Honestly, Audrey Rose, you're far too pretty and too old to be running around like a tomboy," she said. "Bring your needle and thread down after your bath; it's high time we worked on your hope chest."

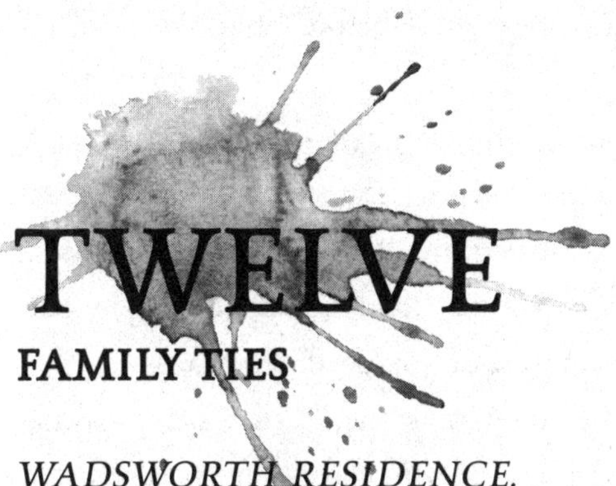

TWELVE

FAMILY TIES

WADSWORTH RESIDENCE,
BELGRAVE SQUARE
13 SEPTEMBER 1888

Nearly two hours and several dainty *ahems* of approval later, my aunt finally retired to bed, satisfied she'd sewn inappropriateness from me one stitch at a time.

It now didn't seem to bother her I'd found a murdered man, so long as I'd created pretty violets and swirling vines to make up for breaking social taboos.

She'd also insisted on having my newest maid add a bit more "powder and polish" to my after-bath routine. When I'd argued that it was unnecessary, I could do fine on my own, she crossed herself and refilled her wine, instructing the maid to attend to my beauty needs each day from there on out.

I resisted the urge to wipe the excess kohl from my eyes, especially when Thomas kept tossing smug glances my way. I enjoyed applying makeup as any other girl my age would, only I did so with a lighter hand.

"Police say a gear was used to slash his throat open." Thomas fidgeted in his seat in our drawing room. I refused to let him smoke in the house, and he was more twitchy than usual while filling me in on the investigation. He slid one of Uncle's medical journals over to me, his fingers lingering a bit near mine before he fiddled with his own notebook.

"How on earth did someone do that much damage with a simple gear?" I asked, moving around in my own chair with discomfort.

It was strange having Thomas in my home without supervision, even though we'd spent time roaming London and Reading by ourselves and my aunt and cousin were only a few floors above us.

I figured once we started discussing the murder, things would become less awkward, but that was proving to be another falsehood.

"Turning something like that into a weapon isn't hard." He lifted his teacup but didn't sip before setting it down again, his gaze snagging on mine. "It's made of metal and has sharp ends. Any madman or drunk can manage killing someone with it. I, myself, have sharpened quite a few."

I did not have the mental energy to ask *why* he had experience or need to sharpen gears. Letting that slide, I kept my focus on the case, drumming my fingers along the journal. "At the first two murders there were gears. It's a bit too much of a coincidence to be unrelated to our own investigation. Wouldn't you agree?"

"Dear Wadsworth. Your association with me is growing more beneficial by the hour. Your intelligence is quite... attractive," Thomas said, raising his brows suggestively and taking in my newly plaited hair. "Let's have some wine and dance inappropriately. You've already dressed the part for me—let's take advantage."

He offered his hand, palm up, a wicked grin set upon his face.

"Thomas, please." I batted his hand away, blushing furiously. Dancing with Thomas alone without a chaperone would be scandalous and was far too tempting. Plus it wouldn't solve this mystery any faster, I reasoned. "Aunt Amelia would perish on the spot if she walked in on such . . . impropriety."

"Hmm. Her untimely end would excuse you from any more embroidery lessons, would it not? Perhaps we should skip the dancing and passionately embrace instead."

"Thomas," I chided. I told myself the sooner we discovered who the murderer was, the sooner I'd be rid of Thomas Cresswell and his devious ways. We'd be kissing in back alleys before I knew it. Then my reputation would truly be in the gutter. I didn't appreciate the twinge of disappointment I felt at the thought of not spending as much time with him.

"Very well, then." Thomas leaned back, sighing. "I believe someone was spying on us in the shipyard. They must've overheard us talking about Mr. Dunlop. It's the only logical conclusion that works. If we can identify him, I'm positive we'll have found our murderer."

"And if I had a crown I'd be queen," I said, unable to stop myself. "Honestly, Thomas, how ridiculous a statement. If, if, if. We need something a bit more secure than a simple *if,* if we're to stop a vicious murderer."

The irony of my last statement was not lost on Thomas. A slow smile crept across his mouth as he leaned forward, our faces dangerously close. "If I purchased a crown, would you run round Buckingham Palace in nothing but your petticoats, demanding the guards let you through?"

"Be serious," I admonished him, but not before laughing at the absurdity of the image. "Can you picture such a thing? I'd be thrown into the Tower and they'd have the key tossed in the Thames for good measure. Good riddance, indeed."

"Fear not! I'd find ways of springing you from your tower prison, fair lady."

I shook my head. "Wonderful. You'll end up in the next cell, dooming us both."

Thomas laughed heartily for a few beats, his gaze straying to my lips and staying there. I swallowed, suddenly remembering we were alone, and I couldn't find one good reason why I *shouldn't* kiss him. I was already trouble in society's eyes. Might as well embrace my role and have a bit of adventure in the process. Cousin Liza would demand every last detail... a bit of gossip might be fun.

Checking my reaction, he slowly closed the distance between us, my pulse quickening as his expression shifted to a sweet unguardedness. Yes, I thought. This was right. I couldn't think of a more perfect first kiss.

A clattering noise from the kitchen downstairs broke the spell. He abruptly sat straighter in his chair, flipping the notebook open with intense interest; the temperature in the room chilled at least twenty degrees.

I blinked at how quickly he shut himself off. I'd half a mind to have a fire made in here, not that it'd help his frigid demeanor.

Straightening my shoulders, I collected my thoughts. Well, then. I could be just as fickle as Thomas, if that's how he wanted our association to be. We needn't laugh or even be friends. In fact, I should never have warmed to him to begin with. I couldn't believe how close I'd been to kissing him. Deplorable beast that he was.

Though, if I were truly being honest with myself, I would admit it was nice having an acquaintance as abnormal in society's eyes as I was. Father hadn't allowed friends into our home while we were growing up, what with influenzas and potential pox contaminations, so I'd never had a best friend before and missed out on those sorts of relationships.

Even with all Father's efforts, disease still found its way into our home.

He hadn't realized how difficult it would make things once I was old enough to accept my own invitations for tea. Now I needed my aunt and cousin to come in and make friends for me. I couldn't be vexed with Father, though. He did the best he could, even when his best was detrimental.

"I'll take that." I snatched another journal from Thomas's side of the table. It seemed he'd grabbed nearly all of Uncle's journals before arriving here and was hoarding them along with his manners.

He didn't bother lifting his head from his own work. Of all the... I set my jaw, and reread the same few sentences, forcing my brain to find a connection between the victims. Two prostitutes, Miss Smith, and a coachman-turned-sailor. Most of whom had a connection to Father, I realized with a start. The only person who couldn't be traced to him was Miss Annie Chapman, and she'd been slain in the most brutal manner.

Everything pointed to the fact that Miss Chapman didn't know her killer, but the others likely did. I swallowed hard, knowing there was something we needed to do immediately.

"Excuse me." I stood, gathering my skirts like silent witnesses, and headed out the door without waiting for Thomas to stand. If he wanted to treat me so coolly, then I'd show him the same lack of respect. I needed no man to empower me. I had my father to thank for that much; his absence in most everyday things had prepared me well enough to stand on my own.

Walking swiftly down the hallway, I paused, listening to sounds of voices drifting up from ornate metal vents in the floor. Once I reached my father's study, I halted to the sound of someone knocking at the front door. *Drat.* I crept back down the hall and slipped into the well-lit drawing room while the first footman greeted the caller.

Last thing I needed was to get caught rummaging through

Father's things, but suddenly recalling something Thornley mentioned had my mind spinning with new questions.

Thomas continued to pore over his notes. I paid him little attention, straining to hear who was calling on us at this hour. Footsteps approached, and I pretended to lose myself in reading. The first footman entered the room, waiting for my acknowledgment. I looked up, eyes innocent and wide. "Yes, Caine?"

"There's a Mr. Alberts here to see you, Miss Audrey Rose. Says he works for your uncle and brings an urgent message. He apologizes for the late hour. Shall I send him away?"

I shook my head. "It's not like Uncle to send someone over unless it's important." Especially if Father intercepted any correspondence he'd want to keep private.

Something must have happened. Perhaps he found a link to the crimes and couldn't wait until morning, or maybe he'd discovered our murderer's identity.

Anticipation raced through my core, erasing all else from my thoughts. "Send him in straightaway, please."

The footman disappeared, emerging again with my uncle's servant in tow. The man gripped a worn derby hat, nervously twisting the brim round and round, looking as if he'd just encountered something awful.

My heart turned to lead, dully thudding in my chest. Perhaps he was simply afraid of encountering my father. Uncle certainly barked loud enough over the last few years about his cruel brother, the miserable Lord Edmund Wadsworth, who hid his darkness behind his pompous title. I hoped that was the cause of his anxiety.

"You have a message from my uncle?"

He nodded, throwing glances toward Thomas as he did so, his unease growing. "Yes, Miss Wadsworth. It's—it's something terrible, I'm afraid."

Uncle's servant wrung his hat until I was convinced it'd be torn in half.

"Do speak freely, Mr. Alberts," I said. "What news do you have of my uncle?"

He swallowed hard—his Adam's apple a bobbing buoy in his throat. "He's been arrested, miss. Scotland Yard's taken him away in a Black Maria and everything. Told us he's the one responsible for them deaths in Whitechapel. Said he's gone mad." He paused, steeling himself against the rest of his news. "A witness come by an' identified him. Said he's the one she seen skulking about the murder. Superintendent said they're taking everyone suspicious in on account of... on account of how awful them... ladies... were cut up."

Notes Thomas had begun scribbling slipped through his fingers, the pages fluttering to the ground like ash after a fire. "What kind of nonsense is this?"

Alberts shook his head, dropping his gaze to the floor, a tremor going through the entire length of his body. "They're rummaging through his laboratory right now. Looking for more evidence to keep him locked away. Say it's only a matter of time before he's found guilty and executed. They say he's... he's Leather Apron."

"Caine, please fetch my coat." My attention shifted to Thomas, who was momentarily taken off-guard, his mouth hanging wide and his eyes blinking disbelief away. We needed to get to Uncle's laboratory now, before they destroyed his life and all his research. "Alberts, thank you for informing us of this—"

"Politeness be damned, Wadsworth!" Thomas bellowed, quickly moving across the room and into the hall. "Let's hurry while there's still a laboratory to save. You"—he pointed at the second footman lingering in the hall—"ready the Hansom cab as if your very soul depends on its velocity."

He grabbed my overcoat from Caine, offering to place it round my shoulders, but I yanked it from his grasp. When the second footman hadn't moved, I nodded at him. "Please do as Mr. Cresswell has so rudely demanded."

Thomas snorted as the footman scampered off to do my bidding. "Oh, yes. *I'm* the villain. Your uncle is being hauled off, his scientific findings most likely being destroyed by barbarians, yet I'm the rude one. That makes perfect sense."

"You're infuriatingly rude. Being boorish and snapping at people won't get the job done any quicker, you know." I pulled my coat on and fastened the buttons with deft fingers. "We wouldn't still be waiting here for the carriage if you'd asked them nicely to fetch it."

"Any other words of wisdom I should take into consideration, my dove?" he asked flatly.

"Yes. As a matter of fact. It wouldn't kill you to be kinder to people. Who knows?" I said, tossing my hands in the air. "Maybe you'd finally find someone who could tolerate you. And, anyway, how twisted your first concern is of the lab and not my uncle's life. Your priorities are hopelessly in disarray."

"Perhaps I don't want any friends," he said, moving toward the front door. "Perhaps I am content with speaking the way I do and care only what your opinion of me is. My first concern is *not* of your uncle's laboratory. It's of their reason for taking him in." Thomas rubbed his forehead. "Thus far they've arrested four other men I can think of. For the offense of drinking too much and flashing a knife. My concern is whether they've taken him to a workhouse or to an asylum."

"Neither is pleasant."

"True," Thomas said, "but he's less likely to be dosed with 'tonic' in a workhouse."

In the next moments, our sleek Hansom carriage pulled around the front of my house, the single black horse looking dangerous. The beast snorted, sending puffs of steam into the already foggy evening. I hoisted myself into the carriage, not bothering to wait for Thomas or the coachman to help.

We needed to hurry. There was no telling how much damage the police were actually doing to Uncle's precious work. And if what Thomas said was true regarding the asylum…I couldn't finish the thought.

Thomas hopped into the small enclosure, his attention riveted on the road ahead of us, the muscles in his jaw tense. I couldn't tell if he was worried about Uncle, or upset I'd insulted him. Perhaps it was a bit of both.

The coachman cracked the whip and we were off, flying through the streets at a gloriously fast pace. We wove in and around larger horse-drawn carriages, moving as agilely as a panther through the urban tangle of London's streets. In what felt like mere minutes, we were pulling up to Uncle's home in Highgate.

I leapt from the cab, my skirts adding bulk and weight to my already heavy footsteps. Police filed in and out of Uncle's home, removing boxes of paperwork. I ran up to a young man who seemed to be in charge.

"What is the meaning of this?" I demanded, hoping I might shame them into stopping. If only for a little while. "Have you no respect for a man who's assisted in finding criminals most of his life? What could you possibly want with my uncle?"

The constable had the good grace to blush, but stuck his impressive chest out a bit more when Thomas ambled up the steps, an obnoxious swagger in his stride. The constable turned his attention back on me, his light eyes showing a hint of remorse. No salty tears spilled from those oceanic blues, though.

"I'm truly sorry, Miss Wadsworth," he said. "If it were my

decision alone I'd send everyone on their way. Believe me when I say I've got nothing against your uncle."

He smiled shyly, something strangely out of character for a man who had the build and confidence of an Olympian.

"In fact, I've always admired the sort of work he's done. Orders came from high up, though, and I can't ignore them, even if I wanted to."

It was hard to imagine someone who spoke so well choosing the life of a simple policeman. I narrowed my eyes, noticing the extra decorations on his uniform; he was a high-ranking officer, then. He was no simple policeman, he was of nobility to hold such an esteemed office at his young age.

My gaze traveled back up to his face. The fine bones and sharp angles of his cheeks and square chin made him quite handsome. He was most certainly highborn. Facially, he looked like a younger, more handsome version of Prince Albert Victor, *sans* mustache.

"What did you say your name was?" I asked.

Thomas rolled his eyes. "He didn't, Wadsworth. But you already knew that. Get on with your flirtation so we might get on with our actual purpose for being here."

I glared at Thomas, but the young man paid him no mind. "I apologize for my rudeness, miss. I'm Superintendent William Blackburn. I'm responsible for the four hundred eighty constables here in Highgate."

His name sounded vaguely familiar, but I couldn't quite place where I'd heard it. Perhaps I'd read it in some paper with connection to our murders.

Thomas interrupted my muddied thoughts. "Seems you've employed every last one of them to trample through this home," he muttered, shoving aside an officer before marching in to assess the situation himself.

I wanted to strangle him for being so rude. Superintendent Blackburn might be able to give us answers we'd otherwise not be privy to. For all his superior intelligence, Thomas could be downright obtuse when it came to dealing with people. If I had to befriend the devil in order to help Uncle, so be it.

I found myself apologizing. "He's a little high spirited, please forgive his impolite behavior. He can be quite..." I trailed off.

Thomas Cresswell was not charming to anyone other than me occasionally, nor was he polite on a good day. Mother would have instructed me to not utter a word when a kind one couldn't be discovered, so that's precisely what I did.

Superintendent Blackburn gave me a sheepish grin and offered his arm. I hesitated for only a moment before looping mine through his. *Play nice, Audrey Rose,* I reminded myself.

"I'll escort you inside and try my best to explain the reason behind your uncle's arrest." He paused and looked around before leaning close, an almost familiar scent lingering on his skin. "I'm afraid it doesn't look very good for him, miss."

THIRTEEN

BLUEPRINTS AND BLOODY BOLTS

DR. JONATHAN WADSWORTH'S LABORATORY, HIGHGATE
13 SEPTEMBER 1888

Walking into Uncle's basement laboratory with uninvited guests rummaging about like scavengers was its own nightmare, plucking at the ligaments between my bones.

Uncle's books, his notes, his journals were all painfully absent. It felt like one of my ribs had been sawed off, leaving me both gasping for breath and missing a piece of myself all at once. Letting go of Blackburn's arm, I slowly turned in place, my eyes two unbelieving orbs in my head. If this was a dream, I hoped to wake from its dreadfulness soon. I had a terrible feeling, however, that this was only the beginning of a series of horrendous nightmares.

The specimen jars were the only items that remained untouched, the dull, preserved eyes watching the chaos with silent judgment. Oh, how I wished I could be like those dead, unfeeling things now.

Anything would be better than the reality I was standing in.

My refuge all these months was destroyed in a few hours by the hands of men who couldn't care less about this sort of work.

"—combined with his history of dissection, and medical

knowledge worked against him," Superintendent Blackburn was saying, but I couldn't concentrate on his words. Thank heavens Uncle wasn't here; his heart would be sheared in half.

I watched helplessly as an officer wrestled a large, gilded tome Uncle had been stroking a few short days ago from the shelf, placing it in a box as if it were a rabid animal ready to snap at him. If only that could happen.

He removed a small box Uncle kept in his desk, the lid slipping off. Bolts and screws clattered to the ground, halting the investigation. The officer bent to retrieve the items, a look of shock and disgust as he rose, holding them up for the superintendent to see.

The bolts were covered in a rusty crimson that could only be one thing. My own blood ceased to circulate as my eyes met Thomas's startled gaze from across the room. "I need to speak with Uncle. I need... I can explain—I just—"

Someone placed a chair next to me and I plopped into it straightaway; it was as if the oxygen had been suctioned from the laboratory with a new steam-powered device I'd seen advertised across London. What was Uncle *thinking*, stealing evidence? Those bolts were from the murder scenes and belonged to Scotland Yard.

Uncle had inadvertently placed himself as the main suspect and I had no idea how to assist him or who to even turn to for help.

Father, though he had the right connections, would rather see his brother hang than assist him in any way. Nathaniel, though he'd want to help, if only for my sake, most likely wouldn't do anything to anger Father or cause an even greater scandal that was bound to fall upon the Wadsworth name. Especially something of this magnitude, sure to hit the papers once reporters caught its scent.

Undoubtedly, Aunt Amelia would throw lavish parties and attend daily services, hoping to distract people from her association with her disgraced brother.

Then there was Grandmama.

She had no ties to Father's side of the family, therefore wouldn't feel obligated to get involved. Not out of maliciousness, but out of a strong dislike for Wadsworth men in general. Grandmama openly blamed Father for Mother's illness and made it very clear that "if a Wadsworth were looking out at a crowd, ready to swing for their crimes, I'd be front and center, watching and cheering" before handing out homemade boondi ladoo treats to everyone in attendance.

Each time we sent correspondence, she searched for excuses to have my bags packed and passage paid to visit her in New York; this would be perfect.

There was no way I'd leave London now.

"Ransack the laboratory, if you must," Blackburn said to an officer. "Just do it carefully."

That snapped me from my reverie. I glared at the superintendent, only partially aware of Thomas throwing a fit over one journal in particular: his.

"You must be mad! I won't hand over my property."

Superintendent Blackburn knelt in front of me, his look no longer light. I stared at the pale strands of his hair. Unlike my brother's careful cut, his hair was too wild to be tamed, curling about his temple like serpents. How fitting for such a cold-blooded monster.

"I know it's a lot to absorb at once, Miss Wadsworth, but I'm terribly afraid there's more." He motioned for the officer fighting with Thomas to give up the one journal since Thomas had brought it into the house with us, and it hadn't been part of their inquest. "We've got witnesses who've stepped forth, placing someone fitting your uncle's description at the scene of the last two crimes."

My attention finally jolted back to reality. I stared at Superintendent Blackburn as if he were the mad one.

"Oh, really? Exactly how many men in London fit my uncle's

description?" I asked. "I can count at least ten off the top of my head, one of them being the queen's grandson, Prince Albert Victor Edward. What? Will you say the Duke of Clarence and Avondale is involved in these murders next? I'm sure the queen would love that. As a matter of fact"—I squinted at him—"you look as if you could be the duke's younger brother yourself. Might *you* be involved?"

Superintendent Blackburn cringed at my inappropriate criticism of his inquest involving the second in line to the throne and himself. I took a deep breath, trying for calmness. I'd be of no use to anyone if I, too, were taken away in a Black Maria on suspicion of being a traitor to the crown.

I steadied my voice. "Surely that's not the reason you've arrested him. You seem much too smart a young man to arrest someone on hearsay, Superintendent."

Blackburn shook his head. "I do apologize for passing along the unpleasant news, miss. I am truly sorry." He shifted on his feet, trying to maintain his balance while still perched on the ground before me.

"We've also found some rather disturbing diagrams and drawings of these mechanisms best described as..." he paused, the tips of his ears turning a slight pink. I motioned for him to get on with it. "Forgive me, I didn't want to overstep my bounds. But they appear to be torture devices. Some ideas fit with mechanical parts Scotland Yard found at the murder scenes. They believe only someone with an intimate knowledge of the crime would be able to construct such... atrocities. As I said earlier, your uncle possesses such knowledge. Now we've got drawings of similar devices found in his laboratory."

He nodded toward the officer who'd just located the hidden bolts. "Then there's the matter of those parts. You're an intelligent girl. I'm sure you can deduce what that dark substance is without my spelling it out. I truly want to believe your uncle's innocent—there are all these things saying otherwise. I cannot ignore what's laid out before me, even if I want to. The public wants this to be over."

"I've heard there are at least four men in custody for the crimes," I said, hoping to shed doubt on their case. "Two of whom are in asylums. Surely that works in Uncle's favor. They all can't be guilty."

"We simply cannot take any chances. He'll be looked after in Bethlem Royal Hospital, I assure you, Miss Wadsworth."

"What?" I couldn't believe this was happening. I gathered my enraged thoughts, corralling them into a cage, willing them to be tamed. Maintaining a sense of serenity was what I needed to do, but it was hard when all I longed to do was shake these men from their shortsighted stupor. Bethlem Royal Hospital, known to most everyone as Bedlam, was horrendous. Uncle could *not* stay there.

"You must believe me," I whispered, angry tears burning my eyes. "I know how it looks, but I assure you my uncle is an innocent man. He's brilliant, and shouldn't be punished for finding the right avenue to search. He lives and breathes a case when he's involved with it. I'm sure he's got plenty of good reason to be in possession of those items. He probably did those sketches after attending the scene. You simply need ask him. This is how he works. You *must* know that."

Superintendent Blackburn gave me a pitying look. I'd find no help here. He was duty-sworn and that was that. Blackburn wouldn't release my uncle based on his denial of being involved alone. He'd need proof, even if it came wrapped in another body shroud.

I clamped my mouth shut and stood. If I stayed a moment longer I was in danger of being hauled off to Bedlam myself. Uncle might be innocent, but I'd definitely be guilty of slapping some sense into these brutes. With my parasol if need be. I motioned to Thomas, who was still glaring at the police collectively, then swept from the room like a storm rushing through the streets, cleansing all the grit in a mad downpour.

To Hell with them all.

An Afternoon Tea, 19th century

FOURTEEN

PROPER LADIES DON'T DISCUSS CORPSES

WADSWORTH RESIDENCE,
BELGRAVE SQUARE
14 SEPTEMBER 1888

Standing in the doorway of our dining room was like gazing upon something familiar yet undeniably foreign at the same time.

There were so many place settings laid out, I felt dizzy. Small topiaries were arranged on the table along with several towering bouquets of exotic hothouse flowers. Pink-and-white porcelain cups were awaiting their warm liquid, while their matching plates stood at the ready.

"You look as if you're expecting the blade of the guillotine, Cousin," Liza said, waltzing into the room. "It's not as if you've been raised by wolves. You've missed only a few months of gossip. You'll catch up in no time," she said. "If you can deal with blood and other horrendous things, a little lace and tea will surely be nothing."

I tore my attention away from the table and looked at my cousin. She sounded like my mother for a brief moment, and my nerves settled. I smiled. If Aunt Amelia was the embodiment of what all proper young ladies should aspire to, Liza was her shining protégé. Except Liza had a fascinating way of flouting tradition when it suited her romantic notions.

Growing up we saw each other only twice a year, but that hadn't prevented her from saying we were the very best of friends. She was three months older, which, in her opinion, made her infinitely wiser on all matters. Especially those of the heart.

Her hair—somewhere between caramel and chocolate—was twisted into an intricate design about her crown. I'd love to fashion mine in a similar way. Her dress was made of watered silk and was of the most gorgeous lavender I'd ever seen. The stitching was superb. A flash of the last cadaver I'd sewn back together crossed my mind. Not to boast, but my stitches had been as good. Perhaps a pinch better.

"Isn't it grand?"

"You could say that," I replied before I could stop myself.

Liza turned to me, grinning. "You can play the gossip game nicely today, then go about your secret detective business tonight. It could be just like a novel!" She clapped her hands together. "How thrilling! Perhaps I'll tag along with you on some of your adventures. Are there any handsome boys to flirt with? There's nothing better than a little danger dashed with some romance."

My thoughts turned to Thomas's face. Liza laughed again, the sound like tinkling bells in a fairy tale. I flushed, struggling to regain my composure. "Not really."

"Don't hold back, Cousin! This is the best part! Oooh, I've an idea. Come." Liza dragged me down the hallway, up the stairs, and into the room we'd set up for her stay. Before closing the door, she quickly scanned the corridor for her mother. But Aunt Amelia was buzzing about near the kitchen, commanding the staff like a colonel at war.

Satisfied we were alone, Liza ushered me over to her dressing table, then pulled out a makeup kit far more complex than my postmortem tools. "So, what's his name?"

She tugged a brush through my hair, pulling and twisting black strands with expert ease. I gritted my teeth, not wanting to show how uncomfortable I was with the harsh primping or topic. Surely if I could sit for Uncle in his laboratory, I could suffer through this. I immediately chided myself. Uncle was trapped in an asylum and I was only having my hair styled. I needed to keep perspective.

"Whose name?" I asked, steering my mind from unpleasant things. For some reason, Thomas was a secret I'd like to keep.

"Stop playing coy. The handsome boy who's stolen your heart, that's who!"

Liza stepped back, admiring her work before grabbing the kohl. I tried not to cringe. I'd already lined my eyes lightly and wasn't keen on being made into something I was not. I'd delicately put a stop to my maid's heavy-handed rouging.

"Tell me everything about him," Liza said. "What he looks like. What color his eyes are. If he wants to run away with you to some beautifully exotic paradise...how many children you're going to have. I hope he plays piano. All good men should be so well rounded. Oh! Tell me he's deliciously smart and writes you romantic poetry. I bet he composes Shakespearean sonnets by moonlight with stars dancing in his eyes, doesn't he?"

I cast my attention down, searching for a way out of the conversation, but my cousin gripped my chin, forcing me to look up while she lined my eyes. She quirked a brow, waiting for my response. Stubbornness was a trait she'd inherited from the Wadsworth side of the family.

I sighed. Wasn't I looking forward to sharing this sort of gossip with my cousin a few days ago?

"His eyes are golden brown when he's intrigued by something. He's regal-looking and handsome, but he's more interested in formulas and solving crimes than he is in me or poetry. He acts devilishly warm one moment, then frigid the next," I said. "So there will be no children or any beautiful paradise in our future. Most of the time I cannot even tolerate his presence. His arrogance is...I don't know. Annoying."

"Silly. Arrogance usually hides something below the surface. It's your duty to unearth it." Liza dabbed my lips with her fingers, then shook her head. "It's truly tragic." She handed me a napkin. "Now blot."

I mimicked her motion of blotting my lips with the napkin, taking careful pains to not smudge the color she'd stained my lips with. When I was done to her satisfaction, she nodded, then pointed to the looking glass on the vanity. "What's tragic?"

She raised her brows. "You're in love with him. And he's most certainly in love with you. You're just both being obtuse."

"Trust me," I said, facing the looking glass. "He's the foolish one."

"Well, we must show your foolish boy *this* girl, then. I'm sure you'd become an equation he'd desperately enjoy solving." She tapped my nose. "Wield your assets like a blade, Cousin. No man has invented a corset for our brains. Let them think they rule the world. It's a queen who sits on that throne. Never forget that. There's no reason you can't wear a simple frock to work, then don the finest gown and dance the night away. But only if it pleases *you*."

I stared at Liza for a few beats, seeing her in an entirely new light. She nodded toward the looking glass again, somehow knowing I hadn't truly seen myself before.

My reflection shone back, lit almost as if the heavens themselves were shining down on me. Dark strands of hair were piled atop my head, my eyes more mysterious somehow with the dark liner, and my lips were the bright crimson of freshly spilled blood. I was beautiful and dangerous at once. A rose with thorns.

I was precisely who I wanted to be.

"Oh." I turned from side to side, admiring the full look. "It's lovely, Liza. You must teach me how to do this."

I thought of my mother and the saris she'd brought me to wear from Grandmama's homeland. I felt just as stunning now as I did then, and the memory warmed me.

Mother used to dress us up and hire a cook to make savory delicacies for us every month, hoping to keep the traditions of India alive in us. Father happily participated in our worldly dinners, eating raita and fried breads with his hands.

We'd drag Nathaniel in for our feasts, but he was always unimpressed by eating without silverware. He'd say, "I cannot tolerate being so messy," then storm out in his little suit. How I missed those simpler days.

Liza ran her gaze over my ensemble, then immediately rummaged through her trunk, tossing dresses and corsets and fabrics over her head until she settled on one.

"What's wrong with my dress?" I asked, touching the rose embroidery on the skirts. "I just had this one made." And it was quite beautiful.

"Nothing's wrong with it, silly," Liza said. "But I'd love to see you in my tea gown. Ah. Here it is."

A cream lace gown with pale pink underskirts was promptly thrown over my head and tied in the back before I even knew what was happening. Liza wiped her hands off in a gesture of finality. Pleased with her efforts. "There. You're darling. I always wished my hair was as dark as yours. Makes the green of your eyes nearly emerald."

I stood there, staring at my image. It seemed a horrid contradiction to the reality of the world and what was going on in it. Here I was, playing dress-up while Uncle was in the asylum and a murderer was butchering innocent women.

Liza was at my side steadying me before I collapsed onto the divan.

"I know," she nodded sagely, misinterpreting my thoughts, "it's a gorgeous gown. You must keep it. Come. It's time to greet our guests. I've heard Victoria and her sister Regina are coming. Their father does something with Parliament and I've heard the most interesting rumors..."

It felt as if I were watching through someone else's eyes the events unfolding before me.

Aunt Amelia sat at the head of the table, a queen holding court during her royale tea. Liza sat on my right while the esteemed Victoria Edwards sat on my left, her button nose turned permanently upward.

A royale tea was different from high tea in that it began with a glass of champagne and did not include supper. That much I remembered. Sandwiches, savories, scones, and sweets were laid out across the table, more riches and delicacies than all of Nathaniel's favorite imported cheeses and fine foods combined.

Uncle's arrest was responsible for my nerves, making me forgetful. It had been only a few months since I'd last attended such a formal tea. And though I didn't care for them, I wasn't normally so distracted.

I stirred my tea then set my spoon behind my cup, as was proper.

Victoria turned to me, a slight smile fixed to her face. "I'm so sorry to learn of your uncle, Audrey Rose. Must be quite difficult having such a ruthless criminal in the family."

I'd just taken a bite of a cucumber sandwich and barely swallowed my surprise down. Liza jumped in, rescuing me with her quick tongue.

"Such a shame. If they can accuse someone as brilliant as our uncle, surely they can accuse just about anyone. Perhaps"—she leaned forward, her voice dropping to a whisper—"they'll set their sights on members of Parliament next. It'd make for a rather sensational story, wouldn't you agree?"

Up until that last point Aunt Amelia had been smiling and nodding, proud of her daughter's appropriate response. When Liza flashed a grin my way, my aunt's face turned a furious shade of red. She straightened, then dabbed at her mouth with a lace napkin we'd undoubtedly stitched.

"Now, girls"—she glanced between us—"let's not allow our imaginations to get away from us. We shouldn't gossip or speculate on such matters. It isn't polite."

"But it's true, Mama," Liza insisted, garnering curious gazes from around the table. "Some royals are under suspicion. It's all everyone in London's talking about."

Aunt Amelia looked as if she'd swallowed an egg whole. After a moment, she threw her head back and laughed, a sound more forced than her thin smile. "See? This is precisely why speaking of such things is a waste of time and energy. No royal would truly be under suspicion. Now, who'd like more tea?"

Victoria, displeased by the turn in conversation, faced me a second time. "You look rather pretty this afternoon, Audrey Rose. To be perfectly honest, I wasn't sure what we'd been invited to. Given all the rumors swirling around about your association with that strange assistant of your uncle's. What's his name? Mr. Cresswell?"

Another girl, whose name I thought was Hazel, nodded. "Oh, yes. I've heard about him from my brother. Says he's got as much feeling as an automaton." She smiled wickedly. "Though I've heard he's quite good looking. And his family *does* have a title. He can't be all bad."

"Mr. William Bradley told me he's got his own flat on Piccadilly

Street," Regina added, looking pleased to involve herself in the conversation. "Honestly, what kind of parents allow their son to live on his own before he's come of age? I don't care how rich they are, it isn't proper." She pressed a hand to her chest. "I wouldn't be surprised to discover he's killed those... women... and hid their bodies away. Maybe Liza's right. Maybe Dr. Wadsworth is innocent and it's Mr. Cresswell who's truly the madman. I bet he's got a slew of unsavory women coming and going there. He might be heir to a good fortune, but who'd marry such an odd fellow? He'd probably murder his own wife."

"Be serious," I said before I could stop myself. "Because he's interested in science hardly makes him a murderer or automaton. In fact, there's absolutely nothing wrong with Thomas. I find him to be quite agreeable."

"Mind your tongue, Audrey Rose!" Aunt Amelia fanned herself. "Addressing a boy by his Christian name is inappropriate. Especially when you're not involved."

If I thought my aunt was upset before, this was a whole new level of emotion. How quickly her tea had turned into discussions of the macabre and impolite.

I held my eye roll in. At least tea was more interesting than I imagined it'd be. The other girls quickly lost interest in Thomas Cresswell and the "tragic and disturbing" murders affecting the lower-class slums.

Conversation moved to more suitable afternoon tea subject matters. Like who was going to be invited to the duke's coming-of-age masquerade in six months.

"You simply must come!" Victoria was saying to me, threading her arm through mine as if we were already the very best of friends and she hadn't just called my uncle a murderer. "Everyone who's important will be there. If you want the right people attending your party, you'll need to make an effort to attend theirs. I hear he's even hired a spiritualist to perform a séance."

As the afternoon wore on, I watched them, noting the role they were all playing. I doubted any of them truly cared about what they were saying and felt immensely sorry for them. Their minds were crying out to be set free, but they refused to unbind them.

Hazel leaned across the table, catching my attention. "Your dress is absolutely divine! Would you be terribly bothered if I had one made like it?" When I didn't respond straightaway she amended, "In different colors, naturally. It's just the design is so gorgeous!"

"If William Bradley doesn't fall to his knees, proposing at first glance," Regina said, smearing a scone with curd and cream, "he's a fool and you need to leave him at once."

Hazel sighed dramatically. "But he's a fool with a title. You really think he'd propose if I wore a similar gown?"

"How could he not?" I teased, holding back laughter at her serious expression. "Surely boys are interested in proposing only to girls in lacy gowns. Why care about beauty *and* brains when they can have beauty *over* brains? Foolish creatures they are."

Hazel drew her brows together. "Why ever would a girl choose anything over beauty? A wife should abide by her husband in all matters. Let him do the thinking." Both Regina and Hazel nodded at that dreadful sentiment before Hazel continued. "Anyway, you truly are the sweetest thing, Audrey Rose. Will you be attending the circus when it comes to town?"

Perhaps I'd been wrong in my earlier judgment. It seemed it'd take a little more time for some girls to free themselves from chains society placed upon them. I bit my lip, thinking of a response that wouldn't offend them further.

Victoria, abandoning her conversation with my cousin and aunt, clapped her hands together. "Oh, yes! You simply must join us. We'll coordinate our attire and everything. People won't know who to look at first, the performers, or us!"

My aunt nodded her encouragement from across the table, her expression threatening something more unpleasant than even Leather Apron could dream up.

I smiled tightly. "That sounds lovely."

FIFTEEN

GREATEST SHOW ON EARTH

WADSWORTH RESIDENCE,
BELGRAVE SQUARE
25 SEPTEMBER 1888

"You're not serious," Nathaniel said, shaking his head at another of my nearly all-black ensembles.

I glanced at layers of black broken up by deep charcoal and silver striped silk, then lifted a shoulder. "Why ever not? There's nothing wrong with the dress."

My corset was pulled tightly over my silky chemise, my gloves were a soft, supple leather with covered buttons running up the sides, and my bustle was annoying me greatly. Judging from how uncomfortable I was, I'd say I was downright stunning this evening. If one could see beyond the dark circles refusing to relinquish their grip on my eyes or the way the midnight colors accentuated how pale I'd become.

The Edwards sisters wouldn't approve of my color choice, but I didn't quite care. I'd attended three more of Aunt Amelia's royale teas, and though they weren't as bad as I'd originally anticipated, it left less time for sleuthing.

"Anyway. It's been nearly two weeks since Uncle was arrested," I said. Neither Thomas nor I had found a scrap of information to exonerate him. "I'll be dressed in the color of mourning until he's freed, and I don't care if it's fashionable or not."

Nathaniel sighed. "I suppose it works well enough for Her Royal Highness. If even the city of London refuses to be anything other than gray and dreary all the time, you might as well act the same."

Blessedly, Aunt Amelia and Liza came down the stairs, looking resplendent in hues of emerald and turquoise, the precise color palette Victoria decided on during our last tea. Nathaniel bowed to them. "Good evening, Aunt, Cousin. You're both visions."

"You are too kind, Nephew," Aunt Amelia replied, feigning humility. "Thank you."

Liza came over and kissed my cheek, shaking her head ever so slightly.

"Your eyes look stunning this evening," she said, looping her arm through mine, completely ignoring the drab color I was in. "I'm so pleased you've taken to the kohl. Thomas Cresswell certainly must be in love. Has he commented on it?"

I thought on our meetings. Thomas pretended to be more arrogant lately, commenting on how I'd made an effort for him. But then I'd catch him staring, as if he were trying to deduce and was unsuccessful for the first time. He wasn't sure if I truly was doing it to entice his affections or for my own purposes, and I suspected it drove him mad.

Before I answered, Aunt Amelia waved the question away like a pesky gnat. "What does it matter? That boy won't amount to anything in society. His family name might be good, but he's destroyed any decent prospects. Audrey Rose has other, more accomplished suitors coming her way. Come, Liza." She tossed her shawl about her shoulders and headed down the corridor. "We'll see you both at the circus."

"See you there." My brother gripped a letter in his hand, crinkling its edges before smoothing it on his pressed pant leg. He reached for his comb but thought better of it. Thank goodness. I was certain if he touched one more strand of hair it'd run away, screaming in protest. The image almost made me smile before I caught myself.

"Are you certain you don't want to change? I thought you were excited for the circus," he said, defeated. "All you talked about for the last several months were the curiosities, menageries—and what of Jumbo? Poor chap's finally coming home and you're greeting him wearing the color of death? What kind of miserable welcome is that for an elephant who's traveled half the world? Aunt Amelia and Liza look like precious stones, while you're making your best coal impersonation. It simply isn't right."

He paced the parlor, hands twitching at his sides. "I've got it! How about we dress you in that horse costume? What was it called? 'The Devil's Auction,' or something equally charming?"

I wanted to smile but couldn't quite bring myself to do it convincingly. Months ago I cared about things like three-ring stages and larger-than-life elephants. I'd even laughed about the postcard we'd found with the strange horse-head-wearing performer.

"There are unsolved murders, and Uncle is being held under suspicion," I said. "Now isn't the time for levity."

"Yes, yes. He along with a slew of other questionable characters," Nathaniel said. "According to the papers, Scotland Yard's throwing any person in a cell until their innocence can be proven irrevocably or until someone more frightening comes about. Uncle will have this sorted out, and you'll have wasted time moping for nothing."

"I'd hardly consider proving his innocence a waste of time." Why police refused to let Uncle out of the asylum, I hadn't a clue. Nathaniel was right: Uncle certainly wasn't the only one being charged with the crimes. "News sources are something else entirely. I can't believe you're reading any of it."

I'd never seen such sensationalist rubbish strewn across every cover. Reporters couldn't get their fill of Leather Apron. They were creating a star out of a madman; glorifying a villain. The lengths people went through to sell a paper was nearly as disgusting as the crimes themselves.

"Awful though they may be, the papers offer some amusement, Sister."

"Honestly," I said. "The whole thing sours my stomach. Why turn a murderer of women into front-page news? I feel sorry for their poor families."

That was enough dabbling in the strange and wonderful for me, thank you kindly. I needn't waste time on distractions.

Nathaniel, however, was on a personal mission over the last twelve days to yank me from the depths of my despair. His answer to my troubles came in the form of two tickets to the "Greatest Show on Earth." Protestations fell upon deaf ears, so I relented.

He'd had a disturbing amount of fabric brought over last week in the hope that a new, colorful frock would chase all the dark clouds away. If only life's problems could be solved with a frilly dress and a pair of slippers. To hell with the world around us, so long as we looked our best.

"Let's be on our way, then," Nathaniel said, checking the grandfather clock. I followed him to the hansom cab, allowing the coachman to help me inside this time, relieved we were taking the fastest means of transportation we owned.

I sat in an inky puddle of expensive silks, rearranging my skirts to make room for my brother in the small carriage, my mind churning with different angles to study the case from.

Nathaniel sat beside me, looking like a child whose favorite toy had gone missing. I was a wretch of a sister. Here I was all wrapped up in my own mind, selfishly ignoring the people who were still very much present in my life.

"You know"—I squeezed his hand—"I'm getting rather excited about the circus after all."

Nathaniel beamed, and I felt mildly redeemed in the court of good deeds, even if I'd lied to get there.

The Olympia was one of the most magnificent buildings in the kingdom; it rivaled even the palace in its splendor and sheer magnitude.

"Look. There it is," Nathaniel said, pointing toward the building.

As our carriage pulled up to the enormous stone and iron compound, I watched a train chug by, puffing white clouds into the atmosphere in dizzying intervals.

Steam was a fascinating source of power; so readily available and used in so many varying applications. I thought again of Father's unique drawings of old toys and war contraptions. They could be on display all across London, perhaps even in the menagerie here tonight, for hundreds of people to marvel at.

That was, if he hadn't stopped making them.

The last train car screeched by and we were off again, making our way to the Olympia's front entrance. People filed in four at a time, all but fighting to catch the first glimpse of the "Greatest Show on Earth."

"Your friends are over there," Nathaniel said. I caught sight of Victoria and her flock of emerald-colored parrots scanning the crowd, but luckily they disappeared into the building without seeing me.

"Shame we missed them," I said. I hoped to avoid them as much as possible this evening. I liked them well enough but wanted to enjoy time alone with my brother.

Taking our coachman's hand, I hopped down from the carriage, my heels catching in the cobblestones as I made my way to the line.

"Do you smell that?" I asked. "Reminds me of Grandmama's home."

Spicy sweet incense wafted over the crowd, spilling out through the arched doorway, filling the warm night air with sultry richness. Against my better judgment, my heart joined the mayhem, soaring between my ribs as if it were one of the pretty ladies on the flying trapeze. Giving into childlike wonder, I grabbed my brother's hand, dragging him through large doors and into the grandest room in the world.

Once inside, I slowly spun in place, my focus riveted on the domed ceiling.

"Nathaniel, it's the most beautiful thing I've ever seen!"

The entire roof was made of glass and iron; each and every last star pricking the sky, it seemed, watched the jeweled crowd—showing off their own dazzling diamond smiles.

"Truly, you should spend more time among the living, Sister." Nathaniel chuckled at my astonishment, but I couldn't quite tear my attention from the mesmerizing night sky.

"Perhaps I will." My hand fluttered to my heart, resting there, as I gazed at slender iron bars arching high above us. I wasn't sure how such a thing was possible. "How can so much glass and metal be supported by a smattering of iron branches?"

It was utterly beautiful, reminding me of looking up through a forest of metal.

"Must be one of those engineering wonders of the world," Nathaniel said, grinning. Somehow, he managed to escort me farther into the chaos.

Swathes of alternating black and brightly colored silk hung from rafters, acting as patricians while billowing toward the crowd, inviting us to come in and be hypnotized by exotic wonders.

Little bells and sparkling beads were sewn into the ends of the fabric with gold thread weighing it down, creating a melodic tinkling whenever someone walked in or out, stirring the breeze.

"Oh!" I gasped. The luxurious panels reminded me of Grandmama's *zardozi* saris, except on a much grander scale. "Remember when Grandmama used to dress me from head to toe in the most elaborate saris? She told the best stories. She said Grandfather had been the British ambassador to India for only a fortnight before proposing."

My younger self loved having the gold and crystal embroidered silk tied about my waist and draped over my arms as if I were a princess holding court in her finest gown. I'd listen intently while she detailed how Grandfather had fallen in love with her, claiming it was all due to her lively spirit. Given the fire that crackled in her soul now, I could only imagine what she'd been like in her younger years.

"Grandmama told me she'd refused him twenty times just for fun," Nathaniel replied. "Said he squirmed like a cobra in a basket. That's how she knew he was in love."

"I'll keep that in mind for future proposals." Those memories warmed me as I took in the rest of the view.

Individual stands stood along the perimeter of the cavernous room, giving one the illusion of being in bustling outdoor marketplaces and bazaars of India. People sold everything from imported silks and cashmeres, to jewels, fragrant teas, and more food than the queen probably had at her Golden Jubilee.

Even little circus trinkets were available to take home, should one desire to do so. I found it hard resisting clockwork acrobats and mechanical tigers, prowling around one table.

"Oh, Nathaniel, look! We must get some." Naan and bhatoora with chickpea curry caught my attention straightaway. My mouth watered with the promise of one of my favorite savory snacks. I couldn't resist its charms, and soon I was dipping flatbread into the creamy chickpea curry and milling about the vendors like a happy child on holiday. I'd spied chicken curry and was certainly going to have some before we left.

"I'm opting for a less... messy version of food," Nathaniel said, paying the vendor.

"Suit yourself." I shrugged as he purchased a box of sweets instead.

After finishing our snacks, we glided through silk doors and feasted on the show. For a little while I forgot about blood and bolts, even asylums, heartache, and all the horror going on in the world—entranced instead by a stampede of around a hundred Arabian horses, prancing about in the most lavish decorations I'd encountered yet.

Gold chains were plaited through their glossy manes, catching the light and reflecting it back in prisms across their sleek faces, while dyed feathers of greens, yellows, and blues curled into the air a foot above their heads.

The horses were well aware of their magnificence, tipping their noses in the air, expecting everyone to *oooh* and *ahhh* appropriately as they passed by.

I shook my head. "If I'd known I'd be out-dressed by a bunch of equines, I might've at least worn a bodice with a few gemstones embellished on it." Nathaniel laughed outright, and I stuck my tongue out. "Least I did my makeup and spritzed myself with that new perfume."

"Next time perhaps you'll listen to your older, wiser brother. Come." Nathaniel gently tugged me from my wide-eyed wonder and led us to a gilded popcorn machine, looking as if it had been commissioned for the queen herself.

Feeling indulgent, we each got a bag, then were ushered to our seats by a silent woman wearing a yellow snake coiled around her throat like a living accessory.

Traditional *mehndi* paint swirled and wrapped around her palms, wrists, and feet. We'd passed a booth where women were being painted with enchanting designs.

"Oh." I pointed it out to Nathaniel. "I *must* have my palms painted before we leave."

The snake stuck its tongue out, tasting the air as we inched by, then hissed. Nathaniel nearly tripped over the man seated beside the aisle, trying to dodge the reptile. I ran my fingers over its large, leathery head as I passed—stifling a giggle as my brother's eyes bulged and he swiped my hand away.

"Are you *mad?*" he whispered harshly. "That beast tried eating me whole, now you're making a pet of it. Can't you be normal and like cats?" He shook his head. "If we make it out alive I'll buy you as many kittens as you'd like. I'll even purchase a farm in the country where you can house hundreds of them."

"Don't be so squeamish, Nathaniel." I playfully jabbed his arm. "Being terrified of an animal a woman's parading around like a scarf isn't very becoming, now, is it?"

With that he huffed, turning his attention on the new act crossing the stage, but I could see a smile curving his lips.

The show was everything it promised to be and then some. There were aquatic acts, more horse acts, and acts taking place high in the sky. Women dressed in outfits made entirely of crystal beads swung from one trapeze to the next—catching their partner's corded arms before letting go and tumbling through the sky, fearless, shining, and free.

I glanced at my brother and noticed he was already watching me.

"It's good to finally see you smiling, little Sister." His eyes misted. "I feared I'd never get to see it again."

I laced my gloved fingers with his. I hated seeing him upset on a night our worries should be continents away. I opened my mouth to comfort him, then snapped it shut as a shadow darkened my view.

An unwelcome patron stepped before us, bending slightly at the waist, before settling his gaze on me.

"Hello again, Nathaniel." Blackburn extended his hand to my brother. "We met during your father's unfortunate... incident. I also had the distinct pleasure of meeting your sister a couple weeks prior."

Superintendent Blackburn offered me a polite smile, then returned his attention to Nathaniel, who sat stock-still. "I'm afraid I must speak with her for a few moments on official police business."

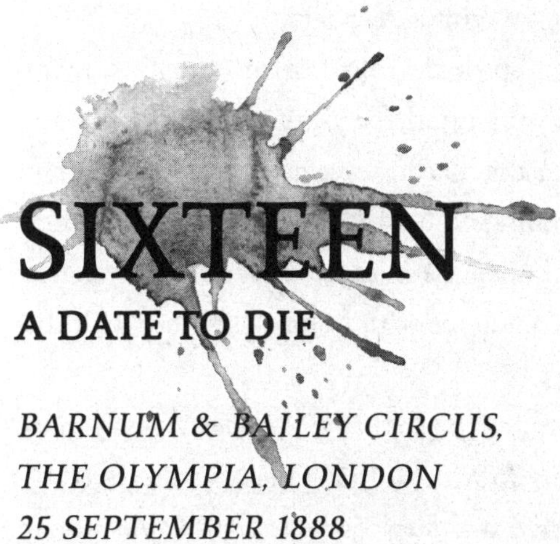

SIXTEEN

A DATE TO DIE

BARNUM & BAILEY CIRCUS,
THE OLYMPIA, LONDON
25 SEPTEMBER 1888

Nathaniel sized the man up with the kind of scrutiny that made even me relieved I wasn't on the receiving end of his look.

It was clear Nathaniel didn't appreciate the intrusion on a night meant to be lighthearted, especially from Scotland Yard, and he wasn't shy in expressing those feelings. Even if the young man standing before us aided Father.

"I apologize, but it's urgent." Superintendent Blackburn swallowed hard, feeling the full force of a Wadsworth's politely controlled wrath, but didn't avert his gaze.

Brave or foolish man. I hadn't quite made up my mind.

Perhaps bravery and foolhardiness were too closely related when it came to him. I narrowed my eyes. Now I knew why his name had sounded so familiar. "Exactly how many times did you save Father from the opium dens, only to send him back to us without any proper treatment, Superintendent?"

"Audrey Rose," Nathaniel hissed, finally returning the firm

shake, possibly a bit harder than necessary, as Blackburn subtly rubbed his hand afterward.

"It's quite all right," the superintendent said.

"My lovely sister's a bit spirited. Your last meeting is a memory that'll be burned into your mind for years to come, I'm sure." Nathaniel's tone implied teasing, but his eyes held no hint of humor. "Apologies, but were you calling on her regarding the awful murders in Whitechapel, then?" He shot me a worried glance. "No matter how strong her heart, I do not agree with bombarding her with this mess, time and again."

"Afraid I can't say much, as the case is still under investigation. But, yes. It has something to do with all that." Blackburn pressed his lips into a firm line. He had a fine face for such a miserable human being. "I—I'm very sorry I was the one who took your uncle away. For what it's worth, I think very highly of him."

Nathaniel straightened his tie, but didn't say another word. I feared he'd reach over and slap the officer with one of his discarded gloves should I show any more outward signs of being upset.

"Might I have a word with your sister now?" Blackburn held his hands up when I made to protest. "It'll only be a minute. Contrary to what you both may believe, I don't wish to disturb your evening."

I couldn't control the laughter from bubbling up my throat. "Oh, yes. Because you're *so* concerned with disturbing people's lives without due cause. How silly of me to forget. Arresting an innocent man and destroying his reputation is rather dull, now that you mention it. Why not ruin his niece's evening as well?" I smiled sweetly. "Then you can add picking on innocent men *and* young women to your growing repertoire. Perhaps"—I tapped a finger against my lips in mock contemplation—"you should kick a child while you're at it. Shall I help pick one out?"

A flash of pain crossed his face, rendering me almost sorry for having said it. Then I recalled *he* was responsible for holding Uncle in an asylum lovingly referred to as *Bedlam*—refusing him any visitors—and any trace of an apology fizzled away on my tongue. I lifted my chin, commanding myself to remain impassive.

From the corner of my eye, I watched Nathaniel fidget with his cuffs. He was getting more upset by the second, and that was something I did care about. His evening shouldn't be ruined by this intruder. He looked at me, a silent question in his gaze, and I nodded. Might as well get this over with.

"After you, Sister." Nathaniel stood, then motioned for me to do the same.

Gathering my skirts in my fists, I moved into the aisle, not waiting to see if Blackburn was following. Once we made it to the main room, Blackburn took my elbow, guiding Nathaniel and me into a smaller area sectioned off by elaborately painted wall screens, serving as the menagerie.

When we were no longer working our way through the crowd, I yanked myself free from his grasp, then crossed both arms over my chest. "I'm capable of walking from one room to the next on my own, Superintendent."

His brows raised a fraction. I didn't care if I was being petty. I didn't care what he thought about me, and I certainly didn't care he was fighting a smile that very instant. I scowled again, wishing on every last saint he'd be struck down for being so blastedly annoying. He coughed into his fist, then glanced at the oddities surrounding us, only succeeding in aggravating me more.

"Planning on getting to the point of your rude interruption soon? Or am I supposed to be swooning and batting my lashes at my uncle's captor and my father's enabler? If that's the case, I'm afraid you'll be waiting until your bones turn to dust." I smiled. "Or, at the very least, until you perish and I'm tasked with dissecting your body to check for a heart."

"Audrey Rose, please," Nathaniel whispered, looking horrified. "Don't aggravate the person responsible for holding Uncle under arrest and keeping Father's secret."

"It's quite all right." Blackburn nodded toward Nathaniel. "She's got every right to be upset."

Blackburn glanced around, making sure the three of us were alone, then drew in a deep breath. An uncomfortable feeling niggled the edge of my brain.

"Don't." I shook my head, begging him to keep whatever toxic words he was about to say to himself. "I don't want to hear anything you've come to say. I've got more than enough to worry about as it stands."

"Audrey Rose." My brother reached for me. "You mustn't—"

"I needn't know a single thing more." I cut my brother's protest off. "Not tonight."

It was childish and I knew Blackburn wouldn't travel all this way only to leave without delivering the message. Still, I hoped he'd spare me an ounce of grief.

His eyes filled with compassion, which was so much worse than his pity.

"I thought it fair to warn you, Miss Wadsworth," he said. "There haven't been any more murders since your uncle's been in the asylum. Some people are keen to find him guilty. They want this whole mess to be done with."

He watched my reaction closely, but I was numb; incapable of responding. It was as if I'd left my body and was watching the conversation take place. Blackburn stared at his feet. "He's tentatively scheduled to hang on the thirtieth of September."

"That's barely five nights from now!" Nathaniel said, ripping me from my shadowy haze. "How can they possibly hold a trial and execution so quickly?"

"Hardly seems legal," I said, searching my brother's face for help.

"That's because it isn't."

Blackburn took another deep breath. "Your brother's correct. There will be a trial but it'll be far from fair. They'll find your uncle guilty and hang him before the ink on his execution order is dry. The public is out for blood, members of Parliament have made proclamations . . . your uncle's the perfect target." Blackburn ticked off each of Uncle's offenses. "He was in possession of bloodstained gears we found near the bodies. Someone of his appearance was seen with the last victim. He has no alibi for either murder. Worst of all, he possesses the skill it took to extract organs."

"For goodness' sake, is that all?" I waved a hand in the air. "I possess those very skills. Perhaps I'm the murderer."

I paced in the sectioned-off room, my hands clenching at my sides. I felt like a wild animal, forced to dance around for people's amusement, and loathed it. Maybe I'd free every last baboon, horse, and zebra in this circus before leaving this evening. Jumbo, too, while I was at it. Nothing should suffer so incredibly at the hands of another.

I turned my attention back on Blackburn. "Can't you stop this madness? Innocent people cannot be hanged, it's grossly unjust. Surely this can't be the end."

He shoved his hands into his pockets, avoiding my eyes as if he'd contract some wretched disease simply from looking upon me. Maybe he could. Hatred was drenching my entire being with its oily residue.

"They've only just closed out the inquest of our former servant," I said, mostly to Nathaniel. "There's got to be some way of repealing this...abomination to our ruling system. They'll have to finish the inquest of Miss Annie Chapman, at least. Shouldn't that offer a bit more time?"

Nathaniel bit his lip, seeming uncertain. "I'm still learning the intricacies of the law. I'll consult my mentor." I stared at him, willing him to make everything better. My brother held his hands up. "I'll call on him now, see if I can get this all sorted out. Try not to worry, Sister. I swear I'll do everything I can to save Uncle. You believe me?"

I nodded. It was all I could do, but it satisfied my brother enough. He turned his attention on the superintendent, his voice cold. "Will you see my sister home? I assume you'll give her a decent police escort, especially after dropping all this into our laps."

It was useless telling Nathaniel I could hire my own carriage home or look for Aunt Amelia and Liza and travel with them, so I kept my mouth shut while he made arrangements with the superintendent.

When my brother was gone, Blackburn cocked his head, a movement showing a new calculating side I hadn't noticed before but knew existed. "Did you say Miss Mary Ann Nichols was your former servant, Miss Wadsworth?"

Excitement radiated from him. I didn't trust him or his new mood, and promptly pressed my lips together. Last thing I wanted was to give Scotland Yard another reason to point their spindly fingers at my family.

Undeterred, he stepped closer, filling the space with his enormous presence, forcing me to meet his inquiring gaze. I swallowed a coil of fear away.

There was something dangerous about him, though it could simply be because he held Uncle's life in his hands.

"You do realize I may be the only person in London other than your family who cares whether or not your uncle lives. Won't you help me solve this case?" Blackburn asked. "Miss Wadsworth... I'm entrusting you to help free your uncle and apprehend the murderer."

He ran a hand through his fair hair, ruffling his already unruly locks. I wanted to help Uncle more than anything; I simply wanted to do it on my own, without involving the person who'd arrested him to begin with. Though it was flattering he respected my intelligence and amateur sleuthing enough to involve me at all.

When I still hadn't uttered a word, he grabbed my elbow, spinning me about. "If you don't want to assist me, let's see someone you do want to help."

"If you don't let go of me this instant," I said between clenched teeth, "I'll be forced to employ a terrible fighting tactic my brother taught me upon your manhood."

Wrestling against his grip, I realized too late he'd eased off because he was smiling. I huffed, tugging my arm completely away. Threats weren't meant to be amusing. I imagine he wouldn't be grinning if I'd actually committed my defense technique, and I wished I'd just done it. "Where is it you think I'm following you to?"

"Bedlam, Miss Wadsworth."

SEVENTEEN

HEART OF THE BEAST

BETHLEM ROYAL HOSPITAL,
LONDON
25 SEPTEMBER 1888

Rumors of Bedlam being haunted by monsters were true.

At least, they felt real enough as we moved swiftly down cold stone corridors. I held fast to my silky skirts, keeping them as close to my body as I could while walking by cells of criminals and the insane.

Arms stuck out like tree branches, searching for things to root themselves to. Or perhaps they were searching for a way out of this dank hell. Blackburn did not hold on to me or offer his arm, trusting I could fend for myself in this abysmal place.

Cries of tortured souls went up all around us, but we pressed on. The stench of unwashed bodies and chamber pots in desperate need of emptying was enough to turn my stomach inside out. The farther we sank into the asylum, the fouler the air became, until I was terrified of adding to the sickness surrounding us.

"This way," Blackburn said, leading us down another bleak corridor.

My mind spun with uncontrollable thoughts. One of the most

terrifying being how to explain my whereabouts to my aunt should Nathaniel return home before I did.

"It's a bit farther," Blackburn said over his shoulder, his footsteps clapping against the flooring as if a giant bell were tolling the hour during an otherwise silent night. "Criminals are kept in the heart of the beast."

"How charming." Chills struggled to unleash their demonic fury across my arms and back. I didn't enjoy thinking of this place as a living, breathing organism, one containing anything akin to a heart.

Hearts usually conveyed compassion, and this place had long since lost that quality. The only beat keeping it going were wails of the damned. I didn't know how Blackburn could stand frequenting a place like this without it tarnishing his own soul.

Inmates sobbed to themselves, speaking in made-up languages and screeching like animals in a menagerie. How my uncle was surviving this mess, I wasn't sure, but he was a strong-minded man. If anyone could be thrown in Bedlam and come out sturdier, it was Uncle Jonathan. He probably found a way of studying different mold specimens growing in patches along the dank walls and floor.

The thought made me smile in the face of fear. That's precisely what Uncle would do in this situation. He'd turn it into a giant experiment to pass the time, never realizing he was actually set inside against his will. I'd probably have to coax him to leave once the time came for it.

He'd say, "Arrested? Are you sure? Perhaps I might spend another day going over my findings first."

Then I'd tell him why that wasn't a good idea, and he'd throw a fit. Once he was invested in an experiment, nothing else mattered.

We walked as quickly as we dared, but I still spied broken men pacing in their cages, looking as feral as panthers. These men were different from the insane. There was a certain air of calculation in their fixed gazes. I didn't want to think of what they could do to me if they were to escape, and sped up until I was practically tripping on Blackburn's heels.

I focused on other things to occupy my mind. I was grateful Nathaniel had departed to speak with barristers prior to our excursion here. I hoped he was already finding ways of repealing Uncle's arrest. He'd put his all into the finest details of the law, never surrendering until he found success.

Finally, we stopped in front of a cell that had only a few rusted bars set into solid stone near the top. Enough to pass food and water trays in, I assumed.

Blackburn removed the ring of keys from his belt—which were handed off from a watchman when we signed in—and motioned for me to stand back. He was a fool if he thought I'd be anywhere but right there when he unlocked the door. I couldn't wait to see Uncle.

Superintendent Blackburn nodded as if he'd already predicted my response. "Suit yourself, then."

With a creak and a groan that would wake things better off left sleeping, the cell swung open in a mocking gesture of welcome. Blackburn stepped back, allowing me to cross the threshold first. What a kind gentleman he was.

A horrid noise emanating from the shadows raised gooseflesh along my arms. Suppressing a flutter of panic, I marched into the lair of a scientist, where the haunting giggles of the newly insane greeted me, freezing at what I saw.

"What in the…" I hardly recognized the creature my uncle had become.

Crouching in the corner of his little stone cell, he rocked back and forth while unearthly laughter poured from cracked lips. An upturned jug of water sat beside him, having run dry a long time ago from the look of it.

"What has happened to him?" I grabbed on to the nearest bar, steadying myself against shock. How did he unravel so quickly? Surely he couldn't have lost *that* much of his mind in just a few short weeks.

Something was very wrong. Blackburn said nothing.

When Uncle wasn't cackling, he mumbled something too low for me to hear. Someone had only given him a thin shift to wear, and it was stained brown and yellow. What little food he'd been given had mostly ended up on his clothing.

"How anyone can treat a person this way is beyond my comprehension," I snarled. "This is...this is *beyond* unacceptable, Mr. Blackburn."

Satan himself must lord over these lost souls. I didn't know what could be worse than Hell, or this place, but wished a thousand terrible deaths on the blackguards responsible for such cruelty. These were people and they deserved to be treated as such.

Grabbing a threadbare blanket from the floor, I shook it out, allowing dust motes to swirl in the pale light streaming in from the bars on the door. The cell was in the supposed heart of this place, yet there was a chill here that hadn't been present in the humid corridor. I approached my uncle slowly, not wanting to startle him, but desperately curious to learn what he was repeatedly whispering.

The closer I got, the thicker the odor clung to molecules in the air. It smelled as though he hadn't bathed in the last two weeks and was using the floor to relieve himself. I fought a bout of rising nausea. His blond mustache was long and unkempt, meeting new facial hair growth in haggard tangles. There was something strange about his eyes, apart from their unfocused, mad glaze. He looked terrified.

After draping the blanket around his shoulders, I knelt down, inspecting him closer. That's when I noticed the upturned bowl of slop and strange consistency of it. My blood turned icy as the Thames in winter, freezing the rivers and tributaries of my veins in sickening waves. I'd kill whoever did this. I would slay the miserable beast so violently, I'd make our Whitechapel murderer seem like a harmless kitten playing with a ball of intestinal string once I was through with them.

"He's been drugged." I glared at Blackburn as if he had a personal hand in the matter. Which, since he'd arrested him, it could be argued he had.

He slowly crossed the room and crouched beside me, avoiding my accusing stare. It wasn't uncommon for the so-called insane to be given tonics to calm their minds, but my uncle was neither insane nor in need of such medication.

"God only knows what this powder is capable of," I said. "Can't you at least protect him while he's in here? What good are you, or do you simply excel at being terrible?"

Blackburn flushed. "In a place like this, intoxicants are often the only way of keeping the peace..." His voice trailed off as I glared at him. "It's inexcusable, Miss Wadsworth. I assure you, it wasn't done with malice. Most everyone here is dosed with... experimental serums."

"Wonderful. I feel *so* much better." I tugged a ribbon from my hair, then tore a length of fabric from the bottom of my skirts and scooped some of the goo into my makeshift cloth bundle before tying it. I'd bring it back to Uncle's laboratory and test it for poisons or lethal toxins. I didn't trust anyone with telling me the truth. It might be a harmless tonic given to "most everyone" or it might be something worse.

Anyone who could administer something like this to a healthy man was too foul and tainted to be trustworthy. Blackburn fell into that same category.

Sitting back on my heels, I peered into my uncle's face. "Uncle Jonathan, it's me, Audrey Rose. Can you hear me?"

Uncle was awake but might as well have been sleeping with his eyes open. He didn't see me or anyone else in the room, only whatever images were playing in his own mind. I waved my hand in front of his face but he didn't so much as blink.

His lips moved, and I could just make out what he'd been repeating since we first stepped into his cell. He was saying his full name, Jonathan Nathaniel Wadsworth, as if it were the answer to all the mysteries of the universe.

Nothing useful then.

I gently shook him, ignoring the wave of disappointment crashing around me.

"Please, Uncle. Please look at me. Say something. Anything."

I paused, waiting for some sign he'd heard me, but he only chanted his name and giggled, rocking back and forth so hard it was aggressive.

My eyes pleaded with him to look at me, to respond, but nothing broke the trance he was in. Tears of frustration welled up. How dare they do this to my uncle. My brave, brilliant uncle. I clutched his shoulders, shaking him harder, not caring how abysmal I must look to Blackburn. I was a terrible creature. I was selfish and scared and didn't care who knew it.

I needed my uncle. I needed him to help me exonerate him, so we could stop a madman from a murder spree that surely wasn't over yet.

"Wake up! You must fight your way out of this." A sob broke in my throat and I shook him until my own teeth rattled. I couldn't lose him, too. Not after losing Mother to death, and Father to both laudanum and grief. I needed someone to stay. "I cannot do this without you! *Please.*"

Blackburn reached over, gently pulling my hands away. "Come. I'll fetch a doctor to watch after him. There isn't anything more we can do for him tonight. Once the drug is out of his system, he'll be able to speak with us."

"Oh?" I asked, wiping my face with the back of my hand. "How can we be sure this doctor of yours isn't the one who administered this... cruelty to begin with?"

"I apologize, Miss Wadsworth. I'm fairly positive it was just a routine procedure," he said. "Know this—I'll make sure everyone is aware there'll be a steep penalty if your uncle is dosed again."

His tone and the expression darkening his features were menacing enough to make me believe him. Satisfied as much as I could be, I allowed Blackburn to guide me from the cell, but not before I kissed the top of Uncle's head good-bye. My tears had already dried when I whispered, "By my blood, I will make this right or die trying."

Once we were back in the carriage, Blackburn gave the driver my address in Belgrave Square. I'd had enough of men telling me where I was going, and rapped my knuckles on the side of the carriage, startling them both. I didn't care what Nathaniel wanted, what Aunt Amelia would say, or what Blackburn would think of me.

"Actually, you can drop me at Piccadilly Street," I said. "There's someone I need to speak with urgently."

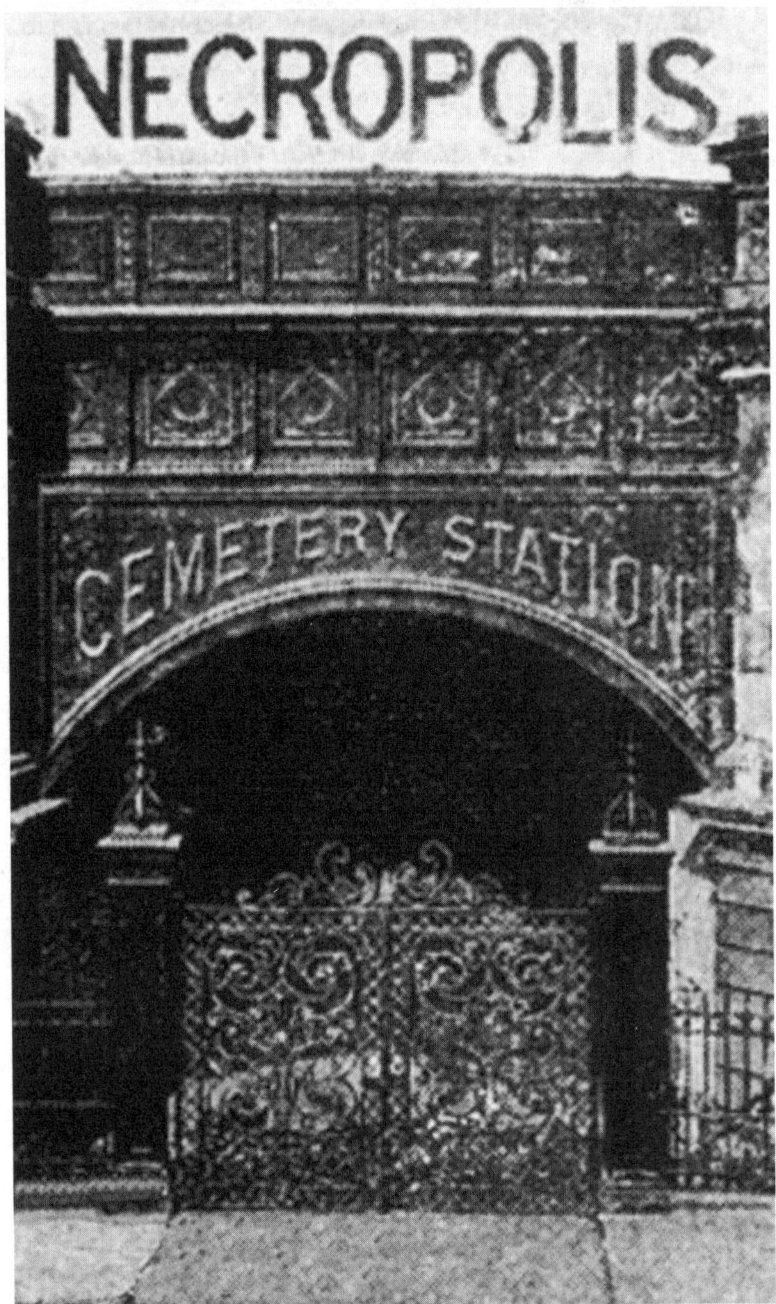

London Necropolis Railway, c. 19th century

EIGHTEEN

NECROPOLIS RAILWAY

THOMAS CRESSWELL'S FLAT,
PICCADILLY STREET
25 SEPTEMBER 1888

I stood half a block away, hiding, as Thomas opened the door to his flat then peered around, looking as sharply put together as if it were nine in the morning instead of nearly ten at night.

I wondered if he ever looked unkempt or frazzled. Perhaps his hair was permanently plastered to the side of his head for less hassle. My brother ought to take a lesson.

I watched silently, gathering courage to walk over to him, but some innate force whispered for me to remain hidden. I half expected him to come marching over, but he didn't notice me standing half in the shadows several yards away.

I'd lied and told Blackburn that Thomas lived two blocks down and had been slowly making my way toward the correct address.

I wasn't sure what I was doing here so late at night and was collecting my thoughts. Silly fears had bubbled up. What if the girls at tea were wrong and he *did* live with his family? They'd be scandalized by my unchaperoned presence at this hour.

It's not as though he'd offered me his address. I'd found it in one of Uncle's ledgers and was contemplating simply going home. Now I was hesitating because he was acting... suspiciously.

I held my breath, certain Thomas had somehow spotted me or deduced my arrival, but his attention never touched on my location. He flipped the collar of his overcoat up, then strode down the gaslit street, his footsteps purposely quiet.

"Where are you off to?" I whispered.

Fog hovered in steamy puffs, obscuring everything from the ground up. All too quickly I lost sight of him. Cool fingers of fear slid down my spine, coaxing gooseflesh to rise. Though it was a fashionable neighborhood during the daytime, I didn't want to be stuck alone when everyone shuttered up for the evening.

Gripping my skirts, I scurried after Thomas, carefully sticking to shadows between the lamps.

A minute later I caught up with him near the end of the block. He'd stopped and was looking one way then the next. My heart crashed into my ribs, and I prayed he wouldn't turn around. Quickly stepping back into the fog, I let its icy wall envelop me.

Thomas cocked his head but continued down the next road, resuming his silent yet fast pace. Exhaling, I counted three breaths then followed, taking more cautious steps.

We traveled through deserted streets, meeting only one horse-drawn cart returning from the park. The scent of manure followed in its wake, and I fought the urge to sneeze, lest I give myself away.

Thomas didn't halt again, his long legs carrying him in great strides toward Westminster Bridge Road and the River Thames. In the distance I made out the stone archway of the London Necropolis Railway Station.

The station had been built thirty years ago to help ferry the dead from London to Surrey, the site of the Brookwood Cemetery. The spread of disease—like scarlet fever and other contagious infections—made extra graves necessary, and the distance from the city helped keep contamination away from the living.

Another chill tangled itself in my hair the closer we drew to the water. I hadn't forgotten the river was one of the places Thomas suggested our murderer had committed his heinous deeds. So why, then, was he stalking that very location this late at night? Before I thought on it too much, a second figure emerged from a sunken access road where carriages delivered corpses to the Necropolis under the river.

I didn't mind the bodies as much as I feared the living, breathing creatures lurking about such a place. I had a terrible suspicion this wasn't some secret meeting of the Knights of Whitechapel. Sneaking into an alleyway adjacent to the building, I craned my neck, hoping for a better view of Thomas and his unidentifiable partner.

Their conversation was hushed, so I couldn't make out any particulars. It didn't take much to garner the gist of it, however. One simply did not loiter outside a place where hundreds of deceased were ferried by railway to Brookwood Cemetery.

Especially when one was studying the inner workings of the human body and needed more test subjects than were volunteered. As if he heard my internal admonishment, Thomas abruptly turned in my direction and I nearly tumbled to the ground.

I closed my eyes and imagined a wall erupting around me, willing Thomas to remain blind to my presence should he investigate this alley. I listened hard, but no sounds of pursuit met my ears. Eventually, I crept back to the corner.

Thomas faced the opposite direction now, deeply immersed in conversation.

The Necropolis had an ominous aura surrounding it, even with its ornate ironwork gate and chiseled stonework doing their best to bring peace to mourners paying their last respects.

Minutes passed, then the two figures disappeared down the

access road. *Drat!* I paced in my spot, caught between wanting to sprint after them and knowing there was no place to hide should I be spotted in that subterranean passage.

If I waited, I could be standing here until dawn. There was no telling if Thomas was getting on the railway to travel to the cemetery or if he was only going into one of the mortuaries or funeral rooms. I'd visited the building on two occasions. Once when I retrieved a body for Uncle this summer and once when my mother died.

I barely remember her viewing, but recall every detail of the room in which she rested before taking her final train ride to the cemetery. I couldn't bring myself to go with Father and Nathaniel to her grave that horrible morning.

On Father's orders Mr. Thornley had escorted me home, safely tucked beneath his arms, sheltering me from the cruel reality of the world.

I stared into the dark, wishing Thomas would materialize and distract me from my memories. I sighed. "Oh, fine. I shall go to you, then."

A leaf crunched behind me. My blood spiked as if a million mortuary needles pricked me at once. I spun on my heel, ready to fly all the way home, then stumbled against the building, my hand covering my heart. "Goodness! You scared the devil out of me."

Thomas leaned against the wall beside me, getting entirely too close for decency. I didn't dare move. I hardly remembered to breathe with his face mere inches away. He tapped his fingers on the stone, never taking his eyes off mine, his lips quirking up. "Well, you terrify *me,* Wadsworth. Seems we're even."

Some of the shock was wearing off, yet my tongue and muscles felt incapable of movement. The way he stole through the night like a thief was unsettling.

I wanted to yell at him, scream about how wrong it was to creep up on someone, but could only stare back, breathing hard. There was something thrilling about being caught by his stare in the dark.

Squeaks of a carriage carrying a heavy load broke the charged silence, and he watched as it passed the alleyway. Once horse hooves clacked against the cobblestones in the distance, he turned his attention back on me.

"I hoped you'd make good on your threats of stalking me." His stare drifted over my ensemble. "Perhaps the style of your hair has had a positive effect on your brain. Beauty and function."

I narrowed my eyes, tucking the fact he'd called me beautiful away for further inspection. "How did you know I was here?"

A devious smile lifted the corners of his mouth. "Tell me something, Wadsworth. Why is it you wriggled in your seat when we were in your parlor, though your aunt was upstairs?" He moved closer, tentatively trailing a finger down my cheek. "Yet you follow me in the dead of night, with no hope of a chaperone to intervene should I try stealing a kiss?"

He focused on my lips, and I was petrified my breaths would snap the stays of my corset. In some ways, he looked as frightened as I felt, his attention flicking back up to gauge my reaction. He certainly wanted to kiss me. Of that I was positive. I couldn't deny my wanting, traitorous heart, either.

"Didn't your family warn you against sneaking around at night alone?" he asked. "Dangerous things linger in the dark."

Now my heart thudded for an entirely new reason.

He leaned in, cupping my face gently before I regained my senses and swatted his hands away. If he wanted to kiss me, he'd have to come up with something a bit more romantic than an alley outside a funeral station. "What are you doing here?"

With great effort, he tore his gaze from mine and stepped back.

"Securing a body for my personal laboratory. What else would I be doing—finding a nice girl to court in the Necropolis?"

I blinked. "Truly? You're thieving a corpse and outright admitting it?"

"Who said I was thieving?" Thomas looked at me as if I were the mad one. "This corpse was unclaimed. I've permission to study unclaimed bodies and bring them back."

I crossed my arms. "Which is why you're sneaking about at night?"

Thomas jerked his chin toward the retreating carriage noise. "I'm here when Oliver's shift ends." He laughed at my confused expression. "Honestly, your imagination is fascinating, Wadsworth. Next you'll be accusing me of the murders."

I noticed his gaze drop to my lips and pursed them in response. "I've never heard of such an arrangement before."

"While it's quite intriguing being holed up in a dark, deserted alleyway with you, arguing about facts," he said, "I have better uses of my time." He paused, taking in my hurt expression. "Allow me to amend that statement. *We* have better uses of *our* time. However, if you prefer we can stay here. I enjoy loitering in darkened places with you fine enough." I couldn't help smiling. He was devilish. "Now then, are you coming? This one's nice and fresh."

He rubbed his hands together, hardly able to contain his dark glee. If I were a good girl I'd go home and pretend I had no inkling of what Thomas was up to. I'd climb into my bed and attend breakfast with my aunt and cousin. We'd discuss the circus and plan another tea while stitching seams and napkins for our future husbands. But I wasn't like my cousin or aunt. I was not wicked, simply curious.

I wanted to study the body as much as Thomas did, even if the acts of human dissection and going home with a boy damned me to a wretched death in society.

Half an hour later we were outside his flat, paying the man who'd delivered the cadaver. He glared at me before pocketing the money. His eyes were two black holes, void of human emotion. It took my entire concentration, but I managed to hold in my shudder. Thomas motioned me inside, then shut the door. I'm not sure what I was expecting, but a simple foyer and a staircase leading to a flat upstairs wasn't it.

"Cozy," I said. A small table was set with a tray of biscuits that smelled as if they'd been freshly baked and laid out within the hour.

Thomas nodded toward the food. "Help yourself. Mrs. Harvey can be quite insufferable when her treats get stale overnight."

I wasn't hungry, but didn't want to offend this mysterious biscuit-making woman he kept hidden God only knew where.

We reached the door to his flat and Thomas hesitated only slightly before pushing it open. Inside, papers and journals were scattered about in haphazard piles, towering three feet high. Taxidermy animals lined the shelves around the room, and scientific tools were lying about in disarray.

A strong scent of laboratory chemicals lingered in the air. In the far corner stood a portable table with the fresh cadaver on it.

I was momentarily speechless. Not because of the body, but because of the room itself. How Thomas found anything in this mess was another mystery to figure out. I was getting used to expecting the unexpected when it came to him, but this still managed to pry a bit of shock from me. His person was so neat and clean, and this... this was not.

"Where are your parents?" I asked, noticing a photograph of a pretty dark-haired girl on a shelf. A fist clenched in my chest. Was Thomas promised to someone else? His family was titled and an early betrothal wasn't out of the ordinary. I didn't care for that thought one bit. I motioned toward the picture. "She's lovely."

He turned his back on me and walked toward it.

"She *is* quite lovely," he said, picking up the photograph. "Enchanting, really. Those eyes, and perfectly proportioned features. Comes from a magnificent family, too." He sighed happily. "I love her with all my heart."

He was in love. How exceptionally wonderful for him. I wished them both a lifetime of misery with ill-mannered children. I swallowed my annoyance down and plastered on a smile. "I hope you'll both be very happy together."

Thomas whipped his head around. "Pardon? You..." He studied the set of my jaw and forced indifference of my features. The scoundrel had the audacity to laugh. "She's lovely because she's my *sister,* Audrey Rose. I'm referring to the superior genes we have in common. My heart belongs only to you."

I blinked. "You have a sister?"

"I assume you haven't come here to ask questions about my personal life, or tell me about the circus you attended with your brother this evening." He glanced in my direction, his grin spreading. "Much to my dismay you've not come here for a clandestine tryst, either."

"How did you know about the cir—"

He cocked his head, taking in the rest of my attire. "Perhaps you'd like to tell me what you learned at the asylum, though..."

I rounded on him. "How do you know I've been to an asylum?"

"The sawdust caught in the folds of your skirts didn't come from time spent at the Olympia. There aren't many places in London a girl would come into contact with said material. I couldn't picture you spending time in a carpentry shop, low-end pub, or morgue this late, so where does that leave us?" he asked without expecting an answer, ticking off each place on his fingers.

"Laboratories, workhouses, and asylums. Narrowing that down further, I saw rust stains on the palms of your hands. Most likely you'd encountered old bars. Then there's the matter of your torn skirt, and the little package you've tucked away." He raised his brows. "It's all right to act impressed. I know I would be."

"Oh, get on with it already."

"Anyway, it didn't take much to conclude you've been to the asylum and have shown up here to discuss your findings," he said. "Another rather obvious conclusion as I assume you were visiting your uncle."

"Show-off," I said, subtly rubbing my palms down my skirt, a memory of hanging on to the bars crossing my mind. I hadn't even realized my hands were stained from such a brief contact. It took every last ounce of energy to prevent myself from rolling my eyes at the smug look on his face.

I offered a slow clap. "Well played, Thomas. You figured out the obvious. Good for you. Now, then, we need to figure out what Uncle was drugged with. If it's standard asylum tonic, or something more sinister."

"What do you mean?" he asked. "How was he acting?"

I filled Thomas in on the evening's events while pulling out my makeshift satchel of the porridge and testing its contents. "It was as if he were lost in some trance."

Thomas watched as I smeared the substance on litmus paper. "The dropper is in the top drawer under a stack of papers on the left."

I followed his instructions and found it easily. I put a drop of liquid onto the paper and watched it turn deep blue. "It's definitely an opiate of some sort."

"They're probably giving it to him in near pure form," he said, pacing in front of the desk. "If they're really moving his trial so quickly, they'll want him as mad-looking as possible. Most elixirs cause hallucinations, which explains his state. Unfortunately, that's not all that uncommon. Could be standard pretrial procedure."

He stopped only long enough to glance at me. "You're positive Blackburn can be trusted? What do you know of him?"

I knew the policeman from only a few unpleasant encounters and wasn't positive about anything. "I think he feels guilty Uncle's in this mess. And I believe he's trying to make up for arresting him by involving me in the case."

"Feeling guilt does not make for a solid basis of trust. If anything, it makes me trust him less." He narrowed his eyes, stalking over to me. "Why has he shown such an interest in your family? If you weren't so taken with him, you'd be more skeptical of his motives. A lot can be hidden beneath a boyish grin."

"I am not *taken* with anyone."

"We agreed we wouldn't lie to one another," he said quietly, then turned away before I could read the expression on his face. "Someone's keen on having your uncle swing for these crimes, Audrey Rose. Let's assume the worst about Blackburn. Everyone must remain a suspect until proven otherwise."

"Should I be wary of even you, Mr. Cresswell?"

Thomas stood before me, all traces of humor gone from his expression. "Yes. It would behoove you to stay on alert at all times. Even with respect to those closest to you."

And I thought *I* was an alarmist. Thomas walked over to a cabinet, pulling two white aprons from within.

I pushed the chemistry set aside, thinking wretched things. "If there's another murder between now and the thirtieth they'll have to set him free. Won't they?" I picked at a thread on my bodice, not wanting to look up. "I mean, surely they wouldn't try him for these crimes if another one occurred while he was in the asylum."

Thomas's attention snagged onto mine. "Are you suggesting we stage a murder, Wadsworth? Are you planning on doing the slashing, or should I handle that part?"

"Don't be ridiculous. I only mean there's always a possibility another body will turn up. I can't believe our murderer will simply give up and quietly fade into the night. You've said so yourself."

Thomas considered this for a few moments. "I suppose. But if we're betting on that theory, then it's also possible I'll invent a sky-traveling steamship before the week's out."

"Are you even trying to build a flying steamship?"

"Absolutely not," he said with an impish grin, grabbing a scalpel from the examination table and handing it to me along with an apron. "You said it yourself, anything's possible." He nodded toward the subject. "Let's get on with this. We've got to return the body by dawn and I'd like to harvest the gallbladder first."

Without hesitation, I split the skin wide with my blade, earning an appreciative whistle from Thomas.

NINETEEN

DEAR BOSS

CENTRAL NEWS AGENCY,
LONDON
27 SEPTEMBER 1888

The sound of typewriters clicking away to the beat of a hundred fingers greeted Thomas and me as we followed Superintendent Blackburn into the busy news agency. Most all of their stories were "sensationalized lies and slander charges waiting to happen," according to my brother. I didn't disagree.

Blackburn had found me locked away in Uncle's laboratory, poring over murder details and evidence being used against Uncle, and insisted I see the latest horror for myself.

Blackburn wasn't eager for Thomas's company, but I convinced him his expertise was very much needed. Thomas would likely spot any detail overlooked, and that's precisely what Uncle needed. Blackburn eventually gave in.

Liza had assisted in fabricating excuses to leave the house, telling her mother we were in desperate need of shopping excursions. Aunt Amelia was thrilled to have me doing "appropriate girl things" and sent us out, humming to herself. I suspected my cousin was willing to help because it afforded her time to sneak away to the park with her newest love interest. Regardless of her motives, I was grateful for her presence and would miss her when they returned to the country.

Anxiety twisted through my limbs. Blackburn wasn't a man of many words, so he didn't spare much on the carriage ride over. All I knew was something came up that could potentially raise doubts about Uncle's guilt or set the noose around his neck for good.

Thomas might not trust Blackburn, but I was desperate enough to take any assistance we could get, even if it meant following the person who'd originally put my uncle in the asylum to the depths of Hell.

We walked by several desks with reporters writing and excitedly chatting over the day's news. A palpable buzz could be felt like electricity running through Edison bulbs.

At the end of the small room stood an office with a stout man seated behind an even larger desk. He was wearing spectacles on his face and stress in his bones.

The etching on the door informed anyone who entered he was the editor. There was a bleak look about him that permeated his every movement and action; it spoke of seeing too much of life's darkness. His attention landed on each of us, seemingly calculating our motives or personalities, before settling on Superintendent Blackburn. He dabbed a cigarette out with pudgy fingers, then motioned for us to step inside and have a seat, his movements quick and jittery.

I watched the tiny embers fade from orange to gray ash that lifted in the wake of our entrance. A thick cloud of smoke took up residence above our heads, as if not wanting to miss out on what we were about to learn.

I couldn't find the will to be annoyed by the toxic fumes, I was too nervous about the news that might exonerate or further condemn Uncle. Thomas, however, appeared ready to jump over the desk and suck the last dregs of tobacco into his lungs.

With unsteady hands, the editor pointed toward the tea set on a buffet near the wall. "If any of you would like a refreshment before we begin, please help yourself."

Blackburn looked at me, brows raised, and I gave a slight shake of my head. I didn't want to stay longer than necessary. This place was overwhelming and the editor made me nervous. "No, thank you, Mr. Doyle," he said. "If you wouldn't mind, I'd like to see the letter you spoke of earlier."

"What you're about to see is rather unpleasant," Mr. Doyle warned, staring at me in particular. "Especially for a young lady."

I smiled, leaning over the desk and used the sweetest tone I could muster.

"In my spare time I flay open bodies of the deceased. Two of whom were victims of Leather Apron. The scent that hung in the room would drop a man to his knees, and I aided my uncle during the postmortems while standing in gelled blood." I sat back in my chair, the leather squeaking its own disapproval. "Whatever you have to show us won't be too much for my stomach to handle, I assure you."

Mr. Doyle blanched, then nodded curtly, shuffling papers lying in front of him. It was hard to tell if he was more disturbed by my unladylike activities or by the way I delivered the message in such a girlish tone. Either way, I felt mildly redeemed for having turned the tables of discomfort around on him.

Thomas snorted, then held his hands up in a gesture of apology when Mr. Doyle glared at him. Blackburn, dropping his air of station, looked as boyish as Thomas and was doing only a slightly better job of hiding his amusement.

I studied this version of Blackburn. Thomas was right, there was something disarming about his features. With one shy glance he earned your trust completely.

Mr. Doyle cleared his throat.

"Very well, then." He opened the top drawer of his desk, removed a letter, then slid it across to where we were sitting in straight-backed chairs. He seemed anxious to be rid of us already. I'd half a mind to inform him the feeling was very mutual.

"This came in the post this morning."

Thomas snatched it before Blackburn or I could and read aloud.

"'Dear Boss, I keep on hearing the police have caught me but they won't fix me just yet.'" Thomas opened his mouth, no doubt ready to say something Thomas-like, so I used the distraction against him, grabbing the letter from his clutches and reading it for myself.

The grammar was atrocious.

I read the shaky, loopy script quickly, my skin crawling over my bones with each sentence my gaze touched. The ink was blood-red, likely to instill fear in the recipient, as if the message inside wouldn't be frightening enough. For all I knew, perhaps it *was* written in blood.

Nothing would surprise me when it came to this madman.

Dear Boss,

I keep on hearing the police have
caught me but they wont fix me just yet.
I have laughed when they look so clever
and talk about being on the right track.
That joke about Leather Apron gave me
real fits. I am down on whores and I

shant quit ripping them till I do get buckled. Grand work the last job was. I gave the lady no time to squeal. How can they catch me now. I love my work and want to start again. You will soon hear of me with my funny little games. I saved some of the proper red stuff in a ginger beer bottle over the last job to write with but it went thick like glue and I cant use it. Red ink is fit enough I hope. ha. ha. The next job I do I shall clip the ladys ears off and send to the police officers just for jolly wouldn't you. Keep this letter back till I do a bit more work, then give it out straight. My knife's so nice and sharp I want to get to work right away if I get a chance. Good luck. Yours truly

Jack the Ripper

Dont mind me giving the trade name

P.S. Wasnt good enough to post this before I got all the red ink off my hands curse it No luck yet. They say I'm a doctor now. ha ha

Setting the letter down, my thoughts swirled together in a maelstrom of hope and dread. While there was no guarantee this alone could save Uncle, it certainly might help.

Thomas and Blackburn took turns reading the letter, then sat back in their chairs. No one said a thing for an eternity until Thomas spoke up. "What joke about Leather Apron? I don't recall police saying anything humorous about it. Unless he knows something we don't."

Editor Doyle and Thomas both stared at Blackburn, waiting for his response, but Blackburn only sighed and dragged a hand down his exhausted face.

Handsome or not, he didn't look as if he'd been sleeping that well since the last time I'd seen him. "I haven't the slightest clue about what the author of this letter is referring to. Perhaps he's talking about the headlines calling him Leather Apron."

I cleared my throat and looked at Mr. Doyle. "The author of this letter said not to show it around for a few days. Why ring Superintendent Blackburn?"

Mr. Doyle turned his world-weary gaze on me. "Even if this letter proves false, sent from some deranged citizen, I could not in good conscience keep it to myself." He swallowed a gulp of tea, then removed a flask from his person and unapologetically took a swig. "I'm holding off printing it, but should he follow through with his threats, I wanted my mind free of guilt."

A haunted feeling suddenly clung to me. Something strange was going on aside from the editor's seemingly remorseful outreach. Something out of place that I couldn't quite touch on. Then it occurred to me; Thomas Cresswell was unusually quiet. This would normally be the part where he had plenty to say or argue over.

He brought the letter close to his face and sniffed. I hadn't the slightest inkling how he'd be able to deduce anything from scent, but knew better than to claim it impossible. The word did not apply to him in any form.

"I assume this was delivered in an envelope," he said, not bothering to look up from his inspection of the letter. "I'll need to see that immediately."

Mr. Doyle tossed a glance Blackburn's way, seeking him to jump in and say it wouldn't be necessary, but Blackburn made an impatient gesture with his hand. "You heard the young man, Doyle. Hand over any evidence he requests."

With a deep scowl settling into place, the editor did as he was asked. He didn't seem like the kind of man who appreciated bending to children's needs. Considering Blackburn himself wasn't much older than my brother, I was certain Mr. Doyle was questioning why he'd involved police at all.

Thomas studied every angle of the envelope, twice, before handing it over to me, his expression carefully composed. "Any of this appear familiar to you, Wadsworth?"

Taking the envelope from him, I silently read it. There was no return address, and the only thing written across it was "The Boss. Central News Office. London City" in the same taunting red ink the letter was drafted in.

The very idea it would be at all something I'd seen before was absurd.

Then a thought slapped me in the face.

Did he think *I'd* written it in hopes of aiding Uncle? Was that what he thought of me, then? I was some spoiled girl, walking about London streets, doing whatever I pleased without regard to anyone? Was my position as a lord's daughter showing itself in my abuse of privilege?

I thrust it back at him. "Afraid not, *Cresswell.* I've never seen this before in my life."

If I was expecting some sort of response by using his surname, I was sorely disappointed. He didn't so much as bat one of his long lashes at me. He studied me for another breath, then nodded. "Right, then. My mistake, Audrey Rose."

"Mistake?" Blackburn glanced between us, a crease forming in his brow. "If rumors are to be believed, since when does Dr. Jonathan Wadsworth's protégé make mistakes?"

"Seems there's a first time for everything, Superintendent," Thomas replied coolly, his attention finally drifting away from me. "Though, as someone with a bit more practice being wrong, I'm sure you can empathize. Tell me, what's it like being—"

I rested my hand on his arm and forced myself to giggle uncontrollably, garnering strange looks from each male in the room. Except Thomas, who fixed his attention on the hand still touching him.

Blasted Thomas. Was I always to rescue him from himself? Blackburn was an untrustworthy annoyance, but he'd proven useful for once. I wasn't in the mood for Thomas to make an enemy of him today, especially when Uncle's life was potentially at stake. I held my hand up. "I do apologize. Thomas has a wicked sense of humor. Don't you, Mr. Cresswell?"

Thomas stared for a beat, then let out a long, annoyed breath. "I admit that's a fair assessment. Though poorly deduced as usual, Miss Wadsworth. Unfortunately your uncle's talent has skipped you entirely. At least you've got an attractive smile. It's not much, but will surely make up for your lacking mental faculties. Well," he amended, his focus straying to Blackburn, "at least for someone equally dull, that is."

I gritted my teeth. "While that may be true, we really should be on our way. We've got that experiment we need to check on in the laboratory. Remember?"

"Actually, you're wrong again, my dear."

I was so mad I could scream some of the worst obscenities I'd heard at the docks at him. He was ruining our exit strategy, and I was most certainly not his dear.

When I thought all hope was lost, Thomas checked his watch. "We should've left precisely three minutes and twenty-three seconds ago. If we don't run now, our experiment will be destroyed. Best if we hail a carriage." He turned to the editor and superintendent. "It's been as pleasant as a fast day in Lent, gentlemen."

By the time they figured out his parting was, in fact, an insult, we were already rushing out through the bustling newsroom and exiting onto the cool afternoon streets. We didn't stop walking for a few streets, silence our only companion. Finally, once we'd made a good enough distance to not be spotted by Blackburn, we stopped.

"What is the meaning of that question?" I demanded, anger swelling back up inside me. I could not believe he really thought so little of me. So much for telling each other the truth no matter what.

"I was not insinuating you had anything to do with writing the letter, Wadsworth," he said. "Truly, you must harness those blasted emotions of yours. They'll just get in the way of our investigation."

I did not feel like having this conversation again. He might be able to act machinelike during our horrid investigations, but ice and stone were not the material forming my blood and bones. "Then what, exactly, were you insinuating?"

"Someone who was wearing Hasu-no-Hana two nights ago was in close proximity of that letter."

I closed my eyes. "You can't be serious, Thomas. That's your major discovery? You think you can identify our murderer by a perfume scent? How can you be sure someone working in the General Post wasn't wearing it?" I tossed my hands in the air. "Perhaps the letter carrier had it next to another letter written by someone's secret lover. Maybe they spritzed their envelope in their beloved's favorite scent. Did you ever stop to think of that, Mr. I Know Everything?"

"You were wearing the very same fragrance two nights ago," he replied softly, staring at the ground, all hints of arrogance gone. "The night you visited the asylum and followed me to the Necropolis. I smelled it on you in the alleyway. I went to several shops trying to find the exact scent..." He looked at his hands. "I wanted to purchase it for you."

If he'd reached out and slapped me, I would've been less shocked. This was what my only true friend in the world thought of me; I was a monster waiting to be unleashed. Maybe he was right. I certainly didn't feel like crying, or begging for him to believe me. I didn't even feel good about his admission of wanting to buy a gift for me. I felt like drawing blood. *His* blood in particular.

"So you *are* suggesting I had something to do with this!" I half yelled, walking away before turning back. He still wouldn't meet my glare. "How dare you? How dare you think such reprehensible things of me. It's the most popular scent in London! For your blasted information, both my aunt and cousin were wearing the very same fragrance. Are you implying one of them wrote the letter?"

"Would your aunt try to protect Dr. Wadsworth? Or perhaps your family's reputation?" He took a deep breath. "She's very religious, is she not?"

"I cannot—" I shook my head. "This is absurd!"

I was through with him.

If he thought I or my aunt or my cousin mailed the letter, so be it.

A new, twisted thought made me smile; Jack the Ripper had done me a favor. His letter, whatever the motive, cast a glimmer of hope for Uncle. At least he had a fighting chance now.

"You know what? You were with me that night, too, Thomas. Perhaps my magic perfume wafted over all your belongings. I wouldn't be surprised if you wrote the bloody letter yourself."

I turned on my heel, a springy bounce in my step, and hailed a carriage, leaving Thomas all alone with his accusations and incredulous stares, blissfully unaware of the horror about to take place in the next nights.

Mitre Square, c. 1925

TWENTY

DOUBLE EVENT

MITRE SQUARE,
LONDON
30 SEPTEMBER 1888

A crowd of angry men and women surged against a barricade made up of police bodies, fear driving their emotions into boiling rage.

I pulled my shawl closer, covering my face from both the early morning chill and from people standing near. I did not wish to be recognized; my family had had enough to deal with as it was.

Father had finally come home last night after almost a month away from his precious laudanum, and I didn't want anyone informing him I'd sneaked out of the house and run here as quickly as I could.

Testing his paranoia was something I hoped to avoid at least until Uncle was freed. Not to mention, I didn't want him rushing to marry me off if I proved too difficult for him to handle. He'd probably already picked a nice, suitable young man who lived far away from the city streets of London. I hated the idea of being trapped away in some gilded cage in the country, but I couldn't fault my father for trying to protect me.

Misguided as his attempts were.

I raised my attention to the surrounding buildings: tall brick monsters that were cold and unmoving. The enormous letters naming the Kearly & Tonge building silently watched the chaos going on below, and I watched the building. If only those letters could speak of the secrets they witnessed last night. I tried absorbing every detail I could, the same way Thomas or Uncle would do, were they here. I hadn't spoken to Thomas in two days, the sting of his accusation still very much in the forefront of my mind.

Mitre Square was the perfect place for a killing. Buildings formed a massive courtyard, keeping prying eyes from main thoroughfares away. From rumors sweeping through the crowd, it was an even better place for a double murder.

Jack the Ripper came back with a vengeance after nearly a month of peace. He hadn't made idle threats in the "Dear Boss" letter. Jack had promised violence untold, and that's precisely what he'd done.

A few men near the front of the crowd shouted for blood, igniting people around them into a blazing fury.

A woman beside me shouted, "It ain't right! We need to catch 'im and kill 'im! Let the madman hang!"

I turned my attention back to the living barricade. Through their limbs, I barely made out a body covered in an off-white shroud, blood pooling around like a red lake near her head. Another body had been discovered a little ways down.

It was the worst thing I could think, but there was no way Scotland Yard could execute Uncle now, not after another two bodies were so prominently displayed for all of London to look upon.

There was a darkness growing inside me that needed to be rooted out. It was the second time that week I was mildly grateful for the Ripper. My own emotions sickened me. How dare I rejoice in someone else's misery. That made me no better than the murderer himself. Still, I was hopeful this crime would at least save one life. Even if that hope made me a miserable thing.

I felt a strong tap on my shoulder and spun around, my skirts twisting about my body.

Superintendent Blackburn shook his head, his fair hair catching the light of the sun. "I'd inquire about the weather, but I'm sure you'd like to speak of other things, Miss Wadsworth." He squinted toward the body, shielding his eyes with his hand. "Seems our boy gave us two more victims."

I followed his gaze, nodding. There wasn't much to add to that, so I stayed silent. Watching and listening to people closest us while they speculated on the vicious Leather Apron, lady killer. Though I'd hardly refer to Jack as "our boy."

There was an essence of unease slowly moving through my body that had nothing to do with the deceased women or frightened crowd. I felt Blackburn carefully studying me, but kept my attention elsewhere.

Something about his manner made me feel as if I were being investigated for a crime I'd no recollection of committing.

"Since I know it'll do no good asking you to speak with me later," Blackburn continued, "I might as well invite you to inspect the scene now. Your uncle obviously cannot be here, and there's no one else I'd trust with giving a proper assessment. Unless, of course, you don't feel you can handle it."

Not quite wrapping my brain around the invitation, I blinked at him. I was merely an apprentice studying under Uncle, but Blackburn seemed eager for my opinion on the matter. And I was willing to set aside doubts regarding him for a chance to examine the bodies. I swallowed, casting my attention around. No one was paying us any mind. "Of course I'll inspect them."

Blackburn focused on me, a hint of uncertainty twitching across his lips. "You may want to prepare yourself regardless. Seeing a body on a mortuary table and seeing a body lying in a bloody pool in an alley are a bit different."

If he was trying to intimidate me, it wasn't working. Little did he know I'd already come across a body in an alley and lived to tell the gruesome tale.

I was more than eager to get a closer look at the scenes, to understand the mind of a man who was brutalizing these women. I imagined it would be one of the most horrific things I'd ever see, but I wouldn't let fear hold me prisoner.

Darkness within me rejoiced for the opportunity of seeing the bodies up close, in the state the murderer had intended them to be discovered. Perhaps I'd find a useful clue.

When I lifted my chin, allowing defiance to wash over my features, Blackburn chuckled. "You're a lot like me." He smiled, pleased with my reaction. "Stay close, and don't speak. I may be keen on having your opinion, but not all men will have the same feelings on the matter. Best you let me do the talking."

"Very well." While it wasn't something I relished, it was the hard truth. I was a young girl growing up in a world run by old men. I'd pick and choose my battles wisely.

Without uttering another word, we pushed our way to the front of the crowd and stood before the line of constables. Women slowly moved away from Blackburn, their eyes taking in his form appreciatively as he passed.

A burly man with a ginger beard and matching bushy eyebrows halted our movement. "No one's to pass by. Orders of the commissioner."

Blackburn stood straighter, nodding as if he'd heard this before, then simply said, "I am well aware of that order, as I was the one who instructed the commissioner to issue it. Thank you for upholding the command so dutifully"—he leaned in, reading the man's name tag—"Constable O'Bryan. I've brought a private assistant, proficient in forensic sciences. I'd like her thoughts before we move the bodies."

The constable eyed me with distaste. I buried my hands in my skirts, gripping the material until I was positive I'd rip it off. Oh, how I despised remaining silent under such awful judgment. I'd like to remind each man who held such poor opinions of a woman that their beloved mothers were, in fact, women.

I didn't see any men running about, birthing the world's population then going on to make supper and tend to the house. Most of them buckled to their knees when the slightest sniffle attacked them.

There was more strength held underneath my muslin layers and well-perfumed skin than in half the men in London combined. I forced my mind to stay focused on our task, lest my emotions show plainly on my face.

After an uncomfortably long pause, Blackburn cleared his throat. The constable shifted his attention back to his superior, color creeping up his collar. "Right. Sorry, sir. It's... we weren't told you'd be coming, and—"

"—and isn't it wonderful I'm informing you directly of my newest plans," Blackburn interrupted, clearly put off by the delay. I wondered fleetingly if this was something he put up with often, given his young age. "Unless you'd like to answer to me later, I suggest you allow us passage," he said. "I'm growing rather annoyed, Constable. Each precious moment wasted here is another moment my scientist loses accuracy."

With that, the man stepped aside. All thoughts of how aggravating he was disappeared when I saw the pale foot sticking out from beneath the nearest shroud.

I wish I'd been disgusted by the sight. Instead, I found myself grossly fascinated, longing to lift the sheet and take a closer look. Blackburn motioned to the men standing guard around the body and they promptly scattered themselves.

Blackburn leaned close. "Take your time. I'll make sure no one disturbs you."

I nodded, then knelt beside the body, carefully avoiding the pool of blood near the shoulders, and gently pulled the sheet back. I held my gasp in, squeezed my eyes shut and prayed I wouldn't drop the covering like a squeamish little child.

Perhaps I wasn't as ready for this as I'd imagined.

I kept my eyes closed, breathing through my mouth until the dizziness eased up. It wouldn't do to faint in front of most of the police force in London. Especially when they already thought me handicapped by my gender.

Gathering my wits, I forced myself to examine the body.

The woman was slight, probably about five feet tall. Her face was badly damaged; blood and cuts disfigured her mouth and nose. She was lying on her back, right knee bent and facing outward, her left leg lying flat. Not entirely unlike how Miss Annie Chapman had been found. A small blue tattoo was on her forearm.

Bolts and gears—smeared in blood—peeked out from beneath her body.

I'd no idea why Jack needed such things. Continuing with my inspection, I focused on what I *could* figure out.

Her entire torso was sliced open down the middle with surgical precision, her intestines thrown over her shoulders. A portion of them even appeared to be cut and draped between her left arm and body purposely. A message of sorts.

I swallowed my emotions down. I needed to get through this examination. I needed to understand the mind of this madman, understand what drove him to such violence so he could never do this to another woman again. I took a deep breath, my focus trailing over the corpse once more, though my heart refused to be tamed.

Like the others, her throat had been slashed.

Unlike the others, however, a slice ran down her right ear. It seemed he tried cutting a piece off. A memory nearly knocked me backward. I called to Blackburn, my voice rising with excitement.

"The letter," I said, thoughts racing along with my pulse as he drew near. "The author of that letter *is* the killer. He said he'd clip her ear—look." I pointed out the disfigurement on her person. "He did exactly as he promised: 'The next job I do I shall clip the ladys ears off and send to the police officers just for jolly wouldn't you.' "

Blackburn's attention drifted over the body, then quickly moved away. "Even if the letter is proven authentic, we've no way of tracing its origin."

I sat back on my heels, contemplating scenarios. I thought about the editor of the newspaper and an idea jumped up, waving its arms in my face. "Well, what if you had Mr. Doyle print a facsimile of the letter? Surely someone might recognize the handwriting. Plus he said he'd run it if it proved true."

Superintendent Blackburn tapped his fingers against his trousers, staring into my eyes so deeply I believed he was trying to send a secret message. I wasn't sure why he was hesitating; it was the perfect solution. After a minute he reluctantly nodded.

"It's a fine idea, Miss Wadsworth." Blackburn smiled, a dimple appearing in his cheek. He pointed toward the body, setting my focus on the horror once again. "What else have you got from all this, then?"

"Well." I stared at the blood spatter, knowing it told a story of its own, losing myself completely in the science. The blood on the left side of the neck appeared to have been spilled first, as it was clotting differently from blood located on the right side of the body. It wasn't hard to deduce her throat had been slashed first before she was split open. I crept closer, pointing each injury out for Blackburn.

"He started with her throat, then probably cut or struck her mouth. I doubt he appreciated what she'd had to say and wanted to punish her." I moved on to the next injury. "Once she was choking on blood, he laid her body out, placing her legs straight out before running his blade over her abdomen. He removes the intestines, probably for easier access to her organs. See? This cavity is too hollow. It's how a body looks after Uncle removes organs during postmortems. I can't tell without getting my hands in there which ones are missing. But I think it's probably her uterus or ovaries, possibly even a kidney or gallbladder as well. What do you think?"

I looked up when Blackburn didn't respond, seeing signs of sickness sprawled across his handsome features. I pressed my lips shut. What a monster I must seem to him. Aunt Amelia would drag me to church and say a thousand prayers if she were here. I watched the column of his throat move in an attempt at swallowing.

He tried maintaining his composure, but gagged when a fly landed on her exposed cavity. I shooed the offender away, watching it land near her bloodied face. They'd need to remove her from the scene before flies began laying larvae.

Blackburn coughed, drawing my attention back to him.

I stood quickly, offering him a handkerchief, but he shook his head, holding a fist to his mouth.

"I'm quite all right, thank you. Possibly something I ate didn't agree with me. Sure it's nothing to be concerned over..."

A small part of me wanted to smile. Here was a young man, one who'd surely seen his share of horror working in this line of business, and here I was, a small, slender girl, offering to be his strength.

"I'll make a few notes, if you wouldn't mind," I said. "Then I'll share them with my uncle. He will be released now, won't he?"

Blackburn shifted from left to right, watching as I removed a small journal from a pocket within my skirts and wrote notes in my best cursive.

I didn't want to appear overly eager or hopeful, but needed to know Uncle would be all right. That he'd be safe and working alongside me before long. It felt as if a year had passed before Blackburn finally answered me.

"I can't see him going to trial after this. Unofficially, I'd wager he'll be out before the night's through." He paused. "Perhaps you'd like to join me for some refreshments? After we look upon the next body, that is."

I glanced up sharply. Was he really asking to see me under these circumstances? How odd. My thoughts must have shown plainly on my face because he fumbled for an explanation. "I mean, perhaps we could have some tea and discuss the particulars of the victims. I'm sure—"

"I'm sure that won't be necessary, William," someone said in a familiar, angry tone. Every single muscle of my body froze; even my heart slowed its beat before accelerating.

Father.

Lord Edmund Wadsworth was a sight a thousand times more frightening than the body lying at my feet. His expression held more warning than a knife placed against my jugular. "When I agreed to let you court my daughter, I'd no idea you'd think it a proper thing involving her in such...vile and masculine matters. I need someone reining her will in and protecting her, not feeding her dangerous curiosity."

Shock punched at me from multiple angles. So many questions begged to be asked. How did he find me here? How did he know I'd left the house? But the most pressing one fell from my mouth first.

"What do you mean? Allowed him to court—" Before I finished my thought, I turned on Blackburn. Confusion giving way to pure anger. "*You're* the one who's been asking Father about a courtship, meeting in secret, plotting?"

Then another thought occurred to me, so obvious I almost laughed. "That's why you want to help Uncle, not because you think he's innocent, but because you're devious!"

"Audrey Rose, please," he started, holding his hand up. "I never meant—"

"Am I wrong?" I demanded.

Blackburn pressed his lips together, shooting a questioning look at my father. It was clear he wouldn't respond without approval, which was never likely to happen now. I fisted my hands. There was nothing I despised more than finding out I'd missed clues all along. What other secrets were being kept from me?

My anger quickly faded when Father motioned for Blackburn's silence.

He pointed his finger at me, bending it in a "come here straight away" motion. If he ever let me out of the house again, it would be a miracle sent directly from Heaven.

How dare Blackburn keep such secrets from me. I cast another furious glare at him before obediently moving to Father's side.

Then, when I thought the surprises were over, my brother skulked over, purposely ignoring the body lying a few feet away from his polished shoes.

He didn't meet my eyes as he made his way to Father's other side. Clearly, he'd turned me in to this overprotective madman. Filthy traitor. Of course the police barricade wouldn't apply to either of my family members. I wondered who they paid for their right to shun the laws or commands of the police.

"Now, then. Let's be gone from this abysmal scene and get you home where you'll be safe." Taking my arm, Father offered me a look only slightly less frightening now that I was under his control. "We've much to discuss this evening, Audrey Rose. You cannot involve yourself with such dangers. I hate to do it, but this cannot go unpunished. Consequences come with a high cost, some more than others."

TWENTY-ONE

THE WRETCHED TRUTH

WADSWORTH RESIDENCE,
BELGRAVE SQUARE
30 SEPTEMBER 1888

The carriage ride home was almost as terrible as bearing witness to one of the mutilated bodies at the double event.

I'd rather be on intestine cleanup duty than suffer through the choking silence sitting miserably with us. By the time we pulled up to our home, I was ready to burst out of my skin simply to escape the anger seeping through my pores.

I was furious with Blackburn for conspiring with my father and not having the decency to mention it, but I was seething over my brother most of all.

How dare he betray me by leading our father to where I was. He had to know how mad it'd make Father, thinking his only daughter was in direct danger.

The East End was rife not only with "improper people" but with disease, which spread quickly because of the deplorable living conditions. What's more, it was foolish to drag Father to an area known for its opium dens.

Every male in my life felt it necessary to put chains on me, and I despised it. Except for Thomas, I realized. He taunted me into acting and thinking for myself. Before I could race up to my room, Father called out to me. "A word please, Audrey Rose."

I closed my eyes briefly before turning around. I didn't want to be scolded or hear about how fragile life was or how foolish it was to place oneself in reckless situations, but saw no way out of it. When Father had something to say, one listened, and that was that. I drifted away from the stairway and the freedom it provided, heading directly toward the den of lecturing.

Aunt Amelia and Liza were out shopping for fabrics to take back to the country with them. Their visit was nearly over, and they'd be leaving first thing in the morning. I was grateful they weren't here to witness my scolding. Aunt Amelia would say the last couple of weeks had done nothing to save either my soul or reputation. She might even suggest a little country air was exactly what I needed.

Leaning against the wall in the corridor, Nathaniel still wouldn't meet my glare, enraging me all the more. What a slithering wimp! Father motioned for me to step into the drawing room and have a seat.

With no other choice, I did.

I settled into a chair, as far away from him as possible, while waiting for my guilty verdict to be delivered and my punishment to be swiftly bestowed.

Father was taking his time, however. Calling for a tray of tea and biscuits, sorting through mail near the fireplace. If he was trying to ratchet up my anxiety, it was working. My heart thudded wildly against my ribs, begging to be set free with each new letter he tore into. The only sounds in the room came from the crackling fire and rustling of paper on paper. I sincerely doubted my sloshing blood could be heard, but it was a sinister symphony in my own ears nonetheless.

I watched the careful way he held the letter opener, the sharp blade piercing the envelopes, before he ripped the letters free with one savage swipe after another. Whenever I scared him, he turned into some foreign person. One who was both frightening and frightened at once.

Folding my hands together in my lap, I waited as patiently as I could for him to calm himself enough to speak with me. My dark skirts were an abyss I'd like to sink into. He sealed an envelope, then handed it off to a servant before finally crossing the room.

"I understand you've been sneaking out of the house for some time now. Studying forensic sciences with your uncle, is that right?"

Without asking, he poured a cup of tea, then offered it to me. I shook my head, too nervous to even dream of eating or drinking when he was so calm and composed. He paused, waiting for an excuse, but I couldn't bring myself to respond. Once an animal's fate had been decided, there was no undoing the crimson necklace they'd wear. It mattered not what I said in my defense, he knew it as plainly as I did.

He sat down, crossing one foot over his knee.

"What, pray tell, did you expect me to do upon finding out? Be pleased? Be... *supportive* of you potentially throwing your life away?" A flicker of rage showed in his chiseled features. He clenched his jaw, then exhaled slowly. "I cannot allow you to tarnish your reputation by indulging your eccentricities and the debauchery you're involved with. Pleasant people who abide by polite society do not find themselves in your uncle's laboratory. Were your mother still alive, it would kill her to see you involved in such... matters."

I picked at the tiny buttons on the side of my gloves, fighting tears with all my might. I was angry with Father for his words, but most of all hated that he might be correct. Perhaps Mother *would* despise the work I did. From childhood, she was instructed to stay away from dreadful things owing to her weakened heart. My unbecoming work might very well have broken it had the fever not done so first. But what of her insistence that I could be both strong and beautiful? Surely Father had to be wrong.

Nathaniel moved from the doorway to stand inside the room. I hadn't noticed him still lingering there but from the stricken expression on his face knew he'd heard every word. I wanted to muster up a decent scowl, but couldn't find the strength.

My heart ached too much.

"From this point forward you shall live according to society's rules," Father continued, satisfied with my obeisance. "You'll smile and be charming to every suitor I deem acceptable to court you. There'll be no more talk of science or of your degenerate uncle." He moved out of the chair and stood before me so swiftly, I couldn't prevent myself from recoiling. "Should I discover your disobedience once more, you shall be turned out on the streets. I'll not tolerate you sniffing around this disturbing case any longer. Have I made myself perfectly clear?"

I drew my brows together. I could not comprehend what had just happened. Father had been mad before, angry enough to keep me indoors for weeks on end, but he'd never threatened to toss me into the streets.

It went against the very purpose he had for keeping me close all my life. Why bind me to our home, only to throw me from it?

I blinked tears back and kept my attention locked onto the swirling design on the rug, then slowly nodded. I didn't trust my voice. I refused to sound weak on top of looking the part so well, and knew my voice would crack under the weight of emotion.

Father must have been pleased, because his shadow lifted from before me, then disappeared from the room altogether. I listened as his heavy footsteps faded down the hall. When his study door slammed shut, I allowed myself to exhale.

A single tear snaked down my cheek and I angrily swiped it

away. I'd held it together for this long, I would not break in front of Nathaniel. I would not.

Instead of rushing to my side as I expected, Nathaniel stayed planted to his post near the door, craning his neck into the hall. It was hard to tell if he was looking to escape or convincing himself to stay.

"What did Father promise you for your betrayal?" His back stiffened, but he didn't turn around. I stood, moving closer. "Must have been extraordinary. Something you couldn't turn down. A new suit? An expensive horse?"

He shook his head, hands twitching at his sides. Any second and he'd grab the comfort of his comb. Stress never looked good on him. I stalked closer, my tone antagonizing. I wanted him to feel my hurt.

"A large estate, then?"

The silver comb flashed in the flickering firelight as my brother ran it through his hair. I went to walk by when he whispered, "Wait."

His tone gave me pause, my silk shoes straddling the threshold. He sounded no louder than a church mouse squeaking inside a grand cathedral.

Moving back into the room, I waited. I'd allow him the courtesy of saying his piece, then be on my way. I plopped onto the chair, exhausted from the day's events, while Nathaniel checked the hallway before closing the door.

He paced, as all Wadsworth men were prone to do, agitation or nervousness shrouding him. It was hard to tell which emotion was getting the better of him. Nathaniel crossed the room to the buffet, removing a crystal decanter and matching glass. He poured himself a healthy amount of amber liquid, drinking it down in a few gulps.

That was very un-Nathaniel-like. I sat forward. "What is it?"

My brother shook his head, still facing the decanter, and refilled his cup. "I can't begin figuring where to start."

The utter loathing in his tone chilled me. I got the impression we were no longer talking about him telling Father I'd sneaked out of the house this morning. My anger dissipated. Was something else wrong with Father? I couldn't take another emotional upheaval. There was too much to sort through as it stood.

"Most start around the beginning," I said, hoping to keep the fear from my voice and force levity into it. "Tell me what's been troubling you. Please. Let me help."

Nathaniel stared at the crystal glass in his hand. It seemed easier for him to speak to it rather than meet my worried gaze.

"Then I'll speak quickly, in hopes of causing you less pain." He took a sip of liquid courage, then another. "Mother wasn't the last person operated on by our loving uncle."

I was grateful he paused, allowing me time to absorb the enormity of his words. Everything else in the room stopped, including my heart. This was a subject we were banned from discussing by both Uncle and Father.

"He... he's been attempting to complete a successful transplant since he and Father were young men." My brother pinched the bridge of his nose. "Father, while dealing with his own demons, reacts in such a way because he knows Uncle keeps secrets from you."

"Secrets? I know all about Uncle's former experiments," I said, sitting straighter in my chair. "His attempt at saving Mother's life is why I started studying under him in the first place."

"Saving her, was he?" Nathaniel gave me a pitying look. "For the good of London, they should've kept him locked away. He's never stopped his experiments, Audrey Rose. He's only gotten better at hiding them."

"That's not true." I shook my head. How my brother could think such a thing about Uncle was preposterous. "I'd know about any experiments."

"I promise you, it is true. I hoped you'd outgrow your desire to apprentice with him, and thought it unnecessary to divulge such... delicate matters." Nathaniel took my hands, squeezing gently until I met his eyes. "Just as I do not wish to burden you with too much now, Sister. If you need some time—"

"Oh, I'm more than ready to learn the truth. The entire truth, no matter how horrid it may be. Do enlighten me further, and make it quick."

He nodded. "Very well, then. The entire truth is this: Your... friend, Thomas Cresswell, he..." Nathaniel sat back and took another sip from his drink. I wasn't sure if the pause in the story was for my benefit or his. My stomach tied itself in knots as I waited for the next horror. "Are you sure you're all right? You look a bit peaked."

"Please, tell me the rest."

"All right, then," he said, releasing a shaky breath. "Thomas's father came to Uncle after Mother's death. His wife experienced severe abdominal pain around that time. He'd heard rumors of Uncle's research." Nathaniel swallowed. "Thomas's mother passed away shortly after ours of gallbladder issues. Uncle tried saving her life, too."

"Wonderful. So you're saying Uncle killed Thomas's mother?"

Nathaniel reached for me, slowly shaking his head. "No, not exactly. Thomas has been obsessed with searching for a true cure ever since. It's all hc talks of when the Knights of Whitechapel meet. I can practically conduct the research myself. He's gone into that much detail."

"He hasn't mentioned anything to me about it at all."

Chills stuck their nails into my back, repeatedly dragging themselves downward. That wasn't entirely true. Thomas had insisted I remove the gallbladder from the cadaver he'd gotten from the Necropolis. A memory of the latest crime scene flashed through my mind—I was almost positive a gallbladder had been taken from one of the victims, too. I felt utterly sick to my stomach.

Could I have been so blind or so wrong about Thomas?

No. I wouldn't accuse him of sadistic murders simply because he was different from other people in our closed-minded society. He was purposely cold and detached working a case, and it was brilliant. And necessary. Wasn't it? My head suddenly pounded. Maybe I was making excuses for him. Or perhaps they were excuses he'd deftly planted in my brain. He was certainly cunning enough to do such a thing. But would he?

Too many emotions swirled through my head to keep track of.

If Thomas experienced the kind of heartache that came with watching as a loved one passed on, then perhaps he might do anything—even murder—to discover answers he'd sought. Then again, didn't I suffer from a similar heartache when Mother died? I supposed it was a decent enough reason for Jack to steal organs. But was Thomas, the arrogantly charming boy I knew outside of the laboratory, truly capable of committing such atrocities in the name of science?

I hardly thought he could become *that* cold and remote. Still...

My head spun. The ladies at tea claimed he was odd enough to be the madman, but that was merely idle gossip. I clenched my fists at my sides. I refused to believe my instincts were so wrong about him, even if there was strong evidence to the contrary.

Which was the exact notion that got the Ripper's victims murdered. I dropped my head into my hands. *Oh, Thomas. How do I sort this mess out, too?*

TWENTY-TWO

SAUCY JACK

WADSWORTH RESIDENCE,
BELGRAVE SQUARE
1 OCTOBER 1888

Early morning light slanted in from the cathedral windows of our dining room, but I could stare only at the two pieces of evidence scrawled in Jack the Ripper's hand while my breakfast cooled.

The days of holding back his ghastly deeds were apparently over. Jack wanted everyone to know he was responsible for these horrendous crimes. He was like an actor or king soaking up the attention of adoring fans and countrymen.

Troubled as I was by Thomas's past, the idea of him being the Ripper didn't sound quite right. The day Thomas Cresswell didn't show off his brilliance was the day I'd find a unicorn for a pet. Jack wanted adoration. Thomas would surely have slipped by now.

Then again, he *did* keep his work with Uncle on transplants secret all these weeks. I cursed my softness toward him. I needed to detach my emotions, but it was proving more difficult than I'd envisioned.

I rubbed my temples and read the paper again. I wasn't surprised the serpent side of Mr. Doyle resurfaced; it was only a matter of time before his paper sensationalized this for all the money it was worth.

"Honestly," Liza whispered while slicing into her breakfast sausage, "I wish we weren't leaving so dreadfully early. I've never seen such excitement in the city! Victoria's throwing a masked ball, encouraging boys to come as the Ripper. Tall, dark, and completely anonymous. It's terribly thrilling, wouldn't you agree?"

I stole a glance at my aunt, who was watching me with a quirked brow. This was a test of good manners. I smiled pleasantly. "It certainly is terrible."

"True. I don't care what people say of those women, no one deserves to be slain like that. You simply must stop whoever it is." Liza stared off, then shook herself into the present. "I'm going to miss you, Cousin. Come and stay with us soon."

I smiled, realizing I couldn't wait to see Liza again. My cousin was smart, unabashedly feminine, and comfortable playing by her own version of society's rules. Her clever remarks and cheerful presence would be missed. "That would be lovely, I will."

I took a sip of Earl Grey, my focus returning to the paper while my aunt and cousin chatted about yesterday's tea I'd missed.

Either Blackburn had kept his promise to seek the editor out and run a copy of the "Dear Boss" letter, or Mr. Doyle had decided to do so himself. I didn't trust Blackburn anymore, so my faith lay with the editor releasing the details.

I reread the letter, getting lost in the manic cursive of the killer's script. Thinking back on the murder scene, there was an eerie number of similarities. The postcard depicted on the same page was something new, however. As it was dated from the night before, it was clear the murderer only recently posted it.

Wretched ideas had assaulted me last night with the growing list of suspects. I didn't know who was responsible, but some memory kept creeping up on me.

Miss Emma Elizabeth Smith possibly knew her attackers. Could that be Uncle and Thomas? In Uncle's notes she'd told investigators one assailant was a teenager. Uncle was betrothed to her... and clearly, it ended in some manner in which she resorted to prostitution.

If Thomas was in on it, it'd explain how the murders continued while Uncle was in the asylum. It also meant I'd been inadvertently working with Jack the Ripper and possibly falling under his spell myself. My stomach twisted.

There had to be something else.

I thought of Thornley, recalling the day Thomas and I had learned of Uncle's connection to Miss Emma Elizabeth. Thomas's shock appeared genuine enough. But was it all a farce? Perhaps he was as talented at acting as he was at flipping his emotions on and off. If only my wretched heart could shut itself off from him completely!

There was something even worse to consider.

My father had connections to most of the victims. It was possible the opium addled his brain in some way, twisting his anguish over Mother into something violent. But was my father truly capable of murder? I wanted to deny it, to scream at myself for thinking such an awful thing, but Father did have a habit of becoming someone else whenever he was afraid or under the influence of his precious tonic. If Father really was innocent, then why did my heart sink at the thought?

Then there was the matter of Blackburn. Did he work with Father? Their association was hidden from my brother and me for God only knew how long. What else might they be keeping to themselves? The murders began again when Father came home.... I stopped my mind from wandering down that bleak alleyway.

I turned my attention back to the postcard facsimile in the paper.

It wasn't very long, but the message was as chilling as the first. The grammar was just as poor, but I had a suspicion it was all for show. The script Jack used was far too clean and careful to be written by someone lacking education. It was a poor attempt at hiding his status in the community.

But which status? Doctor, lord, superintendent, or brilliant pupil?

I was not codding dear old Boss when I gave you the tip, you'll hear about Saucy Jacky's work tomorrow double event this time number one squealed a bit couldn't finish straight off. ha not the time to get ears for police. thanks for keeping last letter back till I got to work again.

Jack the Ripper

The postcard was written in the same hand as the first letter, the loops too similar to be a coincidence. The front of the offending document held no greater clue than the one before it had. It was addressed to:

Central News Office
London City

"Good morning, Amelia, Liza. I believe your carriage is ready." Father strode into the dining room with a paper of his own tucked under an arm and concern set upon his face when his attention turned to me. "Filling your head with safe and appropriate things? Or are you disobeying my wishes so soon, Audrey Rose?"

I lifted my face and smiled, an action more akin to a sneer.

"I was unaware keeping abreast of the daily news was inappropriate. Perhaps I shall spend my time, and your money, on new corsets to bind my will from my lips," I said sweetly. "Wearing something so constricting ought to tether my vocal cords nicely. Wouldn't you agree?"

Father's eyes flashed a warning, but he'd not find me cowering today. I would solve this Ripper case even if it meant awakening the sleeping beast from within whomever it was resting. That same creature was scratching and howling for a chance to be set free from inside me. I promised it all in due time, placating it for the moment.

"Well, then." Aunt Amelia stood, motioning for Liza to do the same. "It's been such a lovely visit. Thank you for hosting us in your absence, dear Brother. You must take some time away from town and breathe in our country air again soon." She turned her attention on me, lips pinched in scrutiny. "Might do Audrey Rose a world of good, getting away from this madness for a bit."

"Perhaps you're right." Father opened his arms to his sister, embracing her quickly before she left the room.

Liza ran over to where I was still sitting, leaned down and gathered me into an uncomfortable hug. "You must write to me. I want to hear more about Mr. Thomas Cresswell and everything regarding the infamous Jack the Ripper. Promise you will."

"I promise."

"Wonderful!" She kissed my cheek, then hugged my father before dashing into the corridor. I was sad to see her go.

Father crossed the room and sat in his chair, ignoring me in a way that accentuated his displeasure with my behavior. Which suited me fine.

After Nathaniel had confessed the truth about our family's secrets, I could barely look at Father. Mother was dying of scarlet fever, and

Father knew of her already weakened heart. He never should have allowed Uncle to operate on her when her immune system was under such attack. He knew Uncle had never been successful before.

Though I couldn't blame him for being desperate to save her. I did wonder why he'd waited so long to ask Uncle for help. I'd been under the false impression that Uncle had operated on her before she'd taken a turn for the worse. I let a sigh escape. Uncle should have known better, but how could he turn his brother away? Especially when Lord Wadsworth had finally broken down and asked for help? The tragedy of what led us here, to this broken shell of a family, was overwhelming, and I feared I'd be as consumed by grief as Father was if I thought too hard on the past.

I received word Uncle was back home late last evening, so I'd stay with him and see what I could discover there.

I opened my paper again, not caring what Father had to say about it.

"Are you so keen to end up a wretch on the streets?"

I took a sip of tea, relishing the bright taste of Earl Grey on my tongue. Father was playing a dangerous game and hadn't a clue. "You'd know a thing or two about wretches on the street."

He dropped his hands onto the table, knocking his flatware askance. His face was pale yet angry. "You will respect me in my own home!"

I stood, revealing my all-black riding ensemble. I allowed a full thirty seconds to pass, letting Father take in my mannish attire, shock and disbelief filtering through his expression. I tugged my leather gloves on as violently as I could, then stared down my nose at him.

"Those who deserve respect are given it freely. If one must demand such a thing, he'll never truly command it. I am your daughter, not your horse, sir."

I stepped closer, enjoying the way Father leaned away from me as if he were just now discovering that a cat, while precious and cute, also had sharp claws. "I'd rather be a lowly wretch on the streets than live in a house full of cages. Do not lecture me on propriety when it's a virtue you so grossly lack."

Without waiting for a response, I swept from the room with nothing but the sound of my heels ringing out against the silence. There would be no skirts or bustles to wrangle with anymore. I was through with things confining me.

Uncle's laboratory was a wreck, much like the man who resided there.

Papers were scattered about, tables and chairs upturned, and servants were nervously cleaning on all fours, their attention flitting between their work and Uncle's never-ending tirade. Whether he was upset because his precious work had been tampered with or because he'd come close to being caught for his crimes, I couldn't tell.

But I was not leaving here without finding out.

I'd never seen him in such a state. Police brought everything back from the evidence chambers when he was released from Bedlam, but threw it back in the laboratory without a care. It seemed Blackburn was no longer interested in winning my affections.

"What miserable fiends!" Another crash reverberated in the small room off the main lab. "Years and years of documentation, gone! I've got half a mind to set Scotland Yard ablaze. What sort of animals do they hire?"

Thomas entered the room, taking stock of the mess. He righted a chair, then folded himself into it, annoyance scrawled over his features.

I studiously ignored him, and he responded in kind. Clearly, he was still put off by our argument. Or maybe he felt my suspicion taking form and pointing a finger toward him.

Uncle didn't remember much from his time in the asylum. The drugs proved too strong for his mind to battle, or so he claimed. He didn't recall mumbling his name repeatedly or any revelation that might have stepped forth from the darkness.

"Don't just sit there!" Uncle bellowed, tossing a handful of papers in Thomas's face. "Fix this! Fix this whole bloody mess! I cannot function like this!"

Unable to watch the madness continue, I slowly approached Uncle with my hands up, as if he were a dog driven mad and cornered. I imagined his nerves were frayed as the tonic they'd given him left his body. Uncle's occasional outbursts were never so loud or disorganized.

"Perhaps"—I motioned around the room—"we should wait upstairs while the maids tend to this."

Uncle Jonathan looked ready to quarrel, but I'd have none of that. My new lack of tolerance extended to *all* Wadsworth males. Even if he proved innocent of the Ripper murders, Uncle had other things to answer for.

I pointed to the door, leaving no room for argument. Maybe it was my new attire, or the stern set to my jaw, but the fight left Uncle rather quickly. He sighed, his shoulders slumping with defeat or relief as he tromped up the stairs.

We settled in the drawing room with cups of tea and pleasant music spilling from a steam-powered machine in the corner.

Thomas sat across from me, arms crossed and jaw set. My pulse spiked as his eyes met mine and sent sparks through my body. I longed to yell at him, demanding to know why he kept things from me, but bit my tongue. Now wasn't the time.

Next order of business was more difficult to bridge. There was a river of lies and deceit that needed to be crossed in a short amount of time.

I looked at my uncle. He'd been raging and throwing things since I walked in until this very instant. Even now his eyes were slightly glazed over, seeing some wretched thing no one else could.

New anger burned quietly under my skin. I hated what Blackburn had done to him.

I went to bury my hands in my skirts, then stopped, remembering I had no skirts to hide in. "I know what happened with Thomas's mother."

Thomas froze, teacup halfway to his lips, eyes wide. I turned my attention on Uncle. The fog surrounding him instantly dissipated, replaced by hardness I'd never really seen in him before. "What are you getting at?"

I met his furious gaze dead-on. "After she died you and Thomas began working together. Performing secret . . . experiments."

Thomas leaned forward, nearly toppling out of his seat. His hawk attention homing in on Uncle's response. If only I could decipher his actions!

Uncle laughed incredulously when he saw the seriousness in my face.

"What does it matter if we did? We haven't performed a surgery in nearly a year. None of this relates to our Ripper. Some ghosts should remain good and buried, Niece."

"And some ghosts come back to haunt us, Uncle. Like Miss Emma Elizabeth Smith."

Uncle Jonathan's expression was as dark as my father's, and I feared he'd send me away for intruding on his memories.

When he sat back, stubbornly crossing his arms over his chest and sealing his lips, Thomas spoke up. "I see. You ought to just tell her."

"You don't see anything, boy," Uncle spat. "You'd be wise keeping it that way."

I walked across the room and slammed the door shut, shifting their attention to me. "If it weren't necessary to this investigation, I'd leave you to your peace. As there's a madman on the loose, ripping women apart, and potentially *trying to use their organs* the way some in this room have done in the past, we do not have that luxury."

"Technically, we've never tried using organs for anything,"

Thomas said, then shrugged. "My mother was too ill for the procedure. We've tested smaller theories out, but as your uncle said, we haven't performed surgery in a year. And that was simply reattaching a severed finger, if you desire the details."

"And you thought it a fine idea to hide this from me?"

"We've been a bit preoccupied with hunting down a murderer, Wadsworth," Thomas said flatly. "Pardon me for not discussing something I find...difficult. Aside from Dr. Wadsworth and now yourself, I've not spoken of my mother to anyone since she died. Especially since my father felt it appropriate to remarry before her body was cool to the touch, and my stepmother cannot be bothered with children who are not her own."

"I—I'm sorry, Thomas."

He shrugged again and looked away. I sat on a velvet settee. I couldn't believe it.

This was the reason Thomas was skilled at being emotionally distant. The root of his arrogance. Liza was right—it did cover pain. My heart raced. Part of me wanted to draw him into a hug and heal his wounds, and part of me wished to ferret out all his secrets and piece the puzzle of him together this instant.

But there was the matter of Uncle and his connection to Miss Emma Elizabeth that took precedence. With great effort, I faced Uncle.

"I need to know what happened with your former betrothed." I could see the gears working in his mind as he tried to avoid telling me the story. "Please. Tell me what became of Emma Elizabeth Smith."

Uncle tossed his hands in the air. "Seems I know less than you."

"Indulge me, then."

"Oh, fine. She made me choose: her or science. When I refused, she severed all connection, saying she'd end up penniless before condoning such blasphemous work."

Uncle put his head in his hands; clearly, thinking of his former love was taking a toll on his already fragile state. A steely determination I was very familiar with seemed to coat his bones then, rejuvenating him within the next breath.

After all, this was the man who taught his students how to divorce themselves from the human aspect of something awful and to charge ahead and seek out the facts without emotions blinding them.

He sat up straighter, doling out facts one after the other.

"Emma could've carried on with her life, but chose not to. Said she wanted me to hurt as much as possible, thought it'd force me into relenting." He shook his head. "Last I'd heard she rented a room in the East End, refusing to take money from her family. Rumors started, as they have a way of doing, that she was selling herself to afford lodging."

Uncle removed his glasses and wiped imaginary smudges from them. I couldn't imagine what his emotions must be like. He dropped his hands into his lap. "I didn't have the heart to find out if that was true. I pushed her from my mind, getting lost in my work, where I've happily lived out my days the last several years."

"What happened the night you saw her body?" I asked quietly. "Does it remind you of the recent killings at all?"

Uncle jerked his head back, looking startled before twisting his mustache. He took a moment, flipping through the notes of his mind.

"I suppose she could be one of Ripper's victims." Uncle crushed the leather case he kept his glasses in, his knuckles turning white as bone. When he spoke, it was through gritted teeth. "I must return to work."

Thomas arched a brow, then set his attention on me. It seemed there were still secrets left to be revealed. I couldn't tell if he was in on them or not but was determined to find out.

TWENTY-THREE

THE CONJURER'S ART

LITTLE ILFORD CEMETERY,
LONDON
8 OCTOBER 1888

Two stone dragons stood sentinel over our carriage as it moved across cobblestones and through the largest of three ogival archways leading into Little Ilford Cemetery.

A heavy mist shrouded a small group of mourners standing around the freshly dug grave of Miss Catherine Eddowes, the slain woman I'd inspected during the double event, blanketing them from the harshness of the day.

Winter was biting at autumn's toes, reminding the milder season it'd be here soon.

As a sign of respect for the deceased, I'd worn a proper gown instead of the riding habit and breeches I'd recently adopted as my ensemble of choice. My simple black dress was eerily similar to what I'd worn the night of Miss Annie Chapman's murder. I hoped it wasn't a prediction of worse things to come.

I felt a strange connection to Catherine, perhaps because I'd knelt over her body and examined the scene where she'd been found.

Papers described her as jolly when sober, singing a tune for anyone who'd listen. The night she was murdered she'd been drunk, lying in the street before being detained by police until shortly after one in the morning.

Ripper found her not long after that, silencing her songs forever.

Uncle stayed at his laboratory, speaking with detective inspectors about the second victim of that bloody night, ushering Thomas and me off in his carriage to glean what we could from Miss Catherine's funeral attendees. He believed killers often visited the sites of their destruction or involved themselves in cases, though like most of his notions, it couldn't be proven. Detective inspectors didn't spend much time convincing Uncle his expertise was essential to solving the case. A little ego stroking on the part of the upper echelons of Scotland Yard went a long way to assuage Uncle's damaged pride.

I couldn't stop stealing glances at Thomas, wondering if the very monster I was hunting was standing beside me. Though his story of his mother's death and father's near-immediate remarriage tugged at me emotionally, perhaps that was his intention. For now I'd watch him, but act as if all was well between us.

Thomas held an umbrella over our heads, his attention focused on everyone in the gathering. There weren't many mourners, and to be honest, none of them appeared the least bit suspicious—except for one bearded man who tossed stares over his shoulder at us. Something about him set caution humming through my veins.

"Dust thou art, and unto dust thou shalt return," the priest quoted from the book of Genesis, holding his arms skyward. "May your soul rest more peacefully than the manner in which you left us, beloved sister."

The handful of people murmured a collective amen before dispersing from the plot. Dreary weather kept their sadness at arm's length and their prayers for the dead short. Moments later the sky opened up and rain flowed freely, forcing Thomas to stand a bit closer with the umbrella.

Or perhaps he was using it as an excuse. He'd been hovering around me as if I were the sun his universe revolved around ever since he'd let me past one of his many emotional walls. Something to ponder another day.

I walked over to the makeshift grave marker, kneeling to run my gloved fingertips across the rough wooden cross, feeling a wave of sadness for a woman I didn't even know. The city of London pulled together, giving her a proper burial and grave. People were always providing in death what they would not do in life, it seemed.

"Audrey Rose." Thomas cleared his throat, and I glanced up, spotting the bearded man lingering a few paces off, looking torn between approaching us and fading into the desolate, gray morning. Unable to shake the feeling he had something important to impart to us, I motioned for Thomas to follow me.

"If he won't come to us," I said over my shoulder, "we'll bring ourselves to him." I stopped before him, extending my hand. "Good morning. My name is—"

"Miss Audrey Rose Wadsworth. Daughter of Malina and—what's that?" he asked an invisible person to his left. Thomas and I exchanged baffled looks.

Clearly, he was unbalanced, speaking to air. But there was something about him knowing my mother's name that unnerved me. He nodded to something we still couldn't see.

"Ah, yes. Daughter of Malina and Edmund. Your mother says you're welcome to the necklace in the photograph. The heart-shaped locket, I believe. Yes, yes," he said, nodding again. "That's right. The one you admired in your father's study. It's being used as a bookmark of sorts."

He paused, squinting at nothing. My heart was very near breaking its way out of my body. Thomas grabbed my arm, steadying me as I swayed on my feet. How could this man possibly know these things? Memories of sneaking into Father's study and looking upon the photograph of Mother assaulted my senses.

I'd been admiring that locket, wondering where it was hidden...

No one knew about that. I barely even recalled it myself. I took a wavering step back, frightened yet not quite believing this was not some act of deceit. Some illusionist's manipulation of the truth. I'd read reports in papers of charlatans and tricksters. Unscrupulous fakers making profit by showing audiences what they wanted to believe. There was some kind of smoke and mirrors game being played, and I'd have none of it.

"How do you know these things?" I demanded, regaining my composure.

Calming my still racing heart, I sought to apply logic to the situation. This man must surely be a skilled liar; he did some form of research, then made educated guesses, essentially the same principle Thomas used while deducing the obvious.

Heart-shaped lockets were popular, practically every woman in London owned one. It was an educated guess, nothing more. For all I knew, the necklace was sitting in a forbidden jewelry box, not being used as an expensive bookmark.

I wouldn't be surprised if he worked for some despicable newspaper. Perhaps Mr. Doyle had sent him to spy on us, desperate to ferret out another story.

"Easy there, Wadsworth," Thomas said, loud enough for only me to hear. "If you shake any harder I'm afraid you might take flight, killing us in the process. While I do not fear death, it might prove a bit tedious after a while. All that heavenly singing would become rather grating, don't you agree?"

I drew in a slow, steady breath. He was right. Getting agitated wouldn't make this situation better. I allowed myself to calm down, before turning my glower back on this liar. He held his hands up, as if he meant no harm—except the harm had already been done.

"Let me begin again, Miss Wadsworth. I—often forget how odd I must seem to non-seers." He extended his hand, waiting for mine to meet his. Reluctantly, I allowed him to kiss my gloved knuckles before sticking my hands back at my sides. "My name is Robert James Lees. I am a medium. I communicate with spirits who've passed on. I'm also a spiritualist preacher."

"Oh, good." Thomas wiped his brow in a gesture of relief. "And here I thought you were simply insane. This'll be much more fun."

I fought a smile as the spiritualist stuttered over his next words.

"Y-yes, yes, well, all right, then. As I was saying, I speak with the dearly departed, and the spirit of Miss Eddowes sought me out almost every night this week, starting from the night she was slain," he said. "My spirit guides told me I'd find someone here who could help stop Jack the Ripper once and for all. I kept getting drawn to you, miss. That's when your mother came through."

I listened with the practiced ear of a skeptic. My mind was very much immersed in science, not religious fads and notions of speaking with the dead.

Mr. Lees exhaled, nodding to that same unseen force again.

"So I thought. I've got it on good authority you're unbelieving." He held his hand up when I opened my mouth to argue. "It's something I contend with most every day of my life. My path isn't an easy one, but I'll not stop my journey. If you'd like to accompany me to my parlor, I'll do a proper conjuring for you."

Part of me wanted to say yes. Sensing my wavering, he continued with his sale.

"Take what you will from our session, leaving anything which isn't useful behind. All I ask is a few minutes of your time, Miss Wadsworth," he said. "Nothing more. Very best, you'll walk away with information about the killer. At the very least, an entertaining story to share with your friends later."

He offered a hard bargain when he put it into those terms.

"If you have information on Jack the Ripper," Thomas asked, holding the umbrella steady, "why haven't you gone straight to Scotland Yard?"

I studied Thomas. His question certainly seemed genuine. Unless he was displacing suspicion. Mr. Lees smiled ruefully.

"They've declined my services on more than one occasion," he said. "It's easier thinking me mad than seriously regarding any clues I might unearth."

I tapped my fingers on my arms, contemplating his offer.

The first part about being a good scientist was remaining open to studying *all* variables, even ones we don't necessarily understand. How little my mind would be if I dismissed a possibility without investigating it, simply because it didn't fit into a preconceived notion.

No advances would ever be made. Scotland Yard was foolish to turn him away. There was the considerable chance he was a fraud, but even the tiniest percentage he could be right should be enough to at least listen to him.

I knew the hope of speaking with Mother was entering both my thoughts and heart, clouding my judgment. Internally I fought myself.

Perhaps one day I'd seek Mr. Lees out when I was ready to confront that emotional mess. Now, with Thomas present, I needed to keep a clear focus.

I took a deep breath, knowing this might perfectly well be a giant waste of time, but not caring. If I had to wave chicken feet at every raven I saw during the full moon to stop this murderer and avenge all the women who were tortured, I'd do it. Plus, one way or another, maybe it would remove any lingering doubt I had about Thomas.

"Very well, then," I said. "Dazzle us with your conjuring arts, Mr. Lees."

Thomas threw an impatient glance at me from across the tiny, battered table in Mr. Lees's séance parlor, his leg bouncing so fast the feather-light table vibrated with his every jitter.

The pinch-lipped look I returned to him was laced with unspoken threat. I learned something useful from Aunt Amelia after all. Thomas stilled his legs before rapping a jittery beat against his arms. Honestly, he acted as if I were dragging him through the streets across a bed of nails, during a winter storm. The mark of a young man with more secrets or simply a bored one? If Mr. Lees was authentic, I might have an answer shortly.

I scanned our surroundings, doing my best to retain an impassive façade, but it was hard. Gray light filtered in through musty curtains, lighting on every speck of dust in the small flat, causing my nose to itch.

Instruments used for speaking with spirits were jumbled in the corners and poked out of cabinets, and dust covered most every surface. A little housecleaning would go a long way. Perhaps Mr. Lees would have more customers if he tidied up a bit.

I supposed, however, one didn't have much time for cleaning when one was speaking with the dead at all hours of the day and night. If his abilities were real, I likened it to being stuck at a party twenty-four hours a day. The thought of having to listen to someone speak that long was utterly dreadful.

My attention snagged on a horn-shaped tube resting atop a rickety-looking cabinet. It was one of the few items in the room that appeared shiny and new.

"That's a 'spirit trumpet,'" Mr. Lees said, jerking his chin toward the contraption. "It amplifies whispers of the spirits. Truthfully, I haven't had any luck with it, but it's all the rage these days. Figured I'd give it a whirl. And that's a spirit slate."

The so-called spirit slate was nothing more than two chalkboards tied together with a bit of string. I assumed it was another tool the dead could use for communicating with the living.

People wanted to be entertained by gadgets and gimmicks, it seemed, as much as they wanted to speak with their loved ones. A haunted atmosphere was ripe for conversation starters amongst the wealthy who knew nothing of poverty.

Thomas coughed a laugh away, drawing my attention to him. He subtly pointed to my leg, bouncing its own anxious beat against the table, then coughed harder at my dark look. I was glad he was so amused; that made one of us.

"Right, then." Mr. Lees situated himself in the middle. "I'll ask the two of you to place your hands on the table, like so."

He demonstrated by placing his large palms facedown, thumbs touching at their tips. "Spread your fingers apart so your pinky fingers touch your neighbor's on either side. Excellent. That's perfect. Now close your eyes and clear your minds."

It was a good thing the table was so small, else we'd never be able to reach one another's hands comfortably. Thomas's pinky kept twitching away from mine, so I quietly shifted my foot under the table and gave him a little kick. Before he could retaliate, Mr. Lees closed his eyes, letting loose a deep sigh. *Focus,* I scolded myself. If I was going to do this sitting, I'd do it one hundred percent.

"I ask that my spirit guides step forth, aiding me on this spiritual journey through the afterlife. Anyone with a connection to either Thomas or Audrey Rose may present themselves now."

I peeked through slitted lashes. Thomas was being a good sport, sitting with his eyes closed and his back straight as a walking stick. Mr. Lees looked as if he were sleeping while sitting upright. His eyes fluttered beneath his lids, his whiskers and beard twitching to some rhythmic beat only he could hear.

I stared at the little lines around his eyes. He couldn't have been more than forty, but looked as if he'd seen as much as someone twice his age. His hair was gray at the edges, receding like the ocean sweeping away from the shore of his forehead.

He inhaled deeply, his facial features stilling. "Identify yourself, spirit."

I latched my attention onto Thomas again, but he didn't crack a smile or an eyelid, politely playing along with our ghost-divining host. He certainly wasn't acting nervous now. I couldn't stop myself from simultaneously hoping and dreading another encounter with my mother so soon. If his opening in the graveyard were to be believed, that was.

Mr. Lees nodded. "We welcome you, Miss Eddowes."

He paused, giving himself time to think of a fabrication or to "listen" to the spirit, his face twisted in concentration. "Yes, yes, I'll tell her now."

Oh, good. We'll get right into it, then. How silly. He shifted in his chair, never breaking contact with either of our hands. "Miss Eddowes says you were present the day her body was discovered. She claims you were accompanied by a man with pale hair."

My breath caught, hope of hearing from Mother momentarily set aside. Could it be true? Could Miss Catherine Eddowes be speaking through this stout, untidy man? This was all very strange, but I didn't necessarily believe one second of it.

Anyone who was at the crime scene that morning would have seen me walking with Superintendent Blackburn. Not knowing proper protocol for this type of situation, I whispered, "That's true."

I glanced at Thomas, but he was still sitting quietly, eyes shut. His mouth, however, was now pressed into a tight line. I turned my attention back on our spiritualist.

"Uh-huh," Mr. Lees said, his tone full of understanding. I wasn't sure if he was addressing me or the supposed spirit hovering about, so I waited with my lips sealed together. "Miss Eddowes says to pass along this message to aid you in believing. She says there's an identifying mark on her body, and you'll know straightaway what she's speaking of."

The urge to yank my hands back and leave this den of lies plagued me for a few beats. I knew precisely what she was talking about.

There was a small tattoo on her left forearm that had the initials TC. That was hardly a secret. Again, anyone could've seen her arm in passing. I sighed, disappointed this turned out to be an act of folly. Before I said a word or broke contact with Thomas or Mr. Lees, he hurriedly continued.

"She said Jack was there that day as well. That he'd seen you." He closed his mouth, nodding again as if he were an interpreter passing a message along from a foreign speaker. "He got close to you... even spoke with you. You were angry with him..."

Mr. Lees rocked in his chair, his closed eyes moving like confused pigeons squabbling back and forth in front of a park bench.

A deep, cold fear wound itself around my limbs, strangling reason from my brain. The only people I'd been angry with were Superintendent Blackburn and my father. Uncle had still been in the asylum and Thomas and I were not speaking.

If this man was truly communing with the dead, that cleared them of lingering suspicion. But Father and Blackburn...

Unwilling to hear more, I drew my hand away, but Thomas reached for it, placing it next to his. His encouraging look said we would see this through together, quieting me for the moment.

Our medium rocked in his seat, his movements coming faster and sharper. The wood creaked a panicked beat, spurring my own pulse into a chaotic rhythm. Mr. Lees stood so abruptly the chair he'd been sitting on crashed to the floor.

It took several seconds for him to reorient himself, and when his eyes cleared, he stared at me as if I'd transformed into Satan himself.

"Mr. Lees. Are you going to share what's troubling you with us," Thomas said, "or are you keeping what the spirits said to yourself?"

Mr. Lees trembled, shaking his head to clear away whatever he'd heard and seen. When he finally spoke, his tone was as ominous as his words.

"Leave London at once, Miss Wadsworth. I was mistaken, I cannot help you. Go!" he bellowed, startling us. He faced Thomas. "You must keep her safe. She's been marked for death."

Thomas narrowed his eyes. "If this is some trick—"

"Leave! Leave now before it's too late." Mr. Lees ushered us to the door, tossing me my coat as if it were on fire. "Jack craves your blood, Miss Wadsworth. God be with you."

From hell

Mr Lusk

Sor

I send you half the Kidne I took from one women prasarved it for you tother piece I fried and ate it was very nise I may send you the bloody knif that took it out if you only wate a whil longer

signed Catch me when you Can Mishter Lusk

From Hell Letter, 1888

TWENTY-FOUR

FROM HELL

DR. JONATHAN WADSWORTH'S LIBRARY,
HIGHGATE
16 OCTOBER 1888

"I see you've thrown yourself another pity party," Thomas said, breezing into Uncle's darkened library. Lifting my head from my book, I noticed his clothing was exceptionally stylish for an afternoon apprenticing with cadavers. His finely stitched jacket fit perfectly to his frame. He caught me inspecting it and grinned. "You've yet to send out invitations, Wadsworth. Rather rude, don't you think?"

I ignored both him and his remark, though I knew he was trying to make light of our situation. Eight days had come and gone since we'd spoken with Mr. Lees, and it had been even longer since I'd last seen my father.

While I couldn't rely on Mr. Lees's spirit testimony alone, Thomas was moving further down the suspect list every day. He pored over notes and details, day and night. I didn't think the stress he tried hiding was an act.

Thomas wanted this case solved as badly as I did. During one particularly troubling evening, I shared my fears regarding my father with him. He'd opened his mouth, then shut it. And that was the end of that. His reaction was less than comforting.

Staying true to his word, Father didn't seek me out, remaining indifferent to my whereabouts. It was so unlike him, letting me out of his sight for days on end, but he'd become a stranger to me and I couldn't predict his next moves.

I hated thinking or admitting it, but he fit several of Jack the Ripper's emerging characteristics. He'd been present for each crime, and absent when Jack had seemingly disappeared for those three and a half weeks in September.

Much as I wanted his opinion, I kept these dark speculations from Nathaniel. Worrying him was unnecessary until I had absolute proof Father was, indeed, Jack.

I flipped through a medical tome, reading over several new notions regarding human psychology and crimes. Father certainly had grief issues and plenty of reason to want organ transplants to be successful. That would explain the missing organs.

Though I couldn't see how it'd help Mother now. Then I remembered his favorite tonic; laudanum might very well explain that delusion.

"You shouldn't waste your precious energies on such rubbish, Wadsworth," Thomas said, reading over my shoulder. "Surely you're capable of coming up with theories of your own. You are a scientist, are you not? Or are you saving all the brilliant work for me to come up with?"

Thomas smiled at my eye roll, puffing his chest up and standing with one foot proudly resting on a chair as if posing for a portrait. "I don't blame you, I am rather attractive. The tall, dark hero of your dreams, swooping in to save you with my vast intellect. You should accept my hand at once."

"More like the overconfident monster haunting my nightmares." I offered him a smirk of my own when he scrunched his nose. He was handsome enough, but he needn't know I thought so. "Haven't you got an organ to weigh, people to annoy, or notes to scribble down for Uncle Jonathan? Or perhaps you've got another patient to experiment on."

Thomas grinned wider, folding himself onto the crushed velvet sofa directly across from me. A fresh body, having nothing to do with the Whitechapel murders for once, was lying on the mortuary table downstairs, waiting to be inspected. First glance said he'd lost his life to the harsh English elements, not to some crazed murderer. Winter was making a few surprise appearances before its official start date.

"Dr. Wadsworth was called away on more urgent matters. It's just the two of us and I'm quite bored of your moping about. We could be taking full advantage of our time together. But no," he sighed dramatically. "You're intently reading rubbish."

I nestled into my oversize reading chair and flipped to the next page.

"Studying the psychological states of humans and how they may or may not relate to deeper, psychotic issues is hardly 'moping about.' Why don't you put that big brain to use and read some of these studies with me?"

"Why don't you talk to me about what's really troubling you? What emotional dilemma needs sorting out?" He patted his legs. "Sit here and I'll rock you gently until you or I or both fall asleep."

I tossed the book on the floor at his feet, then immediately cringed. I was about to tell Thomas I was absolutely *not* struggling with any emotional issues and had shown him differently. One day I'd rein my cursed actions in.

I sighed. "I cannot stop thinking my father's the man stalking the night."

"The moral dilemma being what, exactly?" Thomas asked. "Whether or not you should turn dear old Father in to authorities?"

"Of course that's the moral dilemma!" I exclaimed, incredulous at how obtuse he was when it came to basic human concepts. "How can one turn against their blood? How can I send him to his death? Surely you must realize that's precisely what would happen if I told authorities."

They'd hang Father. Given who he was, they'd make it as public and brutal as possible. Just because blood might stain his hands did not mean I wanted his on mine. No matter if it was right or wrong.

"Not to mention," I added aloud, "it would kill my brother."

I covered my face with my hands. I was not saying the most obvious thing. Not turning my father in would result in more women being slain. It was a horrible predicament to be in and I hated Father even more for subjecting me to it.

Thomas grew very quiet, staring at his own hands. An eternity stood waiting, watching along with me until he banished it from our presence. "What are you hoping to discover between the pages of other men's theories?"

"Redemption. Clarity. A cure for the demon infecting my father's soul."

If there was some way for me to address the issues with his brain, perhaps he could be saved. I listened to the silence stretching between us, the ticking of the clock echoing my own heart's beat.

I lowered my voice. "If it were your father, wouldn't you try anything to save him? Especially after already losing one parent? Perhaps it isn't too late for his salvation."

Thomas swallowed hard, casting his attention to my book. "Will you be using a prop such as religion to deliver him from his sins, then? Sprinkle a bit of holy water and burn the devil out of him? I thought that was your eccentric aunt's domain."

I bent down to retrieve the medical journal, turning back to the last section I'd read. The leather chair squeaked as I shifted my weight.

"I am a scientist, Thomas. Father's salvation will come in the form of tonics working on his physiology. There are great treatises about the effect of chemicals on the neurological pathways of the brain,"

I said, pointing out one of them in the book. "Plus I'll threaten to imprison him in our home. I'll keep him in chains, locked in his own study, if he doesn't agree to have his mind evaluated."

Thomas shook his head—we both knew that was a lie. A weak knock came at the door before he could respond. We both stared at the footman standing half in the hall and half inside the library, a flush creeping up his collar. I hoped he hadn't been lingering there long. If anyone learned of Father's potential identity as Jack the Ripper or the fact we'd suspected him and hadn't turned him in, we'd all be in a world of trouble ourselves.

"Dr. Wadsworth has requested your presence at Scotland Yard immediately, miss." When Thomas and I shot each other glances, he amended, "Both of you."

I didn't care what I looked like to the men standing around Superintendent Blackburn's desk, as I covered my mouth with the back of my lace-gloved hand.

The stench assaulting my senses was almost as bad as what the package contained. Possibly worse. I could deal with most anything gruesome and bloody; rotten meat, however, was something I feared I'd never get used to. No matter how many times I was forced into contact with the foul substance.

"Most certainly it's half a human kidney," Uncle confirmed, though no one had asked. "While it's impossible to tell for sure, we must put some validity to the letter that came with it. Miss Eddowes was missing a kidney. This is a human kidney. From the state of decay, it was taken around the same time as hers was and it's from the left side. Same as our victim. I'll have to examine it further in my laboratory, but from sight alone there seem to be some... similarities."

I swallowed my disgust down. Jack was coming undone, it seemed. Thomas passed the newest note from the murderer to me, averting his gaze as he did so. I wondered if he'd tell the police about my father. I wondered if I'd do the same if I were standing in his place. Guilt wrenched itself deep in my gut. Was I allowing sentimentality to stand in the way of justice? That made me as bad as the Ripper.

Except...what if police had already discovered the identity? I stole a glance at Superintendent Blackburn. I knew nothing of him, really, and remained wary in his presence. Perhaps he'd already seen this organ the night it was removed from its owner. He was rather stone-faced given what my uncle was saying. Which made me wonder if Father committed these acts himself or if he had Blackburn carry out his dark deeds. Was his squeamish reaction at the double event a mere act of deception?

I shook myself out of spiraling thoughts, relieved no one was paying me any mind. The letter was written in the same taunting red ink as the other two notes Jack had sent. I'd recognize that cursive in my nightmares, I'd gone over it so many times, trying to find similarities to my father's own hand.

From Hell.

Mr. Lusk.

Sor

I send you half the Kidne I took from one woman and prasarved it for you tother piece I fried and ate it was very nise. I may send you the bloody knif *that took it out if you only wate a whil longer*

Signed
Catch me when you can
Mishter Lusk

George Lusk was my brother's friend and also happened to be the loudest member of the vigilante group Nathaniel was part of, the Knights of Whitechapel. If Father was indeed Jack the Ripper, sending someone close to our family a piece of evidence was rather brazen. Then again, claiming to have eaten the other half of a human kidney sounded as though insanity had overtaken him.

Cannibalism was a new low for the Whitechapel murderer.

I laid the letter back on Blackburn's cluttered desk. The cursive didn't look like Father's, but that didn't mean he hadn't taken pains to disguise it. Perhaps whatever evil dwelled inside him had its own handwriting.

"I wonder," I said aloud, not meaning to.

Thomas motioned for me to speak, but I wasn't quite ready to. Thoughts and theories were taking shape and forming in my mind. Perhaps if I offered something up, I could study Blackburn's reaction for deceit. A few seconds later, I began again. "Seems a bit odd, don't you think?"

"No, Wadsworth," Thomas said blandly, "sending a kidney through the mail is quite ordinary. I do it at least three times a week to remain fashionable. You ought to try it. Really impress the girls at tea."

I made a face at him. "What I mean is, let's say he's been killing women and trying to perform an organ transplant, why eat her kidney at all? Wouldn't that be a waste of a harvested organ?"

Blackburn's color drained as if he were about to be sick. His reaction appeared genuine enough, but he'd fooled me before.

He ran a hand through his hair. "It's barely two o'clock and I swear I already could use a pint. Is that what you think, Dr. Wadsworth? Jack is using human organs to transplant or sell?"

Uncle stared at the box, nodding absently. "I have a suspicion I cannot shake." Uncle took his spectacles off, wiping them on the front of his jacket before securing them back on his face. "I fear he might've taken an extra kidney, but realized he didn't need it, then decided to keep it from going to waste."

A shudder wracked my body. If Father was Jack the Ripper, where was he keeping the organs? It's not as if they could be stored in jars in our icebox without the cooks and maids seeing them. Was that the true reason why he'd never dismissed Martha, our cook? Was she privy to his monstrous secrets? The thought of having slept in the same house where this kind of horror could have been taking shape a few rooms away was too much.

Blackburn walked around his desk, dropping into the chair behind it and rubbing his eyes. "Perhaps running the estate as my father had wanted isn't such a bad idea. I can handle a vast amount, but this is a bit much. How horrid can a life of leisure and politics be?"

Thomas ignored the superintendent, seeking my uncle's opinion out again. He narrowed his eyes, his angular features sharpening his every thought. "Are you saying he's finished with the killings, then?"

Uncle shook his head, and parts of my skin tried crawling away from my body. He had that bleak look in his eye, the one that spoke of worse things to follow. When he started touching his mustache, I wasn't at all surprised by his next words. "I believe there's one final thing he's in need of, then the murders may stop."

A police officer walked over to Superintendent Blackburn and handed him a file, whispering some message in his ear before departing as quickly as he'd come. Whatever he said couldn't have been too important, as Blackburn tossed the paper onto the desk and fixed his gaze back on Uncle. "I'm not sure I want to hear any more, Dr. Wadsworth. But I'm afraid I do not have the luxury of ignorance. Do enlighten us."

I don't know how, but I knew, with more certainty than I had any right to, exactly what Jack the Ripper was missing. It'd be the most impressive organ to transplant or steal. The words nearly gagged me on their way out, but I said them anyway. "A heart. He'll need a heart before he's through butchering women."

I felt Thomas staring at me, his gaze searing a hole through my conviction to remain silent, but couldn't meet his eyes for fear I'd confess everything I suspected to the police right then and there. Consequences be damned.

But the one thread of hope I held fast to was that Uncle hadn't mentioned a thing about Father to police, either. I'd told him my suspicions last night in the laboratory, and though he was even more skeptical than I was, his face had paled.

Uncle told me not to worry, that we'd uncover the truth soon enough. That Father was simply unwell and everything mounting up against him only a coincidence.

Seeing the truth was never easy, especially when it revealed those closest to us could be monsters hidden in plain sight. If Uncle could hang on to a single string of belief, unraveling as quickly as it might be, that Father was innocent, then so could I.

For now.

TWENTY-FIVE

A VIOLET FROM MOTHER'S GRAVE

DR. JONATHAN WADSWORTH'S RESIDENCE, HIGHGATE
8 NOVEMBER 1888

I pulled the tattered navy dress from a trunk in Uncle's attic; its stitches were coming loose at the seams and the smell of must filled the space as I shook it out in the pale moonlight.

There was no hope of making it fashionable; too much time and not enough care had passed since it was first worn by Miss Emma Elizabeth.

Uncle had gathered nearly all her belongings from a family no longer wanting to be associated with her, taking pains to leave things as she had, frozen in time as if they were captured in a photograph. Except with a thick covering of dust and a few too many hungry moths having had a fine dining experience over the last several years.

The dress was a little too old, a little too ragged, a bit too big.

If I were to wear this ghastly dress out, I'd look as if I belonged in the East End, begging for work to feed my addictions, and Aunt Amelia would surely perish on the spot. I doubted even Liza would be able to make it pretty.

It was absolutely perfect.

Thomas leaned against the door frame, arms crossed, watching me in that silent, calculating way that drove me mad.

"I don't see sense in what you're doing, Wadsworth. Why not confront your father and be done with it? Sneaking about like a prostitute is by far the worst idea you've ever come up with. Congratulations," he said, unlatching his arms and clapping slowly. "You've achieved something memorable, even if it's ridiculous."

"I've *almost* crossed you off my suspect list." I shook out another dull dress. Dust tickled my nose as I laid it down. In its day, the deep-green silk must have been grand. "That's quite an achievement."

"Oh, yes," he said, rolling his eyes. "Another of your fine ideas. As if I'd be messy enough to leave evidence behind. I'm with you practically day and night. Does that not absolve me from being a murderer? Or must we share a bed to prove my innocence? Actually... that might not be a terrible idea."

Ignoring him, I removed a pair of brown lace-up boots from the same leather trunk and inspected them closely. They looked to be around my size, so I added them to my costume pile. Thomas had started following me around two hours prior, milling about and offering up his opinions like sacrifices I didn't care to accept.

"We've done things *your* way for three solid weeks," I reminded him. "Earning us nothing but mounds of frustration. Enough is enough, Thomas."

We'd tried hiding outside my house on Belgrave Square, camping out at all hours of the night, all times throughout the day, but never succeeded in catching Father coming or going. I'd even gone as far as etching his carriage for identification purposes, should we ever see it rolling about at night.

It was as if he always knew when he was being watched, sensed it like a wolf being tracked by something mad enough to hunt it.

Now it was time to test *my* theory out.

"For your information," I said, holding the green dress up, "I am not going as a prostitute. I'm simply blending in."

No amount of discussion would dissuade me from the path I'd chosen. If I couldn't catch Father heading into Whitechapel, I'd plant myself there and wait for him to come to me. It was as fine an idea as any. One way or another, I was determined to figure out if Father was Jack the Ripper.

Thomas muttered something too quiet for me to hear, then marched to an armoire standing solemnly in the corner of the attic, yanking the doors open and rummaging through it with a vengeance.

"What in the name of the queen are you doing?" I asked, though he didn't bother answering. Clothes flew over his shoulders as he tossed them out of his way, searching for something that fit his needs.

"If you'll not be reasoned with I shall have to sneak about with you. Clearly, I'll need an old overcoat and trousers." He made a sweeping motion over his person. "No one in their right mind will think me an East End resident looking as wonderful as I do. I may even don a wig."

"I am not in need of a haughty escort this evening." I scowled even though he wasn't looking. "I'm quite capable of taking care of myself."

"Oh, yes. How silly of me to overlook that." Thomas snorted. "I imagine the women who lost their organs thought themselves quite above being slaughtered as well. They were likely saying, 'It's Friday. I shall go to the pub, find a bit of food, pay my board, then get murdered by a madman before the night's through. How lovely.' "

"He is my father," I said through clenched teeth. "You honestly believe he'll harm me? I do not think even he has a heart so black and rotten."

Thomas finally stopped flipping through the moth-eaten overcoats, turning his attention on me. His expression was thoughtful for a moment.

"*If* Jack the Ripper is your father. You still haven't found definitive proof. You're basing all your bravado on the assumption you are, indeed, related to this monster," he said. "I do not think you incapable, Audrey Rose. But I do know he's murdered women who were alone. What, exactly, do you think you'll do if you discover you're wrong and there's a knife pressed against your throat?"

"I'll—"

He moved across the room so fast, I barely had time to register the object against the sensitive skin covering my throat. Thomas kissed my cheek, then slowly drew back, our eyes meeting. My heart hammered a panicked beat when his attention fell to my lips and lingered there. I couldn't tell if I wanted to kiss him or kill him. Finally, he stepped back, letting the candle clatter to the floor, then picked up a crude walking stick as if nothing had happened.

"Interesting," he murmured, admiring the stick.

Kill him, then. I definitely wanted to murder him. I clutched my throat with both hands, breathing hard. "Have you lost your mind? You could've killed me!"

"With a candle?" His brow quirked up. "Honestly, I'm flattered you think me so capable. Alas, I highly doubt I could do much damage with such a weapon."

"You know what I mean," I said. "If it were a knife I'd be dead!"

"Precisely the point of our little exercise, Wadsworth."

He didn't sound or appear the least bit sorry for scaring the life from me. He crossed his arms over his chest, staring me down. Stubborn mule.

"Imagine yourself alone in the East End," he said. "Freezing like that would've cost you your life. You must be quick to action, always thinking your way out of any predicament. It all boils down to your blasted emotions clouding your judgment. If I were to do it again, what might you do differently?"

"Stab you with the heel of my boot."

Thomas's shoulders relaxed. I hadn't noticed the tension in them until it was gone. "Good. Now you're using that alluring brain of yours, Wadsworth. Step on the insole of someone's foot as hard as you can. There are so many nerve endings, it'll be a decent enough distraction, buying valuable time."

His gaze traveled over me swiftly. It was more an assessment of my attire than a flirtation, but my cheeks heated all the same.

"Now, then. Let's get you ready for a casual night of street walking and be gone. Oh, you can thank me for preparing you any time now," he said, struggling to keep the smile off his face. "I wouldn't protest a kiss on the cheek. You know, return the favor and all."

I glared so hard I feared my face would get stuck that way. "If you ever try anything like that again, I *will* stab you in the foot, Thomas Cresswell."

"Ah. There's something about you saying my name that sounds like a blessed curse," he said. "If you can work up a good hand gesture to go along with it, that'd be exceptional."

I threw a boot across the room, but he'd managed to slip out and close the door before it made contact. I set my jaw, loathing him with each beat of my heart.

Though, he was right. I needed to be more emotionally prepared for my date with Jack. I walked over to the door, picked up the boot, and began dressing. The clouds were rolling in, covering the last sliver of the moon.

It was the perfect night to hunt a murderer on the streets of Whitechapel.

"Why in God's name are you walking with a limp?" I whispered harshly at my idiotic companion, throwing cautious looks at people staring across the street. "You're causing a dreadful scene and we're supposed to be inconspicuous."

Thomas had adopted the asinine lame leg the same time we reached the outer edges of Spitalfields. We'd been arguing about his acting the last few streets, garnering more attention than the queen parading through the squalor in her most expensive attire. Thomas was undeterred by looks and jeers we received.

If anything, he seemed to be enjoying himself.

"You're simply upset you didn't think of doing it first. Now go on and stumble a bit. If you don't act intoxicated, we'll never attract the Ripper." He looked down his nose at me, a smile starting. "Feel free to hold on to me. My arms are all yours."

I grabbed a handful of my skirts, sidestepping rubbish that had been dumped in the gutters, thanking the heavens Thomas couldn't see my blush.

"You've gone and missed the entire point of this evening. I am not trying to lure the Ripper out, Thomas," I said. "I'm trying to blend in and stalk him. See where he's going and stop him from committing another murder. He'll take one look at us and run in the other direction. Lest the lame-legged boy chase him with his walking stick."

"It is a *cane*, and it is quite a handsome cane. The Ripper should be too pleased to be assaulted by such a work of rustic art."

I glanced at the walking stick. It was barely even polished, and had cobwebs stuck in its grooves. It was rustic, indeed.

Silently, we crept through back alleys and squared-off yards, looking for any hulking shadows, and listening for any bloodcurdling screams. It was hard to see anything, though. The night sky was nearly black as ink, no flickering light shined down for us, and what little did from gas lampposts was quickly swallowed by thick fog.

We passed through one dark alleyway, hobbled across another street, and paused in front of a decrepit pub full of discordant music and laughter.

Drunken women draped themselves over the men standing outside, their voices louder and rougher than those of the butchers, sailors, and ironworkers they were trying to entice. I wondered briefly at their lives before prostitution.

It was such an unfair, cruel world for women. If you were a widow or your husband or family disowned you, there were few avenues available for feeding yourself. It hardly mattered if you were highborn or not. If you couldn't rely on someone else's money and shelter, you survived the only way you could.

"Let's go," I said, turning as quickly as I dared. I needed to get away from those women and their tragic lives before my emotions got the better of me.

Thomas eyed the women then glanced at me. I knew very well he was seeing more than I wanted him to and didn't want him thinking me fragile. To my surprise, he simply threaded my arm through his. A silent act of understanding.

My heart steadied. It was such a tiny action, but filled me with confidence in Thomas. Jack the Ripper would never show such compassion.

We ghosted through several more streets, emerging from the fog before hiding in its sanctity once more. Voices carried over to us, but nothing was out of the ordinary. Men talked about their day's work, women chattered about the same.

Thomas gave up his limp the longer we pressed on, having no reason for gimping about when people couldn't even see us.

Gas lamps offered otherworldly glows every few feet, their quiet hissing raising the hair along my neck. The mood of the night was ominous. Death was stalking these streets, staying just out of sight. I couldn't shake the feeling of being watched, but heard no sounds of pursuit and accepted I was simply scared.

"Enough," I said, defeated. "Let's go home."

It was after midnight and I was exhausted. My feet ached, the rough material of my dress itched against my skin, and I was thoroughly finished with walking through all the muck. I'd stepped in something rather squishy a few streets back and was contemplating amputating my own foot.

Blessedly, Thomas didn't say a word as we turned and headed toward Uncle's house. I wouldn't have taken his criticism well in the miserable state I was in.

Lost in thoughts of failure, I didn't hear a sound until our attacker was upon us. A scuffle of boots on cobblestones, the sound of a punch landing true, and Thomas was facedown on the ground, a bulky man kneeling on his back, twisting his arm around.

"Thomas!" Someone else emerged, holding a blade to my throat, shoving me deeper into the alleyway. I tripped over my skirts, but the man wrenched me forward, his fingers digging painfully into my skin. Fear held my senses hostage. My mind shut down, unable to process what was going on. Was this Jack?

"Whatcha got 'ere, boy? Been following you, I been. Think yourself clever, dressing like the riffraff?" The man speaking to Thomas had breath that smelled of rotten teeth and too much alcohol. "Shame. I hafta take from you same as you took from me."

From the ground, Thomas jerked around, his eyes frantic as they fell upon mine. His attacker shoved his face into the stone. My limbs were leaden and useless.

"I assure you. I've not taken from you, sir." Thomas winced as the man forced his head back down. "Whatever your issue with me, leave the girl go. She's done nothing."

"Ain't how I see it." The man spat next to Thomas. "Think taking them from the cemetery is decent? Poor deserve respect, too. My Libby"—his hand shook, the blade piercing my skin—"she didn't deserve to be cut up like that. You 'ad no right. I know what you done. Oliver told me hisself."

A sob broke free of the man's chest. A slight trickle of blood ran down my neck. Its warmth cleared my frozen thoughts. If I didn't act now, we were going to die. Or be maimed. Neither was on my list this evening. Remembering Thomas's lesson on dealing with an attack, I lifted my foot and stomped down with all my might. My heel crunched bone with a snap. It was enough of a distraction, just like Thomas said it'd be.

"Bloody 'ell!" The man stumbled away, jumping on his good foot. Thomas's attacker eased up long enough to watch his friend, allowing Thomas time to flip over and land a swift punch to his gut. The man doubled over, cursing impressively.

Springing to his feet, Thomas grabbed hold of my hand, racing us through the twisted streets as if Satan himself was chasing us down.

We wove in and out of passageways and alleys, running so fast I had to eventually tug Thomas to stop. "What... was... he... talking about?"

Thomas held on to me as if I might turn to ash and disintegrate in his hands if he let go. He glanced up and down the alley we hid in, his chest rapidly rising and falling. There was a wild, untamed look in his eyes. I'd never seen him so unraveled.

On the inside I felt the same, but hoped I was doing a better job hiding it. I took a steadying breath. Thomas was a complete wreck. I gently touched his face, drawing his attention to me. "Thomas. What—"

"I thought I was going to lose you." He ran both hands through his hair, pacing away and coming back. "I saw blood—I thought he'd slit your throat. I thought—"

He covered his face with his hands, collecting himself for a few breaths, then fixed his attention on me, swallowing hard. "You must know what you mean to me? Surely you must know how I feel about you, Audrey Rose. The thought of losing you..."

I'm not sure which of us moved first, but suddenly my hands were cradling his face and our lips were crashing together, propriety and polite society be damned.

There was no Jack the Ripper or midnight attack. There was just Thomas and me terrified of losing each other.

I wove my arms around his neck, drawing him closer. Before I wanted it to end, Thomas pulled back, kissing me sweetly one last time. He tucked a stray lock of hair behind my ear, pressing his forehead to mine. "Apologies, Miss Wadsworth."

I touched my lips. I'd read about dangerous situations bringing about spontaneous acts of romance and thought it foolish. Now I understood. Realizing the very thing you love most could be taken away without warning made you clutch onto it. "I believe I acted first, Thomas."

He stepped back, wrinkling his brow, then laughed. "Oh, no. I'm not at all sorry about kissing you. I'm talking about the deranged lunatic holding a knife to your throat."

"Oh, that." I waved a hand, feigning nonchalance. "He's lucky you had the foresight of preparing me this evening."

Thomas's eyes twinkled with a mixture of amusement and incredulity. "You're truly magnificent. Smashing bones and fighting off attackers in abandoned alleys."

"It's too bad," I said. "Your reputation will be completely ruined once people discover I saved you."

"Destroy it for all I care." Thomas laughed outright. "You can save me again if it ends with a kiss."

"Did you know?" I asked, turning serious. "About the cadavers?"

His jaw clenched. Thomas carefully took my hand, motioning

for us to keep moving. "Unfortunately, I did not. Obviously, the bodies aren't unclaimed as Oliver says. I do not appreciate being lied to or researching on someone's family member without permission. No advancement in science is worth causing pain."

I let go a sigh I was holding. It was all I needed to hear. Thomas was most certainly not involved in the Ripper crimes. He was interested in saving lives, not ending them.

"What will you do about Oliver?" I asked. "He cannot continue lying about the bodies. I doubt you're the only one he's done this to."

"Oh, I'll be having words with him, believe me." Thomas pulled me close. "I despise having put you in unnecessary danger."

"We are stalking Jack the Ripper," I pointed out. "I'm already putting us in danger."

Thomas shook his head, mirth replacing tension, but didn't say more.

Intent on leaving the East End, we trudged across Dorset Street, our attention scattered from the attack, when I nearly walked straight into a hansom cab. I stopped, staring in disbelief. Incredibly, the night took a larger turn for the worse. A snake coiled around my torso, striking at my innards.

A scratch ran down the side of the cab in an unmistakable M, a feature I was very familiar with, as I'd made it myself last week. It was my identification of a murderer.

This carriage belonged to my father.

TWENTY-SIX

BLACK MARY

MILLER'S COURT,
WHITECHAPEL
9 NOVEMBER 1888

I grabbed on to Thomas's overcoat, nodding toward the carriage. Where was the coachman? It would be odd if Father took it himself, leading my mind to stray in a thousand directions. Was it possible we'd had it all wrong? Could John the coachman be responsible for the killings? Or maybe Father had Blackburn take him here. I shook my head, clearing it. Nothing made sense.

"If I were committing a murder," I mused aloud, "why park my carriage outside the scene of the crime? Hardly seems logical."

"Jack the Ripper, whoever he truly is, doesn't appear to be thinking logically, Wadsworth. The man just ingested a human organ. Perhaps he feels invincible, and rightly so; thus far he's gotten away with his crimes."

I glanced up the street: nothing but lodging homes and litter joined us from our shadowy hiding place. Thankfully, our attackers hadn't reappeared and I doubted they would. I was fairly certain I'd broken his foot. I would've felt bad were it not for their malicious assault on us.

Most of the lights were off given the late hour, all except for the lodging house directly in front of Father's carriage. Mumbled voices and bright light poured from two windows facing us. One of them was cracked, allowing the sound to travel into the night.

I pointed to two figures walking back and forth. Making out features was impossible, but the broad set to one of them most certainly looked like Father.

"Come," I said, dragging Thomas into the alley across the street. "Should we fetch the police? Or give it more time?"

Thomas studied the layout of the alley, carriage, and building where the two figures were apparently just talking. The way he scanned the area around us was methodical and exact. After a minute, he shook his head. "Whoever's in there isn't arguing. I say we see what happens."

Something inside me wanted to rush across the street, pound on the door, and scream at Father for all the wrong he'd done, and all the wretched things he still sought to do, and cry for the guilt he was now laying on my shoulders.

"Very well. We'll wait." I settled against the cold stones of the building, waiting and watching. Time dragged by one hour for every second, it seemed.

I was freezing and exhausted from the attack we'd already been through, and scared of the encounter I'd yet to have with Father. I couldn't tell which was making me shiver more. I wanted Father to have an excuse for being here.

I wanted desperately to be wrong about him.

Nearly forty-five minutes later the front door swung open, revealing the two figures from the lodging house—a man and a woman. I strained my eyes, searching for definitive proof it was, indeed, my father standing before us. The couple remained a respectable distance apart, before the man stepped into the lamplight.

Lord Edmund Wadsworth glanced up and down the street, his attention pausing on the alleyway Thomas and I were camped out in, causing my heart to shout a warning. Fumbling in the dark, Thomas grabbed my hand and held it securely between his. The warmth of him steadied my nerves.

I knew Father couldn't see us, but I cringed all the same. I'd never been more grateful for the blanket of fog wrapping us in its cloudy embrace. Father scanned the area again, then climbed into the driver's seat of the cab, cracking the reins and lumbering off toward our home.

"Pay attention to the cab," I instructed Thomas, my own focus flicking back to the woman Father had been speaking to. Now she was standing in the light, speaking to another woman, who'd come from the adjacent building.

I was startled to see how young she was. Though I couldn't make her out clearly, she didn't look to be more than in her mid-twenties. Her hair hung down in long, ginger curls and she was taller than most men.

I hated that Father had sought her out. Nothing good could come from their association, even if he wasn't planning on murdering her. How could my father have so many secrets? After she finished her conversation with the other woman, she reached inside her broken window, then checked the door handle. I drew my brows together. It wasn't a good idea to lock your door without a key in this neighborhood.

She stumbled down the cobbled street, tying a red scarf about herself, singing a familiar song, its lyrics washing over me as they dripped from her honeyed voice.

But while life does remain to cheer me, I'll retain
This small violet I pluck'd from my mother's grave.

The song was "A Violet from Mother's Grave," and the way her voice sounded so sweet while recounting such a horrid occurrence sent chills under my skin. Thomas tugged on my sleeve. "Your father's rounding that corner. Shall we follow him?"

I glanced toward the young woman, then down the opposite way, watching Father turn onto the next street. The same feeling of Death lurking close by caressed my sensibilities. I couldn't shake the feeling something awful was going to occur.

I shook myself out of my daze, then nodded. I was still frightened of our earlier attack. It was nothing more. The young woman singing her sad song would be safe tonight. The monster was heading home.

"Yes." I tore my gaze away. "Stick to the shadows, and be quick."

"City Police have made an official report that a woman was found cut to pieces at a house in Miller's Court, at ten forty-five this morning," I said, collapsing onto the ottoman in Uncle's laboratory, reading the *Evening News* with utter disbelief.

Thomas watched me over his steaming cup of tea, a folded newspaper sitting across his lap. He'd tried comforting me by spouting a bunch of nonsense about how we'd done all we could, but I disagreed.

Now he said nothing and it was driving me mad.

"I don't understand," I said for the fourth time as the same shock kept coming back around, slapping me in the ribs. "We watched Father go straight home. Did he see us, then wait until we'd gone before committing such a vile act? We were so careful. I can't understand how he slipped by."

Still, no response from my companion.

"A lot of good you are," I huffed. "Master puzzle solver, indeed."

I checked the heart clock, my anxiety growing with each tick and tock. Uncle was called to the scene nearly four hours ago. Taking that long to inspect a body was never a good sign. From what the paper had printed, I could only imagine the horror Uncle had walked into. He'd been instructed to go alone, and I was ready to tear hair from my scalp, strand by strand.

When news broke of the murder, Thomas and I confronted Uncle with what we'd seen. He dismissed Father's involvement with a flick of his wrist, saying to keep searching for clues. Lord Edmund Wadsworth couldn't possibly be guilty.

I wasn't as convinced of his innocence but did as I was told.

A woman was found cut to pieces. I read that same line time and again. Perhaps I was hoping it was a mistake and by the thousandth time I'd read it, it'd simply disappear like magic. If only life worked that way.

"This is impossible." I tossed the paper aside and watched the clock again, willing it to speed along and bring Uncle back home already.

I was both sick with worry about who'd been murdered, and fighting the dark curiosity of wanting to know what remained of the woman. How had she been cut up? Did the reporter mean her throat was slashed, or were there actual pieces of her flesh missing? I shouldn't want to know those morbid details. But, oh, how I couldn't control those unseemly questions from springing up like new blades of grass in my mind.

Given the address in the paper, I was fairly certain Thomas and I had spied the unfortunate victim speaking with Father only hours before. Questions married other questions and had theories for children.

"All the unknowing is driving me mad." Now I understood how Uncle felt while waiting for Thomas to come back with news that time several weeks prior. If curiosity plagued him the way it did me, it was a terrible affliction to suffer from.

I shoved myself off the ottoman and paced around the laboratory.

The maids had done an excellent job putting it back together. One would never know Scotland Yard had nearly ripped it apart in their mad search of Uncle's belongings.

I walked over to the specimen jars, looking, but not really seeing objects the murky liquid contained. There was no quieting my mind.

"How had Father managed to throw us so easily from his trail?" I asked. "We were so careful, falling a safe distance behind his carriage, moving from one darkened alley to the next until he arrived home."

Once we hit my street we waited a few breaths before following. We'd just managed to see Father slinking into the house before the lights dimmed.

To be sure he was in for the night, we'd stood guard until three o'clock in the morning. No other murder had taken place that late, so we foolishly assumed it was safe to leave. How very wrong we were. The first rule in tracking a madman should be to never believe their moves were predictable. It was a hard lesson to learn, with astronomically devastating consequences.

I'd never felt like more of a failure in all my life.

"Do you think all that pacing will help the situation out? You're distracting me from my work, Wadsworth."

I threw my hands in the air, making a disgusted sound in the back of my throat before walking to the other side of the room. "Must you be so obsessively annoying at all times? I do not criticize you when you walk about in circles, deducing preposterous things."

"When I pace, it actually results in something clever. You're just kicking up dust and the scent of formalin and it's ruining my tea," he teased. Taking in my sour expression, he softened. "There's nothing to be done until Dr. Wadsworth arrives. You might as well eat something."

I tossed him a disgusted look and kept pacing.

He slathered a scone with jam and held it up. "I've a feeling you won't be very hungry later. Especially if they bring her bits and pieces here for further analysis."

I slowly turned around, noticing he was suddenly standing a bit too close. He didn't bother stepping back, almost challenging me to stay near him, to not care about propriety during the daylight hours, either.

My heart furiously banged in my chest when I realized I didn't *want* to move away from him. I wanted to be even closer. I wanted to stand on my tiptoes and press my lips against his again until I forgot about Jack the Ripper and all the gore.

"You look quite lovely today, Audrey Rose." He stepped forward, staring down at me, and I fought to keep my eyes from fluttering shut. Thomas drew closer until I was convinced my blood would explode from my body like fireworks splattering across the night sky. "Perhaps you should comment on the excellent cut of my suit. I look rather handsome today as well. Don't you think?"

"If you're not careful," I said, brushing imaginary wrinkles off the front of my riding habit and breeches, hoping the flush in my cheeks would come across as anger and not embarrassment, "you'll be the one dragged here in bits and pieces."

Thomas tilted my chin up with a finger, his intent gaze setting my skin aflame. "I do love it when you speak so maliciously, Wadsworth. Gives my heart a bit of a rush."

Before I could respond, the door of the laboratory slammed open and Uncle rushed in, his overcoat stained dark crimson all over its front and sleeves.

Every other thought leapt from my brain.

After all the postmortems and murder scenes he'd attended, he'd never come home so bloodied before. Uncle's eyes were unfocused, his spectacles askew on his face, as he tossed his journal down and took over my pacing. Thomas and I exchanged worried glances but didn't dare speak while Uncle murmured to himself.

"He couldn't have done it. It's too much for him to do. None of the other bodies had the skin removed. And the thighs...why cut the flesh from the thighs like that? Surely they weren't needed for any transplants."

I was fighting down nausea growing inside me. Uncle flipped through the pages of his journal, stopping on pictures he'd drawn of the murder scene.

A minute later a team of four men ambled down the stairs, carrying a body in a shroud. They deposited the corpse on the table, then quickly exited the way they'd come. The whole lot of them looked as if they'd just returned from a holiday in Hell. I'd never seen such unadulterated fear on anyone's face before.

Uncle, still muttering to himself, quickly lifted the cloth, revealing what was left of the victim without any warning.

It was as if time halted in its pursuit of racing around the track of the clock. I didn't want to look but couldn't prevent myself from slowly peering over his shoulder.

I had no one to blame but myself as I ran from the room, searching for a washbasin to vomit into.

I slowly made my way back down to the laboratory, my knees quaking from anticipating the carnage I'd be facing.

I'd never witnessed such sick barbarity inflicted on a person before. The body was barely recognizable as human. If an animal had torn her apart it would've been more pleasant to gaze upon. And less cruel. I could not fathom what kind of terror she must have experienced prior to passing on. Death would have been her welcome friend.

I was glad I hadn't accompanied Uncle to the scene; this was quite enough to deal with. Reaching the end of the narrow staircase, I steadied myself before turning the knob and entering the twisted nightmare once again. I'd do this for all the women who'd been brutalized, I reminded myself.

My attention skimmed over the corpse before sliding on to Thomas, who appeared only slightly more affected than usual, scribbling notes and practically getting nose-deep in the exposed cavity as if it were a Christmas feast to be savored. He cringed every once in a while but quickly schooled himself into neutrality.

Attuned to my presence, he looked up. "Are you all right?"

Uncle lifted his gaze from the body, waving an impatient hand for me to come assist them. "Of course she is. Hurry, Audrey Rose. We haven't got the luxury of pondering life all day. For some god-awful reason Superintendent Blackburn wants the body back in two hours. There's much to do. Now, hand me the toothed forceps."

Why indeed was the superintendent in such a rush? I tied an apron around my waist, then quickly sprinkled sawdust across the floor, following my postmortem preparations. I doubted we needed the sawdust, as the body appeared completely drained of blood, but proceeding as usual helped my mental state clear.

I grabbed the tray of postmortem tools, handing the forceps to Uncle. I wrapped my emotions together, not allowing a single thread to unwind.

It was time to act like a scientist.

I watched Uncle peel back the skin flap on her thigh, seeing nothing but an anatomical diagram needing to be studied. We'd done the same thing to frog specimens over the summer. This was no different.

"The superficial layers of the skin and fascia have been removed," Uncle clinically stated. Thomas rapidly transcribed each of his words onto a medical sheet, his pen hungrily lapping up the ink and going back for more. "The breasts have been excised and were found in various positions. One was located under her head, the other was found beneath her right foot."

I handed Uncle a dissecting knife and Petri dish, taking it back and sealing it once he'd placed a sample inside. He shoved his spectacles up his nose, leaving a smear of blackened blood along the brass. He'd have to address that later. People would start fearing him again if he walked around splattered in gore.

"The viscera were removed entirely and were also scattered about the crime scene. Her kidneys and uterus were found under her head, while the liver was near her feet," Uncle said. "All the intestines were placed on the left side of the body. The missing flaps of skin—both from her thighs and abdomen—were sitting on a small table and are now resting in two bags for further inspection."

Uncle paused, allowing Thomas enough time to capture everything down on paper. When he motioned to continue, Uncle did so, reporting from memory everything as if he were reading from a book.

"A great deal of trauma was inflicted upon her face. Several lacerations were noted—at the scene—in various directions, and her mouth had been cut down to her chin," Uncle said. "Her throat appears to have been slashed down to the bone prior to the removal of her organs."

Using the forceps, Uncle peeled back the flayed skin, inspecting the hollow cavity once containing the life force of this woman. The corners of his mouth tugged down, and he reached for a handkerchief, blotting at his brow.

He set his jaw, then continued with his findings. "Her heart was surgically removed and was found neither at the crime scene nor in her person. It's my belief it was removed for attempted transplant by the murderer."

A large, metallic object clanked to the floor. Uncle motioned for me to pick it up. I grabbed a pair of forceps and lifted the large gear to the table.

"Set it there for the time being," Uncle said.

Something inside me snapped like a brittle twig used for kindling. This had gone on long enough. Murdering women. Taking organs. Now there were gears inserted into their bodies? Each new crime grew more horrific than the last, as if Jack couldn't control the animal rage clawing his demonic soul one second more.

What would the next victim look like if he wasn't stopped immediately?

I refused to find out.

I'd finish this postmortem, then go directly to the source of evil and speak with the devil himself. After witnessing him with this woman last night, all doubt of his guilt was erased. Father had hunted his last victim.

If I had to bring all of Scotland Yard with me, I would. Hope for redemption was as dead as the woman lying on the mortuary slab.

"Wadsworth?" Thomas's brow creased, his tone implying it wasn't the first time he'd called my name and was pretending not to worry. I put on an air of annoyance and he replied in kind. "You look about ready to mount a horse and go gallivanting into some epic battle. Might you pass your uncle the bone saw before you run off and save the world?"

I glared, but gave Uncle the bone saw and rinsed the other tools off in carbolic acid. We were almost done. Since the body had been so badly attacked, there wasn't much for Uncle to sew up. Especially since Scotland Yard wanted another doctor to inspect the cadaver before the evening was through.

"It's a bit strange. Blackburn demanding the body back so soon, I mean," I said. "Could he be the killer, working on Father's orders?"

My uncle stiffened, then lifted a shoulder. "If you're right about your father's whereabouts last night, I suppose anything is possible. We need to be open to all theories. And we need to test Blackburn out."

Uncle placed the skull back together, then got up to wash his hands.

"Are you interested in confronting Jack the Ripper with me?" I asked, checking over my shoulder to be sure Uncle hadn't heard. I didn't want him dissuading me from turning Father in. Uncle was still trying to prove Father's innocence. But I'd seen enough.

Thomas eyed me suspiciously. "Of course I'm interested in confronting the Ripper. What else would I be doing with my time these days? Besides wooing you, that is."

"I'm heading home shortly. Father should be sitting down to supper within the hour. I plan on—"

Uncle thrust a bag at Thomas's chest. "Take this directly to Superintendent Blackburn, will you? Best we immediately hand over any mechanisms lest they toss me back in Bedlam. Be sure to gauge his reaction." Thomas held on to the bloodstained bag, a crinkle in his brow when he glanced from my uncle to me. Uncle huffed. "Get on with it, boy. Make yourself useful and stop staring at my niece like that."

Thomas laughed nervously. Uncle didn't appear as if he were feeling particularly jovial, however, and Thomas's chuckle died in his throat. He nodded at my uncle, then leaned in.

"Please don't confront him alone, Wadsworth. Act as if everything is normal." He straightened when my uncle cocked his head. "Do give your father my regards, though. Perhaps even a kiss on the forehead. I'd like to remain on his good side, especially when I inform him I'm madly in love with his daughter."

Shameless flirt. I watched Thomas run up the stairs, then tugged my apron off and tossed it into the makeshift laundry bin along with the others awaiting their nightly cleansing. Act as if everything was normal indeed. As if I'd listen to that absurd plea! A part of me was sad Thomas would miss the confrontation, but he'd have his hands full with Blackburn. I said good evening to Uncle and trudged up the stairs, letting the door shut tightly behind me, then paused.

It was better this way, actually. It seemed only proper that I'd be the one confronting Jack the Ripper on my own.

Father's reign of terror would cease before a new day dawned.

Of that much I was certain.

TWENTY-SEVEN

A PORTRAIT WORTH CONSIDERING

WADSWORTH RESIDENCE,
BELGRAVE SQUARE
9 NOVEMBER 1888

I stood, hesitating, outside the door to our dining room, the very same room I'd eaten all my meals in, never knowing I'd been sharing food with a monster.

How many times had Father cut into his meat, imagining it instead as human flesh? As fiery as I'd felt on the way over here, the reality of what I was about to do was setting in. Nerves were twisting and writhing through my body, making me jump at every small sound. Even the beat of my own heart was causing a great deal of anxiety.

I had no idea what Father would have to say for himself, or what he might do should I enrage him. The only thought mildly comforting me was knowing my brother would be there, and he'd allow no harm to befall me.

I wished I had the same confidence in Father. But he was past the point of sanity now. Perhaps no amount of reasoning would convince him to hand himself over to detective inspectors. Perhaps I should've gone with Thomas and fetched a constable. I heard a utensil clank onto a plate, the sound muffled from this side of the door.

It was too late to run for assistance now.

I placed my hand on the doorknob, allowing myself a few breaths to pull my emotions together. Falling apart before I even confronted him wouldn't do. If I were to show how scared I was, he'd sense it, lunging for my jugular, no doubt.

I removed my hand from the door, holding it about my throat instead. He could very well murder me. As Mr. Robert James Lees claimed he would. I blinked several times, regaining my composure.

How foolish I didn't bring a weapon of my own! Why would I think he'd spare his own daughter?

Thank the stars Thomas wasn't around, pointing out everything I was doing terribly wrong. Maybe I should creep back down the hall and run out into the night. I was without help, and without anything to defend myself.

An image of Mother's sweet smile flashed before my eyes. Father had inadvertently destroyed her. Weapon or not, I'd not allow him to do the same to me.

I squared my shoulders, steeling myself for the battle I was about to encounter. It was now or never, and I'd procrastinated long enough. I turned the knob and threw the door open, striding inside like a dark angel sweeping down to deliver justice, rage burning behind my eyes as the door shook the wall upon contact.

"Hello, Fath—" Words faltered as the footman dropped a plate, its blue and white pieces shattering across the empty table. I fisted my hands on my hips, as if he were responsible for all the problems in the world, too incensed to feel guilt as he cringed away from my aggressive stance. "Where are my father and brother?"

"Gone, miss." He swallowed hard. "Said they won't be back for supper."

Of all the miserable luck in the universe! I rubbed the bridge of my nose. Of course the night I decide to confront the beast, he'd be packed up and gone. He probably sensed the noose being tied. I realized our footman was still staring, mouth agape.

Perhaps he was more afraid of my ensemble of death. He hadn't seen me in my black breeches and riding habit yet, and that mixed with my raven locks probably painted quite the portrait of darkness. "Did they say when they'd return?"

He shook his head. "No, miss. But I got the feeling he meant they'd be gone for most of the evening. Lord Wadsworth said to leave the door unlocked and dim the lights when we settled in to bed."

I gripped my fists tighter. If Father did anything to hurt Nathaniel, I'd rip him limb from limb before the queen had a chance to order it done herself. I relaxed my grip slightly. No need to worry our footman any more than he was.

"I'll be in Father's study awaiting his arrival," I said, my tone cold and unfamiliar even to my own ears. "I do not wish to be disturbed under any circumstances. In fact, it'd be wise for you all to retire early. Have I made myself clear, then?"

"Y-yes, m-miss. I shall pass your wishes along to the other servants."

I quickly exited the room and ran down the hall, not wanting anyone to see how badly I was shaking. I hated being rude, but that was so much better than having their deaths stain my hands. If they were all in their rooms, they'd be safe.

I tried the door to Father's study. It was unlocked.

This time I wasn't sneaking around, Father would come straight here as he did every evening, so I pushed the door open and lit some lamps around the gloomy space. I scanned the forbidden room; it seemed much less intimidating now than it had weeks ago. His desk no longer appeared to be the imposing monster I once thought it to be. Now it just looked like a large, old desk that had witnessed too many terrible things.

The familiar scent of sandalwood and cigars that accompanied Father also didn't send my heart into spastic drumming. I welcomed it. Let it call his ghost to me now, I dared. My attention drifted over objects passed down in our family for generations, landing on the large, open tome. Recalling the cryptic message from my mother, thanks to the spiritualist, I strode over to it, curious.

There, exactly where he said it'd be, was the locket from the photograph.

I swallowed disbelief down. Turned out Mr. Robert James Lees was no fraud. How tragic Scotland Yard didn't listen to him. Perhaps they could've stopped Father a long time ago. I bent closer, reading the pages of the book that were carefully left open, trying to understand the significance of the passage.

The book was *Paradise Lost* by John Milton.

Upon himself; horror and doubt distract
His troubl'd thoughts, and from the bottom stirr
The Hell within him, for within him Hell
He brings, and round about him, nor from Hell
One step no more then from himself can fly
By change of place: Now conscience wakes despair
That slumbered, wakes the bitter memorie
Of what he was, what is, and what must be
Worse; of worse deeds worse suffering must ensue.

My eyes strayed to the underlined *from Hell* part, recalling the title of the letter sent from the Ripper all too clearly.

The way it was underlined looked like slashes, angry and tormented.

Any residual doubts I might've harbored about Father were gone.

He was comparing his gruesome acts to Satan's in *Paradise Lost*. What a twisted manifesto. The significance of the passage hit me at once. It was where Satan questioned his rebellion—the moment he realized Hell would always be with him, because he couldn't escape the hell of his own mind.

Satan would never find peace or Heaven, no matter how physically close he got, because forgiveness would always be out of reach. He could never change his mind, therefore Hell would be eternal. Acknowledging that, he turns evil into good, committing worse acts in the name of his version of "good."

I stared at the heart-shaped locket once belonging to Mother. Was this all for her, then? I carefully removed the glass case protecting both book and necklace. I'd not allow Father to use her as an excuse to do evil anymore. I placed the locket around my neck, feeling the comfort of it resting above my own heart.

Unable to be near the book, I walked over to the obscenely large portrait hanging on the wall. I still hated the sadistic-looking man with the proud stance of a murderer, the bear he'd slain limp at his feet.

I peered at the brass placard near the bottom. It was smudged with dirt. I reached over, about to scrub it off with my sleeve, when the painting lurched inward.

I yanked my hand back, nearly jumping out of my skin.

"What in the name of God is..." Once my heart stopped ramming against my ribs, I took a step closer. The portrait had been concealing a hidden passage.

An ice-cold breeze blew up from the darkened stairs, lifting wayward strands of hair about my face like the serpents on Medusa's head. I couldn't believe what I was seeing. A curved stone staircase was there, waiting to be explored. Or yelling at me to turn away. It was hard to decipher what the gaping mouth was imploring.

I stood, one foot over the threshold of the unknown, the other planted in the relative safety I knew. A terrible feeling stole over my bones, forcing them to clatter together in dread. This *had* to be the place where Jack the Ripper's prizes were kept.

Indecision clawed at me, confusing my better judgment. I stepped back, closing the portrait. I should run to Uncle's—have him call Scotland Yard and Thomas. Then we could all descend into Hell together. Still, I made no move to leave. I studied the portrait closer, removing the smudge from the placard, then gasped.

My hand flew to my mouth, fear taking on a whole new bodily form. His name was Jonathan Nathaniel Wadsworth the first.

The man both my uncle and brother were named after. Clearly, Father despised his brother, but what did it mean that he'd hung his namesake up in his study, hiding something undoubtedly filled with wretched things?

Was it a secret dig at Uncle? Blaming him for failing Mother? If the secret passage led to Hell, was it Uncle's fault for showing Father the way?

What sounded like a soft moan drifted from beyond the painting. I blinked. Pressing my ear against the wall, I listened harder. There was only the stillness of silence and too many secrets kept. Perhaps I was going mad. The walls couldn't possibly be talking.

Or perhaps another helpless victim was trapped wherever that staircase led. My heart thrashed, and my blood roared through my veins. I *needed* to go down there. I needed to save at least one of Father's victims. I glanced at the clock above the mantel. It was still early. Father and Nathaniel wouldn't be back for hours yet. Or what if... what if it was Nathaniel down there now? What if Father had trapped him?

What a fool I'd been! I couldn't expect Father to play by any rules. Just because he'd said he'd gone out with Nathaniel didn't mean my brother actually left the house. He could be tied up and bleeding to death this instant.

Without further hesitation, I pushed the painting in, then stepped onto the staircase. A whispered noise greeted me from the seemingly endless depths below.

Someone or something was definitely down there.

I went to gather my skirts, forgetting I wasn't wearing a blasted dress, then almost lost my footing as I looked down in surprise. I placed one hand against the cool stone wall, allowing it to act as my guide as I drifted farther into the darkness, my feet flying as fast as they dared over unfamiliar ground.

Grabbing an oil lamp or candle would've been wise. I wouldn't dwell on that lack of foresight now. With each step downward, blackness got lighter instead of more suffocating. A lamp must have been left on for reasons I dare not know.

I shuddered, imagining a million and one horrors about to greet me. My silk shoes raced along the stone, light as a feather as I jumped from one step to the next. I was grateful for the soundlessness they offered. I'd forgotten my boots when I left Uncle's earlier, which seemed like a blessing now. The silken tread would give me time to secure my bearings without revealing myself.

As I neared the end of the stairs, a warm glow reached toward me. The very idea something so inviting could herald the entrance of this pit of hell made my skin crawl. Beyond a final bend, before the room came fully into view, I paused with my back pressed against the wall, listening.

No human noise sounded. But the soft *whirl* and *churn* of steam-driven parts quietly hissed in time to the beat of my heart. It had to be the noise I'd heard.

Whirl-churn. Whirl-churn.

I closed my eyes. Whatever was making that sound could only be wretched.

Whirl-churn. Whirl-churn.

The scent of medical elixirs and burnt flesh wafted over to my hiding place, turning my already queasy stomach. I was not anxious to have my curiosity quelled now, but if my brother was being tortured, I needed to cross that final step.

I sucked a breath through my mouth, seeking to avoid the sickening scent as much as possible, then peeled myself off the wall. It took two tries, but I finally commanded my body to move into the room.

Fear spread its ugly disease throughout my body like rats carrying the Black Death. A laboratory, far more sinister than anything ever dreamed up in novels, was set out before me. As in Uncle's laboratory, shelves lined the walls, filled with specimen jars two and three deep. Unlike in my uncle's laboratory, there did not appear to be any order to these specimens, and the wood looked half-rotten.

I staggered back, bumping into something soft and fleshy on a shelf nearest the wall. The world stopped spinning as I flipped around and saw *flesh* pulled tightly over a mechanical arm, the skin crudely sewn together with large, jagged stitches.

It was as if Father had chopped an arm off at the elbow, and replaced some of the bones in the fingers and forearm with metal before covering it with stolen skin.

Redness surrounded the needle wounds; clearly an infection was leeching into the makeshift limb. My corset felt ten times too tight, and I swayed on my feet, suddenly gasping for breath.

Whirl-churn. Whirl-churn.

This couldn't be real. I closed my eyes, praying when I opened them the world would right itself again. But that was a fool's dream. I swallowed the bile rising quickly in my throat, taking in the full gore of the object I'd bumped into.

Black squiggly lines of sepsis twisted up the monstrosity.

Gray-tipped fingers twitched, the nail beds dried and receding to both metal and bone.

Whatever Father was attempting, he'd failed with this... thing.

Whirl-churn. Whirl-churn.

Steam erupted from the strange device, forcing dead fingers to flex at regular intervals. I was too shocked to even cover my mouth.

At least my heart hadn't lost its senses; I felt its beat throughout my body, pumping so quickly I feared it'd knock me over in its mad rush to flee. Should Father or even Blackburn pop out from one of these dark corners, I'd perish on the spot.

I slowly backed away from the mechanical flesh-covered arm, my attention steadily moving about the room, jumping from one horror to the next.

Whirl-churn. Whirl-churn.

Animals in specimen jars were in various states of decay, their flesh and soft tissues breaking apart in liquid hell. Crude abominations were left on tabletops throughout the room. Birds were ripped apart, placed in the mouths of dead cats, scenes of cruelty in nature displayed in sick tribute to the strong. It reminded me of a much darker version of Thomas's personal laboratory. I stepped closer, unable to stop myself from getting a better look at the horrific creations.

On another shelf I spied a ginger beer bottle filled with a dark crimson liquid. I picked it up, turning it one way, then the other. It had dried and coagulated to a gel. Jack made reference to it in one of his letters. He hadn't lied.

I exhaled, my breath puffing little white clouds in front of me. It was unbearably cold down here. I rubbed my hands over my arms, walking to a machine near the center of the room making the soft *whirl-churn* noise, and halted, nearly stumbling over my own feet when I saw the most sinister thing of all.

A human heart sat under a glass case, and soft noises came from a machine lending an electrical charge to it, causing it to continue pumping.

Pressing a hand to my mouth, I forced myself to stay calm and not gag or scream. Liquid-filled tubes ran out of the organ and over the table, toward something I couldn't quite see without moving closer. I peered at the liquid being pushed through the heart with the transfusion apparatus; it was black as oil and stank of sulfur.

Whirl-churn. Whirl-churn.

I swallowed my revulsion. Father had truly lost his mind. Ghosts of his victims surrounded me, warning me to turn back, run away. Or maybe it was my own innate warning system, commanding me into that fight-or-flight state of being. But I couldn't stop myself from inching around the table—any more than some of the slain prostitutes could resist their drink—too compelled to leave without seeing what the heart was pumping its strange life force into.

My breath came faster, speeding my pulse along with the added oxygen coursing through my system, making me both faint and jittery at once. I could hear myself screaming, No! Turn back! RUN! But couldn't stop moving forward.

Whirl-churn. Whirl-churn.

A closed wooden crate, as long and wide as a coffin, lay on the floor, tubes disappearing into it like worms burrowing into the earth. I did not want to know what that box contained. I paused, feeling the sharp tug of self-preservation dragging me back.

But I cut it away, silencing it.

I mustn't reach for the lid, but knew that was impossible. I was sick with dread, knowing, somehow just *knowing,* what I was about to uncover and being unable to walk away without seeing the truth. I watched as my hand shakily reached down, of its own volition, and lifted the creaky lid.

Inside the makeshift coffin lay my mother.

Her gray flesh—a patchwork of decayed skin with pieces of new—glistened with a sheen of unnatural sweat. The skin over her jaw had rotted away, giving her a permanent sneer. Beneath the grafted skin, something bubbled with artificial life.

Father wasn't trying to complete a successful organ transplant. He was trying to bring Mother back from the dead—*five years after.*

All the fear I'd been containing shattered like glass. I screamed, letting go of the lid and backing away, bumping into the table. The soft *whirl-churn* of the machines grew louder. Or maybe I was about to pass out. I covered my eyes with my hands, trying to rid myself of the image burned there. It couldn't be. He couldn't have done such a thing.

No one, not even the most scientifically mad, would attempt something so ungodly. We'd been so wrong about Jack the Ripper's motives. Even Thomas couldn't have predicted such a thing.

I kept trying to drag myself away, prevent my gaze from lingering on the rotten face and decayed body. But I couldn't move. It was as if the horror was so intense it had frozen me in place. Time didn't seem to move. Life outside of this hell didn't exist.

But the worst part was my emotions. I was disgusted, through and through, but part of me wanted to finish the work he'd started. I hated that piece of me, hated that I yearned for my mother back so much I'd condone this madness. Who was more a monster, my father or myself?

I was going to be ill. I turned, finally listening to my primal instincts, and ran for the stairs. As I rounded the steps, I slammed into a mass of flesh. *Warm* flesh.

It gripped me back hard and I screamed again. Only when I lifted my gaze did I breathe a sigh of relief.

"Oh, thank God," I panted, clutching on for dear life. "It's you."

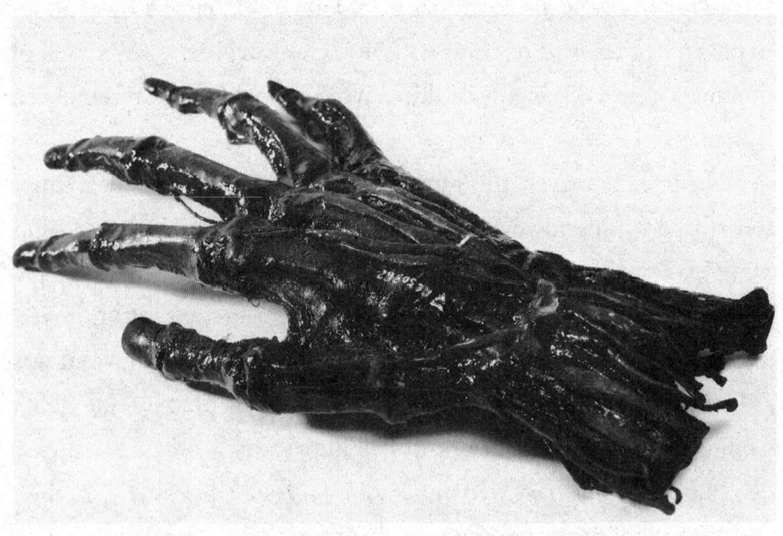

Human Hand Anatomized and Preserved, 19th century

TWENTY-EIGHT

JACK THE RIPPER

WADSWORTH RESIDENCE,
BELGRAVE SQUARE
9 NOVEMBER 1888

"Hurry," I urged, tugging my brother toward the staircase with the kind of super strength awarded those in the throes of deathly terror. "We must leave before Father comes back. Oh, Nathaniel. He's done terrible things!"

It took several moments to realize my brother wasn't moving. He was standing, frozen in place, eyes drinking in our surroundings. I grabbed the front of his long overcoat, shaking him until his wide gaze landed on me.

His hair was a wreck, standing out every which way, and it appeared as if he hadn't slept in days. Dark shadows hung beneath his eyes, giving him a sunken expression. He looked no better than the corpse of our dead mother.

Or whatever that creature was in the coffin. That abomination.

Another shudder wracked my body, almost dropping me to my knees. I couldn't let him see that. He'd never be the same again. Getting ahold of myself, I stood straighter, easing the boning from my ribs.

"Nathaniel," I said sternly, taking hold of his hand. "We must leave here at once. I'll explain on the way to Scotland Yard. Please, let's hurry. I do not wish to meet Father down here."

My brother nodded, seeming too shocked to do much more. I led him toward the stairs, our feet reaching the first blessed steps, when he stopped again.

I turned, exasperated, unable to convey the importance of leaving swiftly. If I had to slap him unconscious and drag him up the stairs, so be it. "Nathaniel—"

He latched onto my wrist with a viselike grip, yanking me away from the stairs and deeper into Jack the Ripper's lair. I struggled against him, not understanding his need to be difficult, when he threw his head back and laughed.

Gooseflesh too terrified to even erupt lurked just under my skin, tinkling with the promise of new fear. He tossed me into a chair near the corner of the room, still chuckling to himself. I blinked. My brother had never handled me so roughly before. Father must have drugged him somehow. It was the only explanation. I rubbed my lower back. A bruise was already forming where I'd hit the chair when he'd thrown me into it.

He didn't seem to notice. Or care.

"Nathaniel," I said, trying to sound as calm as possible while he paced in front of me, slapping the side of his head as if silencing voices only he could hear. "Once we leave, I'll fix you a tonic. It'll cure whatever's ailing you. Whatever Father gave you, we'll make better. Uncle will know precisely what to do. You have to trust me, all right? We stick together. Always. Isn't that right?"

Nathaniel stopped laughing, his gaze zeroing in on me with an icy precision. He lowered his hands from the side of his head before cocking it. Right then he was a predator in every sense of the word.

"Dear, dear Sister. I'm afraid you've got it terribly wrong. For once, Father isn't responsible for what's afflicting me. This is all my doing."

"I don't understand...you've been taking elixirs yourself?" I shuddered. "Have you... have you been abusing laudanum, too?" My brother had been under severe stress. I wouldn't be surprised if he turned to the cure-all tonic. Hallucinations weren't unheard-of when it was taken in large doses. "It's okay," I said, reaching for him. "I can help you. We'll both go to Thornbriar until you're well."

Reaching his arms out to either side, he spun proudly in place. Acting as if this were all his...

"No." I shook my head, blinking disbelief away. It couldn't be. Life wouldn't be so cruel. It just wouldn't. Tears pooled in my eyes before rushing down my face. This could not be. I was going to be sick. I lurched forward, clutching my stomach and rocking.

Nathaniel paced in front of me, removing a concealed knife from his sleeve. It was roughly six or seven inches in length. The exact size Uncle had predicted Jack the Ripper's weapon to be.

He ran his fingers tenderly over the bloodstained blade, then set it on the table with the taxidermy bird being ripped apart.

Memories of my brother saving animals, feeding them more than they could hope to eat, crying each time something died in spite of his efforts, filtered into my thoughts. The sweet boy who'd vowed to protect me against our grief-stricken father. This could not be the monster brutalizing women. I would not allow it to be. This lab was not his. These weren't his experiments. He was not the one who'd done this to our mother.

"Tell me this is a nightmare, Nathaniel."

Nathaniel knelt before me, wiping my tears away with such gentleness, I sobbed harder. I shook my head again. This *was* a nightmare. Surely I was sleeping and I'd wake up in Uncle's house and discover this was a terrible dream.

What a rotten sister I was! Dreaming such things about my beloved brother. The real Nathaniel would never do this. He'd know it would kill me to lose him. He would never do something to hurt me so. He'd never hurt *anyone*. He just wouldn't.

"Shhh," he cooed, smoothing loose hair from my face. "It's fine now, Sister. I promised you everything would be all right. And it is. I helped exonerate Uncle with those letters. Didn't I? Though, admittedly, it was rather fun seeing the chaos a bit of bravado and red ink caused. Couldn't help myself from sending more."

"You... what?" I felt my nerves unraveling. "This can't be real."

Nathaniel lost himself in some reverie before shrugging the memory away. "Anyhow, I think I've discovered why you and Mother got sick, and Father and I didn't."

He sat on his heels, looking around the room again, exaltation and wonder etched into his normally sunny features.

"Took some time figuring out, and I wish you would've waited before coming down here, but no matter." He smiled, patting my hand. "You're here now and it's perfect. I've worked out the final touch. All that's left is a little prick of blood and a bit of electricity. Like in the book. You remember the one, don't you? Our favorite."

Another tear slid down my cheek. I wasn't dreaming, I was sitting in Hell. My brother fancied himself Dr. Frankenstein, and I'd never allow our mother to become his monster. "You cannot bring Mother back from the dead, Nathaniel. It isn't right."

He shoved himself away from me, pacing in the orangey glow of his devil's lab, shaking his head. "What makes it wrong? You, of all people, I thought, would appreciate and understand. This is a breakthrough in science, dear Sister. A feat people will speak of for all time. Our name will forever be attached to the unimaginable. Uncle's a shortsighted fool. He wishes only to conduct a successful organ transplant. I've got something much bigger in mind."

Nathaniel nodded, as if it were all the convincing he needed. He punched his fingers into an open palm, exposing cuts on his fingertips. I couldn't recall the last time I'd seen him without gloves on. Now I knew why.

"Until now, people didn't believe it could be done. Only authors and scientific visionaries like Galvani dared imagining such a wonder. Now I've accomplished it! Don't you see? This is something worth celebrating. People will never forget the scientific breakthrough I've made."

"What of the women you killed?" I asked, wringing my hands in my lap. "Is it worth celebrating their deaths?"

"The whores? Why, yes. I think it's doubly worth celebrating now that you mention it." He stood, hands fisted at his sides, eyes darkening. "Not only have I rid our streets of the blight attacking it, but I've just about brought our beloved mother back from death."

He paced in front of me again, his tone growing more hostile with each step he took. "I've put the wretches out of their misery and their sacrifice will bring back a good, decent woman. Please, inform me of my wrongdoings. Honestly, Sister, you make it seem as if I were a common monster preying on the helpless. Mother herself was a God-fearing woman. She will understand."

I had no words. The women he murdered did matter. They weren't rubbish to be tossed away in the streets. They were daughters and wives and mothers and sisters. And they were loved as we'd loved our own mother. How dare he pass such judgment. My brother was so lost to his own fantastical science and sense of justice that he totally missed the mark of what it meant to be human. Which sparked something in my brain.

"What of the gears left inside the bodies?" I asked. "What sort of message were you sending the police?"

"Message? There was no intended message. I simply left them

where I'd dropped them." Nathaniel ran his fingers over his hair, attempting to smooth it down but achieving the opposite. He continued pacing, growing more agitated that I wasn't applauding his unforgivable behavior. "Is that truly all you care about? The blasted gears inside the wretches?"

"They did not deserve to die, Nathaniel," I whispered.

"These women did not deserve to live!" His voice boomed in the small space, making me jump. "Don't you see? These women are a disease. They destroy lives. I offered them a chance at redemption—death for life!"

He walked around to the coffin, then threw the lid back, tears filling his eyes. "Her life was destroyed by disease. Disease spread widely in part by whores coughing and infecting good men. So, no, Sister, I won't feel an ounce of sorrow for cleansing our city of a few of them. Would that I could, I'd set the entire East End ablaze and be done with them all. As it stands, I took only what I needed for my experiment."

"How very noble of you."

"I know." My brother missed the sarcasm in my tone. He smirked, like it was high time I saw his reasoning. "Truthfully, I'd not intended to kill so many, but the organs shut down before I could work on them. The bolts proved difficult to master in the dark, so I started carrying a medical satchel with ice and inserted the bolts and gears here. Watch."

He hoisted a large luggage case over, unfolding it into a portable table and setting it beside the glass-encased heart in the center of the room. Hand and leg restraints dangled from the edge of it. Nathaniel walked over to a gear on the wall and cranked it until a long, needle-type device hovered above the table. This must be his electrical source.

Something that felt a lot like fear stirred in my blood.

To my utter horror, he bent down, dragged Mother's corpse onto the makeshift table he'd set up, then shoved her hands and feet into the leather straps.

I closed my eyes as her lifeless head lolled to the side, feeling a rolling wave of nausea wash over me. She'd been deceased for five years and I hadn't a clue how she was more than just bones.

"I had the foresight to keep Mother partially frozen in a special icebox down here." Nathaniel stared at the slightly decayed corpse, tenderly pushing her hair aside, and answering the question I never asked aloud. "Shame I didn't think of preserving her immediately. It was hard enough sneaking her out of her grave and bringing her here without Father's knowledge. That's where the laudanum came in handy."

Nathaniel dropped a glass specimen jar, then cursed, rousing me from denial. I couldn't reconcile the Nathaniel I'd known all my life with this beastly version before me. And I couldn't even think about the pains Father would experience should he see our mother now.

Mother had been dead enough years that strands of her long, black hair fell onto the floor. Nathaniel picked up large pieces of glass, discarding the clumps of hair that caught in them as he tossed them into a rubbish bin. He was completely unaffected by the ghastly scene in front of him, cleaning up his mess as if the corpse of our mother were not rotting on a table before him.

Had I not already expelled the contents of my stomach earlier, I'd be doing so this instant.

"How did you discover this room?" I gripped my hands together, refusing to look at Mother again. I was so close to losing my nerve, so very close to losing my own sanity, it wouldn't take much to cripple me now.

Whirl-churn. Whirl-churn.

Nathaniel flicked his attention to me. "You recall the secret passages in Thornbriar?"

Memories of playing in secret passageways each summer flipped through my mind. Jonathan Nathaniel Wadsworth the first was a bit of an eccentric. He'd had more secret passageways built in the cottage estate than were in the queen's own palace. I nodded.

"A few summers ago I found a map of this property at Thornbriar," he said, shrugging. "Father was already abusing his tonic, so I added extra laudanum to his brandy at night. It wasn't hard to ensure Father remained... sedated and unaware of my use of his precious study. What was a bit more opium to an addict?"

"You... fed Father opium, knowing the consequences?" Clenching my teeth, I watched my brother walk over to the table with the steam-pumping heart. The urge to cry reared up, but I silenced myself. Nathaniel removed a scalpel from a medical kit under the table, then set it down beside the organ. He took another bag out and placed several locks and bolts out in a row.

Little puzzle pieces finally clicked into place.

Nathaniel was the only one other than Father who knew how to craft such intricate steam-driven toys. He'd been there with Father nightly as a child, watching and learning from the best. Then there was the matter of his short medical apprenticeship before he switched to studying law. Both of those previous hobbies had aided with his dexterity. And precision.

While I fought with the image of a loving brother I knew and the monster before me, he lit a burner on the table and heated the metal up, fusing bolts and gears together as if it were second nature.

Another memory slid into the forefront of my mind. My brother had been disturbed when he'd discovered I'd snuck into Father's study. I'd thought him worried for me, should our father ever find out I'd been snooping through his things. When in reality, Nathaniel had worried I'd find *his* secret lab.

Nathaniel peered over at me, smiling menacingly as he worked furiously on his newest invention. I watched in silence while he created a metal cage, still unable to think straight. My logical brain knew I had to think and act quickly, but my body felt leaden and crushed by devastation. I couldn't move.

"It's going into Mother's chest cavity. It'll keep her new heart protected." He nodded several times to himself. "Think of it as an artificial rib cage of sorts."

My body finally shook itself free of shock. Chills dipped their fingertips into buckets of ice, then darted wildly over my back. Everything made sense. The look of fear when the detective inspector showed up with me at the door after Father's dismissed coachman had been murdered. The same fear-frozen gaze when Superintendent Blackburn interrupted us at the circus.

A million clues had been sitting right before me, and I chose to ignore them.

My brother was the kind one. The sensitive one. I was the monster. The one who sought to pry secret knowledge from dead flesh. How had I not seen the same curiosity in him? We were composed of the same inheritance.

He held the contraption up to the steam-powered heart, measuring it for size, laughing to himself and muttering incoherently. I could not ignore his sick deeds anymore.

Once the metal cooled, Nathaniel carefully placed the steam-pumping heart within the rib cage, then fused the metal together with more bolts. He cranked the gear on the wall, adjusting the electrical needle until it touched the metal cage, then stood back, admiring his work. Satisfied with this new grotesque device, he walked over to the table and picked up a syringe, tapping its side with his forefinger.

"You must cease this madness, Nathaniel."

"What's done is done, Sister. Now"—he turned to me, brandishing the syringe as if it were a holy relic—"I only need a bit of your blood to inject into her heart, then we'll flip the switch together. If dead frog legs can be made to move by dint of electrical current, we can do the very same on a grander scale. We have the benefit of having more living organs. That's where Galvani and all his intelligence went wrong," he said, pointing to his head. "He should've invested in live tissues for his cadavers. Then he need only add a little voltage. Metal in the gears will help transfer the energy. That's why I'm fusing them with flesh. It's brilliant, you'll see."

I followed his gaze as he admired the electrical needle dangling from the ceiling and disappearing into Mother's chest. This needed to end now. I could not bear to see him do another wretched thing to Mother's body. I allowed all the emotion I was suppressing to seep into my voice.

"Please, Brother. If you love me, you'll stop this experiment. Mother is dead. She's not coming back."

I swallowed hard, tears streaming down my face. I recoiled at the small part of myself wishing to see if it *could* be done; if he could animate long-dead flesh. If he could bring the mother I missed so much to life again.

But the human part of me would never allow it.

"You've achieved so much. Truly," I said. "I've no doubt you'll surpass any scientist you choose to, but this, this is not the right path."

Whirl-churn. Whirl-churn.

Nathaniel shook his head, pointing at the steam-driven heart. "We're so close, Sister! We're mere minutes from speaking with Mother! Isn't that what you've wanted?"

He'd shifted from being angry to looking like a sullen child. All he needed to do was stomp his feet and cross his arms to complete his tantrum. Instead, he stood completely still, and that was somehow more eerie than watching him pace like a rabid animal.

"This is all for you!" he shouted, exploding from his stillness, taking a few giant steps toward me. "How can you turn this gift away?"

"What?" I wanted to sink to my knees and never get off the ground. My brother had killed all those women because he thought I'd be selfish enough to see only the beauty of the end result.

The room spun when I realized the choices now laid out before me. If I called upon Superintendent Blackburn, he'd kill Nathaniel. There would be no asylum or workhouse. No trial. No hope for life.

What was I to do about my brother, my best friend? I couldn't stop myself from crying out, from rushing across the room and beating his chest.

"How could you do this?" I screamed while he stood there, accepting my hysteria with that same frightening stillness. "How could you believe murdering women would make me happy? What am I going to do with a dead brother and mother? Don't you see? You've ripped us apart! You've killed me, you might as well have torn my heart out, too!"

The proud gleam in his eyes was replaced by a slow sense of understanding. Whatever madness had gripped him over these last few months seemed to release him from its grasp at last. He staggered back, steadying himself against the table.

"I—I don't know what evil has overtaken me. I—I'm sorry, Audrey Rose. It will never be enough, but I'm . . . truly sorry."

He allowed me to pound his chest until I grew tired. Tears slowed, marginally, but the ache of what he'd done was a weight I feared would never lift.

My brother. My sweet, charming, beloved brother was Jack the Ripper. Emotions threatened to drown me where I stood, but I fought the flood of them back. I couldn't be consumed by grief yet.

I needed to get Nathaniel help. And I needed to get out of the room where my mother was trapped somewhere between life and death.

"Let's go, Nathaniel. Please," I said, urging him toward the stairs. "We'll have some tea. All right?"

It took a moment for him to respond, but after a few breaths, he finally nodded.

When I thought he'd finally seen reason, he painfully gripped onto my arm, brandishing the syringe. " 'Long is the way, and hard, that out of Hell leads up to Light,' dear Sister. We must continue our chosen path. It's too late for turning back now."

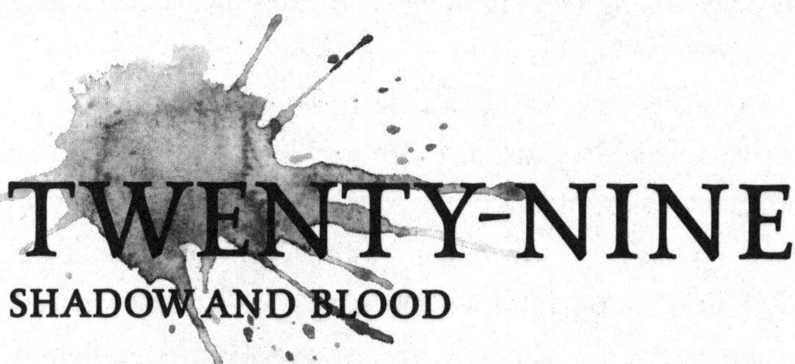

TWENTY-NINE

SHADOW AND BLOOD

WADSWORTH RESIDENCE,
BELGRAVE SQUARE
9 NOVEMBER 1888

I clung to my brother in the midst of our shared hell, not wanting to step away and make this nightmare real.

Dragging me back across the room, he threw me into a wooden chair next to our mother. "Look what you've done! Now I must tie you up for your own safety, Sister."

I sat there immobile, unable to comprehend what he was saying, which cost precious time. Before I could react, he yanked my arms behind the chair and swiftly tied my wrists together. No matter how hard I strained against the rope, there was no escaping my new prison.

Nathaniel had secured me so soundly the tips of my fingers were already turning icy cold. I tugged and pulled, managing only to scrape my skin raw with each panicked attempt to break free of my bonds.

I screamed, more out of shock than hurt, as he thrust the syringe into the thin skin on my inner arm. "Stop it, Nathaniel! This is madness! You cannot revive Mother!"

My pleas didn't stop him from sinking the plunger in and drawing out my blood. His first attempt failed and he drove the needle in a second time, ripping a yelp from me. I clenched my teeth and gave up struggling, knowing it wouldn't do any good.

He was too far gone. Science had overtaken his humanity.

Once he'd filled the glass tube with my blood, he smiled kindly and blotted at my skin with a cotton swab he dabbed in alcohol.

"There, now. That wasn't so bad, was it? A little prick, no more. Honestly, Sister. You act as if I was torturing you. Half the women I freed from their chains of sin didn't cry so much. Have some dignity, would you?"

"What have you done?"

Nathaniel jumped and I jerked in my chair, startled by the sound of Father's voice at the edge of the stairs. He hadn't shouted, making it all the more terrifying. I cringed, more from habit than from true fear at being caught doing something potentially dangerous. I was strangely less intimidated of Nathaniel, even knowing the atrocities he was capable of, than of Father when he got angry.

Perhaps I was simply used to the daily mask of a good son and brother that Nathaniel wore. Father never hid his demons, and maybe that scared me more.

"You... you..." I watched Father's gaze leave my bindings then linger on the steam-powered heart, the muscle in his jaw twitching ever so slightly as his attention moved onto who the organ was residing in.

Father walked over to the contraption, then lifted one of the tubes carrying the black substance. He followed the tube around the table, halting when he got close to Mother. In that moment I saw an entirely new side of my father. Here before us was a man who seemed as if he'd been fighting a battle for years and had just realized it was close to coming to an end. He sucked in a deep breath and turned his attention back on me, his gaze locked onto my arm restraints. "How could you do this, Son?"

It disturbed me how still we all were. Nathaniel seemed to be stuck to the floor, unable to move his feet even the slightest inch, while Father shifted and quietly stared at his wife with growing horror and denial.

Without turning around again, Father said, "Untie your sister. Now."

"But Father, I'm so close to waking Mother..." Nathaniel squeezed his eyes shut at the glare Father shot at him. "Very well, then."

Finally, my brother faced me, jaw clenched and eyes still defiant. I followed his gaze taking in my bound wrists and tear-stained cheeks. He nodded curtly. Once. The heavy charge electrifying the room seemed to build to a crescendo.

For a few tense seconds he glanced between the syringe and our mother, his chest rapidly rising and falling to the same manic beat of the steam-powered heart.

"Very well." He peeled his own fingers away from the syringe, then set it on the table. A sob broke out of my chest and he turned to me once again. I steeled myself against my fear as he slowly stepped closer, mumbling.

"Be quick about it," Father barked.

Nathaniel took a deep breath, then nodded again, as if comforting himself about something before finally loosening the ropes at my wrists.

I stared at my brother, but he simply hung his head. Whispered voices cried, "Run! Run!" but I couldn't force my feet toward the stairs.

Father lifted a lock of Mother's hair, his expression wiped clean of all emotion except for one: disgust. "I've never claimed to have succeeded in taking care of either of you. As parents, we only do what we think is best. Even if we fail miserably at our duty."

Tears collected in the corners of his eyes as he continued staring at my mother's ruined face. I swallowed, unsure of where to go from here. It seemed my family relationships were not at all what they appeared to be. Nathaniel moved closer to our father and gazed down at Mother. It was too much. I had to leave this place.

Monsters were supposed to be scary and ugly. They weren't supposed to hide behind friendly smiles and well-trimmed hair. Goodness, twisted as it might be, was not meant to be locked away in an icy heart and anxious exterior.

Grief was not supposed to hide guilt of wrongdoing.

In what sort of world could such vast dichotomies co-exist? I longed for the comfort of a scalpel between my fingertips, and the scent of formalin crisp in the air. I wanted a cadaver that was in need of forensic study to clear my mind.

My attention strayed back to my mother. Perhaps I should focus on healing the living from now on. I'd seen enough death to last ten thousand lifetimes. Maybe that's precisely why Uncle and Thomas started experimenting with organ transplants.

Thomas. With a sudden jolt, I realized how much I loved him and needed to be with him. He was the only truth left in the world I understood.

"Where do you think you're running off to?" Father asked, a demanding edge in his tone.

Even now, in the face of this sinister lab and all that was revealed, he wanted to protect me from the outside world. He was too mad to see this place was exactly the kind of thing he'd been keeping me from all my life.

A disease much worse than pox or cholera or scarlet fever lived here. Violence and cruelty were something else entirely.

"I'm going upstairs, and I'm locking Nathaniel in here," I said, sparing my brother one last glance as he petted Mother's hair. "Then I'm paying Scotland Yard a visit. It's time each of us owned our truths, no matter how twisted and horrendous they are."

"You can't be serious," Nathaniel gasped, looking to our father for assistance. I moved across the room, studying Father. He seemed torn between wanting to do right and wanting to protect his child. Indecision lifted from his features.

"They'll have your brother hanged," he said quietly. "Could you honestly watch that happen? As a family, have we not suffered enough?"

It was an arrow shot straight through my heart, but I couldn't bury the truth. If I didn't go to the police, I'd live a thousand lifetimes in regret. Those women did not deserve to suffer at all. I couldn't ignore that.

"Mother would expect me to do the right thing, even if it's brutally hard."

I looked at my father, feeling sympathy for him. What must it be like, knowing you raised the devil? It probably felt the same as knowing you sat by a monster day in and day out, never noticing the blackness of his soul.

Father gazed at me for a long moment, then nodded. I offered him a weak smile before facing my brother. Even though he'd committed wretched things, I still couldn't find it in my heart to hate him. Perhaps we were all mad.

"Wadsworth? Audrey Rose!" A panicked shout rang out from the stairwell, followed by a clatter of feet banging down the stairs. A second later Thomas dashed into the room, looking rumpled for the second time in his life. He halted before me, his eyes running over my face and body, pausing on my wrists. "You're all right?"

I stared at him, unable to answer his question. Unable to comprehend he was actually standing here with me. There was a flash of relief in his face before he looked away. He eyed Nathaniel as he moved farther into the room.

"I suggest you leave before Scotland Yard comes for you." He glanced from my father's stunned face to Nathaniel's, his tone as somber as their expressions. "You didn't honestly believe I'd show up unprepared, did you?" Thomas smiled sadly at me. "I'm truly sorry, Audrey Rose. This is one instance I hate being right."

"How did you—" Nathaniel began asking.

"How did I discover you're our infamous Jack the Ripper?" Thomas interrupted, moving closer to me, sounding more like himself. "It was quite simple, really. Something had been bothering me from the night Wadsworth and I followed your father home from Miss Mary Jane Kelly's flat."

"You what?" Father flashed an incredulous look our way.

"Apologies, sir. Anyway, there are no such things as coincidences in life. Especially when murder is involved. If your lordship was not involved, then who?"

"Who indeed," Nathaniel muttered, not very impressed.

"I studied Superintendent Blackburn this evening, finding his actions genuine. Plus, he was missing the biggest clue I'd come across. When I went over details in my mind a thought occurred to me—our murderer might be involving himself in our case somehow. Lord Wadsworth and Blackburn, though good leads, were not involved. I could not find a single motive for either of them. Nor could I locate a particular clue I'd unearthed to implicate them."

Thomas moved directly in front of me, planting himself between me and my bloodthirsty brother, who looked as if he was about to rip Thomas's limbs from him.

"You, however, were quite curious about the case. Starting that vigilante group was a nice touch," Thomas said almost appreciatively. "Then there was the pesky matter of those women with connections to your father. Since I'd ruled Lord Wadsworth out, that allowed my mind to stray. Your uncle has this theory, fascinating, really, about career murderers killing those they know. At least to start with."

Nathaniel's attention flicked to the blade he'd left near Mother. I gripped onto Thomas's arm, but he wasn't through showing off his deduction skills.

"While on my way to Scotland Yard tonight, I remembered seeing drops of blood on our last victim's flayed skin. From the way the drops had fallen, it was obvious it didn't come from Miss Kelly. Leading me to deduce our murderer would've sustained injuries of his own."

"And how, exactly, did that lead you here?" Nathaniel asked, moving toward the knife on the table.

Thomas was not intimidated, though I was about to shout or jump for the weapon myself. "I recalled seeing cuts on your fingertips a few weeks prior. At the time it didn't seem important enough to comment on. As I mentally walked through your last crime, I finally understood where you were hiding your weapon."

He allowed a knife to fall from the inside of his own overcoat, surprising us all as he held the weapon up.

"I was able to replicate the very same wounds on myself. See?"

Nathaniel clenched his fists, staring at Thomas like he was a rat that needed to be exterminated immediately. "You must feel extraordinarily clever."

The smug expression normally kissing Thomas's face was absent when his eyes found mine. "The only thing I feel is extraordinarily sorry you've hurt your sister so deeply." Thomas glanced around the room, then checked his pocket watch. "I wasn't jesting about Scotland Yard. I told them a crime was being committed in this house. Either stay and accept your fate or start again new. Be the brother Audrey Rose thought you to be, and the son your father deserves."

Father looked upon Thomas with appreciation gleaming in his eyes.

Thomas was offering my brother a chance at life. A chance to atone for his sins and still know the police would be looking for him. It wasn't right, but it was a chance I was willing to take for my family.

I took a deep, shuddering breath and faced my brother. "Either your reign of terror is over, or your life is over. You decide."

Nathaniel released a nervous bark of laughter before his expression turned cold. "Here's a warning for you, dear Sister. Should you ever threaten me again, I'll destroy both you and your idiotic friend before he ever dreams of finding me."

"Nathaniel." Father shook his head. "Do not intimidate your sister."

Nathaniel's words stung, but not as badly as the icy look he gave me. All the warmth that made him my brother was absent.

Sensing my hurt, Thomas reached for my hand. He was offering me his strength and I gladly accepted. It was time to be finished with this nightmare. I turned to give my brother one last look, hoping to remember him exactly as he was before I walked away. Only he was no longer watching me with those cold, dead eyes.

Grabbing the syringe, he flipped the electrical switch, intent on finishing his unseemly work. Blue and white light hissed and fizzed, cracking the air with its power as it whipped along the needle and into Mother's coffin. Something wasn't right, though.

There was disorder to Nathaniel's process. He was doing things all wrong. He was *supposed* to inject Mother with the blood first, then flip the switch. But why? My mind whirled as the electrical buzz filled the air.

Nathaniel raised the metal syringe, a startling realization crashing through my mind exactly one second too late.

"No!" I shouted, my voice sucked away with the clamor. Thomas held fast to me as I struggled in his arms. I needed to run

to my brother, to save his miserable life. Nathaniel stared, unseeing, through me, and I cried out for him again. "*No!* Nathaniel, you mustn't! Let go of me!"

The buzz was overwhelming. It set my teeth clattering and made breathing nearly impossible. My brother appeared unaffected. I shouted again, to no avail.

"Stop this madness, Nathaniel," Father growled over the din. "I said—"

My brother thrust the syringe into our mother's chest, metal connecting to metal with nothing protecting him from its surge. Mother's body lurched forward before collapsing back onto the table and twitching. I tore my gaze from her, desperate to help my brother.

"Nathaniel!" I screamed as he shook in place, unable to drop the metal syringe and disconnect himself from the malevolent current.

A bloody stream poured from his nose and mouth at the same time smoke rose around his collar. I wrestled and kicked like a wild animal refusing to be tamed.

"Let go, Thomas! Let me *go.*"

"You cannot help him," Thomas said, his arms fused around my body, caging me. "If you touch him now, you'll suffer his same fate. I'm sorry, Audrey Rose. I'm so sorry."

I sunk against Thomas, knowing he'd never let me fling myself into death. It felt like years had passed when suddenly Nathaniel flew back from the force, his body smashing into the wall and crumpling in a heap of smoldering clothes.

Silence blanketed the room like freshly fallen snow. Everything was too quiet and too loud all at once. Even the machines had finally stopped pumping.

Mother's body jolted once more, then fell still.

I blinked, needing to focus on one horror at a time. My attention shifted to my brother. Nathaniel's head hung at a fatal angle, but I couldn't accept it. I wouldn't. He'd get up. He'd be sore and bruised, but he'd live. My brother was young and he'd survive and make up for his sins. He would apologize and seek help to fix whatever had made him violent. It'd take time, but the old Nathaniel would return to us. I waited, holding my breath. He would rise. He had to.

The scent of burnt hair filled the space and I suppressed rolling nausea.

I watched my father slowly collapse to his knees, covering his face with his hands and sobbing, "My precious boy."

It was too much to take in. I felt myself swaying but had to be sure of one thing before I lost myself. I peered at Mother's body, relieved she wasn't moving. Then a terrible sadness crushed me: Nathaniel's rampage had been for naught.

"Please. Please get up." I stared at my brother's ruined hair. I wanted him to stand up and reach for that blasted comb. He needed to fix it. He'd hate it if someone saw him that way. I silently counted to thirty. It was the longest he'd ever gone without addressing disastrous hair. When I reached thirty-one he still hadn't moved.

I fell to the ground, dry-heaving as realization sank in.

Nathaniel would never care about his hair again. He'd never drink another bottle of imported brandy. He'd never picnic with a hamper from Fortnum & Mason or help me escape Father's pretty cell. He'd done horrific things, then left me to pick up the shattered pieces of our lives. Alone.

I screamed until my throat was raw. Thomas tried soothing me, but all I could think was: Jack the Ripper was dead. My brother was dead.

I continued screaming until darkness held me in its welcome embrace.

THIRTY

DEATH TO LIFE

DR. JONATHAN WADSWORTH'S LABORATORY,
HIGHGATE
23 NOVEMBER 1888

"Use the larger bone saw to cut the cranium."

Uncle's hands twitched, but he didn't reach for the blade. He knew I needed the distraction more than he needed to perform this postmortem. I took a deep breath and pushed with all my might, moving the serrated edge back and forth.

This time I wore a facial mask to avoid breathing in bone dust.

I'd watched Uncle do this procedure many times now and had learned there were some things I did not wish to be exposed to.

Two long weeks had passed since we'd buried Nathaniel next to Mother. Father was more remote than ever and I was slowly losing myself to insanity. The house felt empty, sullen, as though mourning its own loss. It was amazing how much one person could fill up a space and leave it so hollow when they were gone.

Nothing was the same, nor ever would be again. Not only did I lose my brother, I had to suffer through the knowledge of the murderer he'd been the last months of his life. Lord Edmund covered up

Nathaniel's involvement, I didn't ask how. One day I'd let everyone know the truth, but the pain was too raw now.

A tear slid down my cheek, but I continued sawing into the skull, not bothering to wipe it away. Some days were better than others. On good days I only cried myself to sleep. On the bad I found myself tearing up randomly throughout the day.

"Good. Now lift the top part of the skull up," Uncle said, motioning toward the top half. It reminded me of the small side of an egg. "Might offer some resistance at first, but it'll suction off with the right amount of pressure. Stick the scalpel in and pry it."

I did as I was instructed. The top of the skull pulled off with a slurping noise, not unlike a sealed jar being opened. An unpleasant scent lingered in the space around us, apparent even through my mask.

Thomas coughed, drawing my attention briefly to him. Truthfully, I'd forgotten he was even here. He'd been quietly perched in the corner of the laboratory, writing notes and studying my brother's journals. I couldn't bear to read them just yet, though from what I'd heard they contained breakthrough science.

My brother's Autumn of Terror might end up being used for good one day after all. It was Thomas's hope he'd be able to perform a successful transplant on a living person during his lifetime. I didn't doubt it.

Uncle handed me a tray and I set the upper portion of the skull on it. "Now, you'll want to remove this little piece of the brain... here." Uncle used a scalpel to point out the specimen.

I plucked the scalpel from his hands and brought it to the brain when a knock came at the door. A servant popped her head in and forced her eyes to the ground. I couldn't blame her; there was nothing beautiful about decay.

"Lord Wadsworth is in the parlor. He'd like to speak with Miss Audrey Rose, sir."

Uncle made an exasperated sound and tossed his hands in the

air. "Then tell *Lord* Wadsworth he'll either have to wait or bless us with his presence in the laboratory. This cannot hold."

The maid dared a glance at the mortuary table where I was standing, my apron bloodied and my hands stained in death. I could see her throat bob when she swallowed. "Very well, sir. I'll tell him."

Before Uncle could utter another word, she disappeared back up the stairs. Thomas met my gaze and offered a wary smile. If Father was here, that meant I was in trouble and would be dragged back to my gilded prison, kicking and screaming if need be. I sighed. Father was bound to notice my absence sooner or later, and I was hardly hiding my activities from him as I used to.

"I might as well go to him, Uncle. Thomas can finish this lesson for me."

I untied my apron and pulled it over my head. There was no need to give Father another reason to shout about my unladylike fascination with forensic medicines. I went to place the apron in the laundry bin, and Thomas gently took it from me, his fingers lingering on my gloveless hands. I lifted my gaze and found him staring down into my eyes. Even in the wake of all I'd lost, my heart found the will to beat rapidly at his touch.

"It'll all work out," he said softly, then grinned. "I could always have a word with your father. I'm not surprised he fancies me. I am rather hard to resist."

I snorted, removing my hand from his. "I should like to see you sit down to tea with my father. Perhaps you could even tell him how many times you've indecently asked for a kiss."

"You mean how I've successfully received a kiss, I believe. If that's what the lady wants, I shall act immediately." Thomas shrugged and made to walk up the stairs, but I grabbed him and pointed to where Uncle was huffing across the room.

"If you don't go over there and assist him"—I nodded in Uncle's direction—"I fear he may start throwing things."

"Admit it. You're afraid your father *will* love me and we'll be betrothed before the night is through." Thomas leaned closer, his lips tickling my ear in the most inappropriate manner as Uncle cleared his throat. "I rather fancy the thought of more adventures with you, Miss Wadsworth."

I shook my head. Of course now he'd address me properly. The fiend. He pressed a chaste kiss to my hand, then stalked off toward my uncle, taking my place near the exposed brain.

I watched him remove a piece of it before silently making my way upstairs. I'd miss him terribly and a new wave of grief flooded my system. Nathaniel was gone and now Father would banish me from my apprenticeship, taking Uncle and Thomas from me as well. I had nothing.

I reached the top of the stairs and halted. Father's broad form blocked the doorway, imposing as ever. I twisted Mother's ring, all too aware it probably had droplets of dried blood on it.

Father glanced over my shoulder, then settled his attention on me. He needn't say a thing. His emotions were clearly written across his face. Anyone could read their meaning. I held a hand up, tired and defeated.

Nathaniel involved himself in science and ended up buried. Perhaps it was a sign I needed to give it up as well. I was tired of fighting both society and life. Giving in felt weak, but the gaping hole in my chest swallowed any burning desire to carve my own path.

"Please. Spare me from the lecture this once. I am a shameful creature who does not deserve our good name." My breath hitched in my throat. I'd not cry now. Not like this. "You were right, Father. Nothing good can come from such wicked pursuits. Perhaps if Nathaniel hadn't been obsessed with such things he'd still be alive and well now. I will not disobey your wishes again."

For the first time, I meant what I said. I was not crossing my fingers behind my back, or willing to beg forgiveness later. I'd find another profession and another path to take in life. I did not fool myself into thinking I'd ever be content with staying home and tending to the house, but I'd search for some other way to fulfill my soul.

Father reached for me and I flinched. His eyes grew misty. "Have I been so cruel that you fear me?" I shook my head. He'd never hit me, and I felt a new wave of shame for flinching away from him. "I've been doing some thinking."

He pulled an envelope from his overcoat pocket and inhaled deeply. "After your mother died, it was as if each shadow grew talons and claws and was threatening to steal away everything I loved."

Father stared at the envelope in his hands. "Fear is a hungry beast. The more you feed it, the more it grows. My misguided intentions were good, but I'm afraid they didn't turn out as I'd planned." He tapped his heart. "I thought by keeping you close, keeping you safe in our home, I could protect you from such monsters."

A few moments passed and I longed to reach out and hold him. To say something, but couldn't. There was something about this moment that felt too fragile, a bubble of soap floating above bath water.

He stood straighter and finally met my gaze. "Did you know I spoke with your uncle last week?"

I drew my brows together. "I'm afraid he didn't mention it."

A genuine smile tugged at the corners of Father's mouth. "It's about time the ornery fool listened to me." He handed me the envelope. "I asked him to put in a good word for you. You're brilliant and beautiful and life has countless possibilities for you. Which is precisely why I'm sending you away."

The stairwell spun before my eyes and I nearly swayed backward. This was so much worse than I could've imagined. Panic cinched my lungs together.

"You cannot send me away!" I cried. "I promise I'll be good. No more corpses or postmortems, or police investigations. I swear!"

Father came forward and did the very last thing I expected him to do. He wrapped me in his arms and kissed the top of my head.

"Silly child," he said, not unkindly. "I'm sending you to a forensic medicines school. It's one of the very best in Europe. Took all of my connections *and* your uncle's good word to secure you a place in the class. You leave for Romania in a week."

I pulled back enough to look Father in the eyes. There was something there that stole my breath and boosted my spirit: pride. My father was *proud* of me, and he was giving me the freedom I so longed for. This time when the tears came they were for an entirely different reason. "Is this truly real? Or am I dreaming?"

I must've looked like a fish taken from the water, gulping at air. I shut my mouth and stared at Father. How he approved of this was truly miraculous. Or a delusion. I studied him, trying to decide if he'd been abusing the tonic again.

He chuckled at my worried expression. "Thomas has assured us he'll watch out for you while you're both away. He's quite the responsible young gentleman, from what I hear."

My brows shot up. "Thomas is... he's going, too?"

Father nodded. "It was his idea."

"Oh?" I couldn't believe it. Thomas had won over my father just as he said he would. Clearly, this meant the end times were near. I hugged my father, still not quite believing my luck. "This is all wonderful, but... why?"

Father held me close. "I've tried in my own way to protect you from the harshness and diseases of the world. But men—and young women—weren't meant to live in gilded cages. There's always a chance some contagion will find a way in. I trust you to change that. In order to do so you must venture out into the world, my sweet girl. Promise me one thing, will you?"

"Anything, Father."

"Always foster and grow that unquenchable curiosity of yours."

I smiled. That was a promise I fully intended to keep.

AUTHOR'S NOTE

Historical and Creative Liberties Taken

Newspapers first used the term *Leather Apron* in regard to Jack the Ripper on September 4, not on August 31, and they referred to suspect John Pizer by name on September 7. I adjusted these dates to better serve my purposes and removed Pizer's name altogether to avoid muddling the plot with extraneous characters.

On September 10 there really was a vigilante committee that formed, called The Whitechapel Vigilance Committee. Using that idea, I involved Nathaniel and Thomas, giving them a solid reason to be trolling the streets in the nights following the crimes as part of the Knights of Whitechapel. I had them out and about on September 7 (the real-life evening before Annie Chapman's body was discovered), however, which is another embellishment of the historical timeline as far as the vigilante group is concerned.

I also don't mention that John Pizer was arrested on September 10 as "Leather Apron." There were so many men arrested as suspects, I feared it wouldn't add anything to the story line other than confusing readers with too many names and dead ends. Arrests were made of the following men in September alone:

John Pizer
Edward McKenna
Jacob Isenschmid (accused of being the Ripper and sentenced to the asylum)
Charles Ludwig (arrested after reportedly threatening two people with a knife)

Mary Ann "Polly" Nichols had no history of working for upper-class families in London that I could find while researching her background. I took the liberty of fictionalizing what her life *could* have been before she left her husband, becoming a prostitute and alcoholic and moving from workhouse to workhouse in the early 1880s. I wanted to show the human side of these women, not just the horrific crime scenes they were a part of at the end of their lives. They were wives, mothers, sisters, and daughters, not just forgotten prostitutes, remembered only in death.

Emma Elizabeth Smith was someone else I fictionalized greatly. There are conflicting theories of whether she was actually an early victim of Jack the Ripper, but I really wanted her included in this novel because I was fascinated by the vagueness of her life before she became a prostitute. While there are rumors of her coming from an elite background, there's no concrete proof she was highborn. People who knew her claimed she spoke differently, meaning she had a firm grasp of proper language, which was rare for people living in the East End at that time. She said next to nothing about where she came from, which made me ask the all-important question, What if? What if she really was part of the aristocracy? There are reports that she may have known the perpetrators who had attacked her, giving me the spark of an idea to create a new background for her. The mystery surrounding her life and death was a blank canvas that I could really explore through my imagination.

Annie Chapman's murder date and details of what she was wearing were as close to accurate as I could make them. She'd been drinking heavily and had used her rent money for alcohol. The lodging house deputy refused her board until she could pay, so she went out to earn some. Her husband had been paying her ten shillings a week, but that ended in 1886, when he passed away, not in 1888, the year of her death.

Elizabeth Stride is not mentioned by name in this novel, though she was one of the victims of the infamous double event.

Catherine Eddowes was the second victim in the double event. I kept the date she was buried and embellished the rest about Robert James Lees meeting Audrey Rose and Thomas at the grave. He offered his assistance to Scotland Yard at this time, so I reimagined it as him offering his assistance to Audrey Rose and Thomas instead.

Mary Jane Kelly was someone I tried keeping as historically accurate as possible. Some of Jack and Mary Jane Kelly's conversation and descriptions of what she was wearing the night of her death are included in the novel, although I embellished the times and sequence of how they occurred a bit. She was heard singing "A Violet from Mother's Grave" once she was already inside her apartment with the Ripper, not outside on the street. She was wearing a red shawl, according to one eyewitness.

The home on Miller Street wasn't accessible by carriage during this time, but for the purpose of my story, I made it so, allowing Audrey Rose and Thomas a decent hiding spot for their midnight spying excursion.

Facsimiles of the "Dear Boss" letter and the "Saucy Jack" postcard were actually printed on October 4 (in the *Evening Standard*), not October 1. Earlier printings of the letters were text only (on October 1 and 3, in the *Star* and *Daily News*), not picture copies of the actual letters.

The Barnum & Bailey circus didn't come to London's Olympia until November 1889 (the fall following this story), but since the queen was a fan of it, and hundreds of Victorian circuses traveled across Europe during this time period, I decided to include it. Poor Jumbo the elephant also passed away in 1885 and wouldn't have been entertaining the crowds.

Clairvoyant and spiritualist Robert James Lees was an actual man who offered his assistance to police on several occasions for the Jack the Ripper killings. While spiritualism was still quite popular across the United States and Europe (even after some spiritualists and mediums were proven to be frauds), Scotland Yard did not accept his assistance. It has never been confirmed, but there are rumors he also communicated with Prince Albert for Queen Victoria and had even resided in the palace.

I also tried keeping all medical terminology and practices as close to the date they were used as possible. Books using the term *forensic medicine* or *forensic science* were really printed in the 1800s. And doctors/medical examiners used things such as body temperature to determine time of death, though they were also aware that blood loss and cold temperatures would affect the accuracy of their estimates. Joseph Lister developed the idea to sterilize instruments during surgeries in the 1860s using carbolic acid, and fingerprint identification was discovered in the early 1880s. Though they didn't have all the tools we have now, police scoured a crime scene and collected evidence much the same way in the nineteenth century as they do today.

As stated on the New York State Troopers website (under "Crime Laboratory System: Forensic Science History"), the following practices were applied during the 1800s:

> In the 1800s the field of forensic science saw substantial progress. The decade saw:
>
> - The first recorded use of questioned document analysis.
> - The development of tests for the presence of blood in a forensic context.
> - A bullet comparison used to catch a murderer.
> - The first use of toxicology (arsenic detection) in a jury trial.
> - The development of the first crystal test for hemoglobin using hemin crystals.
> - The development of a presumptive test for blood.

- The first use of photography for the identification of criminals and documentation of evidence and crime scenes.
- The first recorded use of fingerprints to solve a crime.
- The development of the first microscope with a comparison bridge.

Forensic science was significantly applied in 1888, when doctors in London, England, were allowed to examine the victims of Jack the Ripper for wound patterns.

Any other historical inaccuracies not mentioned were artistic liberties I took to enrich the world of *Stalking Jack the Ripper* and better serve my characters.

ACKNOWLEDGMENTS

Without the help of the fiercest agent warrior in the world, Barbara Poelle, these acknowledgments wouldn't exist. Thank you for unleashing Godzilla Bunny for me, B. We did it! To the entire team at IGLA for being the best agency. To Heather Shapiro for getting my book into the hands of readers across the world.

Huge thanks to my whip-smart editor and fellow Victorian dress enthusiast, Jenny Bak, for expert precision with making Audrey Rose's story come to life. My book's so much stronger because of you. I can't thank you enough for taking a chance on me and a cadaver-wrangling girl. Excited to see what new adventures Audrey Rose and Thomas take us on next! To Sasha Henriques, for comments that always made me smile. (Gruesome and sexy!)

To James Patterson for the amazing foreword, and for making me and my novel feel right at home with your imprint. JIMMY Patterson Books means the absolute world to me, and I'm thrilled to be a part of it. To Tracy Shaw, whose gorgeous cover caused a flurry of exclamation points and dancing GIFs. To Erinn McGrath, for the exquisite publicity plan. Ned Rust, Sabrina Benun, Peggy Freudenthal, Katie Tucker, and the entire team at JIMMY Patterson Books and Little, Brown and Company—your hard work and dedication are truly humbling. I've had the *best* debut experience because of you all.

Mom and Dad, thank you for always encouraging me to reach for the stars (or scalpel or paintbrush or pen) and never thinking something was unattainable because of my gender. I know the word "impossible" can be broken down into "I'm possible" because of you both. Kelli, you're my favorite sister. (Not because you're my *only* sister.) Thanks for styling me with Dogwood Lane Boutique clothing for every event and for being my best friend. I'm so very proud of your accomplishments. Love all of you!

I dedicated this to Grandma but need to add this: My entire world is built on books and she laid the foundation. I can only hope that she would have adored this story—and the strong female who solved one of the biggest whodunits in history—as much as I do.

To the Belascos, Cuthbertstons, Diakakises, and Loews—love you! Paula, Jeff, Mike, Matt, Daniel, Anna, Juliet, Katie, and Ben, thank you for all the laughter and shared food. I'm blessed to know each of you. Jacquie, Alyssa, Shannon, and Beth—BFFs, always. There's no place like home. To fur babies Toby, Miss Libby, and Oliver for their names.

My mews, Bella, for constantly keeping Mommy on track with writing and giving me the belly, and Gage for being adorable.

Early readers: Renée Ahdieh, A. G. Howard, and Leah Rae Miller, infinite thanks for your time and insight. Beta team extraordinaire: Kathy and Kelli Maniscalco and Ashlee Supinger, you're the best. Critique partners Precy Larkins and Alex Villasante—my words and life are richer because of you. To Traci Chee, who, two weeks before Christmas, brainstormed like a complete badass—even though she was under her own deadline—and offered amazing notes and feedback. I'm thrilled to share this journey to publication with you. #goatwub to the goat posse who are the best writing group. The Sweet Sixteens—what a ride! To Stephanie Garber for being my BEA buddy—so happy we got to share the fun in Chicago. Dresses and comfy shoes forever!

Renée Ahdieh and Beth Revis, your blurbs made my life. Much love to you both!

Readers, book bloggers, librarians, booksellers, social media friends, and Ava + the Knights of Whitechapel: I owe you piles of gratitude for your incredible response! Thank you for rallying behind a scalpel-wielding girl who adores fancy dresses and justice for women. I'd pluck the stars from the skies for you.

First, she stalked Jack the Ripper.
This time, things are about to get even bloodier.

Following the horrifying revelation of Jack the Ripper's true identity, Audrey Rose Wadsworth flees her home in Victorian London to enroll as the only female student in Europe's most prestigious forensics school. But when a series of troubling deaths brings whispers of Vlad the Impaler's bloodthirsty return, Audrey Rose and her sharp-witted companion, Thomas Cresswell, must unravel the cryptic clues that will lead them to the shadowlike killer—living or dead.

Could it be a copycat—or has the depraved Prince Dracula risen from the grave?

Read on for a sneak peek at

HUNTING PRINCE DRACULA

By Kerri Maniscalco

AVAILABLE NOW!

Bucharest, Romania, c. 1890.

GHOSTS OF THE PAST

ORIENT EXPRESS
KINGDOM OF ROMANIA
1 DECEMBER 1888

Our train gnashed its way along frozen tracks toward the white-capped fangs of the Carpathian mountains. From our position outside the capital city of Romania, the peaks were the color of fading bruises.

Judging from the heavy snow falling, they were likely as cold as dead flesh. Quite a charming thought for a blustery morning.

A knee struck the side of the carved wooden panel in my compartment *again*. I closed my eyes, praying that my traveling companion would fall back asleep. One more jitter of his long limbs might unravel my fraying composure. I pressed my head against the plush high-backed seat, focusing on the soft velvet instead of poking his offending limb with my hat pin.

Sensing my growing annoyance, Mr. Thomas Cresswell shifted to tapping his fingers against the windowsill in our compartment. *My* compartment, actually.

Thomas had his own quarters but insisted on spending every hour of the day possessed in my company, lest a career murderer board the train and unleash carnage.

At least that's the ridiculous story he'd told our chaperone, Mrs. Harvey. She was a charming silver-haired woman who watched over Thomas while he stayed in his Piccadilly flat in London, and was currently on her fourth nap of the new day.

Father had taken ill in Paris and had placed his trust and my virtue in both Mrs. Harvey's and Thomas's care. It spoke volumes as to how highly Father thought of Thomas, and how convincingly innocent and charming my friend could be when the mood or occasion struck. My hands were suddenly warm and damp inside my gloves.

That feeling vanished as my focus slid from Thomas's dark brown hair and crisp suit to his discarded Romanian newspaper. I'd been studying the language enough to make out most of what it said. The headline read: HAS THE IMMORTAL PRINCE RETURNED? A body had been found staked through the heart near Braşov—the very town we were traveling to—leading the superstitious to believe in the impossible: Vlad Dracula, the centuries-dead Prince of Romania, was alive. And hunting.

It was all rubbish meant to inspire fear and sell papers. There was no such thing as an immortal being. Flesh-and-blood men were the real monsters, and they could be cut down easily enough. In the end, even Jack the Ripper bled as all men do. Though papers still claimed he prowled the foggy London streets. Some even said he'd gone to America.

If only that were true.

An all-too-familiar pang hit my center, stealing my breath. It was always the same when I thought about the Ripper case and the memories it stirred within. When I stared into the looking glass, I still saw the same green eyes and crimson lips—both my mother's Indian roots and father's English nobility apparent in my cheekbones. By all outward appearances, I was still a vibrant seventeen-year-old girl.

And yet, I'd taken such a devastating blow to my soul. I wondered how I could appear so whole and serene on the outside when inside I was thrashing with turbulence.

Uncle had sensed the shift in me, noticing the careless mistakes I'd started making in his forensic laboratory over the last few days... carbolic acid I'd forgotten to use when cleansing our blades. Specimens I hadn't collected. A jagged tear I'd made in ice-cold flesh, so unlike my normal precision with the bodies lining his examination table. He'd said nothing, but I knew he was disappointed. I was supposed to have a heart that hardened in the face of death.

Perhaps I wasn't meant for a life of forensic studies after all.

Tap. Tap-tap-tap. Tap.

I gritted my teeth while Thomas *tap-tap-tapped* along to the chugging of the wheels. How Mrs. Harvey slept through the racket was truly incredible. At least he'd succeeded in drawing me from that deep well of emotions. They were the kind of feelings that were too still and too dark. Stagnant and putrid like swamp water, with red-eyed creatures lurking far below.

Soon we'd all disembark in Bucharest before traveling the rest of the way by carriage to Bran Castle, home to the Academy of Forensic Medicine and Science, or *Institutului Naţional de Criminalistică şi Medicină Legală,* as it was called in Romanian. Mrs. Harvey would spend a night or two in Braşov before traveling back to London. Part of me longed to go back with her, though I'd never admit it aloud to Thomas.

Above our private booth, an opulent chandelier swung in time to the rhythm of the train, its crystals clinking together and adding a new layer of accompaniment to Thomas's staccato taps. Pushing his incessant melody from my thoughts, I watched the world outside blur in puffs of steam and swishing tree limbs. Leafless branches were encased in sparkling white, their reflections shimmering against the polished near-ebony blue of our luxury train.

I leaned closer, realizing the branches weren't covered in snow, but ice. They caught the first light of day and were practically set ablaze in the bright reddish-orange sunrise. It was so peaceful I could almost forget—*wolves!* I stood so abruptly that Thomas jumped in his seat. Mrs. Harvey snored loudly, the sound akin to a snarl. I blinked and the creatures were gone, replaced by branches swaying as the train chugged onward.

What I had thought were glinting fangs were only wintry boughs. I exhaled. I'd been hearing phantom howls all night. Now I was seeing things that weren't there during daylight hours, too.

"I'm going to . . . stretch my limbs."

Thomas raised dark brows and leaned forward, but before he could offer to accompany me, I rushed for the door and slid it open.

"I need a few moments. Alone."

"Try not to miss me too much, Wadsworth." Thomas sat back, his face falling slightly before his expression was once again playful. The lightness didn't quite reach his eyes. "Though that might be an impossible task. I, for one, miss myself terribly when asleep."

"What was that, dear?" Mrs. Harvey asked, blinking behind her spectacles.

"I said you ought to try counting sheep."

"Was I sleeping again?"

I took advantage of the distraction, shutting the door behind me and grabbing my skirts. I didn't want Thomas reading the expression on my face. The one that I hadn't yet mastered in his presence.

I wandered down the narrow corridor, barely taking in the grandiosity as I slowly made my way toward the dining car. I couldn't stay out here unchaperoned for long, but I needed an escape. If only from my own thoughts and worries.

Last week, I had seen my cousin Liza walking up the stairs in my home. A sight as normal as anything, except she'd left weeks earlier for the country. Days later something a bit darker occurred. I'd sworn a cadaver craned its head toward me in Uncle's laboratory, its unblinking gaze full of scorn at the blade in my hand, its mouth full of maggots pouring onto the examination table. When I'd blinked, all was well.

I'd brought several medical journals for the journey, but hadn't had an opportunity to research my symptoms with Thomas openly studying me. He'd said I needed to confront my grief, but I wasn't willing to reopen that wound yet. One day, maybe.

A few compartments down, a door slid open, dragging me into the present. A man with primly styled hair exited the chamber, moving swiftly down the corridor. His suit was charcoal and made of fine material, apparent by the way it draped over his broad shoulders. When he tugged a silver comb from his overcoat, I nearly cried out. Something in my core twisted so violently my knees buckled.

It couldn't be. He had died weeks ago in that awful accident. My mind knew the impossibility standing before me, striding away with his perfect hair and matching clothing, yet my heart refused to listen.

I gathered my cream skirts in my fists and ran. I'd know that stride anywhere. Science could not explain the power of love or hope. There were no formulas or deductions for understanding, no matter what Thomas claimed regarding science versus humanity.

The man tipped his hat to passengers sitting down to tea. I was only half aware of their open-mouthed stares as I bounded after him, my own hat tilting to one side.

He approached the door to the cigar room, halting a moment to wrench the outer door open to travel between cars. Smoke leeched from the room and mixed with an icy blast of air, the scent strong enough to make my insides roil. I reached out, tugging the man around, ready to toss my arms around him and cry. The events last month were only a nightmare. My—

"Domnişoară?"

Tears pricked my eyes. The hairstyle and clothing did not belong to the man I'd believed they did. I swiped the first bit of wetness that slid down my cheeks, not caring if I smudged the kohl I'd taken to wearing around my eyes.

He lifted a walking cane, switching it to his other hand. He hadn't even been holding a comb. I was losing touch with what was real. I slowly backed away, noting the quiet chatter of the car behind us. The clink of teacups, the mixed accents of world travelers, all of it a crescendo building in my chest. Panic made breathing more difficult than the corset binding my ribs.

I panted, trying to draw in enough air to soothe my jumbling nerves. The clatter and laughter rose to a shrill pitch. Part of me wished the cacophony would drown out the pulse thrashing in my head. I was about to be sick.

"Are you all right, *domnişoară?* You appear..."

I laughed, uncaring that he jerked away from my sudden outburst. Oh, if there was such a thing as a Higher Power, it was having fun at my expense. "*Domnişoară*" finally registered. This man spoke with a Romanian accent. He wasn't even English. And his hair wasn't blond at all. It was light brown.

"Scuze," I said, forcing myself out of hysterics with a meager apology. "I mistook you for someone else."

Before I could embarrass myself further, I dipped my chin and quickly retreated to our private car. I kept my head down, ignoring the whispers and giggles, though I'd heard enough.

I needed to collect myself before I saw Thomas again. I'd pretended otherwise, but I'd seen the concern crinkling his brow. The extra care in the way he'd tease or annoy me. I knew precisely what he was doing each time he irked me. After what my family had gone through, any other gentleman would have treated me as if I were a porcelain doll, easily fractured, and discarded for being broken. Thomas was unlike other young men, however.

I came upon my compartment and threw my shoulders back. It was time to wear the cool exterior of a scientist. My tears had dried and my heart was now a solid fist in my chest. I breathed in, and exhaled. Jack the Ripper was never coming back. As real a statement as any.

There were no career murderers on this train. Another fact.

The Autumn of Terror ended last month.

Wolves were most certainly not hunting anyone on the *Orient Express*.

If I wasn't careful, I'd start believing Dracula had risen next.

I allowed myself another deep breath before I slid the door open, banishing all thoughts of immortal princes as I entered the compartment.

IMMORTAL BELOVED

ORIENT EXPRESS
KINGDOM OF ROMANIA
1 DECEMBER 1888

Thomas kept his focus stubbornly fixed on the window, his fingers still drumming that annoying rhythm. *Tap. Tap-tap-tap. Tap.*

Unsurprisingly, Mrs. Harvey was resting her eyes once again. Her soft snuffles indicated she'd fallen back asleep. I stared at my companion, but he was either blissfully unaware or likely pretending to be as I slipped into the seat across from him. His profile was a study of perfect lines and angles, all carefully turned to the wintry world outside. I knew he sensed my attention on him, his mouth a bit too curved in delight for mindless thought.

"Must you keep up that wretched beat, Thomas?" I asked. "It's driving me as mad as one of Poe's unfortunate characters. Plus, poor Mrs. Harvey must be dreaming awful things."

He shifted his attention to me, deep brown eyes turning thoughtful for a moment. It was that precise look—warm and inviting as a patch of sunshine on a crisp autumn day—that meant trouble. I could practically see his mind turning over brash things as one side of his mouth tugged upward. His crooked smile invited thoughts that Aunt Amelia would find completely indecent. And the way his gaze fell to my own lips told me he knew it. Fiend.

"Poe? Will you carve my heart out and place it beneath your bed, then, Wadsworth? I must admit, it's not an ideal way of ending up in your sleeping quarters."

"You seem awfully certain of your ability to charm anything other than serpents."

"Admit it. Our last kiss was rather thrilling." He leaned forward, his handsome face coming entirely too close to my own. So much for having a chaperone. My heart sped up when I noticed tiny flecks in his irises. They were like little golden suns that drew me in with their enchanting rays. "Tell me you don't fancy the idea of another."

"First and last kiss," I reminded him. "It was the adrenaline coursing through my veins after nearly dying at the hands of those two ruffians. *Not* your powers of persuasion."

A wicked smile fully lifted the corners of his mouth. "If I found a dash of danger for us, would that entice you again?"

"You know, I much preferred you when you weren't speaking."

"Ah"—Thomas sat back, inhaling deeply—"either way, you prefer me."

I should have known the scoundrel would find a way to turn our conversation to such improper topics. In fact, I was surprised it had taken him this long to be vulgar. We'd traveled from London to Paris with my father so he could see us off on the impressive *Orient Express,* and Thomas had been a complete gentleman the entire way. I'd barely recognized him while he chatted warmly with Father over scones and tea.

If it weren't for the mischievous tilt to his lips when Father wasn't looking, or the familiar lines of his stubborn jaw, I would have claimed he was an imposter. There was no way *this* Thomas Cresswell could possibly be the same annoyingly intelligent boy I'd grown too fond of last autumn. I tucked a loose wisp of raven hair behind my ear and glanced out the window again.

"Does your silence mean you're considering another kiss, then?"

"Can you not deduce my answer, Cresswell?" I stared at him, one brow raised in challenge, until he shrugged and continued drumming his fingers on the windowsill.

This Thomas had also managed to convince my father, the formidable Lord Edmund Wadsworth, to allow me to attend the Academy of Forensic Medicine and Science with him in Romania. A fact I still couldn't quite accept. My last week in London had been stuffed full of dress-fittings and trunk packing. Which left too much time for them to become further acquainted, it seemed. When Father had announced Thomas would escort me to the academy along with Mrs. Harvey due to his illness, I'd practically choked on my soup course while Thomas winked over his.

I'd barely had time to sleep at night, let alone ponder the relationship budding between my infuriating friend and usually stern father. I was eager to leave the dreadfully silent house that ushered in too many ghosts of my recent past. A fact Thomas was all too aware of.

"Daydreaming of a new scalpel or is that look simply to charm me?" Thomas asked, drawing me away from dark thoughts. His lips twitched at my scowl, but he was smart enough not to finish that grin. "Ah. An emotional dilemma, then. My favorite."

I watched him take note of the expression I was trying too hard to control, the gloves I couldn't stop fussing with, and the stiff way I sat in our booth that had nothing to do with the corset binding my upper body, or the older woman taking up most of my seat. His gaze fixed itself to my own, sincere and full of compassion. I could see promises and wishes stitched across his features, the intensity of his feelings enough to make me tremble.

"Nervous about class? You'll charm them all, Wadsworth."

It was a mild relief that he sometimes misread the entire truth of my emotions. Let him believe the shudder was entirely from nerves about class and not his growing interest in a betrothal. Thomas had admitted his love for me, but as with many things lately, I was unsure it was real. Perhaps he only felt beholden to me out of pity in the wake of all that happened.

I touched the buttons on the side of my gloves. "No. Not really."

His brow arched but he said nothing. I turned my attention back to the window and the stark world outside. I wished to be lost in nothingness for a while longer.

Our new academy was set in a castle located atop the frigid Carpathian mountain range. It was a long way from home or civility, should any of my new classmates be less than welcoming. My sex was sure to be seen as a weakness amongst male peers—and what if Thomas abandoned our friendship once we arrived?

Perhaps he'd discover how odd it truly was for a young woman to carve open the dead and pluck out their organs as if they were new slippers to try on. It hadn't mattered while we were both apprenticing with Uncle in his laboratory. But what students at the prestigious Academy of Forensic Medicine and Science would think of me might not be as progressive.

Wrangling bodies was barely proper for a man to do, let alone a highborn girl. If Thomas left me friendless at school, I'd sink into an abyss so deep I feared I'd never resurface.

The proper society girl in me was loath to admit it, but his flirtations kept me afloat in a sea of conflicting feelings. Passion and annoyance were fire, and fire was alive and crackling with power. Fire breathed. Grief was a vat of quicksand—the more one struggled against it, the deeper it pulled one under. I'd much rather be set ablaze than buried alive. Though the mere *thought* of being in a compromising position with Thomas was enough to make my face warm.

"Audrey Rose," Thomas began, mussing the cuffs of his overcoat then removing his hat before running a hand through his dark hair, an action truly foreign to my normally arrogant friend. Mrs. Harvey stirred, but didn't wake.

"Yes?" I sat even straighter, forcing the boning of my corset to act as if it were armor. Thomas hardly ever called me by my first name unless something awful was about to occur. During an autopsy a few months back, I'd lost a battle of wits to him and had to grant him permission to use my surname. A privilege he also allowed me, and something I occasionally regretted whenever he'd call me "Wadsworth" in public. "What is it?"

I watched him take a few deep breaths, my focus straying to his finely made suit. He was rather smartly dressed for our arrival. His midnight jacket was tailored to his frame in a way that made one pause and admire both it and the young man filling it out. I reached for my buttons, then caught myself.

"There's something I've been meaning to tell you," he said, moving about his seat. "I... think it only fair to disclose this before we arrive."

His knee knocked into the wooden panel again and he hesitated. Perhaps he was already realizing his association with me would pose an issue in school for him. I braced myself for it, the snip of the cord that tethered me to sanity. I would not ask him to stay and be my friend through this. No matter if it killed me. I focused on my breaths, counting seconds between them.

Grandmama claimed stubbornness should be inscribed on all Wadsworth tombs. I didn't disagree. I lifted my chin. The clatter of the wheels now counted off each amplified beat of my heart, pumping adrenaline into my veins. I swallowed several times. If he didn't speak soon, I feared I'd be sick all over him and his handsome suit.

"Wadsworth. I'm sure you...perhaps I should—" He shook his head then laughed. "You've truly possessed me. Next thing I'll be penning sonnets and making doe-eyes." The unguardedness left his features abruptly as if he'd caught himself from falling off a deadly cliff. He cleared his throat, his voice much softer than it had been a moment before. "Which is hardly the time, since my news is rather...well, it may come as a slight...surprise."

I drew my brows together. I'd no idea what he was about to say. He was either going to declare our friendship unbreakable or cast it aside for good. I found myself gripping the edge of my seat, palms dampening my satin gloves.

He sat forward, steeling himself. "My mother's f—"

Something large crashed against the door of our compartment, the force nearly cracking the wood upon impact. At least it sounded that way—our heavy door was closed to keep the noise from the nearby dining car at bay. Mrs. Harvey, bless her, was still fast asleep.

I dared not breathe, waiting for more sounds to follow. When no noises came, I inched forward in our booth, forgetting entirely about Thomas's unspoken confession, heart pounding at twice its normal speed. I imagined cadavers rising from the dead, beating down our door in hopes of drinking our blood, and—*no.* I forced my mind to think clearly. Vampires weren't real.

Perhaps it was simply a man who'd indulged in one too many spirits and stumbled into the door. Or maybe a dessert or tea cart got away from an attendant. I supposed it was even possible that a young woman had lost her footing with the motion of the train.

I exhaled and sat back. I needed to stop worrying about murderers stalking the night. I was becoming obsessed with turning every shadow into a bloodthirsty demon when it was nothing more than the absence of light. Though I was my father's daughter.

I heard the sound of another commotion outside our little chamber, followed by a muffled cry, then nothing. Hair stood straight up on the nape of my neck, craning itself away from the safety of my skin as Mrs. Harvey's snores added to the eerie atmosphere.

"What in the name of the queen?" I whispered, cursing myself for packing my scalpels in a trunk that I couldn't readily reach.

Thomas lifted a finger to his mouth, then pointed to the door, stalling any more movements. We sat there while seconds passed in painful silence. Each tick of the clock felt like an agonizing month. I could scarcely stand one more breath of it.

My heart was ready to burst from its confines. Silence was more frightening than anything as it stretched seconds into minutes. We sat there, focus fixed to the door, waiting. I closed my eyes, praying that I wasn't experiencing another waking terror.

A scream rent the air, chilling my bones to their very marrow.

Thomas reached for me across the compartment, and Mrs. Harvey stirred. I knew this was no figment of my imagination. Something very dark and very real was on this train with us.

ABOUT THE AUTHOR

Kerri Maniscalco grew up in a small town just outside of New York City, where her love of the arts was fostered from an early age. In her spare time she reads everything she can get her hands on, cooks all kinds of food with her family and friends, and drinks entirely too much tea while discussing life's finer points with her cats. *Stalking Jack the Ripper* is her debut novel, and it incorporates her love of forensic science and unsolved history.

For more information, visit Kerri online at kerrimaniscalco.com and follow her on Twitter and Instagram at KerriManiscalco or on Facebook at KerriManiscalcoAuthor.

JIMMY Patterson Books for Young Adult Readers

James Patterson Presents

Stalking Jack the Ripper by Kerri Maniscalco
Hunting Prince Dracula by Kerri Maniscalco
Escaping from Houdini by Kerri Maniscalco
Capturing the Devil by Kerri Maniscalco
Gunslinger Girl by Lyndsay Ely
Twelve Steps to Normal by Farrah Penn
Campfire by Shawn Sarles
When We Were Lost by Kevin Wignall
Swipe Right for Murder by Derek Milman
Once & Future by A. R. Capetta and Cory McCarthy
Sword in the Stars by A. R. Capetta and Cory McCarthy
Girls of Paper and Fire by Natasha Ngan
Girls of Storm and Shadow by Natasha Ngan

The Maximum Ride Series by James Patterson

The Angel Experiment
School's Out—Forever
Saving the World and Other Extreme Sports
The Final Warning
MAX
FANG
ANGEL
Nevermore
Maximum Ride Forever

The Confessions Series by James Patterson

Confessions of a Murder Suspect
Confessions: The Private School Murders
Confessions: The Paris Mysteries
Confessions: The Murder of an Angel

The Witch & Wizard Series by James Patterson

Witch & Wizard
The Gift
The Fire
The Kiss
The Lost

Nonfiction by James Patterson

Med Head

Stand-Alone Novels by James Patterson

Expelled
Crazy House
The Fall of Crazy House
Cradle and All
First Love
Homeroom Diaries

For exclusives, trailers, and other information, visit jimmypatterson.org.